# THE RASH ACT

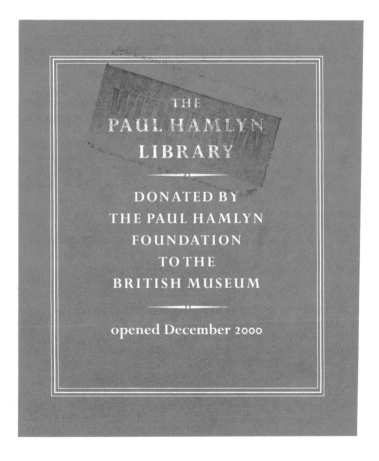

Also by Ford Madox Ford from Carcanet

*A History of Our Own Times*
*Ladies Whose Bright Eyes*
*The Ford Reader*

# FORD MADOX FORD

........................................................

# *The Rash Act*

'The rash act,' the coroner said, 'seems to have been inspired by a number of motives, not the least amongst which was the prevailing dissoluteness and consequent depression that are now world wide.'

*Times Law Report,* 14 JULY 1931

CARCANET

First published in Great Britain in 1933
and reprinted by Carcanet Press in 1982.

Paperback edition published in 1996 by
Carcanet Press Limited
402–406 Corn Exchange Buildings
Manchester M4 3BY

A CIP catalogue record for this book
is available from the British Library.
ISBN 1 85754 285 1

The publisher acknowledges financial assistance
from the Arts Council of England.

Printed and bound in England by SRP Ltd, Exeter

# INTRODUCTION

WRITING to Ezra Pound on 8 March, 1933, a fortnight after the publication of *The Rash Act*, Ford Madox Ford said that the book 'is more like what I wanted to write than anything I have done for years', adding that he had 'put more into it' than, as it were, he 'could afford . . . in the way of mental fatigue.' Six months later, in a letter to Caroline Gordon: 'it was my best book —more, that is to say, like what I really wanted to write than anything I have yet done.'

Ford was sixty, with *The Good Soldier* (1915) and the Tietjens books (1924-8) far behind him—and how many books besides! It is not only the number of Ford's volumes of novels, memoirs, criticism and poems which makes it difficult for readers to get a view of him. The fact that they *all* contain something of himself, that there is no page, even in what pass disparagingly as the poorest of them, which does not bear traces of his invincible passion for good writing, has itself been a drawback. For it would have been convenient to be able to assume that all but a few of the books are unreadable; but that is not the case. All are readable, some more, some less. But there are limits to human endurance, and even the Ford addict has to admit that, in many of these volumes, there is, if not repetition, at least ceaseless re-vamping of matter which at times becomes so thinly spread that it has to be conceded that they are marginal—though, to have a proper view of Ford, one must have read *some* at least of these marginal books. Where does *The Rash Act* fit in the general scheme of things?

The most generally accepted view of Ford's works—accepted perhaps largely on the authority of Graham Greene—is that 'Ford will be remembered as the author of three great novels',

1

the *Fifth Queen* trilogy, *The Good Soldier* and *Parade's End*—this last being the Tietjens books with the exclusion of *Last Post*. This is certainly too restrictive. As to the exclusion of *Last Post*, we know that Ford wrote to his agent Pinker saying that he did not like the book and 'always intended the series to end with *A Man Could Stand Up*'. We know that in the Dedicatory Letter to the novel there is more than a suggestion that Ford was pushed into writing it. None the less, it is an exaggeration of more than Fordian proportions, on Greene's part, to say that 'it is a better book, a thousand times, which ends with the confusions of Armistice Night, 1918', that is with *A Man Could Stand Up*, rather than with *Last Post*. The twentieth-century conventions which require a novel to end 'with no absolute certainties about the past . . . or about the future' are not self-evidently superior to the conventions of the happy ending, and are now as worn. *Last Post* is the weakest of the four books, but it contains too much of the essential Ford to be cast aside. It may be added that, considerable though the merits of the *Fifth Queen* books are, they are vitiated by traces of post-pre-Raphaelite language as well as by a little of the cardboard effect rarely absent from historical novels. In any case, it would be a pity if The Bodley Head Ford Madox Ford was regarded as a sort of canon. *The Rash Act* must be ranked very high among the omissions—and put higher than the *Fifth Queen* trilogy, which is included. If it is not Ford's 'best book' simply, it certainly deserves attention as 'more like' what he wanted to write than anything he had done 'for years'.

That the book is a technical masterpiece is beyond question. The structure of the novel was the subject of all others to which Ford had given continuous and restless attention for over four decades. He had set up novels in various ways; he had talked endlessly with his fellow-practitioners, of whom Conrad was only the most distinguished; the corner of his writing-table was rarely free of the typescript of some beginner who was seeking advice. No doubt mere technicalities, in any art, are nothing

2

except where there is the matter to engage them, and Ford did not always find that matter when he sat down to elaborate one more 'affair'. He found it in *The Good Soldier* and in the Tietjens books. He found it, assuredly, in *The Rash Act*, the book of a singularly fortunate moment in his affairs when he was able so to speak to gather up the whole armful of his acquired skills and match them to almost the whole range of the matters most dear to him. The book lacks the agonies of *The Good Soldier*, the profound worries of the Tietjens books. It is a work of great ripeness which would have been impossible without those earlier agonies and worries—the work of a man about to descend into Avernus—a few more years only—but for the moment poised within reach of happiness. The whole course of Ford's errors, mistakes and pleasures, from years back to his then present, are here in play. So also is that passion for the French Mediterranean world, and for the ancient world as reflected in it, which was his gravitational centre. And here all those elements meet with the words, the forms of chapter and of book, which would enable him to set them down as comprehensively as he was ever able to do. *The Rash Act* is certainly one of Ford's key books. If not the most profound of them, it is the most central—and it is one of the most profound too. No one who cares at all for Ford's work should leave it unread. Few of those who read it will not want, over the years, to return to it more than once.

For all his talk of technique—important because the shapelessness of the English novel had got beyond all bounds—Ford understood the primary importance of subject. He wanted 'nothing either high-brow or recondite', as he says in *The English Novel* (1930); 'the nearer you are to your fellow-man who differs from you only in not having literary ambitions or gifts, the nearer you are to universality'. 'You must therefore,' he continued, 'write as simply as you can—with the extreme of simplicity that is granted to you, and you must write of subjects that spring at your throat. But why subjects appeal to you you will have no

3

means of knowing.'—The subject, that is to say, has nothing voluntary about it; it is what you cannot help. Ford had a proper contempt for the novelist who wrote a book to point a moral or assist a cause. The subject of *The Rash Act* did spring at his throat. When he tried to define it, as a matter of practical necessity to publishers and the like, he was inclined to make out that it was a novel of the Great Depression, and Henry Martin 'the typical man of the period'. It was to be 'the beginning of a trilogy that is meant to do for the post-war world and the Crisis what the Tietjens tetralogy did for the war'. Ford did in fact write a sequel, *Henry for Hugh*, which took up some of the themes, but when he came to write it he found that he had 'omitted' some motives that would have made the sequel easier to write. The fact is that *The Rash Act* is a singularly rounded work which is complete in itself, and the Crisis is of no more than incidental importance in it. The manner of Henry Martin's stepping off the felucca—or of his intention to do so—was suggested by the death of Hart Crane, but that too is little more than a drama of the surface. What really make this book what it is are the themes which invoke all Ford's deepest loyalties and uncertainties: the relationship between Henry Martin and the impeccable and casual Hugh Monckton he would like to have been; the appreciation of certain characteristics in women; the sense of the remaining solidities of European civilisation; a Latin reading of Love and Death which is as much Roman as French and which is akin to the matter of *Great Trade Route* (1937) and *Provence* (1938). It is as if, before the writing of *The Rash Act*, the whole of the past—personal and historical— which the author had digested, was simultaneously swirling round in his capacious stomach. The nourishment thereby imparted to the fine and finely-trained nervous system of this incomparable writer is given us in a form which only years of attention to the craft of fiction could have achieved.

There has been, on the part of critics of more than one generation, a tendency to make light of Ford, as if some personal weaknesses, mere absurdities even, gave the critic a moral superiority. Let those who write better throw the first stone. It is the artist that matters, and Ford was a considerable one. The game of making more of the life than of the work is one of the hallmarks of the inferior critic, as the preference for reading gossip about an author, rather than reading his books, is the mark of an inferior reader. Of course we all like gossip—Ford liked it—but one ought to recognise that there is an impenetrable barrier between us and any subject of gossip whomsoever, whereas the work is there, to be read and enjoyed—and if it cannot be enjoyed it had better not be read. From this book one can promise pleasure: 'You have at your disposal'—to use words from *The English Novel*—'heredity, environment, the concatenation of the effects of one damn thing after another that life is—and Destiny who is blind and august.' And the novelist sees 'that line by line and filament by filament, the reader's eye is conducted to' the culminating point.

The clarity of Ford's vision, at this moment of his life, must have been very great. He seems to move through his own past— seen under various disguises—with great sureness of touch. The surface appearances may be as type-cast as figures in Ben Jonson —Monckton with his stylised slang and mannerisms, the *sale flic*, the *poules*—but under all this the narrator moves among his most solid realities, the treasures collected in his sixty years: it is rather as if Hugh Monckton had opened all those packing-cases intended for the Victoria and Albert and were handling the articles. The book is, for all its narrative movement, in the end a piece of contemplation under the guise of fiction; excellent as fiction but recording, as it were, a long look in the Mediterranean sunlight. It is a pagan world the author sees, and to which he has given his loyalty, and because this is truer to his appreciation of things than the evocation of George Herbert in the Tietjens books, *The Rash Act* has a seriousness which goes further and deeper than that of the great tetralogy. Life and fate are in appearances. A roll of silk, a red sail, the glitter of the sea, these are the absolutes.

5

The Roman boy who 'danced and gave pleasure' exists by and for his dancing, and the pleasure is for the spectator. For the spectator all external things, people included, are there not for their own sakes, or for God's, as in one part of the western tradition, but for his own contemplation and use, for the brief time that he enjoys in the sunlight. There is a chill in that view of things and the author's assent goes to the accomplished suicide of Hugh Monckton, not to the evasions of Henry Martin, even though the latter thereby accedes to brilliance hitherto denied him.

'Means of escape,' Hugh Monckton said. 'The world's full of them. Only one is genuine.'

It is not thus that suicide is regarded in the Tietjens books. The world has changed, and Ford has noted the symptoms.

He has not made a final statement; there are no final statements, according to Ford. He himself went on, to expire, six years and eight books later, at Deauville, on 26 June, 1939. Madame Biela records* that, 'thanks to a drunken grave-digger, he was erroneously buried in a plot of ground reserved for temporary graves.' 'That was Ford all over,' she comments.

*See her contribution to *The Presence of Ford Madox Ford*, edited by Sondra J. Stang (University of Pennsylvania Press), 1981.

PART ONE

THE morning seemed to herald a glorious day. The motionless silver of the sea was ruffled in irregular streaks like watered satin. The light mists were rising from the horizon and the islands. Sunlight from over the stone pines just touched the end of the jetty so that there was a triangle of gold. A boat, anchored beyond, brooded, motionless. On the translucent water it seemed to be suspended in the air. It became vivid – a melon slice of incandescent white, a curved stripe of scarlet. Another, parallel below, was of azure. The boat should have caught the light first. It was further out than the end of the little pier.

The phenomenon was no doubt occasioned by the irregular outlines of the pines. Or perhaps a beam pierced an interstice in their tops. The prow of the boat stood up, white, shaped like half an open fan. The sail, untidily housed on the curving felucca-yard was lambent maroon. Then all the light went out of the whole caboodle.

It was as if he had been vouchsafed a chromolithographic close-up of a prehistoric craft. In miniature the thing had been one of the thousand ships that Helen's face had launched and Homer catalogued.

What a thought for that moment!

He was suspended as this boat had been – between nothing and nothing. There was nothing to think of but visible objects. The sea, level: blue at the edges. The stone pines bent, red-trunked. The umbrella pines brighter in colour.

The sunlight was falling on the islands now . . . a landscape without mercy. It smiled with the heartless smile of syrens. Infinitely without the quality of pity.

He imagined that Mlle Simone, the chambermaid, would find his bedroom tidier than usual. He was always tidy. Now there would be not a scrap displaced. Not a cigarette paper. She would perhaps think him considerate! Tuberculous: that was what she was. You could not be so thin without being tuberculous. She might even think that nothing in his life became him like the leaving it.

An aged man in improbably soiled ducks came down the inclined plane leading from the Douane. Why should the white Douane building be as large as the barracks for a detachment of soldiers? No other house in the place was larger than a pill-box and the whole port consisted of not more than twenty pill-boxes. The port was no larger than the mainsail of a schooner-yacht. At one time bands of smugglers had landed there. Coming from Corsica, their brows bound with handkerchiefs. Long flint-lock muskets behind their backs. They needed detachments of troops with which to drive off the picturesque bandits. Picturesque days! – Helen! Homer! Bandits! Salee rovers! Centurions! The landscape with its heartless smile had seen them all with the same equanimity. With the same it regarded him: him Henry Martin Aluin Smith: free, male and twenty-one. Rising thirty-six, that is to say. It is all one, twenty-one or thirty-five if you are called Henry Martin Aluin with 'Smith' to top it off. . . . If you are going. . . . But a less grotesque name would have given more dignity to the occasion or to a cross!

He was at least spared the indignity of Aluin-Smith. On his passport, which, along with his letter to Alice, he had obligingly wrapped in oiled silk that also enveloped a fifty franc note, 'I, the undersigned, Secretary of State of these United States' had boggled at the task of inserting a hyphen between his last two names. That would perhaps let his grizzled boar of a father out. Presumably his grizzled boar of a father would not like to have the name 'Aluin-Smith' on a cheap metal cross looking over the Mediterranean. His father had achieved the name Aluin-Smith with some difficulty on his candy wrappers. Early specimens that Henry Martin had seen had borne the legend 'Alcyone A. Faber.' That had become, presumably as his father had lived himself into the life of Springfield, Ohio, 'A. A. Smith.' *Faber* is after all the Latin for the more American 'Smith.' At last, on marriage it stood up boldly as: 'A. Aluin-Smith.' . . . Mother had been the daughter of a 'pharmacist' who in those old-fashioned days called himself Smith the Chymist – with a 'y'. A rigid New Engländer he had been and claimed to be a man of science, no tooth-brush or pop corn pedlar.

Henry Martin wondered too about his tombstone. His father would no doubt attend to that. He would probably waver between having the remains thrown into the common fosse of the paupers of St. Jean du Var and a lump of Vosges rock that would be smoothed to a glassy finish as to one panel which would be inscribed: H.M.A.S. *UN ETRANGER.* 15 AUG. MCMXXXI. His father would not be one to omit the date. An orderly, if truculent, man fond of making memoranda! His packets – even his one cent pre-war packets of Pisto-Brittle had been decorated with a slip inviting the complaints of purchasers. The slip would bear a facsimile of his father's signature, a number running into millions and a date.

H.M.A.S.
*UN ETRANGER*
NOYE
*3.*
Le 15 Août MCMXXXI

The inscription would be in good Roman capitals.
'Leaded caps' was perhaps the technical word! Presumably there would be no religious addition. That
would be frowned upon by ecclesiastical Authority. It
was singular that his father had never become Protestant
Episcopal. It was held in Springfield that Catholicism
was a cult only for nursemaids. They gave to the priest
their hard-earned pennies out of little leather purses. This
he had heard time out of mind in prep-school where the
boys had been nearly all German Lutheran. Possibly it
was Moravian. At any rate Springfield was a great
centre for the production of German Lutheran clergy.
The training college on its insignificant mound had had
architectural features. As a boy he had been awed by
them. . . . Well, if Henry Alcyone Aluin had become
Protestant Episcopal – or even Moravian – he, Henry
Martin Aluin, might have had a pious aspiration carved
on that polished granite panel. As it was, there would
be none now. It might as well run:

HIC
EXIT
SMITH'S
PISTO-BRITTLE
– drowned in the Mediterranean 15.8.31!

There would be no one to carry on that sticky dynasty.
Brother Hal as an engineer with a fine if laborious career

in the Klondike would not want to be bothered. Nor certainly would Heldenstamm, Sister Carrie's husband. He would want to go on hunting wild boars in Luxemburg. . . . A precipitous country. All rocks, streams and trees. That was why his father made his family tombs out of boulders. The habit shocked the inhabitants of Springfield. When it had merely been a matter of Aunt Hedwig, Comtesse de Pralinghem, it had not so much mattered. But when father buried mother under a similar lump Springfield had said that had been un-American. If mother had been alive she would never have stood for it. But it had looked like good publicity. When father had first come to the country he had manufactured peanut brittle. Then mother – before the marriage – had suggested that pistachios were more genteel than peanuts. But father had continued to manufacture peanut brittle after he began making the other. Henry Martin could remember as a tiny boy standing behind the counter in the drug-store. His father would be laughing at his attempts to wrap up tablets of Pisto-Brittle. They were thinner than the peanut concoction, trays of which stood by the first cash register. That you cut with fat, sharpened pincers that opened like crocodile jaws and bit out chunks of the rocky candy. There was another candy made with almonds. Some called it almond rock.

On a Saturday afternoon he, Henry Martin, would be allowed to cut up the candy for customers. The country folk came in and bought it to take to their children though old folks said they liked sucking it themselves. It reminded them of their courting days before they had lost their teeth. They turned it round in their toothless jaws and chuckled.

His father let him have on such Saturday afternoons every exact ounce he could cut out with the pincers at one cut. He never managed many. Hardly ever more than two cuts in an afternoon. Well he was earning a large lump of almond rock! Really such a tombstone much resembled that candy. When it was cut it had sides like polished granite – for the inscription. The almonds on the other side had the ruddled appearance of the reddish boulder from Luxemburg.

The proudest moments of his life he had known, not inside but on the sidewalks, on winter evenings, outside that drug-store. With a woollen cap and mittens, a small sled dangling behind, the parti-coloured lights falling on the trodden snow from the great red, blue and yellow bottles. The other boys goggling up at them. That was pride . . . his proprietary interest . . . those flaring demijohns! Really of course they were mother's. Father had only come into the drug-store on the marriage. That accounted for mother's social ambition. She had to give father a hoist. She had married below her even by American standards. Her father had been Smith the Chymist! Father had started his career as far as Springfield was concerned in a wooden shed with a shutter that pushed up and displayed his candies. On a vacant lot on Main Street.

There was nothing to be ashamed of in that. But it was kept in the background. Only; when they took grave walks with father on Sundays down Main Street he had been used to stop opposite what had been successively Parke's, the butchers', Gurney's, the booksellers', and the Ohio Electric Corporation's show-store. Henry Martin believed it was now the First National. Or perhaps the First National had failed. So many had in the last few months.

Father would point out that there he had started his career. In a shed. Hal and Henry Martin in their creak-

14

ing boots – Sister Carrie in her rustling starched petticoats that stuck out all round her tartan stockings – they would stand goggling whilst father pointed his gold-knobbed cane at the shutters – at first of Parke's, then of Gurney's. The Electric Corporation did not have shutters even on Sunday. Nights, they had a light burning so that you saw the copper wind fans and nickel irons! 'Ready for service,' night and day. Father, with his top hat and white waistcoat with mother-of-pearl buttons would expatiate on the fact that there he had had his first shed. Occasionally he would stop a passer-by – two passers-by or three – and tell them, too, the tale. He would swell – they would all seem to swell and smile cordially – at the thought of the growth of Springfield.

Presumably that was how the news of father's Sunday afternoon habit had reached the ears of mother. At any rate father was told that it would be better for the children's health if they were taken into more rural surroundings on a Sunday. So, for a time they were taken along the ridge where villas and porticos and stoops were beginning to arise among the apple orchards.

So father, by all accounts, had been the better American, even if his name had at first been Faber and even though mother had come of one of the first families in New England. They heard that from both father and mother often enough. Grandpa Smith had emigrated to Springfield from Fall River . . . oh, a great many years ago. So mother had been born over the coloured bottles in Springfield. But to be born in a stable does not make you a mare if you are a lady and the daughter of a scientist. It was said to have broken Grandpa Smith's heart when, by the pressure of his wife and daughter, he was forced to give up a section of a counter to his son-in-law's candies. At any rate he had died within a year of the marriage, not living to see Henry Martin who had come into the world two days after the old gentleman's death.

If he had known that the Smith family would one day have two visible countesses in it it might have heartened him up. No other family in Springfield could show the like though nearly every one of them had non-visible liens that attached them to Royalty, Durchlauchts, Serenities, and Archdukes. Many of them, they whispered in moments of expansion over their sewing, if they or their husbands chose to exercise their rights, might well be sewing coronets on their teacloths. But they were too democratic. Most of mother's napkins and finer face towels did have coronets. That was because they were presents from Aunt Hedwig and Sister Carrie.

But Aunt Hedwig had not arrived in Springfield until many years after Grandpa Smith's death, though she had lived to see the marriage of Sister Carrie to her nephew Van Heldenstamm who now, in the Ardennes, hunted wild boars from a castle rejuvenated by Pisto-Brittle profits.

Auntie Hedwig had arrived in Springfield as a refugee from Luxemburg a very few months after the outbreak of the European war. Apparently her husband, the Comte de Pralinghem, had had his ancestral ruin desecrated by invaders and had died of apoplexy. A certain veil had been drawn over that part of her career. Until the United States had entered the unfortunate struggle Springfield had been markedly Central Empire in complexion, and, after the Comtesse de Pralinghem had made an incendiary speech in German about atrocities committed in the Grand Duchy of Luxemburg, there had been some talk of riding her on a rail out of town.

That at least had been Brother Hal's story. Henry Martin had been at Dartmouth and, being at that time on bad terms with his father, had not seen his relation till later. What he had seen of her had not increased his pride of race. She had seemed a nasty, toothless, dirty, very aged woman who took snuff, smelt of brandy and talked French with a hideous accent. Hal said she had bought her husband, the deceased Count, with money sent her by father and he made disobliging surmises as to the Count's past.

The aged man who had been descending the stone stade was clattering on the flat rocks at Henry Martin's side. He was toothless, wrinkled and aged like Aunt Hedwig. His neck was as deeply set in his shoulders as a chimpanzee's, his arms as long. He squinted up with difficulty at the skies and raising his arms as if they had been a marionette's, flapped them, ill-jointedly, up and down, up and down, with, at the end of them, hands like powerless hooks.

Henry Martin wondered whether it had not been the old man's mahogany-coloured, wrinkled face that had reminded him of his aunt. The wrinkles were ingrained with dirt. But they say that men about to drown see their whole lives with extraordinary vividness. He had certainly just seen Springfield much more plainly than he had ever wanted to see it again after he first left it. He could have sworn he had just been standing by the level-crossing over the railway with the gates shut and the inextricable jumble, in that squalid thoroughfare, of automobiles and horse-trucks that the cops never succeeded in reconciling. There were all sorts of white marks and lumps in the roadway. There were more of them pro rata in Springfield than in all New York with Chicago thrown in. Why did provincial cities have to go to these excesses?

Brother Hal said nothing in the world would induce him to drive his Buick down those streets again. He himself would certainly never again tread its unrepaired sidewalks. He had once or twice returned there – at the dictates of conscience – after he had broken irrevocably with the old man. Hal, he presumed, had inherited their father's impetuous, wild boar's obstinacy. He himself had perhaps more of his mother's New England conscience and determination. It worked out at something very like irresolution. Few people – certainly few young men of his generation, free and male, had by the age of thirty-five made as much of a muddle of their lives. He seemed never to have been free for a minute till that moment. He presumed he might call himself male.

But at that moment he was being resolute enough. The old man – Marius Vial, the proprietor of the inn and half the boats in the harbour – was undoubtedly urging him not to go out. He was reciting the long incomprehensible sorty of seventeen boats that had been sunk by a *trombio* off the end of Cap Cépet, at the end of the peninsula of St. Mandrier. Out there! . . .

He hooked a claw into Henry Martin's forearm and waved his other flibbertigibbet arm at the distant promontory with its slopes of fir woods.

Henry Martin considered that, to the old man, he must present an aspect of inflexible Nordic valour. He had laughed, disengaged his arm and continued striding towards the land end of the little pier. The old man might be right – but again he might be wrong. He had grappled himself to Henry Martin's side every day for an hour or so during the past serene-weathered week and had recited the story of the *trombio* – a local dialect version of the word *trombe* which means a cloudbreak. And every day he had dissuaded Henry Martin from going out. That might be sympathetic fear. It might also be just business. Henry Martin had hired the boat for a week from Olive, Marius Vial's grandson – but the boat, like the hotel and every stick in it, belonged to the old fellow. The old fellow might very well want him to get as little hire out of it as the recital of the storm could make him. On first hearing the story he had actually not gone out. But during the succeeding twenty-four hours there had not been a breath of wind on the glassy sea. This time he was going!

He was, however, worried about the boat. What would happen to it? It was, it is true, insured. Old Marius Vial had seen to that before he would begin to think of letting his grandson hire it out to a visitor. He would be doing the Vials no harm. But the thought of the boat, drifting empty, was very disagreeable to him. You should not treat boats like that. A boat manned had a dignity, as if a purpose. Even anchored or hitched to a buoy its dignity does not desert it. It waits; it broods; it retains a personality. It is all right hauled up on a beach. It has stability. But drifting, lurching clumsily to an unexpected wave, exhibiting parts usually hidden, a boat is degraded. You should not degrade boats any more than you should mishandle tools or maltreat animals. A boat adrift is like an ownerless dog, the tail and ears drooping, the gait furtive.

The problem of the boat had worried him a great deal. A story he had heard had returned to him again and again whilst he had been pondering the problem at odd moments during the last six or seven days. He had heard the story in Lowland Scotland – from a red headed Scotsman married to a Chicago girl. The girl had had a name that in Chicago stank of dollars and eatables. Henry Martin had wondered that Ferguson had had an ancient

and battered car of an extinct model. Ferguson had explained that the chauffeur would not let him have a new
one. The car was the chauffeur's pride. He wanted to
drive it for ever, scattering nuts and bits of radiator all
over the countryside – to show what he could do! He said
he would prove that he could get more out of it than the
chauffeur of the people on the next estate who had a
brand new, silver Rolls-Royce.

Ferguson had told him the story as a comment on his
chauffeur and on how people regarded their implements
and vehicles once they had got attached to them and
credited them with individualities. An aviator – or at
any rate a man who had owned a plane for a long time –
had also a wife to whom he was as attached as to his
plane. He found his wife had a lover. Life ended for
him. He invited the unsuspecting lover to take a flight
with him. He intended to smash the plane and put an
end to both of them.

He couldn't do it – not because he was afraid of Death
but because he could not bear to put a slur on the fair
fame of his plane. People would think she had failed him.
And, still more, he could not bear to make her do wrong
because she would feel humiliation.

Henry Martin had felt the same about his boat. It is
true that he had run her only about a fortnight – but a
fortnight of continual society is ample to make you intimate with boats or people. He had loafed, drifting all
about such of the sea as was there visible, doing nothing –
as if he had been immured in the boat. Shut in on himself! It had not perhaps been good for him. But what
did that matter? He was beyond good and evil.

He had chosen with great deliberation the place at
which he would step off the boat. The great harbour had
a mole – if that was what you called it? – a sea wall with

two openings for the passage of warships. At each opening was a little lighthouse with a guardroom for signallers. It was their duty to watch events in the harbour. Therefore Henry Martin had resolved to end it about fifty yards from the left-hand lighthouse – fifty or a hundred.

A certain fastidiousness may be allowed to one in the choice of the place of one's end! In any case he assumed that right, and there was no one to stop him. He had passed over the chosen spot several times in the course of the last week. Once he had put the boat about three or four times on a course of a couple of hundred yards. If it had been murder he was planning you could with full warrant have said it was premeditated.

He had gone close in under the terrace of the little lighthouse. The sentry had called to him to stop and had asked him if he were practising for the speed boat races. That proved that they watched the proceedings of even the smallest boats. For smugglers, no doubt!

He had answered, No, he had dropped a pocketbook overboard and had been trying to recover it. . . .

Was one, then, as fastidious in lying as in the choice of the place of one's end? Wouldn't it have been just as easy to accept the lie the sentry had provided for him? It was in any case what the Jesuits would justify as a lie of necessity. He could hardly have told the fellow that he had been cruising back and forth over the place where he intended to end his life. In order to insure that the last landscape his eyes would see would be agreeable to him. It would certainly be agreeable. On the one hand the island towered up, near by, dark with pines and chestnuts because it was the north slope. Close to him would run the white mole that kept the heavier waves of the open sea from the harbour . . . and, far beyond the waters of the outer harbour, the façades of houses, irregular in height, white as a general colour and basking in the sunlight. Arid mountains towered up behind.

He had disliked the cold sea that you saw from Nantucket or Portland, Maine. That was perhaps due to his inland birth and inland origins. You could hardly think of an inhabitant of Springfield or the descendant of Luxemburgers as a sailor. But he had had, in his time, a cruising yawl and then a speed boat on Lake Michigan and, to the little, glassy, azure, sunlit Mediterranean coves and harbours he had taken exactly as a duck takes to water.

The sentry, leaning over the balustrade that surrounded the lighthouse had jeered at him for letting his pocketbook go overboard and, still more, for thinking he could recover it from the sea. He had said that it might be washed on to the landing steps and asked Henry Martin for his name and address. Henry Martin had replied:

'Henry Martin Aluin Smith, Hotel Belle Vue, Carqueiranne,' and the sentry had waved his hand as the boat drifted away.

Perhaps the fellow really took him for a smuggler trying to pick up a buoy. Or a spy trying to observe details of the fort whose semaphore showed white on the outline of the island. Well, he would learn the truth if he ever walked in the cemetery above the railway behind the town. There would be the name on the lump of almond rock. . . . Or perhaps the sentry would read of the case in the papers. Or perhaps he had not caught the name at all. Or perhaps he would see him, Henry Martin, male, free and thirty-six, step over the side of the boat.

Perhaps, too, his father might refuse to go to the expense of the tombstone. There was no knowing what his father would do. In his thirty-odd years of acquaintanceship he had never sized his father up. He was like a wild boar – like a mountain. Slumped down in his round-backed office chair as if he would never move again, but occasionally lifting a heavy hand and dropping it. Behind his little, watchful eyes his thoughts ran round and round – actively, no doubt. He was tyrannical, cunning, intelligent, sentimental, vindictive and completely without shame. He must be rising sixty – but still of immense physical strength and very little bowed.

He could not be said to have modelled himself on the old-school American Merchant. He was too obtuse to model himself on anyone. But it worked out like that. Perhaps the Europeans who came to America had to be fitted to work out true to type if they were to succeed. To the type, mental and physical. Father certainly made a good, representative American of the old-school – even to the remorseless, overhung jawbone. He was indomitable and passionate – but Henry Martin had never felt settled in his mind as to what was his father's ruling passion. It was no doubt centred in Smith's Pisto-Brittle. . . . But what did he see in that simple business edifice? There was no knowing. He hardly seemed to wish to extend its fame to the extreme corners of the continent. Once he had said to Henry Martin:

'Don't you believe you're going to come into a lot of millions. I shall never die worth more than a million and a half!' So that even if Henry Martin pleased him to the day of his death he could not expect to have more than three-quarters of a million. It was not a great sum to receive after having played the sedulous ape . . . for fifty years. There was no reason why father should not see eighty.

The reward had not seemed good enough – either to Brother Hal or himself. Hal had simply cut and run – into engineering. He seemed to lead a riotous and successful life with a good humoured, healthy Swedish girl he had picked up – mostly on the Alaska-Canada border. When the couple of them hilariously descended on Springfield – usually, of course, in the winter – they united in windy vitality to make fun of that city, of the old man, of Henry Martin, and of Sister Carrie if she happened to be there for Christmas. How the old man regarded Hal and Greta there was no knowing. When they actively displayed their satisfaction with each other and turned the house upside down the old man merely blinked – as if at sunshine in a high wind. He said nothing. Sister Carrie kissed him good night on the bald forehead. He blinked. It might be pleasurably; it might not.

But when he, Henry Martin, had had his tumultuous affair with Wanda, the old man had said:

'One sixty-horse power Swedish nightingale is quite enough sunshine in the American home.' So he might have been jeering at Greta. But he might not. It might have been as if he had said – as he did say – that such and such a proportion of milk-butter was a good thing in Pisto-Brittle de luxe, but too much spoilt the crispness.

Equally, you couldn't tell how he took the Van Heldenstamm family. When Aunt Hedwig had imported that beetle-browed, lanky, greasy-accented piece of Belgian aristocracy to Springfield with the avowed intention of marrying him to Carrie, the old man had uttered no objections. Mother had been delighted. Poor mother! She had pointed out the analogies that existed between old New England families and the European aristocracies. They – she and her children – through the Huntingdons of Dorchester, Massachusetts, were undoubtedly, if mysteriously, descended from the Earls of Huntingdon. The most famous of that family had been the great Robin

Hood – who was certainly a democratic figure in that what he took from the rich he gave to the poor.

But no doubt a great part of the pleasure that poor mother had taken in the anticipated noble alliance had come from the fact that it put her level with father. She was to have an authentic Countess of her own blood to score against Aunt Hedwig. That some sort of rivalry existed between poor father and mother was indubitable. It manifested itself on her part in half tones of the voice; on his part, in chuckles that were barely audible. These symptoms might be presumed to occur when either had scored off the other – as if each, on occasion, should say: 'I told you so!'

Henry Martin had not the least idea what it was all about. . . . No doubt about minute points in the housekeeping, the cooking, father's indigestion. Or his clothes and behaviour on social occasions. They were obviously the best of friends, but father's tastes in ties and trouserings were flamboyant and he stuck to his gold-headed cane long years after the habit of carrying such articles had passed from the Middle West. If the cane had been of malacca with smooth, rich-looking gold for its handle it might have passed. But it was of ebony and had elaborate gold-chasings in the worst style of the eighteen-eighties. The perfectly genuine gold extremity looked as if it were the cheapest of gilt brass.

At any rate, when the gorgeous wedding in the Roman Catholic church was over, father let the cane be wrapped up in tissue paper and put away in the mahogany chest of drawers in the bedroom. And he gave up railing at the New England vegetable plates and pot-roasts that poor mother insisted were essential to his health. That was the symbol that poor mother was, for the rest of her life, to dominate him completely.

It might have been indeed that he had lost all spirit when he lost Carrie. He was probably deeply – deep-rootedly – attached to her.

At any rate, before consenting to the marriage, he had called her into his office and, fingering her necklace pathetically as she stood before him, had asked her if she really knew what she was in for if she married Van Heldenstamm. He drew for her vivid pictures of the habits of the Belgian aristocracy. They were apparently the only aristocracy left that were aristocratically outrageous in the old style. They carried off each other's wives on coal-black chargers, shot injured husbands across the moats of châteaux, kidnapped the children awarded by courts to injured spouses, flogged their butlers, maintained harems in Brussels, Ghent, Antwerp or on their properties under the nose of their wives. They had, the old man said, all the black properties of the old-time Spaniards and Netherlanders from whom they drew their blood. And he pointed out that if Van Heldenstamm proved an exception Sister Carrie couldn't expect to find in Europe the freedom and the affection that young American girls expected as theirs of right. At best the life of a European château is one of unceasing calls on you. There are the servants, the priests, the peasants, the poor neighbours, making perpetual calls on your purse, your needle, your poultry yard and, above all, your time. He would not want a daughter of his, if she was to occupy a prominent position in a country bordering on one that had been his own to occupy that position with any want of dignity. . . .

As far as Henry Martin could see, the old man had come with more dignity himself out of that interview than out of any other that he had had with his children. Perhaps he had felt it more! With Henry Martin and

Brother Hal he had never come off well. Brother Hal had simply defied him at every turn. He had done what he wanted, never asked his father for a penny and had prospered boisterously in half-opened territories and markets. He had worked on bridges in Spain, Mexico, Sweden, Buenos Aires, and New Mexico – on the machinery of gold mines in Ballarat, South Africa and now, in the Klondike. He had earned good money and had even now a good sum invested in one or two inventions that, in spite of the times, were beginning to do well.

His own career Henry Martin was shy of recalling in this his final review of it. He was strolling desultorily along the pier. Old Marius Vial, having given up the struggle to dissuade him, had hobbled forward to gloat over the boat as he gloated over all his property.

What was the good of reviewing a career that was so soon to run inside a lump of pink granite with one polished side? As if it were an automobile running into its last garage. He didn't want to think of his perpetual wanderings with Springfield as a base – the town to which he had as perpetually returned to make new beginnings. And new excursions under the sardonic eyes of his father. . . . Surely if father had loved his wife he would have shown more sympathy with the aspirations of her son!

He had never seemed to.

Their first wounding and atrocious quarrel had come just after Henry Martin's return for the first time from Dartmouth. He had still been a freshman and still had ambitions to become a writer. Over that they had not directly quarrelled. Not ostensibly!

If he was now thirty-five he ought to have been born in 1896. Actually he had been born in 1895. He would be thirty-six in three months' time. . . . But he would

27

not, of course. 'He would have been' was perhaps the way to express it. It was a mistake to have been born in the nineteenth century when the whole of your life was to be passed in the twentieth.

Carrie had been born on July 11th, 1894. It was just over a month since he had sent her his last birthday telegram. Hal had been born on January 9th, 1901. . . . It was perhaps a mistake to have been born between an early maturing, soft natured sister and a brother much smaller than oneself. He had no doubt been rendered soft by his sister's solicitude. . . . It was not good for a boy to go to his first socials under the wing of an elder sister. It had got him into the early habit of relying on women for advice and support.

Carrie had been married early in 1915 – when she had been just under twenty-one. He had been at Dartmouth . . . was it a year, then? He was not certain. These dates confused themselves. There were too many of them.

Mother had died in . . . yes, in late 1915. She had only had a countess of her own blood for four months! And a son at Dartmouth for fifteen.

He had come home for her death. She had, it then appeared, only just kept up for the wedding and had been under opiates for most of the time since then. The old man must have suffered like hell all those months. But to Henry Martin he had seemed merely callous.

Coming home from the funeral he had gone straight to the kitchen door and had shouted to the cook in Luxemburg Flemish that she would cook Luxemburg fashion from then on. He had afterwards gone up to his bedroom, opened the drawer and taken out from its tissue paper his gold-knobbed cane.

Coming straight back from college triumphs Henry Martin had regarded that as an offensive assertion of

28

recovered freedom. At Dartmouth he had been quite popular. He had had money to throw away. He stood already six feet in his gym shoes and was very large boned. Taking college life with immense seriousness he had united to a studiousness sufficient to make him stand very well with the English teaching staff, a zealous observance of fraternity necessities. He had, too, a great devotion to athletics. He was light of foot in spite of his weight, very muscular and of remarkable balance for a cub. He knew that he was already under observation for the Rhodes Scholarship list of 1916.

Three days after mother's funeral father had sent for him to the office and had told him that he would not be going back to Dartmouth. His blinking eyes had watched Henry Martin's face with the effect of a medieval executioner taking stock of the emotions of a victim to whom he had announced sentence of death. He had said simply:

'You won't be going back to Dartmouth.' Without any breaking of the news.

Henry Martin had stood like a pole-axed ox. Swaying.

After a long time father had added:

'You will be going to learn the business from the bottom. American fashion. Stoking. Boiling. Cutting. Packing. Carting, travelling, retail selling. Boy clerk. Head cashier. . . . Partner. . . . Sole owner.'

Henry Martin did not think he had shown himself wanting in resolution. Then, or ever! Then why did he seem like Hamlet to himself? He was now bronzed to the shade of a quadroon, over six feet in his stockings. He was perhaps too aware of his height. It had done him no good.

Conscious of his own prowess on the football field he had asked his father: Was wrapping candy the job for a fellow who stood over six feet? His father had heaved his great bulk humorously back in his chair. Henry Martin had been conscious, then, that he had behind him he did not know how many generations of ancestors all, like his father, six feet two and over. And – back into the remotest recesses of time! – they had all wrapped toffee in the Grand Duchy of Luxemburg.

He had no instinctive repugnance for the trade. Even in the social stiffness of Magdalen College, Oxford, England, he had not felt ashamed of his descent. Not amongst the descendants of a hundred belted earls.

He had got his Rhodes Scholarship all right – at the cost of working as a dishwasher and cleaner in his off moments at Dartmouth. Or a little perhaps because of it! The governing authorities of that place of education had no doubt looked with a kindly eye on that gentle six-footer who indomitably washed dishes and scrubbed floors -- in the determination of being a scholastic and athletic honour to his Alma Mater.

He had got to Oxford all right. But he had not stayed there long. He had found the dreaming spires as disagreeable as the Lutheran College of Springfield, Ohio. Not as painfully sordid but more minatory. He felt that he would turn pudding-faced and rice-milky in the brain. The war had been on then, of course, and the contents of the cloisters and courts was distinctly what was there called off-colour – or too coloured. He had found himself a lanky giant amongst copper, coffee, or saffron-hued midgets – from Paraguay, the hinterlands of Bengal or Monrovia. Or else they were odd-come-shorts from obscure London suburbs with grotesque names.

Other colleges indeed had been more highly-coloured in spots. Once the Queen had been dining at Balliol and the more truculent spirits of Magdalen had paraded before that college shouting: 'Bring out your black man,

Balliol.' Balliol had amongst its undergraduates at the moment the coal blackest negro that those climes had ever seen.

In the return party Balliol had paraded before Magdalen yelping:

'Bring out your white man, Magdalen.'

And they had seized on tall, white Henry Martin and dragged him along the High whilst little, yellow and parti-coloured fellows had tried to rescue him.

He had frequently wondered whether that confusing experience had not considerably influenced his life. For the worse! At any rate it had been there that, as far as he could remember, he had for the first time wished seriously to be someone else. He had wished intensely to be a certain broad-faced Japanese – a little man with an immense mouth over-filled with gigantic teeth!

It was the measure of his discontent with himself that he should have wished to be something so completely unpresentable. To have wished to be a Japanese was unthinkable. But to have wished to be such an ugly one! . . .

Yet on the face of it he had at that date nothing to be ashamed of. He might, had he wished it, have been Smith's Pisto-Brittle, Junior. That was a position equivalent – not to that of a crown prince or an archduke heir-apparent. . . . But equivalent to that of a quite considerable earl's eldest son. Or he might have been well in the running towards representing his country at the next Olympic Games – and so a world hero, though at that date the Olympic Games had seemed remote enough.

But he could have had his father's money if he had chosen to pretend enthusiasm for his father's business. Or if he had chosen to take a little trouble in the way of wire-pulling he could have had the support of the professional speculators in brawn and muscle who turn you into the meat of which heroes are made. . . .

On the face of it his record when he had again faced his father and Springfield had been one of sufficient toughness! He had toughly defied his father, the dons of Oxford, the sergeants of a British regiment. He had toughly followed the true national tradition in performing menial functions in a café whilst proving himself a credit to the place of his education.

Where then was the snag?

He was walking along the pier . . . towards suicide. Suicide is an act of despair. Still more it is a confession of ineffectualness.

Yet it calls for resolution. . . . No, he had never been wanting in resoluteness. . . . Then. . . .

It was as if he were not all of one piece. It was perhaps that. Born in the nineteenth and having lived the great part of his life in the twentieth century.

Resolution was the note of the nineteenth, mental confusion of the twentieth. Perhaps it was that.

He remembered motoring in a public motorbus in the Pyrenees last year. An incredibly arid region of bare, piled up rocks. He had been even then not so far from his bedrock bottom dollar. 'Anacondas' were hovering at the thirty mark. He had bought at 115 – as an investment. With the highest possible advice. The man who had advised him was said to have lost seventy million – out of one hundred and twenty. It was very likely true, too . . . 'Kennecotts' had been even worse than 'Anacondas'.

Well, that arid region like one of the circles of Dante's Hell, had made him think prophetically of 'Anacondas' at 15. . . . And passing their dividend as like as not! . . . So he had said to the fortyish lady next him in the bus.

'What would you do if you found yourself on the roadside here? Without a cent!'

His mind had run through a number of expedients. You could wire to people across the Atlantic for funds, you could find the nearest American Consulate and apply for relief. . . . At that time he could still have cabled to the First National. . . .

The grey, firm-looking lady with brown eyes had gazed at him with amazement.

'Do?' she had answered. 'What should I do . . . I should find a job!'

He had felt crushed to abashment. . . . That was the nineteenth century speaking. America of the nineteenth century. . . . She was five . . . or at the most seven years older than he. A few years more spent in that hardier century had sufficed to give her the gift of incisive resolution. And Valour. She was ready to take her life in her hands and establish it in that arid waste. At a moment's notice. . . .

What then was the matter with him? . . . He had had quite – a time – a full year, whilst Anacondas and the rest wavered slowly down to 15 – 14 – 13 . . . like a flock of sheets of paper dropped from a height and darting sideways; to right, to left, inward, outward . . . but always down. He had had a full year in which impatiently to watch that decline and to know that destitution approached. He had known that he would ultimately find himself where he now was. . . . In a stern, if not arid, district of the South. . . . Without a cent. . . .

That lady had looked out over the side of the bus at the pink rocks and, without a moment's hesitation, had declared that she would find a job. . . . He had hardly

33

so much as written a line. It had been before the publication of his unfortunate book. Yet he had gone to Paris and settled there . . . as a 'writer.'

On the occasion of his momentous and quivering interview in 1915 – sixteen years ago – he had told his father he intended to 'write.' . . . He was going to get a Rhodes Scholarship and then with the requisite culture behind him follow in the footsteps of . . . Shakespeare . . . Goethe. . . . Possibly Sainte-Beuve. . . .

His father had looked at him with little, twinkling, chuckling eyes. For a long time. Then he had said:

'My boy . . . if you want to hitch your wagon to a star you can. But not on my money!' He had lifted his hand and dropped it heavily on the desk. He had added:

'Never!'

Henry Martin, at Dartmouth, had found himself attracted to the group that ran the collegiate periodicals. They had all announced themselves as having the intention of 'writing.' . . . Just writing, without much intimation of whether they intended to produce verse or prose, novels or volumes on metaphysics.

His father had chuckled again and had repeated:

'Yes, my boy. Hitch your wagon to a star. But not on my money. . . . You come of an honourable line of sugar boilers. . . . I assure you they would all turn in their graves. . . . Yes; turn in their graves if they thought the tombstone of one of their family would say "lousy ink-slinger" . . . Yes . . . "Lousy ink-slinger." '

In his rare anti-American, or rather anti-New England moments when debating with mother, father was accustomed to cite the phrase about the wagon and the star with derision as proof of New England craziness.

34

. . . It was the product of a New England writer. . . . Holmes maybe. Or Emerson.

'Hitch your wagon to a star!' he used to exclaim, rolling his shoulders against the back of his chair. 'Who ever heard of such nonsense! Ain't hitchin' posts good enough for Fall River?'

Poor mother, who was reduced to silence when father really kicked over the traces, would say that the sentiment was allegorical and beautiful. The old man would go on jerking in his chair till he had become motionless and exclaimed earnestly, leaning forward and demonstrating with his short fingers:

'Why, if you hitched your wagon to a star it would go flying away. Maybe it would knock other stars out of their places. Then your candy would fall all over the world. . . . A nice figure you would look! And they'd carve on your tombstone: "Phaeton of Fall River fell in the river."'

His mind ran on tombstones. European Teuto-Frankish minds still did. Father, in private, thought Holbein's 'Dance of Death' the finest humour in the world. . . . And, when Henry Martin came to think of it, he was not averse from thinking of tombstones himself. There was a mural inscription at Antibes, a few miles from where he then stood. It was on the wall of the Roman Theatre – to the memory of a boy dancer who had died young.

'SALTAVIT. PLACUIT. MORTUUS EST.'

'He danced. He gave pleasure. He is dead.'

It would be nice to have that on one's tombstone. But he never would. That would no doubt make his real epitaph – that he had never given pleasure. He

35

had certainly danced. Only last night he had danced – well enough. But he could feel that he gave no pleasure to the little, depressed French *poule* who was in his arms. . . . He could not attribute many sins to himself. But he had never given pleasure. Not to his father; not to his college friends: not to his Magdalen tutor: not to the sergeants of his British regiment. Not to Wanda . . . certainly not to Alice. Not on necking parties in the corners of woods with girls who had to neck someone or socially fade. . . . Well, he had danced, he had given no pleasure. He would certainly be dead. In an hour and a half maybe.

The sun was now gloriously up. He was at the end of the pier. Long, glutinous flakes of brilliance were reflected from folds of the glassy water. In its translucent depths beneath his nose the negligible *oursins* were like remote doorknobs. One of them was dead. It was not brown but skeleton grey. What could be more negligible than a dead sea-urchin? The most negligible thing in the world!

He was going to step off the half-deck above the motor of the boat – a hundred yards from the opening through the mole. . . . Step off. Like a sentry on his beat. Stiff! In a soldierly manner.

That was how he had arranged it with himself.

You could not dive effectively off a boat. Or he could not. To slip over the side would, considering the circumstances, be undignified. Like shuffling out of the world. . . . But to step stiffly, find nothing for the foot and chance what came. . . .

HUGH MONCKTON ALLARD SMITH had strolled across the floor of the little *dancing* to where Henry Martin had sat beside the silent and depressed *poule*. Hugh Monckton, who had been rolling a cigarette as he walked, looked down on them from his considerable height, and, still rolling, had remarked nonchalantly to Henry Martin:

'Met you somewhere, haven't I? Know your face. Because it's damn like my own.' He added: 'Would you pay for my drinks? I find I've left my note-case at home.'

Enviable! . . . That was what he was. He seemed to have no shadow of a doubt that Henry Martin would produce the money for his bill.

'If I were that fellow!' Henry Martin had said to himself with a sigh. . . . He had been wishing for a couple of hours that he were – that he could actually become – that easy fellow.

Hugh Monckton had been all evening with Gloria Sorenson and her glorious back. When she had strolled away from him every half hour or so to take her turn in the Casino next door they would hear the applause. She would be back beside the fellow before it had quite ceased. He had gone on sitting easily in his place. He had the air of a graceful bridegroom.

He had sat, when she was there, with his brown hair mixed in the golden waves of hers. They had gone on talking ceaselessly, her glorious bare shoulders against his admirable polychromatic tweeds. Occasionally, as if enclosed within a sphere of their own, they had got up and walked between the tables to the floor. At once the crashing of the Russian Orchestra died to nothing.

There were four fellows, always laughing, at a table in the corner of the floor. Two had violins, one a ukulele. He was a high yellow. And one had a miniature saxophone. He was pure negro. The violinists were white, but black haired. They laughed all the time and all the time inaudibly played with their instruments. Only, when Gloria Sorenson went to take her turn, they strolled after her, still laughing. And when she stood up with Hugh Monckton you suddenly heard their incredible music which had been going on all the time beneath the coarser noises of the Russians. These became as suddenly almost mute.

No wonder that fellow could dance. Those two moved in each other's arms with rapt expressions, as if a transparent sphere surrounded them. To the measure of those extraordinary, laughing players.

Henry Martin thought: 'I dare say I dance as well as that fellow.' But he had never had such music. Those two moved about with their own musicians, ready to play to them at any moment, with that little, low, lilting, exciting music that in no way interfered with your talking. Except that it seemed of itself to lift your feet off the floor. He couldn't keep his own feet still. He wanted to kick his legs about like a nigger at a barn dance.

The little *poule* beside him made desultory and mournful remarks about Gloria Sorenson when she danced. She deprecated her gleaming shoulders, the great expanse of her white back. She suggested that anybody could be Gloria Sorenson – if only they had the chance to be born *une étrangère*. . . . In a foreign country. No one had any use for French women in France nowadays. . . .

38

Decidedly the conversation of the young woman had not been exciting.

She seemed to be suffering from the world depression as badly as anyone between there and Wall Street. She had drunk two gin fizzes in the course of the evening. The only spark they seemed to elicit from her had been the surprising information that an unpresentable figure who sat motionless the whole evening at a little table next that of the glorious couple was Gloria Sorenson's husband.

Henry Martin had combated this idea. It seemed to him unthinkable. But the girl had insisted on it with vehemence . . . almost as if with vindictive pleasure. Gloria Sorenson might be an *étrangère*. Her contemptible dancing and exaggerated legs, her shamelessly bare back and the imbecility of men might, in combination, have made her the cynosure of half the world. But *that* was her husband. All the city knew it.

The man was unbelievable. He was bullet-headed, immensely obese, with an expression of lachrymose despair. He sat over the table, humped on one support-ing elbow as if he had been a sack-like marionette that someone had thrown down there. From time to time, when Gloria Sorenson had been away, the glorious young man had addressed smiling remarks to him. Before him was an immense beer glass. That from time to time the young man would fill – half from a champagne bottle and half from a bottle of stout. Neither the young man nor Gloria had drunk anything all through the evening. Yet there were three empty champagne bottles and three empty stout bottles on the table in front of them. The old fellow gulped off his liquor with extraordinary velocity, humping down in the same attitude between chair and table as soon as he had finished it.

The presence of the husband – if it was indeed the

husband – seemed in no way to depress the young man. Nor did it make Henry Martin in the least less inclined to wish that he and that fellow could exchange identities.

It occurred to him as odd that, hitherto, when he had wanted intensely to be someone else that someone had always been of ignoble position, or apparently rather unfortunate. At the time of the Magdalen-Balliol rag he had wanted to be a Japanese; once he had desired to be a French policeman; once, a man selling papers outside the Metropolitan Opera. . . . These obsessions had always come to him vividly at times of immense depression. During the Oxford rag, apart from the noise and confusion of the moment, he had been worried by his tutor, by the thought that Oxford was bad for his psychology, by his position in regard to the World War. He had wished to be a Paris policeman at a time when he had made simultaneously two disastrous discoveries. One had been that he was not suited for the career of a writer, the other that Alice was insupportable for vulgarity of mind, manners and elegance. The newspaper seller had synchronized with the eighth or ninth month of the Wall Street Crash. . . .

In each of these cases he had desired to become someone presumably humbler than himself. . . . Now he found himself intensely wishing that he were a lord of the earth. . . . Why?

That was simple. Whilst he had possessed anything at all or any hope of a future he had been willing to make a pact with Providence. He had been ready to surrender his possessions and future in exchange for fewer possessions and hopes. On condition that he could be released . . . from the worry of the World War, of Alice, and of the financial perplexities of the Stock Market crashes and eddies. . . . But now that he had nothing and no hopes there was nothing left but to pray to Providence to give him something for nothing. It was as easy for Omnipotence to make him a lord of the earth as a crossing-sweeper. . . .

He tried to lose himself in imagining what it would be like if he became actually that fellow. . . . There would be a feeling of physical lightness. . . . The numbing sensation of the brain and eyelids would not be there. It came with worries connected with finance and women. This fellow was undoubtedly immensely wealthy. In the gossip of the town – as reflected by the little *poule* at his side – the fellow was said to be negotiating the purchase of Madame Hauvrant's celebrated *Le Secret* – the famous yacht whose very tall spars and black hull were such a feature of those seas. Possessed of that vessel he was going to assume final control of the blazing Gloria and detaching her from both her contracts and her husband, to sail away towards endless bliss and idleness. In tropical seas. . . .

Physical lightness. . . . You could stretch your limbs. You could command things to happen at a distance. You could feel as if you possessed the wings . . . the wings of a dove, to flee away, flee away, and be at rest!

No wonder you could give pleasure with your dancing. . . . There was not a thin, numbing stream of lead within all your limbs.

Who the fellow was Henry Martin did not then know. The inhabitants of the city – the *poules*, waiters, commissionaires, *chasseurs* knew him as Smeez, *un américain* – which was no doubt 'Smith' phonetically rendered. Like all bearers of that unfortunate name Henry Martin was sensitive to the extent of tracking out distinguished 'Smiths.' There were Smiths in America who were distinguished in all trades and occupations. But he could not think of any that was overwhelmingly distinguished. This fellow seemed to have the consciousness of over-whelming distinction in every gesture.

Yet, ironically, Henry Martin imagined that they must be physically very much alike. They must have been both almost exactly six feet in height. They were both loose-limbed and erect. They could both be said to have broad, as it were, frank brows, earnest, slightly frowning, brownish eyes: brown hair waved slightly over the foreheads and they had rather short-clipped brownish moustaches. . . .

Henry Martin had never had any but a vague idea of what he himself would look like to an outsider. He was little given to looking at himself in glasses though at times when he had still considered himself as a 'writer' he had consciously scrutinized his reflection to see if it showed any traces of genius or talent. Or even of intelligence! He had never been able to discover any. But when you look into mirrors you stiffen your features. When you think you discover expressions of genius in others their faces are usually in motion.

It occurred to him to consider that if he hadn't had the idea of being a writer he would not be there. He would never otherwise have settled in Paris. Alice would have had no excuse for urging him to that step. It had seemed to offer to her unlimited chances of high-balls, exhibiting herself, and exchanging dubious stories with dubious companions. . . . And of embroiling him still more deeply with his father. . . . Pisto-Brittle was one of the few things that seemed to have flourished all the more because of the Wall Street Crash. The inhabitants of Springfield and the surrounding territory had by chewing more candy consoled themselves for having to do without more costly pleasures. . . .

In any case, it had frequently in the old days occurred to him that if he met himself in the street he might well not recognize himself. On the other hand, if he met that other fellow he might very well imagine it was himself he was meeting.

There was nothing very remarkable in that. They were both ordinary – in the sense that they were of not unusual types and had undergone identical trimmings and parings. They had probably sat under the same manicurists, barbers, tailors, tutors and preachers. He seemed certainly to have met the other sometime, somewhere. . . . That fellow was probably Princeton – a product that much resembled what Dartmouth turned out. . . . Princeton and then very possibly Oxford, too. With just a touch of the World War. . . . There was certainly a slight look of the soldier about him. Indeed, vaguely, Henry Martin found himself connecting him with the associations of the short, troublesome period he had passed before being turned out of the English Army. . . . He had been perpetually in trouble with the sergeants on parade. He had been in those days stubborn and it had not seemed to him as of infinite importance in the winning of the World War that a free born American citizen – free, male, and twenty-one – should stand motionless with his feet at an angle of forty-five degrees, his thumbs exactly in contact with the seams of his trousers . . . until someone entirely uneducated barked a noise that meant you to jump to it!

Fortunately it had been discovered that he wrote an excellent hand, could add correctly, was sober, cleanly and athletic. So he had gone little on parade but had been kept in what they called orderly room, sitting on wooden benches covered with horse blankets, making out endless returns. He had considered that that in itself was a symptom of the way Fate was inexorably determined to display him as ineffectual. He had enlisted in the British Army with the idea of showing that America though officially neutral was, at heart, just as ardently determined as anyone else to make this a world fit for free men. . . . But Fate decreed that he should be put to almost exactly the same ignominious sort of job as that offered him by his father.

He tried to take it out of Fate by being as undisciplined as he could. But undiscipline had been difficult to exhibit. If he didn't there call officers 'Sir,' they didn't bother about it. If he got out of his bed late no one bothered as long as he did his returns all right . . . and he did not get his breakfast. His buttons and kit were always irreproachable because, at the very beginning of his service, he offered a poor devil a dollar a week to look after them. The poor devil had had an aged Welsh grandmother whom he helped to support, so Henry Martin had never had the heart to take away his employment. And as he was by a long chalk the most redoubtable half-back of the battalion's football team and was indeed spotted as quite likely to play for the Welsh against England in the Army team, officers taking orderly room would merely shake their heads at him if he were charged with being late returning to barracks.

He had in those days – for the only time in his life! – been something of a hero. The low-class scum who were his comrades considered him a devil of a fellow – lawless, desperate – and as wealthy as Croesus. . . . He could at least say for himself that during those months – *saltaverat* . . . he had jumped, in the football field had given pleasure . . . to scum! . . . You could translate *saltavit* by 'jumped' as well as 'danced.' The Roman youth had no doubt done both.

44

He didn't know why, at that moment, these associations should come so strongly over him. . . . What was that absurd period of five months to him . . . now? He was at the end of his trivial tether. If he were going to commit suicide on the morrow it was as much perhaps because of the dread of the French police as for any other reason. Yet he was merely at the end of his money. And humiliated. He was no kind of criminal. He did not suppose he would mind being a criminal. He simply wasn't one!

In his army career – when he had won fame! – he had certainly arrived at being a military criminal. He had been absent for a whole night which he had passed in a hotel in Newport, Mon. The military police had taken him back to his battalion under escort and he had passed a week-end in cells – the bloody clink, as they called it.

He had discovered that he had not liked that . . . And the discovery had humiliated him. At the beginning of the exploit – whilst throwing his money about in the Newport bars – he had been inclined to regard himself as resembling his ancestor – by his mother's account – Robin Hood, Earl of Huntingdon. He had imagined himself defending the poor, bloody Welsh Tommies against the ignorant brutal oppression of their English superiors. He could not see why men should be made martyrs to spit and polish or why they should have to jump to it when an English N.C.O. barked. That seemed no way to make the world free for Democracy. It had appeared to be merely aping the Enemy Nation. He imagined that if the United States had entered it they would have gone into it heads down, waving guns and swearing . . . as Colonel Roosevelt's Rough Riders had done with satisfactory results, at Guantamarro . . . or perhaps it was not Guantamarro. . . . At any rate in

the war for the liberation of Cuba from tyranny. . . .
He had boasted a good deal about that in the Newport
saloons. And he had boasted about it still more to the
Red Caps – the regimental military police – He had even
said that he being an American citizen they could do
nothing to him.

But in the bloody clink he had got cold feet. The
clink was merely a perfectly impassive, clean, cube of
space enclosed in three-ply boarding. There was no
cruelty about it: it was merely impassive. The lightly-
barred windows gave on to a green park where the men
did exercises. When they didn't, the white peacocks of
the Marquess of Bute walked about there. The Marquess
had been a rather nervous Tommy, employed like himself over accounts in the battalion orderly room. He had
been accustomed in secret to think it was some orderly
room. It employed not only the heir to Pisto-Brittle but
the premier Marquess of England.

Then, in the clink, looking at the white peacocks with
their mincing gait, he had suddenly had a revulsion of
feeling . . . after all, this system employed in its lowest
jobs the great of the earth. . . . No doubt, since they
were intelligent, sober, and since *noblesse oblige* they ought
to prove disciplined. Then they should surely be given
opportunities of distinction: of proving themselves useful
on a larger scale. . . . His thought of that day had of
course been youthful. But he was already a little ashamed
of himself. He had arrived at the conclusion that the
Ruling Classes should stick together wherever they found
themselves. After all it was they who controlled the
bloody clinks, whether in Springfield, Ohio, or South
Wales.

The orderly officer's usual round, inspecting prisoners,
had rather confirmed than interrupted his train of thought.

46

He had marched, he remembered, up the cinder path and had stood before him at attention, a great deal more smartly than he had ever stood before. The officer had looked at him rather sorrowfully after he had asked him if he had any complaint. He had said, slightly shaking his head:

'You're an American citizen, it appears . . . you allege it.'

Henry Martin had enlisted as a Canadian to account for his accent.

'Then,' the officer had said, 'you're obviously White Man Smith of Magdalen.' He had added that he had been instructing the Balliol O.T.C. at the time the rag had occurred. He said he would speak to the colonel about it.

He remembered having envied the young officer – who nevertheless appeared sad. He was also called Smith . . . Lieutenant Smith. He had envied him – he had not wished to exchange identities with him. The young fellow – just his own age – had had an ease, an assurance, he himself appearing gawky and raw! . . . In the orderly room when he pushed his hair back, puzzling over some return, you saw he had a scar on his right temple – and some medals. . . .

In front of the clink the fellow had talked to him sadly. Henry Martin, he had said, was a man of some intelligence. Why did he behave like this? He gave trouble to the officers who had enough, God knew, on their hands. He gave trouble to the men, setting a bad example. . . . He was doing the work of the Enemy Nations. . . . Every case of insubordination that he put up might be said to make the Enemy Nations or their sympathizers rejoice. He didn't suppose that Henry Martin wanted that. . . .

47

Henry Martin hadn't wanted that! The thought of the Teutonic sympathizers of Springfield, Ohio, patting him on the back when they heard of his exploits was remarkably distasteful to him. . . . Disagreeable old spectacled ladies and harsh-voiced Lutheran novices. . . . They would do that. . . . The people who had proposed to run his old Aunt Hedwig out of town on a rail. . . . They were the great majority in the city. . . . He had not liked his old Aunt. She smelt of brandy. . . . Still. . . .

He had said to the officer in front of clink that he certainly did not want enemy sympathizers to rejoice.

Some of his emotion in those days was even then very vivid in his memory. He sat in a little dancing room of the Côte d'Azur, with tinsel decorations and a Russian orchestra in white smocks with scarlet embroidery. But he saw the green boughs of the trees over the lightly barred windows of clink!

It had been a confused time. . . . That was no doubt what was the matter with him. He was perhaps one of the *génération perdue* that the French talked of. The Lost Generation. . . . They were said to have been so disturbed in their equilibrium by the distortions of the late war that they had no sense of the values of life. . . . That might of course be the case. But he could not see why he should have been affected. He certainly had not taken the war hard. He had shuffled, really, through it. Not of his own will. He had not asked for easy jobs. They had just been given to him.

It came back to him as a period of fever. After fevers you do not remember *what* has happened. Or you remember most things only dimly. Then some things with great clearness. . . . You wake up in the

48

night with an unbearable headache. The water glass is at a great distance. You cannot get at it.

That had been just his case in the war. He could, he supposed, disentangle its chronology if he tried. But he had never bothered to try. He remembered the declaration of war in Springfield. Or rather he didn't – because he had been recovering from a dull carouse with some girl. Shut up in her father's house and afraid to stir out in daylight for fear the neighbours saw him. . . . And he remembered the end of the war. . . . Hearing of it in a mountain valley in the Cevennes where he had been in charge of a saw mill and a canning factory. Why should they have set up a canning factory in the Cevennes? There was no knowing. Perhaps because of water power. Most likely it was just a piece of graft. But why should he have been in charge of it? . . . Well, that was because he had made for his Captain a portrait that his Captain had found satisfactory. . . . A fat man with a blue grey walrus moustache – bulging out above and below his new belt. . . . The Captain had detailed him to look after the saw mill and the cans. . . . He had taken up Art by that time.

That had been to please Wanda. . . . Or to please the memory of Wanda. Because, of course, Wanda had given him up by then. At the request of his father and her husband. . . . Still he had gone on making watercolours. Without enthusiasm. . . .

There had not been any vividness about Armistice Day in the Cevennes. Snow had already begun to fall up where the saw mill was. One of the men had broken his leg and he had gone up with the syphilis inspector to see about it. The saw mill had been higher up in the mountains than the canning factory. . . . Félicité had raised Cain about his going up. Because of the snow

49

and because he had promised to take her in to Valence. She had raised Cain. She had been certain he would fall down a ravine and be hidden by the snow until next May. Then what would become of her if, as she suspected? . . .

What in the world did they want with a U.S. Inspector of Syphilis in Troops in a lost valley in the Cevennes? There weren't any troops. Henry Martin had a corporal in charge of the saw mill. That was the fellow who had broken his leg. And an artillery quartermaster at the canning factory. . . . Why artillery? Were they going to use canned salmon for shells? . . . In the Argonne? . . .

The syphilis inspector had turned out to have no medical qualifications. He was a poet by profession. Stoutish and chuckling. He turned out doggerel about the local legends by the hundred lines an hour. . . . Legends about the religious wars of the district. . . .

'And so the battle this and that way goes. . . .
Hurrah for something in the mantling snows. . . .'

The Inspector said that he had been marooned there because he had discovered things that the Great Medical Staff had not wanted spoken about. Henry Martin had strongly suspected they had put him there because they could not bear his verse. . . .

Anyhow their arts had done them proud. . . . They had lived warm, quartered in a good farm, low down. They had written verses and made water-colour sketches and played craps and spit in the ocean day after day. Félicité – who was well educated – would recite Victor Hugo in her pink robe de chambre at bedtime.

50

'Enfant si j'étais roi je te donnerais l'Empire
Et mes flottes et mes something et mes something et
mes something . . .
Pour un baiser de toi. . . .
Enfant si j'étais Dieu. . . .'

He would give something else. . . . It was Félicité's
way of suggesting that he did not requite her kisses with
sufficient passion. She wasn't mercenary. But her old
mother would have coerced him into marrying her if he
hadn't kept his head. Or course she hadn't been with
child. . . .
What had become of Félicité? A little clean brown-
eyed filly. Or the Syphilis Inspector? Or the Captain?
Or all the crowd? . . . Hundreds and hundreds with
whom he had rubbed shoulders. Friendly nearly all.
Loud voiced. Roistering. . . . Or even Wanda? She
did not appear to have made good. At Hollywood or
anywhere else. Yet undoubtedly she had talent. . . .
This Gloria Sorenson reminded him of her – deep chested
with luminous flesh, large nostrils and wide mouth.
She might have made a man of him if father hadn't
butted in.
Of all of them he had only kept track of Leopold
Kuhn and, God, he wished he hadn't. . . . Though if
it hadn't been Anacondus and Kennecotts it would have
been something else. . . . As corporal in charge of the
Y.M.C.A. canteen in that accursed White Star transport
Kuhn had seemed a mighty potentate.
A hell of a ship with all those starving thousands on
board! He didn't even know whether it had been the
fault of the shipping company or merely of the grafters.
He had had indignant ideas of exposing the affair – but
they had died away. He couldn't be said to have suffered

himself. His art had saved him. He had passed the voyage on the poop – painting, in water-colour, portraits of the officers of his regiment. That had cured him of ever wanting to paint again. The sight of a tumbler of discoloured water still made him inclined to vomit.

But his occupation had assured him of the right of access to the canteen and the society of Mr. Leopold Kuhn when he wanted it. Kuhn struck him as the calmest person and one of the greatest *savoir-faire* that he had ever met. He cleaned his canteen-zinc with great master-strokes whilst talking of continental literature. The impassivity with which he had his canteen cleared of the starving, yelling soldiery by the Marines was enough to make you respect him permanently. His canteen would be packed with the upper parts of the poor dough-boys six deep. They yelled and gesticulated, their faces convulsed. Mr. Kuhn served them with extreme deliberation in complete silence for the ten minutes that the canteen was open. Then he would make a half-visible sign to the Marine corporals and those pugilists would fall on the miserable doughboys and heave them out of the confined space, down the pitch black companion.

He would remove his great spectacles, close and open his eyes a great many times, readjust his spectacles and begin throwing craps with the Marines for who should cook the corned beef-hash or *chile con carne* whilst the others played spoil five and drank cocktails made from the applejack of which Mr. Kuhn had a couple of casks beneath the zinc.

It wasn't till the vessel had been some days out that Henry Martin had discovered the real state of affairs. Mr. Kuhn saw that the Marine corporals who were detailed to help him and that Henry Martin and one or two other fellows who were officially scheduled to him as helpers but who really did odd jobs for the officers – Mr. Kuhn saw that these were lavishly fed by the canteen. But there were no stores at all on board for the soldiers. The holds were completely filled with typewriters and sewing machines. Even some of the cabins were occupied with that merchandise.

So that the men were actually starving. They had for dinner a piece of bread – begged by the cooks from the British sailors – of about the size and not much more than the thickness of a playing card, and watergruel made with coarsely ground corn that the cooks stole from the mangers of the horses on board. For supper they had a couple of spoonsful of the same gruel.

The ships had been driven up north of Scotland in the evasion of enemy submarines so even those rations had been halved. And when Henry Martin had pleaded with Mr. Leopold Kuhn to let the canteen be open a little more than for the two periods of ten minutes which was all that he allowed, Mr. Kuhn answered phlegmatically that it was forbidden by all the articles of his association and the Secretary of State. Mr. Kuhn admitted that it seemed a shame. But a deputation of the Women's Clubs of – Mr. Kuhn thought – Ohio, Missouri and North Dakota – had waited on the department and extracted that promise in the interests of the poor boys themselves. The canteens were of course bone dry. But they purveyed cigarettes. Some ladies of these states considered that cigarettes were nearly as pernicious as drink. . . .

The effect of that voyage, Henry Martin was now aware, had been to cure him of all respect for the louder virtues. . . . Perhaps for all virtues! It – and all the enterprises connected with it – seemed to be like a vast smudge across the landscape of his life. . . . He could almost mark the very moment when the sunshine of virtue – and of vice – had gone out of it. That was of course unsophisticated. But it had marked the last glow of conscious patriotism in him. Of patriotism as a glow – and even of adultery as a glow!

It had been very shortly before his going out to France. He had been sent as clerk to an officer who was supposed to arrange for the embarkation of Ohio and Middle Western troops. At New York. As the officer had not given more than half an hour a day to his duties – which had been taken over obligingly by an officer once a partner in the firm which belonged to the family to which Mr. Leopold Kuhn belonged – Henry Martin had had the whole inside of a week to himself. He had been very flush of money and having hired a car had amused himself with exploring the State of New York.

It had occurred in a dilapidated village below Redding Ridge – rather towards Danbury, Conn., than the other way. He had persuaded Wanda to spend three days – and two nights – with him in a summer boarding place on the Ridge. They had been waited on by the most perfectly elegant coloured girl with a most amazing head of unkinked hair. All around them at separate tables had sat elderly ladies overflowing with sentiments of goodwill to the young hero and his war bride. It had not been his first adultery. It had certainly been his most glorious. Wanda had given to his nights raptures that could only be read into the ends of fairy tales.

By day, a rather faded, blue woollen Norwegian garment masking the extraordinary glow of her glorious flesh and most of her amazing hair being hidden by a knitted purple cap like a tam o'shanter, she had resembled a bird of Paradise before it dressed up for a party. She had a good, Scandinavian, utilitarian tinge to her day-

54

time personality. She believed in employing the shining hours. Henry Martin had been compelled to paint in water-colours the decayed villages that were sprinkled over the countryside, whilst Wanda sat on a tree stump beside him and memorized a new part in which she was understudying Miss.—— But Henry Martin could not remember the name! . . . That gave to the last shining days of his youth a feeling of duration and domesticity as well as of glory.

He couldn't remember, either, the name of the village. It had not been far from the Mark Twain homestead. They had smashed the car up on the extraordinarily bad sunken road that ran along under the ridge – near a pile of stones in a ragged little wood where a huge bunch of rattlesnakes were sunning themselves. You might have expected Norwegian Wanda to be scared of rattlesnakes. But she hadn't been. She had pelted them with small rocks, leaning forward to see where they fell and opening her large, healthy, rosy mouth in great gusts of laughter when the sinister, dry, churning sounds answered her efforts. . . . She had been glorious, with her large mouth and shining eyes that were in her moments of merriment, like those of a fine dog that laughs when you wave a bit of stick as if you were going to throw it. . . .

They had walked on until they came to the village. They found a farmer who agreed to take a couple of horses and tug the car after them. Henry Martin had carried his colour and sketching board, Wanda the blue-paper covered parts. The village had consisted of a broad street of dust with, on each side of it, a border of grass and then, beneath very tall, thin-leaved elms, the unusually high gables of brown-shingled, dilapidated houses. As far as he could remember the village had once been much more prosperous. It had been the centre of a cotton-spinning industry that had long since died. Or perhaps it had not been cotton. It might have been wool – or lumber – or chair-making. . . . But there were the high, mournful, shadowed gables, suggesting very old European villages. And Henry Martin remembered thinking that, if your prosperity had departed, it was all one whether that had happened forty years ago or four hundred. You were a relic of the past. There must, however, have still been some inhabitants. In the street were a general store, a drug store and a little one-windowed store where 'Miss Twisden, Dressmaker,' manufactured and showed for sale, baby linen, or at least crocheted caps.

Henry Martin wondered idly whether Pisto-Brittle could be bought in either of the stores. But he remembered to have heard his father say that he had never been able to penetrate into New England. And they were just across the border of New York State – in Connecticut.

An ice-cream wagon had come lumbering through the flat dust of the road to the steps of the drug store. It had been then that Henry Martin had felt his glow of patriotism. He did not believe that any of the other nations taking part in the war had ice-cream delivered daily in its remotest villages. This seemed to him the high-water mark of civilization. The starving millions of Europe could not any one of them show the like of that. Let alone the other continents.

The episode remained among his other memories like a bright spot.

Thunder had descended on his head immediately afterwards. One of the old ladies at the boarding house had written to father to congratulate him on his daughter-in-law. The old man had stormed down to war-time New York, seeming to add new noises to that already sufficiently noisy city. He had however relapsed into his wild boarish good humour as soon as he learned that Henry Martin was not married to Wanda.

Henry Martin could not see what it mattered to his father whom he married. Father let him go roaming about the world – or necking in Springfield. He even appeared to have no views on masculine sexual morality. His character did not hang together. When it came to this marriage he got raging on to his hind legs. Why?

He blinked at Henry Martin with his inflexible little eyes and said over and over again:

'No, sonny. It isn't this star that you're going to hitch your wagon to. Not this star! You go find another. . . .'

Henry Martin had treated his father with cold indifference. He did not see what his father could do about it. He was free, male and still twenty-one. He imagined that, when the war was over, he would be perfectly capable of supporting Wanda. In the meantime she would be quietly getting her divorce. Her husband was a frank undesirable – a possibly Norwegian violinist who led an unspeakable life in Paris.

Two days later the troopship had sailed.

His father had seemed to get busy pretty soon. For quite a time Wanda had written to Henry Martin every day. He had got her letters in bundles in various odd corners of England and France to which his military jobs had taken him. They were always connected, ingloriously, with commissariat or supplies. He had never come within two hundred miles of the enemy forces.

It had been difficult, even at first, to gather much about the state of Wanda's feelings. She wrote singularly

57

foreign English considering that in her small parts on the stage she had no noticeable accent. Her endearments which were unusually phrased might have meant the deepest of passions; her assurances of fidelity might have meant equally the deepest of passions. . . . But they might have meant nothing of the sort.

Gradually her letters began to mention his father. The old man seemed to have gone to Detroit to see her company play. They must have become as thick as thieves. After all, they were both European. It became a European sort of an intrigue. Father had gradually persuaded her that the marriage could not possibly be a success. Henry Martin had no means. He was a trifler. He was, moreover, several years younger than the girl. . . .

The effect of these conversations penetrated gradually to Henry Martin in his Cevennes valley. They had driven him nearly mad. He had written: he had cabled – two or three times a day. . . . It was an infamous lie to say that he was without means. Being of age he had come into a third part of his mother's property. It consisted of the drug store of her father and a small piece of real estate. The drug store which was managed by a company was by now a good property. He expected to draw from it as much as four or even five thousand a year. On that they ought to be able to live comfortably when these troubles were over. . . .

Wanda's letters could not be said to grow colder. But they did begin to allow weight to his father's arguments. She was certainly three – nearly four – years older than he. At the time that seemed a small matter. But as the years went by the difference would be more perceptible. A young man of twenty-five married to a woman of thirty was considerably handicapped.

Henry Martin had answered everything he could think of.

He remembered he had written frantically' and had indeed gone almost out of his mind, shut up in the valley with his saw mill. At the same time he was living with Félicité. . . . If you had told him that it was possible to be in love with one girl and live with another he would have said that you lied. Yet the books were wrong. Indeed when Wanda had come over to Paris definitely to break with him he was already living with Alice.

Wanda had walked into the apartment on the Rue des Saints Pères while Alice was laying the table for lunch. She had left her almost incapable husband propped up against the wall outside, drumming a tattoo with his hands behind him. The sun had shone into the apartment and on the white, orange and blue of the Breton crockery on the table.

A little, as he remembered, to his mortification she had hardly taken any notice of the presence of Alice . . . though Alice was not altogether unnoticeable. But Wanda had talked to him as if the other did not exist. That was partly due to her stage habit of mind, partly to her Scandinavian earnestness. She had not only ignored the existence of all women who were not on the stage, she ignored the existence of all human beings who did not practise one or other of the arts. That point of view as a pious expression of opinion was not unknown to Henry Martin. He had heard it at Dartmouth amongst young men who intended to 'write' and at Magdalen from a small clique who had called themselves the Ten, but were better known as the Yellow Pants. These choice souls had all expressed the opinion that a person who did not practise one of the arts belonged to the outer darkness and was merely stuff to fill graveyards. All these young men, however, had either gone into their fathers' businesses or one or other trade or calling that they would once have called bourgeois. So that, with the exception of two who had stuck together and become reporters on a Brooklyn paper, Henry Martin was the only one who had so much as used the Arts as an excuse for a purposeless life.

It was upon that that Wanda had pitched as an excuse for breaking with him. She had said that if he had followed the writing career he had first professed to desire, or that of a painter into which she had tried to urge him, the idea of breaking with him would never have occurred to her. Henry Martin had reminded her that there had been a war and that he had been a soldier. The war indeed was still in being and he still in the service. It was the period of the Armistice and he was doing commissariat work for such American troops as remained in Paris, escort work for funerals or at state appearances of diplomats. It was not glorious employment, but, such as it was, it was his duty to see it through. He was at the moment engaged on a laborious correspondence between the Army Department and the French Authorities as to payment for the sewing machines and typewriters that had filled the hold and cabins of the transport in which he had come over. Mr. Leopold Kuhn had indeed turned up again looking extraordinarily slim, athletic and graceful in a handsome, modified, staff-officer's uniform. It had by now reached Henry Martin's intelligence that his presence on board that vessel had been far more connected with seeing these munitions of war through the European Customs Houses – where, of course, they paid no duty – than with the supply of cigarettes and coca cola and stationery to the unfortunate troops. He was now interested in making the French authorities pay for them, but in the meantime found plenty of leisure for compiling a work on copper as employed in German industries. . . .

To the various excuses that he got out of his present occupations, Wanda blazing in the bright room had replied merely that she had been shocked. . . . She pronounced it: 'Stchocked!' from which he gathered that she was actually feeling some emotion. When she was quite calm she watched her English accent very carefully.

She had been shocked by the nature of his arguments in his letters. When he had replied to his father's statements that he would be unable to support her properly he had never once mentioned his pen or his brush. He had proposed to keep her out of his four or five thousand dollars a year. For what did he take her? She was an actress in demand. Perfectly well able to support herself with considerable luxury, but perfectly ready to leave the stage had Henry Martin's career as either artist or writer needed that she should remain beside him. But she was not ready to sit at his side in an apartment in the Bronx or a suburb of Christiania. Nor yet whilst he pursued the career of a stockbroker.

She had gone out several times during her long harangue or his interruptions to place her husband in different positions – against the wall, against the banisters, or on the stairs.

She said that if Henry Martin had proposed to follow an artist's life – in a garret, a cottage in the wood or beside a glacier – she would contentedly have followed him. She would even, if the necessaries of life had proved lacking, have returned temporarily to the stage to keep them going for a period.

She broke off to go and fetch in her husband whom

she deposited in a roundbacked armchair. He was an extraordinarily emaciated fellow. He came back to Henry Martin as having had whitish rings round soot-black eyes. He stood apparently for the arts and looked very nasty, sunk down in his chair, his hands incessantly drumming on its legs as they drooped beside them. A violinist he was. A marvellous violinist. And doped to the eyelids.

She appeared to have brought him there as an exhibit. Exhibit A. The sort of man a woman ought to devote herself to. He, Henry Martin, was Exhibit B – the sort of man to whom a woman ought not to devote herself.

It seemed queer to Henry Martin. There he was: free, male and twenty-one. Six feet in his stockings. The picture of health and moderation. He had indeed been thinking of taking up athletics again and had lately visited several training places in Paris.

The other fellow just gibbered, leaning forward in his chair, smiling as if with intense friendliness at the rest and making gay remarks in an entirely unknown tongue.

It was no doubt the mothering instinct in Wanda.

She had eventually removed her husband and Henry Martin had understood that the separation was to be final.

He had not even had time to make a remark to the completely silent Alice. She had gone on laying and re-laying the table. During the intervals of Wanda's apostrophes he had been conscious of her moving a table-spoon or putting the jug of yellow flowers in another place on the table. With an abstracted manner, as if she had been reflecting deeply upon the pattern made by the table service or weighing in her mind the arguments put forward by Wanda.

They would no doubt have talked. But before the sound of Wanda's voice was quite out of Henry Martin's ears the door which she had left ajar was pushed open by the shoulder of Henry Martin's father.

He stood in the doorway, a round, Dutch-looking pillow of tightly encased flesh. His eyes rolled. He was exceedingly out of breath. At last he brought out triumphantly the words:

'Another star!'

Henry Martin had never made up his mind whether by that father had meant that Henry Martin would now be pressed to find another star or that in Alice he had found one. . . . He stayed to lunch, lumping down into the chair that had been vacated by Wanda's husband and wolfing down great quantities of the *blanquette de veau à l'ancienne* that had been admirably made by the *femme de ménage*. . . . Henry Martin had to attend a parade at the Arc de Triomphe at two. He went, leaving the old man with Alice.

He had by then been promoted to the rank of top-sergeant, but, since he had great difficulty in remembering which was his right hand and which was his left, appearances on parades – which at that time were rather frequent as A.E.F. troops were returned home – were rather disagreeable to him.

The old man spent nearly two months in Paris. He had seemed to have the time of his life which, for a Luxemburger in Paris, was not difficult. There he had a rustic air which was not noticeable in Springfield, Ohio. He looked like an enriched farmer from one of the French northern departments and he showed – for a gentleman who had not seen Europe for over thirty years – an astonishing knowledge of how to amuse himself in Paris.

63

The mainsprings of his character had remained enigmatic to Henry Martin in spite of that period during which they were together for large parts of the day. His father and Alice were alone together even more often, but Henry Martin never quite knew, either, how they got on. They visited museums, galleries, theatres, operas, variety shows. When Henry Martin could get leave for sufficiently long they hired motors and visited such of the battlefields as were then visible. Those of the Argonne where the A.E.F. had been so mercilessly hammered were not available, Henry Martin believing till the present moment that the French wanted to clear up those spots a little so that Americans should not too plainly discern how remorselessly Mangin had used up their troops. So Henry Martin never saw scenes of patriotic interest to him. But they got once as far as Luxemburg, a queer, suburban principality that very little stirred the pulses of Henry Martin. His father – and indeed Alice – had nevertheless what his father called a high old time there amongst the friends of his boyhood and their sons and daughters.

Sister Carrie came into the town to see them. Her husband, because of a presumably too great toleration of the occupation of the Grand Duchy by the late enemy, was not encouraged to visit the capital of a state that was now enthusiastically pro-Ally. On the other hand, as an American, Sister Carrie did not seem to have had too good a time, at any rate after the United States had declared war. She appeared worried, or at least abstracted. But, if she confided in her father, he did not transfer her confidences to Henry Martin. She was beginning to acquire the European veneer of the great lady that was afterwards for a time to make her seem disagreeable to Henry Martin.

In the Grand Duchy Alice was accepted as – or at any rate presumed to be – the fiancée of Henry Martin.

What the old man thought about it there was no knowing. After his first visit to the apartment in the rue des Saints Pères he had never come there again. They on the other hand never penetrated further than the entrance hall of a magnificent hotel in the Champs Élysées where the old man installed himself. It was rather presumed by Alice and Henry Martin that he had there found some sort of feminine companionship. There seemed to be no reason why he should not have. He led a lonely enough life in Springfield. Once, from the promenade of the Folies Bergères they saw him in a box in company with a platinum-haired blonde who was covered with diamonds. He began to grow obviously tired and to talk of Springfield with some complacency. . . .

It had flashed suddenly through Henry Martin's mind that the fortunate young man was the Lieutenant Smith who had interrogated him outside the regimental clink. . . . That, then, was why his thoughts had taken their tone of wartime reminiscence. . . . The curves of his features must have awakened them.

Henry Martin's definite wish that he could become that accomplished and elegant fellow redoubled itself. He at least had knowledge of the world, assurance, and, in the companionship of Gloria Sorenson, indisputable good fortune. How differently he could look around the room and how differently the room with its bright papery decorations and shining floor must seem to him! Worry – more particularly financial worry – and the curse of ineffectiveness can take the brightness out of any colours. To the other Smith the scarlets of the Japanese paper umbrellas and the Chinese lanterns must be a blaze – a gay, vivifying blaze.

And Gloria Sorenson . . . the idol of a dozen capitals! . . . By the quick pang at his heart every time he caught sight of her without having looked for her, he knew that Wanda, in his memory, had lost none of her physical glow. He had been astonished by that unsuspected constancy in himself. It pleased him momentarily because he thought it must make him an interesting figure. He had apparently cherished a passion for twelve – nearly thirteen – years. . . . But he should not have been pleased. It was nothing to write home about. It was merely that the four or five women with whom he had more or less transitorily to do since then had been mentally and physically mediocre. Except perhaps Mrs. Percival. . . . But he had never . . . 'enjoyed her favours,' was the phrase. She might have married him, though, . . . if Anacondas had stopped say at 75. . . .

But mediocre persons would be his lot, drifting into bored or warmed-up adultery because it was the fashion of the times. Passion . . . that was not for him or for his day.

That fellow Smith . . . Molesworth Smith . . . Moulton Smith . . . no, it was Monckton Smith because he was connected with the Shreiner-Monckton aero-engines . . . Monckton Smith had always for Henry Martin gone about in an atmosphere of awe. . . .

A draught from a wind-fan raised the fellow's brown hair from his tanned right brow. There was the jagged weal of an old wound. . . . It immediately brought back to Henry Martin the Cockney pronounced words:

'E'll come into er million an a arf, E will. What price our chanstesses of a million an er arf?'

Evans, one of his fellow clerks in the battalion orderly room had said those words and they had, even then, filled Henry Martin with envy. They had been looking at Monckton Smith sitting at the adjutant's table with his elbows on the grey blanket that covered it. His fingers were pushed into his hair. He had been frowning over some incomprehensible order from headquarters. . . . The jagged scar had become visible.

'Bloomin' Fortunatus!' the clerk Evans had said. 'Some 'as *hall* the luck.'

'A million an er arf' represented at that date seven and a half million dollars. Father had told Henry Martin that he never expected to cut up for more than a million and a half at his death. . . . Not more than five hundred thousand apiece for Sister Carrie, Brother Hal and himeself. Even if they got it! . . . And the Monckton engines had gone ahead like blazes since that day. . . . They had extended most extraordinarily in times when nothing else had. The extremely wealthy put down their Packards and Napiers. And bought Moncktons. . . . When all the world . . . all the *bloody* world . . . dreaded starvation, that fellow was scooping in more millions. . . . What a hope!

Some 'as indeed hall the luck! That fellow had had the luck to go out with the first battalion of the regiment, to distinguish himself in the petty little war of movements that began the game. And to have a piece of his skull clipped off by a cavalry sabre. Nothing less! Other men had to be hit by pieces of shell or old tin. That fellow could be incapacitated after a month or two of fun in fine weather. By a sword wound. . . . Gallantry and romance! With three or four ribbons, bright on his tunic. And the sword wound to give him for ever the chance that women would say of him:

'One of the Old Contemptibles, my dear. One of the Old Contemptibles.'

That was the swanky title that those fellows gave to themselves who had gone out with the first hundred thousand British troops. Because the enemy leader had called them in the earliest days: 'The contemptible little British army.' He should not of course have done it. It gave them a chance of exciting awe. Even Henry Martin felt a certain awe as he looked at Monckton Smith!

It was awe, of course, not for that military achievement but for that amazing continuance of good fortune. From a sword-cut on the Marne to the bed of Gloria Sorenson. . . . And who knew how many others! An immensely powerful God must be behind that fellow. If you came within his sphere you might be under the cognizance of that tremendous Power. For good or ill! . . .

He himself had come into the town that night which was to be his last night on earth with the hope of some of the glory that attached to sharing the bed of someone with some of Gloria Sorenson's blazing flesh. For her flesh seemed to give off lights of its own. And no doubt incandescent heat and perfume. As Wanda's had done. She was extraordinarily like Wanda. Larger as it were, in the way that in ancient hieratic pictures the important personages were represented as large, the less important as exactly the same shape but smaller.

Wanda's fate had been even similar, if smaller, too. From paragraphs or inspired articles in entertainment columns during her rare visits to Paris Henry Martin had gathered that she made starring tours in Scandinavian, Dutch, or North German towns and in the smaller cities of the United States where the populations were mainly German or Scandinavian. She travelled with her husband, the distinguished violinist called Pipperogios or something like it. Apparently a Greek. Apparently he conducted the small travelling orchestra that she took about with her. Sometimes he played solos between her turns. The French papers said that she was noted for the 'seriousness' of her conduct, her avoidance of the fashionable world and the devotion to her career that her husband, Mr. Pipperogios, displayed. According to the photographs she had become astonishingly more beautiful. . . . She had danced . . . had given pleasure. . . . It was he that was to be dead.

The last time he had seen her she had come bearing white flowers because she thought he *was* dead. Well, he hadn't been. He had tried to see her after that. On the stage of a theatre on the outer boulevards when she was being unusually successful. Presumably because she was so *sérieuse*, avoided the fashionable world and no doubt because of her husband, Paris had never taken to her like Berlin or Copenhagen or, say, Chesterton, Indiana. . . . He had not been able to go and see her. Alice had been away visiting. But the woman to whom he had been temporarily attached had taken grippe and he had taken it from her. That was the sort of thing that would have happened to him. But never to Monckton! . . .

He examined critically the *poule* at his side. She had a cold. That was all you could say about her. . . . There were much better looking girls in the room. Dark creatures with high colours and hat-brims that hid flashing eyes. If you wanted to go out in a blaze of sexual glory you could have taken one of them. At least he supposed you could have. He was really unacquainted with the etiquette of the place. They were perhaps only dancing partners. He didn't know. In New York he had once penetrated into a public dancing hall on the corner of Twenty-Third Street and Sixth Avenue. They had handed you out rolls of strip tickets at a quarter apiece. Each ticket gave you the right to dance with a girl for three minutes. Or to sit out and treat her to soft drinks for three. He did not exactly know. He had danced with a rather pretty, fairish girl in a pink dress, though he could not remember how it had been cut. Only it was pink. Or perhaps mauve. Apparently he had not given much pleasure to her with his dancing. Because, after a couple of turns they had sat at a table for a long time and talked. . . . About Estonia. She was an Estonian by birth. In Estonia she had had a

70

swing that her father had put up between two fir trees. And a cat called something or other. He could not remember what. It was a peculiar name. After he had talked with her for some time about Estonia he had handed her his roll of strip tickets. It had cost four dollars. He had expected her to take what she was entitled to, but she had put the roll into her bag and gone away without thanking him. Four times four were sixteen. He did not think he had talked about Estonia for forty-eight minutes. At any rate he still did not know where Estonia was. Somewhere in the north of Europe, very likely. He didn't equally know whether he was expected to invite the lady home with him.

He didn't even know whether the present *poule* wanted him to go home with her. He had given her drinks and danced desultorily with her two or three times already. That was his luck. He didn't know that world any more than he knew the world of lower Sixth Avenue dancing saloons. He did know that she was the last person in it that he would want to go home with. But he began to think that he knew nothing in the world about anything – or at least about life. People's lives. How did they live? . . . Even where! He was pretty sure he had given up the novel he had once begun because of that. He could imagine characters but not how they lived. He could not imagine their surroundings at home. Of course the novel had been about the war. And if you write a novel about the war there will have to be lots of characters in it. But he didn't know anything about the war. From the inside. He had seen nothing of it.

This girl now. What sort of room did she live in? He had not the ghost of an idea. She was tidy. Neat about the ankles. Then perhaps her room – in the Red

Light quarter no doubt – was very neat. He had once gone home with a French *poule*. Her room had been unusually clean. Its chief adornment had been a first communion card. Her own! Except for that it had seemed to be nearly all wax flowers. There had been hundreds of wax flowers of every colour and shade. And the astonishing thing was that there had not been a speck of dust on any of them. She must have gone over them, probably every day, with a feather duster if not with a polishing cloth. . . . But he had never had much to do with that class. They said that it had died out in America. They said that amateurs had put up too much competition for the professionals to be able to make a living any more. That had certainly been his dreary experience. The amateurs had seemed to stand like a wall between him and the professionals. He imagined that that particular underworld might have proved amusing if he could have tried it. Perhaps it wouldn't. The samples he had seen had been dreary enough. But he might have been unlucky.

He seemed to have a knack – it was perhaps merely a weakness – for forming attachments. People attached themselves to him. Then it was hard to get rid of them. It had been the case with Alice; with Mr. Kuhn, with the miscellaneous collection of people at his hotel. . . . And now with this young woman. . . . The dreariest sort of attachments.

If he ever came to this world again he would see that he kept out of them.

He had picked out this uninteresting young woman three weeks ago. He gave her gin fizzes and danced with her once or twice in the course of each evening. He had picked her out for these invitations because he had been feeling depressed, and to-night she looked depressed. She had proved so. She accepted his invitations without smiles or any evidence of satisfaction. He wondered whether he ought to have given her money. He presumed it to have been unnecessary because she had continued to dance and sit with him without either comment or unwillingness.

So he was cut off from any blaze of physical enjoyment on the last evening of his life. There was a girl in the hall – with quivering nostrils, dark – very dark – tragic in expression. She might have fulfilled the requirements. He looked at her at intervals. She was well dressed – in black with an attractive hat. Her looks certainly moved him. She sat with other girls rather disdainfully or talked to men without obviously throwing herself at them. She was different – as if she knew unusual things. His *poule* told him that that girl had lately come out of prison after six months. She had been engaged with others in selling 'snow.' . . . It was not on the face of it a repulsive offence. . . .

But his *poule* stood like a damp wall between him and the other. The other sat most of the evening alone. Part of the time she was at a table with a little old man with grey curly hair and a rather sulky countrified-looking other girl. . . . As the evening went on she seemed to grow in attraction. He thought of going over, asking her to dance, and in the course of the dance suggesting that he should go home with her. . . . But he had heard of ensanguined scenes in the Red Light quarter of the town. A man he knew, called Preston Hartman, from Lincoln, Nebraska, had had his nose nearly cut off there. It is true that he had innocently hired a room in a house of ill fame, taking it for a respectable boarding house. The rest of the affair had been wrapped in mystery. . . .

73

But French women of that class certainly did fight for the man they considered themselves to have a claim on. He had seen it happen at the Dôme in Paris. He had at least witnessed the row and was told that was what was the matter. An American woman in a slightly canned state had smiled at a man sitting with a French woman. They and their sympathizers on the one side and the other had broken quite a lot of furniture and a district call had had to be given for the police and fire brigades. He didn't want to distinguish his last night on earth by an affray of that sort.

Besides he did not want to hurt the feelings of his *poule*. She might consider that she had established a claim to him. She probably had as these things go. He began to wish that he had given her something or that he had something to give her now. He literally hadn't. His entire wealth was reduced to three hundred and ninety-four francs. He couldn't die without a sou in his pockets.

He wanted to leave, wrapped in a piece of oiled silk, in his identity card case, a fifty franc note. And a memorandum asking whoever found his body to send a cable – deferred – to his father. And a wire to Alice in Paris. Thirty-seven francs for his father: ten or eleven for Alice. Perhaps the finder would just steal the fifty francs. Then they would have to learn it from the paper . . . or perhaps the papers would not consider the matter of sufficient importance to notice it. A down-and-out young American drowns himself. Thousands of bundle-stiffs got rid of themselves every year unsung – between the California desert and – oh, say Fall River.

Fifty francs for the oiled sack. . . . He was paid up till after lunch at the hotel. Forty-five francs in lieu of notice. . . . Ninety-five – he had meant to give the dark girl a hundred and fifty. . . . Much more than the current rate there. But as far as *poules* were concerned he wanted to think of himself that nothing in life became him like the leaving of it. . . .

But he wasn't going to die in the dark girl's arms after all. . . . It was perhaps just as well. Perhaps going out in a blaze of physical glory might turn out to be an overrated pleasure. You obviously couldn't – as a gentleman – really die in the lady's arms. You would have to go out and do it somewhere else. In the tide of reaction. . . *Post coïtum tristia* – As if she had danced. And had not given pleasure. And he had died.

Besides, it might be held up against the girl. They might jeer at her. They would say he had enjoyed her favours and immediately gone out and drowned himself. That would not be fair. Especially to a girl who had just come out of prison for supplying stupefiants. . . . As if the narcotic had been inefficient. . . .

Across the room the dark girl was using her vanity case – with quick, impatient dabs. Her lips blazed scarlet. Her cheeks glowed. He felt he was ready to throw all these considerations to the wind. He would pay for the gin fizzes and throw all that remained into the dark girl's lap.

The depressed *poule* would be all the more depressed. He couldn't help that. Just before going out of the world you owed it to Providence to say that you had used your body gloriously. It was the cock due to Aesculapius. . . . He might even give pleasure to the dark girl. Then indeed nothing in life would have become him like the leaving it!

She was pulling on her suède gloves. She was going. He would pay the bill. He tried to attract the attention of the waiter. That nonchalant man in the white coat walked out at the back of the hall. . . . It was always like that. By the time he had got that bill paid the girl would be gone. . . . He would follow her out into the street: he would hurry up one street and down another. But there would be no trace of her. His life would be robbed of its last glory! . . . By a waiter. . . . It had always been like that with him. That was his life. In epitome!

It had been at that point that Hugh Monckton had strolled over.

The little paper slip that he dropped nonchalantly on the table showed a total of three hundred and twenty-one francs. . . . Three bottles of champagne and three small ones of stout. With the tip say three hundred and fifty. And his own bill: thirty. . . . Three hundred and eighty. . . . He could just do it.

He pointed to the chair on the other side of the table.

'Sit down,' he said, 'have a drink.'

The dark girl had not gone. He wasn't however going to go with her. The duties of hospitality come before the duty to the body that Providence has given you! If he didn't go with the girl it was because he had to pay the bill for this Godhead. He must be Apollo at least. It was the story of Philemon and Baucis. . . . Without Baucis, of course. . . .

The least the fellow could do would be to reward him with an inexhaustible cruse. . . . A self-filling beer jug. . . . He wouldn't, of course.

Hugh Monckton said:

'Thanks. Can't. Wish I could. Ever since I stopped one! Mine for the water-wagon. As I believe you'd say.'

He was of course referring to the wound on his fore-head. . . . It was as if there were that drop of bitter in his sweet cup. But no doubt it wasn't. After all it's a blessing not to drink. You feel brighter. Henry Martin was pretty abstemious. But even at that he felt better when he had drunk nothing at all for a week. . . . Better. . . . Fitter. . . .

'A very little drop,' Hugh Monckton said, 'gives me sometimes. . . . Not always. . . . Sometimes. What you'd call precious like an epileptic fit. No knowing what you mayn't do. . . . Better not to chance it in these tiring times.'

Henry Martin said:

'You don't look tired! . . . You're Lieutenant Hugh Monckton Smith.'

'Oh, I'm tired enough,' Hugh Monckton said. 'No end tired . . . of the whole bally old game.'

He sank gracefully down on to the vacant chair. Henry Martin asked the *poule* if she would like another drink and called the waiter. The *poule* said: 'No.' Then 'Yes. Geen feez is beneficial to a cold.'

Hugh Monckton said:

'Rum is better. But gin's good, too, mademoiselle.'

Henry Martin was piqued to see that the girl bridled pleasantly before the other's amiable nonchalance.

'For us who desire to remain *plutôt maigre*,' she said, 'gin is better if less efficacious. Mademoiselle Gloria can no doubt drink rum. She will no doubt exercise herself. All day and all night.'

'Perhaps she will,' Hugh Monckton said. 'No doubt perhaps she will." He added. 'You're of course White Man Smith of Magdalen. You got out of that old show early. Some people have all the luck.'

Henry Martin dropped the ineffectual-looking French notes on the table. . . . Three hundred and fifty for Hugh Monckton's bill: forty for his own and four more francs to the unimpressed waiter. Three hundred and ninety-four francs! He was penniless. Literally *sans le sou.* The long downward course of Anacondas and Kennecotts was finished. It had begun in the Algonquin Hotel on the fifth of August two years before. Mr. Kuhn had brought his famous uncle to gaze on the literary heroes. And to give him, Henry Martin, a financial tip or two. The great man had said:

'Buy Anacondas at 115. They will go up to 135 by Christmas. Sell out and buy New York Central Bonds. You'll be settled for life. If that's what you want. . . .'

With his usual aloofness a little tempered by the awe-inspiring presence, so that he had the air of a distinguished top-salesman in an expensive department store, Kuhn had asked his uncle if there was no chance of copper dropping. Germany was coming into the market as a producer. Cape copper was being reorganized under American auspices so that its production might expect to be doubled.

The great man had said flatly:

'I've given you my advice. You can take it or leave it. It's good. Unless the bottom of the world falls out. But sell out at Christmas.'

The bottom of the world had fallen out. The last penny of his mother's legacy had gone. He had sold out his shares in the drug-store and followed that advice. Two years and ten days ago. By Christmas, 1929, Anacondas had been at 95. Now they were 13. He had not even a few francs to give the depressed *poule.* When she learned of his death – if she did learn of it – she would be more depressed still. Not because of his loss. That would probably mean nothing to her. But because the last chance of getting something out of him would be gone for good.

Hugh Monckton said:

'If you'll walk down with me to the Port I'll give it you back.'

Henry Martin said it was nothing. It didn't matter.

'You American Croesuses!' Hugh Monckton exclaimed good-humouredly. 'You must not corrupt us beggared Europeans with charity. I'll go and get the money.'

He added:

'Oh, but walk down with me. I'd be glad to talk with you. . . . About old times, of course!' he added rather hastily. . . . 'Unless,' he began again and he waved his hand toward the *poule*. . . . 'In that case if you'll tell me where you're going, I'll send the money there in two two's after I get to the Port.'

Henry Martin rose wearily.

'I'm coming,' he said.

As he put up his hand to open the swing door he noticed his signet ring on his little finger. It had been mother's gift to him on his fourteenth birthday. For twenty-three years it had hardly been off his finger. Except for once when he had had it enlarged. It was so part of himself that till that moment he had never thought of it as a separate entity.

It was no doubt worth some dollars. It might give him two or three more days of life. But he was not sure that he wanted two or three days more of life. Besides, you should not pawn your mother's presents. On the other hand, how would the ring like visiting the bottom of the sea? His body might drift out and never be found. There was a strong outward current under St. Mandrier. . . . That was no way to treat a ring. A ring was meant to be kept warm by human flesh. It wouldn't like the ooze of the sea-bottom.

He asked Hugh Monckton to wait and went back into the hall. The dark girl was making herself up again.

Gazing rather fiercely into the mirror in the flap of her bag. He dropped the ring under her nose. It spun round, the hoop of gold gleaming. The bloodstone was like an oval of red candy. She looked up at him enigmatically.

'I have seen you throwing glances at me,' she said.

He said:

'It is because you danced and gave pleasure.'

She laughed and said:

'Oh! Oh! . . . I have not danced since I came out of the . . . the cruel place.'

He said:

'It was before then. . . . Fifteen hundred years before then.'

She laughed again.

'A thousand and half a thousand . . .' she said. 'You cannot escape that inscription here. If you came to my room you would see it on the wall. . . . All the same I am not yet dead.' . . . She said. '*Saltavit et placuit. . . .* But not *mortuus est.* . . . It is *mortua* in the feminine.'

He said:

'I shall be dead before I come to your room.'

She said:

'Courage, mon vieux. . . . Courage, my friend. . . . I am not so repulsive. I have a little friend, a seamstress. . . . She became the mistress of the governor of Cochin-Annam. . . . But before then. . . . Elle m'adorait! . . . She crocheted me some curtains. . . . If you came to my room you would see them. The likeness of the tomb. . . . In crochet-work. . . . *Saltavit: Placuit: Mortuus Est.* . . .'

She pronounced it:

'Schltahvee. . . . Plahssüee. . . .'

He said:

'I regret . . . I have a friend waiting. . . .'

She laughed again: throwing her head back. Her teeth were white but reddened by her lipstick.

'Naturally,' she said. 'We have all of us friends waiting.'

He thought to himself:

'If I were Hugh Monckton Allard Smith and had all the wealth of the Indies I might pass ravishing hours with that creature. . . .'

The Russian orchestra with their white blouses, scarlet stitching and black top boots were playing 'Frankie and Johnnie'. . . .

'It is astonishing, the education of these creatures,' he said. He was crossing the floor. He had in his ears her words:

'Vous êtes gentil, quand même,' as she put his ring on to her reticule.

He seemed to have given pleasure.

Probably her education was not so astonishing. That was the motto of that region. Naturally she would know it. Her little friend had been the mistress of the governor of French Cochin-Annam. A romantic but steel-hard commercial region where you danced and gave pleasure. If you didn't give pleasure you went down into the ooze of the sea-bottom. But if you did you become immortal. On a tombstone or as Laïs Corinthiaca . . . a once fashionable prostitute.

PART TWO

CHAPTER I

HUGH MONCKTON said:

'Do you know anything of the Foreign Legion? . . . You're a man of the world. I daresay you know everything.'

They were walking in the tepid sirocco night, in the solitary blaze of the electric lights, down the Place du Théâtre.

'Romantic spot,' he continued. 'Palm trees and painted house fronts. . . . What does *Aux Délices* mean?'

Across the salmon-pink upper part of a house that had a chrome yellow *rez-de-chaussée* had been painted the words '*Aux Délices*' in immense black capitals.

Henry Martin said:

'It's a tart shop. A very good tart shop . . . *Aux Délices* means . . . oh, that you'll be delighted with their candies. . . .'

'Ah,' Hugh Monckton said: 'Some people have all the luck. . . . You can pronounce French like a . . . oh, a French actress you know. . . . You fellows are so educated. . . . Rose Scholars and all. . . .'

Henry Martin said:

'Rhodes . . . Rhodes was an Englishman . . . I don't know a great deal about the Foreign Legion. . . .'

'The point is,' Hugh Monckton asked, 'is it an escape? . . . A means of escape? . . . You fellows are so damned modest. . . . You get it both ways. . . .'

They plunged, across the light of the Rue Jean Jaurès, into the deep shadows of old houses in a black canyon.

'Of course I can say *arma virumque cano*. . . . And *conticuere omnes intentique ora tenebant* . . . oh, five or six hundred lines of the *Aeneid*. . . . But you. . . .'

'I can say . . . *Saltavit* . . . *Placuit*. . . .' Henry Martin said grimly.

His face invisible in the shadows, Hugh Monckton caught his arm:

'That's it,' he said, 'You know all those queer things. . . . The Greek Anthology, I dare say. . . . And yet you manage to look like us. That's a damn nice suit of Harris tweeds you've got on. I wish I had known your tailor. It might have made a difference.'

Henry Martin said:

'Good God. . . . It's a reach-me-down from the Galeries Lafayette.'

Their footsteps echoed from the high fronts of the houses, black beneath bright stars. They walked with regular steps as if marching.

'That's precisely it,' Hugh Monckton said. 'You fellows – no, you in particular. . . . American Croesuses can go into any jolly old department store. . . . That's what you call it, isn't it?' . . . Henry Martin could go into the Galeries Lafayette and say: 'Give me any jolly old suit.' And at once he looked like one of us. . . . Damned smart! . . . But of course Henry Martin had been in the Forty-First. Not a bad regiment. . . . But there it was. . . . Several millions was a good thing to have. But not the equal of. . . . Oh, *savoir-faire!* Some people had all the luck.

He himself had pots of money rolling in. You couldn't stop it. Henry Martin and his Johnnies – if Henry Martin would excuse him – were duds at accumulating the shekels. He himself, Hugh Monckton, would be . . . oh, pots . . . richer next week. If he were alive next week. Which he didn't plan to be. Unless information about the Foreign Legion seemed satisfactory. . . .

Henry Martin said he knew a man who had been in the Foreign Legion. William Budells. He had written a book about it.

They had come out on the *rade* – the platform of stone level with the harbour water. The reflections of lights quivered in an infinite, black placidity.

'There you are,' Hugh Monckton said. 'You have all the books at your fingertips. . . . And all the . . . department stores, isn't it? . . . You can't make money. As my people make it for me. But if my people make more money in a week than you will see in your life you can have your shoulders padded in a way to attract the neatest little filly . . . a damn neat little filly . . . I ought to thank you for being walking with me instead of . . .'

He broke off and exclaimed:

'I'm not drunk . . . I've not had a drink in a week of Sundays. But I'm going to be. And . . . what do your French friends say – *Vogue la galère*. . . . Which means: take it hot and chance your innards. . . . But you can get a nicely padded-shouldered suit at the Galeries Lafayette and pick up a neat little filly . . . and I. . . . Oh, damn it. . . . You're not a business man. You don't know what business is. I . . . my people . . . could make . . . double . . . triplicate . . . your fortune between now and sunrise . . . Yet I can be shown the door by a . . . a large-mouthed . . . oh, female descendant of the Viking who discovered your country. . . . Your jolly old country. . . .'

He broke away from Henry Martin's arm and marched to gaze into the depths of the water that was blackly and gluttonously lapping the stones of the quay. The regularly

87

architectured houses went up into blackness. He hurried back and said:

'Sorry, old bean . . . I'm going to give you some *Fine de la Republique* your friends the French call it. I bought it in your city. . . . I suppose you're a New Yorker. . . . Of a fellow whose great-grandfather had been ambassador to Napoleon. . . . Seventeen-ninety-two. . . . I brought it down for . . . Oh, a large mouth that likes good liquor. . . . I beg your pardon for . . . what is it? . . . intruding intimate details on your attention. . . . But we may as well finish it. . . . The Republican *Fine*, I mean. Good stuff, *fine* if you haven't had a jolly old crack on the skull. . . . If you have it's not so good. . . . But if you've been shown the door. . . . Well then, it's good.'

He said:

'Escape. . . . Means of escape from your jolly old self. . . . They say there are books called literature of escape. . . . I have not found any . . .'

He spoke low, earnestly and with great distinctness. He was certainly not drunk. There was not much light on the quay. That is to say, there were lights that looked bright but had practically no illuminative quality. So his face was not very plain. But he seemed as calmly smiling as he had been in the dancing hall.

He said: 'Come along here,' and went away, a hundred yards or so to the edge of the quay. His firm footsteps echoed. The English don't wear rubber heels. Henry Martin's footsteps were noiseless.

Hugh Monckton was gazing at a vessel moored stern-on to two cannon in the dockside. Four or five French bluejackets were also gazing at her, their hands in the pockets of their tight trousers. The water lapped musically on the squared stone and on the side of the ship.

88

'Means of escape,' Hugh Monckton said. 'The world's full of them. Only one is genuine.'

Henry Martin read the gilt inscription on the black stern above the rudder.

'It's *Le Secret*,' he said. 'It's always seemed to me her spars were terribly tall.'

*Le Secret*, tall and black hulled, was one of the most familiar vessels of those seas. Hugh Monckton said:

'If you only use canvas in the lightest breezes it doesn't matter. They say she has the finest auxiliary engines in the world. I don't know, of course. You can have her for me. You would know.'

Henry Martin said:

'You're going to buy her. . . . They say so. . . .'

He said:

'Buy your grandmother. . . . I'm not going to!'

He went on again:

'What should I do? On a yacht? I don't care for the sea. Not to yearn for it. Scandinavians do. But if you're not a Scandinavian and not going to have one with you. . . . What a hope!'

His vast, dim bedroom in the mouldering hotel, was mountainous with leather luggage and some packing cases. He stood astride a grip and looked absently around him.

He said:

'Ah, the Republican *fine*. . . . It's. . . . Not here.' And bent over another grip. He could bend with a straight back from his hips. And undo straps with the back still unbent. He said: ,

'What's your jolly old name? . . . It's like mine. . . . And your jolly old business? And address?'

He kept his face averted, over the grip he was opening.

He handed Henry Martin a polished leather case, shaped to fit over a bottle. He said:

'Amuse yourself with that. . . . It's the *Fine de la Republique*. . . . 1792! I want to write a note.'

He sat at a rickety bureau and pulled out letters and letter paper. He smiled at Henry Martin.

'Try it,' he said. 'It isn't dope. . . . There aren't three quarts left in the world. . . . There's half a pint there. . . . Take a sip and keep the rest. . . . For special whoopee. . . . With your best girl. . . . You unscrew the top with a right hand turn. . . . That's my device for dealing with butlers.'

He began to write scratchily. He said whilst he wrote: 'Of Monckton-Warminster,' and some name Henry Martin did not catch, then: 'Salop, England. . . .'

He said: 'By Jove, you've no glass. . . .'

He produced from a round-topped blue closet two vast, thin tumblers, gleaming bell-shaped on their stems.

'I've got amazing things in that valise. You wouldn't believe. . . . I'll drink with you when I'm finished. . . . Akervit I call it. . . . But the proper name is Akvavit. . . . Made by trolls. Bogys, you know. . . . In the something mountains. I can't pronounce 'em. . . . Amazing things. . . . A pint of attar of roses. . . . Haschisch made for the last Shah but one. . . . He was a connoisseur. . . .'

He smiled friendlily down on Henry Martin who was sitting on a horsehair sofa. He could see through the windows the searchlights of battleships. He had got the curious square bottle of old, dim glass out of the new leather case. About an eighth of the contents remained.

' "And I on honeydew have fed," ' Hugh Monckton said, ' "and drunk the milk of. . . ." Oh, I don't mean me. They were meant for other lips. . . . Pour a little . . . a very little. . .'

He held the tumbler under the bottle. Henry Martin

poured a few drops. Odour rose from the glass. Astonishingly it made Henry Martin see the line of villas with the white pillars and stoops at the top of Main Street in Springfield, Ohio.

Astonishingly, because when he had first smelt brandy in the breath of his Aunt Hedwig, Comtesse de Pralinghem – and it was of that of course that he was being reminded – those family hives had not yet been built. Alice came from one of them.

'Amazing things!' Hugh Monckton said. He waved a hand towards his luggage. . . .

'Good stuff that *fine*. . . . Take a tiny sip. Close your mouth. Swallow. Breathe out through your nose. . . . That's the way to taste liquor. . . .' He said: 'You see: when you swallow there's no sensation in the throat. . . . No burning. . . . You might be drinking perfume. . . . Amazing things. . . . The folly of me! . . . And having them turned down. As if they were modern Japanese. . . .'

He began:

'Why, there's a Nuremberg Bible. . . . And a psalter from Mount Athos. . . . And a quite good Second Folio. . . . The best that was on the market. . . . And an Ibsen manuscript. . . . That's for the highbrow side. . . . The highbrow travellers. . . . Must have something highbrow for a long voyage.'

He paused and swung his body round without moving his feet – looking vaguely at the packing cases.

'Oh, yes. . . . Adornment. . . . Art. . . . I tell you I looked through the *Encyclopaedia Britannica* for the headings. . . . There are some jewels of jolly old Tutankhamen and a tiara of the Empress Eugénie. . . . Then Art. . . . There's two . . . Oh, Simone Martini's . . . And a Raphael drawing of a jolly old Pope. . . . And paintings of the South Seas by that fellow. . . .

You know: We were making for the South Seas by the way of the Islands of the Blest.'

He drifted again towards the ramshackle desk.

'You don't have to laugh,' he said to Henry Martin. 'You're man of the world enough to know that it's wise to be provided with objects of interest if you're going to . . . filer le parfait amour as your French friends say.'

He sat down again, stiff and long and again took up his red cornelian pen.

'Well, well. . . . Filer le parfait amour,' he said. . . . He asked: 'Ever do it? . . . I never did. . . . Some people have all the luck. . . . Try the 'fifty-seven brandy on the table. It'll taste like paraffin after the other. But it'll get better as you drink it till you think it a damn fine brew. . . . Le parfait amour, indeed!'

He re-read what he had already written.

'You see,' he said, 'everything ought to be . . . oh, rich and strange. . . . Try that '57. There's no reason why you should not get a bit blotto. . . . I mean to. . . . I won't be two minutes. Then I'll run you to Carqueiranne in under the quarter. . . .'

He began to write in earnest, muttering:

'Rich and strange: rich and strange. . . . Shall suffer a jolly old sea-change.'

He seemed to be able to mutter these things whilst writing something else; for he looked around at Henry Martin and said:

'Henry Martin Aluin . . . one "l" . . . Smith. . . . No "y" or "e" nonsense. Of course not. . . . Of Highcrest. . . . Springfield, State of Ohio, United States of America and the Pisto-Brittle Works, same place, same state, at present . . . Oh, residing at the Hotel Bellevue, Carqueiranne, Var, France. . . .' He repeated, 'Henry Martin Aluin – one "l." . . .'

Henry Martin supposed him to be writing to an aunt and describing his meetings. It seemed a queer job to be doing at nearly midnight. . . . But the *Bremen* was sailing on Saturday. It was no doubt an American aunt to whom he was writing. These fellows intermarried no end. . . . Going where money was. . . .

Hugh Monckton said suddenly:

'Henry Martin Aluin Smith . . . Hugh Monckton Allard Smith. . . . We could pass as cousins with the French authorities. . . . If there were any trouble about Death duties. . . .' Then he said: 'But what two jolly old names for tombstones!'

He began to write again, his pen scratching in the silence. The searchlights whirled and whirled behind him.

The shock to Henry Martin had been quite considerable. It was as if that fellow had been spying on him and knew his plan. That, of course, was absurd. He had confided in no one. It had been only that afternoon that he had received his father's jeering cable. Certainly none of the friendly old maids at the little hotel could consider that he had been depressed. He imagined that to them he must seem as unconcerned – as fortunate even – as Hugh Monckton. They were extremely poor maiden ladies – three English, one French, one American: they crocheted and pawkily twitted him with having designs on old Marius Vial's granddaughter-in-law. The granddaughter-in-law was an extremely tightly dressed Parisienne, always in brand new black even at half-past seven in the morning, with remarkable black curls *à la d'Artagnan* and always with a perfect, artificial strawberries and cream complexion. She was sharper on the *sous* than an Airedale terrier on rats, and in secret sighed for Paris. That is to say, that unknown to the grand-

93

father she unceasingly nagged at her husband, young Olive Vial, because she had to superintend the linen and the *caisse* of the tiny hotel instead of one just as tiny in the rue du Cherche Midi, in the metropolis. Henry Martin would just as soon have designs on her as on a beautiful, stuffed parakeet – but the jocular old maids insisted that nothing else could keep him – gay, young and Pisto-Brittle apparent in a tiny nest. At that season the little port was malodorous on account of the myriads of dead Portuguese men-of-war that the east wind drove in. That at least was how the Vials accounted for the odour. They said it was salubrious – as witness the vigour of old Marius who was eighty-two and had the sight of a hawk and the volubility of a radio announcer. As was singularly the way with him, all these people except the French old maid had attached themselves to him. As if he had been a member of all their families. They confided in him so, all their incomes and the troubles of their married sisters and nieces – but they knew nothing about his complete lack of income or that he had a married sister – the Comtesse Van Heldenstamm with troubles of her own.

So that there could have been no leak from that little port and that fellow's speech about tombstones must have been made merely to pass the time away.

You couldn't think of that fellow as contemplating suicide. He was perfectly cool, as ruddy as a peach and as good-humoured as a nice dog. Besides the coincidence would be too absurd – that about midnight between the fourteenth and fifteenth of August there should be in the same room two Smiths, each contemplating suicide and each considering how similar names would look on a tombstone.

He didn't know how popular the contemplation of their own tombstones might be with the inhabitants of

Europe. He had spent a great deal of time in Europe – of the last fifteen years he must have passed nine, possibly ten there. Nevertheless he knew next to no Europeans. . . . Well enough to get at their psychologies. Americans he knew avoided the thought of death . . . of passing over. About three years ago the papers and more particularly the magazines had had lots of articles asserting that America had abolished death. That did not of course mean that no one died. But the whole country sang in chorus: 'Oh, death where is thy sting? . . .' Europeans apparently, arranged life with an eye to death. They built, still, rather for their heirs, put down wines that would only come to their best after they themselves had passed over. They wrote books for posterity; attempted to establish dynasties or by their testaments to cabine with iron bands the careers of their descendants.

All that was very un-American. The trouble with Henry Martin was that he could not satisfy himself as to precisely how American or un-American his father was. He, Henry Martin, free, male and over twenty-one sat there, will-less, numbed, in the presence of a stranger – because of some manifestation of his father's will. That was indisputable.

He sat there, rather improbably, because his father had numbed him. Exactly what he was doing there he didn't know. That fellow – Hugh Monckton – scribbled furiously away as if he were rapidly finishing some job before the two of them set out upon some piece of concerted whoopee. But nothing had been concerted between them. Ostensibly he had come up to Hugh Monckton's vast, maritime room in the maritime hotel in order to receive 394 – no, 350 francs. But why did the fellow keep him waiting?

He did not himself care. He didn't even want the money. To be completely – absolutely and completely –

95

without a *sou* had a not disagreeable, chloroforming effect. As long as he had had that small sum, action of a sort had been open to him. He could have cabled to his father for 37 francs 50: 'Must irrevocably suicide if no remittance received twenty-four hours.' Or he could have bought several sacks of oranges from the Spanish schooner in the harbour and have retailed them in the babbling market place. Or he could have bought the favours of the dark girl whose face was still vivid to him. Or have lived for four days longer in the little hotel – and had the use of the boat. As it was there was nothing that he could do. He could not indeed even pay for a taxi back to Carqueiranne – twenty-eight kilometres. Well, he could just as well spend that stifling night in walking back. Twenty-eight kilometres was nothing in particular to him. . . . Then why was he waiting? He didn't want the money.

He made a movement half to rise. The horsehair hissed under him, the wood creaked dryly. Hugh Monckton said:

'A minute or two more and we'll have a good drink. After that I'll run you to your bugwalk. It's very good of you to wait.' He ran his eyes over what he had been writing, pointed with the end of his pen at the packing cases behind him.

'Those,' he said, 'are to go to the London Museums, you understand . . . South Kensington. The National Gallery. The British and so on. According to common sense and their needs. . . . I understand the National Gallery is short in the article . . . Gauguin. . . . That's that painter's name, isn't it?'

'You aren't going to take them in the *Secret?*' Henry Martin asked. 'Oh, come. . . . If you'll excuse me . . . Gloria . . . Mrs. Sorenson. . . .'

96

Hugh Monckton said:

'Excuse *me*. . . . For my private affairs getting in your way. . . .'

He broke the long carnelian holder of his pen and tossed the end in among the valises.

'No sea-change for them,' he exclaimed. He was still smiling. 'As we used to say, you remember. *Na poo finny*. Mamma say *no bong!* . . . The poor bloody Huns used to say *Kaput*. . . . Cut is the branch that might have grown full straight.' He hesitated and said:

'And the least little sensation brings you those perfectly damnable headaches. . . . You wouldn't believe. . . .'

He ran his hand round the dim blue cornice of the room.

'Rum sort of place to be in,' he said, 'Pico della Mirandola or Pavlova. . . . Or it may have been Casanova used to hang out here. Or perhaps it was Melozzo da Forli or Taglioni. . . . So I had to put up here. . . . To represent the artistic side of the party. . . . Our Norwegian friend – Bjumstumja Bjumblepupple don't room here, of course. They have to go to the Grand for his poor dear health. The fiddler fellows room in the Golfe at Hyères. . . . Catch them rooming in this rat-trap of a place. But someone had to do honour to Pico and the rest. . . . Try it on the dog, you know. . . . *In corpore vili*. . . . I'd prefer Duke Street, Cardiff, at any time. . . . Remember Duke Street on a Saturday night? . . . With the miners coming up from the Rhondda Valley. . . . Gay by comparison. Seemed rotten then. . . . But I can't believe there was ever a poet in Cardiff.'

He wrote three words: then he said:

'His name isn't Bjumstumje Bjumbleppple of course. That's what I call him. He's really someone else. But the only Scandinavian poet one ever heard of was called

Björnstjerne Björnson. Of course there were Thorwaldsen
and Andersen . . . and Ibsen. All Scandinavian glories.
Northern lights. . . . This poet has to be . . . *dorloté*
your French friends call it. . . . Done up in cotton wool.
. . . But all this doesn't interest you. Laugh and the
world laughs with you: weep and you weep alone. . . .
Damned alone. . . . Not chick nor child nor light o' love
shall charm thee to that sweet sleep that thou owedst
yesterday. . . . You don't know the feeling. . . . Remember the three dropped goals you kicked against the
7th Monmouthshires? You were heavier then. . . .'
He asked suddenly:
'Doesn't the world seem duller to you now? . . .
Like the half-warmed fish that Spooner Johnny said
when he meant half-formed wish? . . . Not much fun in
women. . . . Too easy to come by. . . . Not much kick
in wine. . . . So they say. . . . I don't know much about
it. . . . But you're an authority. . . . What do you say?
. . . Try that '57 cognac. . . . It won't taste so bad
now. . . .'
It was true that the '57 cognac did not now taste so
bad. It was almost as oleaginous as the *Fine de la République.*
Left almost as little sting in the throat. And it was much
more warming. You could feel it go all through your
limbs – like courage.
He suddenly found himself wishing intensely that he
were that fellow. . . . More intensely than before. . . .
By now Hugh Monckton seemed less of a demi-god. . . .
But it was more reasonable to wish to be something less
than a demi-god. . . . Apparently he had lost Gloria
Sorenson. To her husband. There was nothing very
singular in that. Married women in Europe seemed to
think they still had duties to their legitimate spouses.
It made them no doubt more piquant. Apparently if

you had an affair with a European woman the husband always had a fifty-fifty chance. Or more. Seventy-thirty, say.

He himself had had an exactly similar experience. Wanda, of course, was a European in the end. Though the European men were fish-like enough, the women made up for it. Their manners and customs were singular, apparently. . . .

The '57 *fine* was certainly warming. . . . He had read a book by a Frenchman, Beadle, or something like that. About Scandinavian women.

Yes, it made that fellow a more human person to want to be. . . . He had lost his Gloria. . . . Or no doubt she was only holding out on him for a higher allowance for her husband. . . . Apparently that lump was a Scandinavian poet. . . . Very like himself and Wanda – their affair. She seemed to have told him . . . *just* like Wanda – that she must look after the old man. . . . Like thousands of European women. . . . Like Madame de Récamier. *She* had to go back to Récamier. After Prince Henry of Prussia, and Benjamin Constant . . . and a doctor fellow. . . . He had lately been reading a life of Madame Récamier.

No doubt if he were in that fellow's skin at the present moment it would not be exactly gay. He would be feeling it outrageous that she should have left his muscular six feet to return to that five-foot-eight lump. . . . But he would have the conviction that he could buy her back at any time. With all that wealth. . . . It was only complete want of wealth that rendered you impotent.

When he went to the window Hugh Monckton looked round at him disquietedly.

'Only ten minutes more,' he said. 'I assure you not more than ten. . . . You can be in bed by one. One's not late for a whole man. . . . I'm supposed to be in bed at ten. . . .'

The searchlights waved desperately. When they were at certain angles the black water of the harbour existed because of their reflection. At other times it was completely invisible. Then all the great arms converged. Where they met was a tiny, golden dragon-fly. They had spotted their plane. . . . They performed these exercises ceaselessly in those waters. The mass of a battleship showed itself in the harbour against pale glow. . . . A dull business, spotting planes in a world that had lost glory.

It was certainly a duller world. It had been the eve of the Assumption, but you would hardly have noticed it. . . . There were the small figures of small French bluejackets. Down on the quays their absurd white caps and tight white trousers ran about. They lifted their arms noiselessly in the glare of the arc-lights. . . . That was all there was to the eve of the Assumption, as far as he could see. Small bluejackets had late leave. . . . What was the good of them? Even war had appeared a dull affair. . . .

Dull wars; dull women; dull wine. . . . Hostilities lacking glory; adultery lacking sin; drink a mere means to a hangover. . . . Hugh Monckton was undoubtedly right. . . . But if you were in a position to do these things very expensively! . . . That might give an edge to dullness. . . . He wished himself again, intensely, Hugh Monckton.

It wasn't such a terrible affair to lose a Norwegian. . . . He had done it himself. . . .

Wanda had expected – in Paris, that time – that he would commit suicide, the same evening. He hadn't. When Wanda had come next morning with a sheaf of white flowers to lay upon his bier he had been – dully of course – in bed with Alice. He could not remember what his feelings had been like but Wanda had thrown back her head and laughed for five minutes. He and Alice had watched her with the sheet up to their chins. No doubt they had felt awkward. Then Wanda had thrown the flowers on their feet.

She had been laughing at herself. . . . Presumably for having expected passion and despair from him. . . . But the modern man was incapable of passion. He could know despair. When Anacondas dropped to 12 and passed their dividends. . . . But passion . . . Europeans might know what it was. But you couldn't call them modern.

It had been whilst arranging Wanda's flowers in a yellow faience jug that Alice had first asked him to regularize their union. She said it was disagreeable to have strange women walking into your bedroom. Not to have authority to tell them to go away. That was apparently what the sacrament of marriage meant for her. There had been nothing to their union, regularized, or before.

It had come about – had been drifted into – on the Christmas after the Armistice. Leopold Kuhn had a staff-car. A great Packard. He had suggested that they should spend Christmas day and the day after at Chartres. And take a couple of girls.

Henry Martin had known only one girl. And she had not been available. He had not been long in Paris at the time and knew few people. Leopold Kuhn on the other hand moved in expensive, peopled circles, mostly American. Paris was full of Americans then. Kuhn was at the time attached to a dark girl from Baltimore. But his attachments had not lasted long.

He had turned up with the Packard at the door of the apartment in the rue des Saints Pères. When Henry Martin had gone down, Kuhn had been standing by the door of the car with two girls – the dark Baltimorean and a fair, small, rather sulky-looking younger girl. She was introduced to Henry Martin as Miss Alice Heinz of Springfield, Ohio. . . . She had given only one look at him from rather resentful blue-grey eyes and they had all got into the car. The men were in the front seat. Kuhn said that he had chosen for Henry Martin a girl from his home town so that he might feel safer and have a more Christmassy feeling.

As soon as they were outside the city they changed places. The Baltimorean sat with Leopold Kuhn who embraced her from time to time while he drove. In the rear seats Henry Martin and Alice Heinz had told each other their middle names. That used to be the phrase in those days.

Of her associates in Springfield he had known very few. Of his she had known practically none. That was hardly astonishing. Springfield was a small city; they had nevertheless moved in entirely different spheres, hers having been one that his mother's associates would have called almost the underworld . . . until three years or so before. Her father had been a North German farmer who had emigrated to Indiana before her birth. He had done badly. Having had insufficient capital to last out three bad grain years he had found himself reduced to a four-horse team as almost his only possession. He had made an indifferent living by taking hauling jobs for neighbouring farmers and small townsmen until horses had been nearly superseded. He had then acquired a heavy motor lorry and had continued at his work. That might have been in '97 or '98. The bad times were

passing. Hermann Heinz came with a load to Springfield. He had come across the mother of Alice – a cook,
from Hamburg. He had never liked the neighbourhood
of Chesterton, Indiana, where, till then, he had been
settled. There were too many Swedes and Norwegians
there: not enough Germans. He had removed himself
and his lorry to Springfield. With the good times the
building trade had revived. Springfield was growing by
leaps and bounds. His lorry was never idle. With the
savings of his wife he bought another lorry. A brother
of Alice's mother drove that. The two men remained
simple peasants. Alice's mother ran the office. She was
a master woman with a head for figures and social ambitions. She had served in the best families in Springfield
and knew their ways.

By the birth of Alice they had five motor lorries and
were the foremost transporters in the city. Mrs. Heinz
was already an official of the Americanization League.
She was very active in turning hyphenated Americans
into hundred-per-centers. Her husband and brother
remained rather obstinately peasant in speech and appearance. They were at least neither Irish, Negro, Jew,
nor Catholic and could on occasion be got to assert that
they despised the lot. Mrs. Heinz would explain that
Hamburgers were not like other Germans. They were
more like Anglo-Saxons. Cosmopolitan. Resembling
English and Americans of pure blood. Because of their
independence and descent from the Hanseatic traders.
She herself was a Hamburger.

Alice had been to school and high school in Springfield – but she had just gone to Chicago University when
the war broke out. In 1917 she had been nineteen. She
was extraordinarily lazy and more than a little untidy –
but not at all unpopular in Chicago. In Springfield she

had not got on very well. The girls had not asked her to belong to any of their clubs. That was perhaps because of the uncouthness of her father or because her mother had cooked for the mothers of other girls at her schools. One day she had appeared with the initials B.Y.C. on her tunic. She had refused to explain them for a long time. Then she said they were the initials of a powerful secret club. A little later she had explained that to be a member you had to be able to hang from the bough of a certain tree by your toe-nails. This assertion, together with her complete reserve as to any other details had gained her a certain notoriety.

The explanation was this. . . . Being more or less ostracized she had passed the greater part of her time in her backyard with her cat. She had formed herself and her cat into a club – the Back Yard Club. The cat could hang by its claws from a bough of the one hickory tree in the yard. Alice herself, as perpetual president, did not have to possess this qualification for membership.

Apparently Alice had had no idea of the humorous aspects of this arrangement. She had no sense of humour. She had had a deeply serious desire for revenge and for mortifying those of her school comrades who could be mortified at being unable to penetrate her secret. To be extraordinarily taciturn was no trouble to her. The greater part of her mental broodings were even at that day unknown to Henry Martin himself. It was only when she was very drunk on alcohol that she would at all open her mind and then only to a female intimate – hardly ever to Henry Martin. It was only when one or other of these intimates openly or unwittingly had discussed her with him that he had acquired what little insight he had into her hidden character. It had been from the Baltimore girl who had accompanied him to

Chartres that he had had the story of the Back Yard Club. The Baltimore girl had at that time been anxious to make Alice seem attractive to him.

She was in Paris of course because of the necessity for the German-descended to do War Service, though she appeared contented enough to be there because she had a passion for looking at pictures. Her mother had had no great difficulties to meet in Springfield in spite of her enemy origins. Springfield was preponderantly German in population. Nevertheless she had thought it as well to let Alice go to France – as an auxiliary nurse.

For that Alice had proved herself entirely unsuited: she was too hopelessly untidy, not so much on her person as with her belongings. She had at last been pitchforked into a job where the defect was no particular obstacle – that of assisting an older woman in distributing to French hospitals the supplies that benevolent America sent over in vast quantities.

She had been stationed with this woman at a depot near Blois. They had French *poilus* attached to them to help in unpacking crates; they lived in a small, old-maidish house in the shadow of the castle and drove great distances every day in an old car lent them by the French authorities. This life seemed to have suited Alice as well as any other. She appeared to have no very decided tastes. She liked as well as anything to sit still in a straight-backed chair, saying and doing nothing. But she liked driving an automobile which she did with great coolness and preferably at the highest speed to be obtained from the car which she happened to be driving. At intervals more or less regular, of a fortnight or two, she would visit museums or art galleries. She would do so with avidity for about ten days. The next fortnight she would spend apparently in digesting what she had seen – sitting still with her hands in her lap and looking straight in front of her. She never appeared to make any use of her knowledge.

She was rather small – which was singular since both her father and mother were very tall – she was fair but not very fair; her mouth was small and very red-lipped; she pouted naturally which gave her usually a sulky expression except on the rare occasions when she smiled. Her eyes were grey – not very large – with the brows strongly marked. Several curling strands of rather luminous brown hair usually came out from under her hat beside her cheeks. Her equanimity was always absolute. She never lost her temper except with high winds which she detested or when asked to tidy up a room with speed. Then she would make a sound like 'Tcht! Tcht!' between her teeth and make the confusion of what she was tidying seem more hopeless. . . .

During the drive to Chartres Henry Martin had gathered very little about her. She was not interested in such few common friends as they had. She had apparently made the acquaintance of the girl from Baltimore at a boarding house at which they had both lived after the armistice. After the Baltimore girl had gone to live with Kuhn at an hotel she had come almost daily to take Alice to the Louvre in Kuhn's car. Alice had apparently been going through the pictures century by century. The Baltimore girl had stayed with her when she found interesting the pictures through which Alice was plodding. When she did not like them she drove Mr. Kuhn's automobile round the Bois and returned to pick up Alice at closing time.

Henry Martin had gathered that Alice had had a lover at the boarding house – a Frenchman who had picked acquaintance with her at the Salon Carré in the

Louvre, and had taken up his quarters at the *pension* for the purpose of sleeping with her. He did not appear to have gone about with her during the day or to have identified himself with her in any way. Apparently as soon as her freshness had gone off for him he had broken with her, had told her that she did not interest him any more, and had left the boarding house. It had been immediately after that that the Baltimore girl had suggested to her that she should go on the trip to Chartres . . . .

Henry Martin had not heard of Alice's former liaison until after he had been married to her for some time. If he had heard of it earlier it might have shocked him but, by the time he did, he was already accustomed to the change in the point of view that had overcome the world as he was to know it. Drink had no doubt had a good deal to do with it. After Alice had been to the Louvre, the Baltimore girl returning at closing time from her driving in the Bois would take her to the Ritz bar. There they would meet Mr. Kuhn and, amidst the noise of the polyglot but pre-eminently English and American crowd, they would drink so many cocktails that it had never been either the Baltimore girl or Alice who had driven home. Mr. Kuhn on the other hand practically never exceeded, but the two girls seemed to pass every evening in this state of definite intoxication or mental haze.

His union with Alice had presented no aspect at all of romance. At Chartres they had visited the cathedral, walked rather noisily about the town in the dusk, dined copiously at a restaurant, played auction whilst drinking champagne and *fine* in a private sitting-room at the hotel. The girls had become very intoxicated and had sung French songs. He remembered some necking with Alice and that he had certainly kissed the Baltimore girl.

His necking with Alice had been rather timid on his part. He had not known exactly what part he was supposed to play with a girl of rich parents from his own town. By her it had been received rather sulkily but without repulsion or reproof. He imagined afterwards that she was resenting the Frenchman's desertion.

Next morning they had found themselves in bed together. Henry Martin had no idea of how they got there nor, as far as he knew, had Alice. She had exhibited a sort of exaggerated sulkiness during the following morning, and at lunch she had expressed her intention of returning at once to Paris. But after they had visited the cathedral and attended Benediction she had said no more about it. They had drunk almost as freely at dinner and during the subsequent bridge but they had remained sober enough to know that, before they went to sleep she had become, almost without preliminary endearments, his mistress.

They had spent the two ensuing days in driving round the flat country about Chartres. Alice drove at horrifying speed in country lanes at the bottoms of valleys, then cresting ridges always to see the distant blue spire of the cathderal, brooding, like a finger pointing upwards, over the December plains . . . And Alice brooding over the sight. . . .

She told him once afterwards in Springfield, driving back more than a little tight from the Country Club on a New Year's morning, that the lot of them had never been so near their deaths as on that period of driving. She said, if it hadn't been that each time she had  wanted once more to see that spire, when the car had been doing over eighty she would have given a twist to the  wheel. He shivered sometimes still when he thought of it. He shivered at that moment. But he never knew whether it was for hatred of himself and his companions – and she came afterwards to hate Mr. Kuhn very furiously, at least in her cups – or whether it was out of despair for the loss of her Frenchman. She had told him once, too, that if it had not been for the blue glass in the great rose window of the cathedral just before Benediction that Christmas day he would never have possessed her. She said once that if she ever found him attractive it was when she used to imagine she saw him silhouetted against that blue haze amongst the dark columns.

That was almost as much as he knew ever about her attitude towards himself. They had once had almost a gay period together. It was when, coerced into acting as traveller for Pisto-Brittle by his father and herself, they had been driving to little places round Chicago. She had driven almost as fast as she had round Chartres and had almost uttered exclamations of delight when the pile round the Spearmint building had from time to time appeared, grey-blue, against the sky, above the plains. They had imagined at the time that she had been with child but that had not proved to be the case. He did not know whether she did or did not want to have children. At first they had taken precautions against it happening. But they had given these up, partly out of listlessness and partly because they interfered with such physical pleasure as they got out of their intercourse. They had, however, never had a child.

Henry Martin imagined that that might be because she had procured an abortion whilst she was the mistress of the Frenchman – or earlier. But he had no means of knowing. The physical disability might well be in himself. He had no reason to suspect that. But he had never had a child as the result of any of his affairs and both his Sister Carrie and Brother Hal were childless.

He sometimes thought that Alice was heartbroken over the sterility of their union – that that might account for her queernesses. But that too he had no means of knowing. . . .

When they got back to Paris from Chartres Mr. Kuhn had just simply clumped Alice's grips down in the apartment in the rue des Saints Pères. That seemed to mark for Henry Martin the degree of promiscuity that his world had reached. For himself he had till then been on the side of the angels. Mr. Kuhn talked a great deal more than Alice; in spite of that, his motives and point of view were not much less inscrutable. He seemed to mark the passage of time. Henry Martin learned that the French authorities at first and then gradually the French in general were becoming extremely unpopular. He knew that, because whatever Mr. Kuhn said represented what was felt in the most correct circles. Mr. Kuhn's uniforms grew daily more decorative and resplendent; his conversation more and more to lay stress on the fact that his part in the war had been strictly non-combatant. His task of assuring the welfare and comfort of perhaps misguided soldiers had been fulfilled. He was careful to inform hearers gathered together in the Ritz bar or more democratic drinking places across the water that his present function was merely to ensure that the United States got her dues out of the iniquitous grafters who ruled the lately allied republic. He was merely engaged in attempting to obtain early payment for typewriters and sewing machines. They had formed the cargo of the transport that had brought over himself and Henry Martin. But only Henry Martin knew that.

Thus almost the same moment Henry Martin learned that it was good form, or going very shortly to be good form, to dislike the people among whom they lived, and that it was becoming more and more the fashion for males to regard females as little more than the casual furniture of a man's apartment. You could acquire women as you acquired divans, mattresses or central heating and replace them by other patterns when their attractiveness made them seem a little shop-soiled. . . . And women, of course, if their means permitted, could behave exactly the same by men. . . . A well-dressed woman who had been sitting at his table whilst Alice was dancing with her husband at the Bal Tabarin had said to him:

'You seem to be a niceish sort of a fellow. I'm a nice woman. Why don't we divorce our husband and wife and get married?'

She had been of course more than a little lit – but it would not have much astonished Henry Martin if the proposal had been agreed to by Alice or the husband who was a prominent member of the younger set of Providence, Rhode Island. Henry Martin had never known their names. They had struck up a friendship, with practically no introductions, at Harry's bar in a crowd all more or less acquainted and had gone up to dance at the Ball Tabarin because it was relatively in-expensive and both the men at the moment rather broke. . . . He had never seen that couple again.

If her union with Henry Martin had done her any good it was fortunate for Alice that first Wanda and then his father had arrived in the apartment just after they had had a very late and fairly wet night at Mont-martre. They had only just got up and the apart-ment had been like a new pin. The *femme de ménage's* tidying had had no time to be undone by Alice. She had not even opened her *Saturday Evening Post* or dropped the wrapper in the butter dish.

The *femme de ménage* had been an elderly lady with

only one eye, in a rusty black dress and perpetual carpet slippers. Her other eye had been put out by a fragment of the bomb that had destroyed her husband, one of her grandchildren – and a number of other worshippers in the Church of St. Gervais on Good Friday, 1918. She had a singular high voice, like a horse's laugh, and she and Alice played a perpetual game of catch-as-catch-can.

It had amused him at the time. He imagined now that that amusement had given Alice a certain claim on him. It was perhaps all the claim she had really ever had.

He had been in his apartment nearly two months. Every day at least once the old lady had stood with her back to the doorpost of the kitchen, leaning a little back, holding a fork and telling the story of how she had lost her husband and grandchild at the same moment. On a Good Friday. At Mass. God be thanked, they might be considered as having gone straight to Paradise. They, if anyone ever, would be in a state of grace. The thing that troubled her was that it would be many years before she would see them again. She was a good woman after her lights. *Sérieuse*! But she could not expect to escape many years at least in Purgatory. Unless God took into account her being an old woman who had been hard hit. Sorely tried! She had put all her savings into the hands of the Christian Sisters. The Government had seized all the property of the Christian Sisters. So at seventy she was without a sou.

Henry Martin had eaten in his apartment at least once every day. His office had been next door to the Ministry, on the boulevard round the corner. She had talked to him whilst he ate.

In that way she had acquired a proprietary interest in him, and showed a great deal of devotion. Naturally Alice had torn that a good deal. In spite of her untidiness she was a masterful housekeeper. A saucepan, a slipper and a hairbrush would stand among his papers on the bureau but she scrutinized Madame Eugénie's accounts with the fierce conviction that she would find the old lady overcharging by at least ten cents a day. . . . And a dime a day meant a dollar every ten days. Thirty dollars a year.

The old lady stood that with a good deal of humour. She would stand respectfully behind Alice whilst Alice compared her books with her receipts. But suddenly her one eye would fall on the saucepan amongst the papers. She would wander with it, her felt slippers dragging, away into the kitchen. When Alice would look up with a fierce question as to the price of a T bone she would be gone. When she came back, Alice's torrents of impetuous French would be incomprehensible to her. In the middle of a long speech her attention would wander and she would go away with the hairbrush or the slipper. Sometimes it would be a stocking draped over the Quimper pottery teapot on the mantelpiece or a bathrobe under the sofa.

Her untidiness was extravagant considering that she was really very careful of her personal appearance. It was to be accounted for by her mental concentration. She would take the saucepan in order to make coffee – for she considered that the French could not make coffee. She would have been reading a letter from a girl friend when she went to get the saucepan, so she would drop the several pages of the letter into a bowl of salad in the kitchen sink. With the saucepan in her hand she would remember that she had meant to make a note of the date of a painting by the court painter to Louis XIV – Rigaud . . . Rigaudin, some such name. So she would stand the saucepan in among the papers on the bureau and become engrossed in a long note on French art of the seventeenth century.

He had once or twice asked her why she did not take up painting herself. It might occupy her leisure moments. She had at first said that she didn't care to. She wanted to be a good housewife. One day, in a real temper, she had blazed out at him: Did he mean her to shame her mother? Her uncle's children – four of them – were all musical. Each of them played an instrument. All good musicians. . . . But did he want her to shame her mother by comparison with them? They were good musicians. But once their instruments were bought that was an end of the cost. Their music they got from the symphony society to which they belonged. . . . But consider the cost of this painting. . . . Brushes. Mediums. Palettes. Easel. . . . A whole paraphernalia every time you moved. She had a girl friend. Ida Schlemberger! She painted and it was a shame. She was for ever going to her parents for money for this and that. . . .

When Alice was angry she had little quick movements. They were attractive. When she was angry with Madame Eugénie she jumped from side to side in her chair as if she were avoiding thrusts. It reminded him of a film that he had seen of a mongoose evading the strokes of a cobra. Not that Madame Eugénie was like a cobra. She seemed amused by Alice. Or it may have been only that her peculiar voice gave her the effect of laughing. Anyhow, when they had left Paris she had sighed. She had said that you got used to people's way and then, as soon as that happened, they went away.

Alice detested her. She found her invincibly dishonest because she could not catch her in dishonesty. If she could have caught her she would have liked her better, for she would have gained a cent or two. But she could not. She began to detest all the French. Every morning and afternoon she came back with a story of how one shopkeeper had robbed her over a pair of stockings. Another had called her *sale américaine*. She considered that she ought to be admitted free to State collections of pictures. As if she had been a copyist. She said she memorized the pictures – which was just as good.

Looking at the matter from that distance Henry Martin considered that the fact that she went on paying her francs for admission to the Louvre proved that her ruling passion was not acquisitiveness. She certainly at that moment possessed all the money that remained to him. But she had acquired it so wordlessly that it had the air of having been a natural process. Money flowed to her as water goes down the hole in a bath. It went invisibly, apparently very slowly. Then the bath was suddenly empty. His suicide was to be, as you might say, the rather indecorous noise usually made by the last waters of an emptying bath.

He didn't resent it – any more than he resented any other great natural phenomenon. She was now, as things went, comfortably situated. She must have six thousand a year or so all invested in New York Central Bonds. In addition she had inherited from her mother. No doubt in the end her investments would feel the frost. At the moment they were almost unaffected. With six thousand a year she could do well in Paris and no doubt, as soon as he was dead, father would come to her assistance. He had said as much in answer to a letter Henry Martin had written him from Paris four months ago. Henry Martin had said that he was no longer in a position to support his wife. Father had answered that he, Henry Martin, could always return and again take up drumming for Pisto-Brittle. As long as he did not he would have to support his wife. If on the other hand he died, father would see that Alice was properly provided for.

It began to worry him that, with all the time he had had for thinking about it, he had never got his relationships straight in his mind. Not with his father. Not with Alice. . . . What was at the bottom of his father? Determination to break him, Henry Martin, to his will? The desire to continue the dynasty of sugar bakers? . . All he knew was that, all his life, he had felt against him a tremendous obstinacy. Willing him to do something.

And, for the matter of that, what was at the bottom of Alice? Avarice? Some unknown passion? . . . All his life with her he had felt himself to be up against an obstinacy only equalled by that of his father. But he could not feel that it willed him to do anything. It was as if he hardly existed for her. . . .

It burst like a shell in his mind that she might be a Lesbian.

He knew next to nothing about Lesbianism. Alice had certainly had a great deal to do with women and practically nothing to say to men. Their presence always seemed to make her sulky. . . . Sudden excitement filled him. He felt as if he ought to investigate. . . . As if he had been wronged. As if he had wrongs that he could declaim about. He had always wanted to have wrongs. . . . To be in a position to declaim about them. . . .

Hugh Monckton said:

'Finished writing, old bean. Be ready in a minute. . . . Then we'll drink!'

The dim blue room and the window with the whirling shapes of light became important again to Henry Martin.

But he was too excited not to return immediately to his brighter images. . . . Paris and Springfield. Those were what were really material. . . . He was haunted by the level-crossing over the railway where there had always been a traffic jam. His father had walked them, as children, down there. Passing the store that had the electric fixings. Grandfather Smith's drug-store had been at the upper, left hand corner. A little girl called Gretchen with two flaxen pigtails had cried because he had shooed her away when she wanted to look through the coloured demi-johns.

He was convinced that he had suffered a great wrong. That was a queer thing to discover a few hours before . . . his end. If you discovered a great wrong it ought to be about the middle of your life. So that you would have time to track it down. . . . It was true that he knew nothing about Lesbians – their practices, beliefs, private conversations. New York swarmed with them. There were numbers in Paris. They did not seem to be so thick on the ground there as in New York. Parisians disapproved more; they were more old-fashioned. No doubt the Lesbians did not show themselves so much.

Some man in New York – at a stag party at Hieronymo's – had once said to him:

'How can you wonder at it? Look at the male New Yorker. He's a crass beast. There must be eleven nice, educated, clean girls in New York to every decent man. . . . No wonder a nice girl prefers to take up with another girl. . . .'

It seemed plausible. When he looked at the table full of lit men with whom he had been in company he could not imagine anyone wanting to take up with anyone of them. They had been the larger Pisto-Brittle New York distributors. Giving him a farewell dinner before one of his returns to Springfield. . . . That look had indeed decided him – for the last time – to have done for good with Pisto-Brittle and Springfield. . . . He had had that farewell dinner under false pretences. He hadn't gone back to Springfield – or only to pack his grips.

Instead, immediately afterwards he had gone to see Mr. Kuhn who lived then in an apartment in West Forty-Second Street. Mr. Kuhn happened to be in. He suffered from hay fever and was of the opinion that the pollen of the ragged herbs and loose-strife that grew on the vacant building lots of the city were the cause of his malady. He therefore stuffed the cracks of his windows with medicated cotton and sat all day with his radio going.

Henry Martin had decided to take definitely to 'writing.' The sight of the Pisto-Brittle agents embattled and all more or less lit, round the speakeasy table, had certainly had something to do with that determination. But no doubt it had been coming on. Mrs. Percival must have had something to do with it. She was tall, cool, with beautiful wrists and she seemed to him to be always shadowy. In a hat with feathers drooping over the brim. At any rate she did not seem to belong to the age of Pisto-Brittle agents. . . . *Any* other age!

When they weren't adolescent and high-voiced the Pisto-Brittle agents were pendulous-jawed, greyish-faced and bass-voiced. Their personal linen was profuse, they sucked huge cigars with fat lips, slapped the beaming adolescents on the shoulders with enormously heavy fat white hands and roared in harsh voices the glories of various fellows who had extended the sales of Pisto-Brittle. The thin adolescents beamed at having their shoulders struck by those tallow thunderbolts and said:

'Yes, Mr. Schmalz! Sure, Mr. Schmalz!' in the blue smoke of the great cigars and the fumes of straight alcohol disguised as Burgundy. They made an incredible row considering that they had nothing but Pisto-Brittle to talk about. . . . Certainly Mrs. Percival had nothing to do with an age that contained them. . . .

She herself had been born in Stuttgart of quite pure American parentage. Her parents had been in the diplomatic service. Her husband treated her badly. He was a novelist of South Dakota origin, but his people, who had been farmers, had moved to Springfield where they had engaged in the shoe trade and become very wealthy. Percival, the novelist, was by then well known. But outrageous. A bad man. The parents sided with Mrs. Percival against their son, and she came to make them a protracted visit. The mother, at fifty, had taken to writing free verse of an extremely modern type. She was grey-haired and thin and was understood to have French blood. After she took to writing free verse she built a studio over the back garden. It was in two tiers with a sort of gallery like a stage. On this, the musical society to which belonged the cousins of Alice performed every Thursday night. The studio was adorned with very modern art from Paris. There was even a Picasso drawing. The Percivals' house was thus quite an art centre. Father and Alice's uncle Heinrich and Mr. Percival, Senior, used to play cut-throat quietly in an alcove in the studio on Thursday evenings. They all liked music with their cards. Alice's father was not allowed to play with them on these evenings. He could not be taught not to shout as German players shout over skat. So on those evenings he used to go through his accounts with his antique head-clerk over two immense seidels of what passed for near-beer. . . .

Quite an art-centre! A little Paris! . . . Nearly everyone who went to the Percivals' on a Thursday evening could talk of the Place de la Concorde. It gave them indeed a background that most of them at one time or another had lately banked there. . . .

Henry Martin exclaimed suddenly:

'That's it. . . . That was exactly it!'

There were people in the room. . . . Hugh Monckton's English chauffeur and a girl in a kimono like the wings of powdered butterflies.

He remembered that Hugh Monckton had pushed open the communicating door of the next room and had said something in French. . . . But the shock of his discovery or possibly the two shots of '57 *fine* that he had swallowed down made it difficult to keep his mind on Hugh Monckton and his companions. . . .

When they had all three gone off to Paris two years or so ago, Alice and Mrs. Percival had been going together. . . . It was outrageous. But he remembered twenty things that showed it. . . . Old Mrs. Heinz's disproportionate rage at their going. . . . Old Mrs. Heinz had made a special visit to the Pisto-Brittle works to warn Henry Martin that if they went to Paris Alice would go to the devil. He had thought at the time that the fiery-moustachioed grenadier of an old woman had meant: because of the drink.

Alice had been becoming more eccentric at that time when under the influence of liquor. Henry Martin had thought himself that Alice had wanted to go back to Paris so that she might without censure can herself and display her person in public places. . . . Since Mrs. Percival had been in Springfield Alice had taken dancing lessons from her. . . . Mrs. Percival had been a pupil of some celebrated Russian. She could almost have been a professional. Once when Percival had gone off to Latvia for three months he had left Mrs. Percival without a cent. She had supported herself by dancing Russian dances in one of the Parisian Palace Hotels. . . .

It was outrageous!

Hugh Monckton was standing by the little bureau. The chauffeur was seated at it. Hugh Monckton had one hand down on the paper before the man. He said :

'You'll recognize this document, Phelps. . . . You see the underlined words. NOW THIS CODICIL WITNESSETH . . . You'll recognize Mademoiselle!'

He was saying to the girl who had her back to Henry Martin:

'Veuillez vous approcher un peu, petite, que Phelps puisse vous reconnaître?'

The girl had her handkerchief up to her face. Either she was crying or ashamed. . . .

The girl probably did not sleep with Hugh Monckton or he would not have *vousvoyé'd* her. You probably say 'toi' to French girls you sleep with. He himself had certainly always *tutoyé'd* Félicité. . . .

Mrs. Percival's face came before him. . . . Her earnest face and deep voice when he had been begging her to divorce Percival and marry him. She had said. . . . He heard her saying it:

'No. No. It's unthinkable. It would be too hard on Alice.'

He had argued with her incredulously. Other people divorced and re-married. It was already settled that he and Alice were divorcing. There was no reason why she should not divorce Percival. She was not living with him since she was living with them. They had then a very nicely furnished house in the rue des Quatre Vents.

. . . Provençal armoires in brown wood with bright steel hinges and ornamentations.

One of Alice's undergarments had been lying on a brown wood settee. Mrs. Percival had said:

'But this would be different . . . unthinkable. . . .'

He had taken Alice's garment and thrown it furiously into her bedroom. She was at a dancing lesson. . . . Outrageous.

Hugh Monckton said amiably:

'Heigh, old man. Turn on us the light of your counting-house for a second. . . .'

He pointed Henry Martin out to the chauffeur.

'That's Mr. Henry Martin Aluin Smith,' he said. 'You'll recognize him if you meet him again. One of the best.'

The man blinked at Henry Martin.

'Your cousin, sir,' he said. 'No difficulty in recognizing 'im. The spitting image of you, sir.'

The scrutiny destroyed Henry Martin's subconsciousness. Hitherto these persons had seemed dim and in miniature. At the end of a diminishing glass.

Hugh Monckton said to the girl:

'Regarde-toi bien ce monsieur, veux-tu, petite?'

He was *tutoy*-ing her now! But it was perhaps because she was crying. She held her handkerchief over her eyes and shook her head behind it when asked to look at Henry Martin. Hugh Monckton said:

'A nice little filly. A decent piece. A bit watery because she's been deserted by the Governor of French Cochin-Saigon.' He added: 'A pair of us, you see. Both deserted. Two inconsolables!' He said: 'Excuse me,' and began to give directions to Phelps.

Phelps was to take the silver Rolls-Royce and drive like hell to Biarritz. He was to get to Biarritz station before Madame Bumblecuppy Bumblecumbske. Madame Bumblecuppy Bumblecumbske's train would just about be starting.

'There's a drive and a half for you, Phelps,' he said. 'You like driving like that.'

Phelps was to present Madame Bumblecuppy Bumblecumbske with this dressing-case full of souvenirs and five hundred francs' worth of roses that he would buy in the town. After that he was to make his way as fast or as slowly as he liked to London and put himself under the orders of Mr. Cyril Monckton. Mr. Cyril would no doubt find jobs for him.

'You're too good a man to lose,' he said.

Phelps asked if he might drive by Paris and pass a day or two there. There was a little piece in that city.

'You'll never drive Madame Bumblecuppy Bumblecumbske again,' Hugh Monckton said. 'Nor me either, very likely. I'm to wear the jolly old willow.'

Phelps's immobile face became more immobile. He said, 'Oh, come sir, there was a plenty of nice little pieces on sea and on land . . . Madahmahsell there, now. She'd soon stop raining. One day again they'd be up and away through the Khyber Pass to the Atlas Mountings.'

Hugh Monckton said:

'No. No, Phelps. It's good of you, Phelps. No more little pieces for me. Nor large ones. Napoo finny. Mamma say No Bong! I shall get me to a monastery.'

'Those are my sentiments,' Mr. Phelps said. 'But there's pleasure to be got out of little pieces if you don't let them wind around your heart strings.' He said reflectively:

'I shan't be sorry not to be driving Madame Sorenson again. . . . Nervous she was. Not that she demonstrated! But little shrieks, going round corners. . . . Distracting . . .' Suddenly he said earnestly:

'You ain't comtemplating nothing. . . . Not rash, sir? "The rash act" . . . the coroner said. . . . That's how the papers put it.'

'You'll have to drive damn rashly if you don't start,' Hugh Monckton said. He was pushing the chauffeur out of the room with friendly pats on the shoulder.

THE girl was still sitting beside the bureau . . . a parti-coloured butterfly. Patches of vermilion, blue and emerald green. Her too Hugh Monckton propelled across the room with friendly pats. She had still her handkerchief to her face. She had never looked at Henry Martin.

All these actions were dim to him. The room was dim, lit only by the battered, shaded green lamp on the bureau that diffused a little light with its reflections. Hugh Monckton had his right arm round the girl. With his left hand he was forcing into the fingers that held together her kimono a closely folded wad of paper.

'Vous me ferez le plaisir . . . la faveur . . . l'honneur, he said, 'd'accepter cela . . . oh, comme souvenir, you know. Vous avez été bonne pour moi.'

At the door she turned. Her right sleeve elevated itself. She was like a butterfly about to take wing. With the awkwardness of a woman throwing violently her hand came forward. The little packet flew from it and dis-solved into slowly descending sheets of paper. Pinkish. . . . Large French bills they were. They fell among the packing cases.

'You speak French like a native,' Henry Martin accused him.

He was labouriously retrieving the notes from among the cases. He came up slowly.

'Mustn't speak French too well unless it's necessary,' he said. 'It isn't done. He was counting the notes. 'A damn lot of things aren't *done*,' he grumbled. 'Most of the jolly things.' He added: 'That little piece can't get over the ex-Governor of French Cochin-Shanking-Saigun. . . . Whatever it is. . . . Not a very savoury-looking bloke, you'd say. But she can't get over his . . . oh, defection. . . . Wonderful things some women are. . . .'

He took up a large envelope and put it down again.

'May as well go with the others and save stationery.'

He had inserted the notes into another large envelope that was already addressed. He closed it and sealed it with a great red wafer that shone on the white like a gout of blood.

'The girl's to have the notes,' he said. 'Enough to keep her for a year. At her own computation.' He added: 'She told me what the ex-Governor ought to have done if he'd done what she might have expected he would have done. . . . Name of Becquerel,' he said. 'Mademoiselle Jeanne Becquerel. . . .'

He was standing astride the great, strapped, eccentrically striped grip from which he had taken the leather case of the *Fine de la Republique*. He looked a little wan.

'You'll think me a damn reckless fellow,' he said. 'But I take plenty of precautions. I have this kit bag looking like a harlequinade because any luggage-snatcher would think twice before carrying it through the streets. It's bolted to the floor too and lined with flexible steel.' He said absently: 'Plenty of precautions. . . . Plenty of . . . ' Then he exclaimed:

'My damned head. . . . It's difficult to think of what I do want to say. . . . Like neuralgia of the worst. . . .'

He picked out of the grip a polished pig-skin case and pitched it across to Henry Martin.

'Open it,' he said. 'Count them.'

Henry Martin had never seen a thousand-pound note.

126

There were like magpies and rustled. There were twenty of them.

'Part purchase money for *Le Secret*,' Hugh Monckton commented. He added: 'Come over here. . . .'

He put the leather case into a fold of the grip. 'I've warned the agent. . . . Lamoricèire. . . . I've seen you talking to him . . . that the purchase will not go through.'

He closed the grip.

'Nothing will open it now,' he said. 'But look here. The "M" of my initial goes over a stud. . . . The nail head. . . . If you pull it out. . . . See?'

The grip opened with the unctuous sound of good leather. He said:

'You noticed that. . . . The "M" of my . . . *our* initials. . . .'

He repeated again:

'All these precautions. . . . All these precautions. . . .'

Then more briskly:

'But you'll know now. . . .'

He exclaimed suddenly the one word: 'Unless. . . .'

He looked earnestly at Henry Martin. He seemed almost appealing:

'Unless you'd care. . . . If it would give you pleasure. . . . As a lark you know. . . . Don't you say "whoopee?" . . .'

He retreated rather wearily to the sofa, his square shoulders rolling as he bestrode the luggage.

'It was meant to give pleasure . . . that money!' he said. 'Incalculable pleasure. . . . And they say that non-active capital. . . . Frozen reserves . . . are the curse of to-day . . . I'd like to think. . . .'

He was suffering some emotion. It was perhaps only British inarticulateness. He said:

'We'll drink now. . . . The '57 is good enough, isn't it? . . . For a last binge? . . .'

It occurred to Henry Martin that it was not nice that Hugh Monckton should drink. The glass of a motor might crash and cut your face. He felt extreme dislike at the idea of having his face cut by the splintering glass of a wrecked automobile. . . . This fellow had said he went cuckoo after the smallest drink. He was going to drive back to Carqueiranne! . . .

It was, all the same, folly to bother about what happened to your face if, in a few hours. . . .

It was now well past twelve o'clock. He had meant at 6.30 sharp to step: like a sentry. . . .

It was odd the kind of delicacy that prevented your really uttering . . . oh, the word for . . . passing over. Even when you're fully determined. . . .

If he did not get to Carqueiranne till two. Say, half-past two. . . . It would hardly be worth while to go to bed. There would be nothing to occupy him if he did not. All of his papers were destroyed and all his clothes packed into his two grips. Along with the souvenirs for Sister Carrie and Brother Hal. . . . And of course Mrs. Percival.

Sister Carrie was having a bad time with that black-guard foreigner . . . he wished he could tell that fellow off. . . . He wished he could have told Mrs. Percival off. . . . Because that had been a monstrous discovery for him to have made. At what you might call the eleventh hour! . . . It was too late to do anything about it. The queer thing about. . . .

Hugh Monckton said:

'Death. . . .'

He was pouring the '57 brandy into a smallish tumbler. He was doing it with the care of a chemist transferring a liquid from one phial to another. His head was bent down, his eyes frowning seriously at the liquid as it went over the neck of the bottle into the glass.

He looked up and smiled ingenuously at Henry Martin:

'We'll drink,' he said. 'I don't suppose you want to get blotto? It'll make two good goes. . . . The ice pail is in the wash-stand.'

When Henry Martin came back from the end of the room with the frosted pail Hugh Monckton on the sofa had stretched his long legs before him. He had the air of resting after a great labour and of being determined to make a long and luxurious sitting.

'As I was going to say,' he began, 'death is a queer thing. . . . Your . . . one's own death. . . . Queer to think about. . . . It will leave you. . . . *one* . . . so impotent. . . . Powerless, you know.'

He made room on the sofa.

'Let's suppose you are in the trenches. . . . You are timed to go over. . . . In say six hours. . . . It's twelve-thirty now. . . . Say at six-thirty a.m. . . . You say to yourself. . . .'

He said suddenly:

'I beg your pardon for saying "you". . . . It's probably disagreeable. You aren't preparing yourself for death. . . . I ought to say "one" all the time.'

He took a sip of his iced brandy and soda. He savoured it luxuriously, rolling it over his tongue.

'The queer thing about contemplating death is the feeling of absolute impotence it gives you. . . . Supposing I mean, that you're in complete health. . . .'

He was still smacking his lips a little.

'Damn good *fine*, this,' he said 'That just illustrates what I mean. I don't excuse myself for commending my own brandy. I may tell you I haven't tasted any.

. . . Not, you know, to have a binge. Not in donkeys'
years. Tyranny of the doctor fellow, you know. . . .
I always seem to feel my Johnnie standing at my elbow.
. . . "Two fluid ounces of alcoholic liquor diluted to
four in eleven," he seems to say . . . Sir Pumpleby
Pumpleby, you know. Physician-in-ordinary to His
Majesty. . . . That sort of name. Standing at your
elbow when your butler fellow pours you a glass of '14
*Château Pavie*. . . .'

He tapped a fat cigarette end on his thumbnail.

'Illustrates what I mean,' he repeated. 'This is the
last of my '57 . . . I say to myself: "I must tell Cyril"
. . . Cyril's my cousin. And factotum. . . . Bit of a
tyrant too. Like the doctors. . . . Damn it, you'd
think he'd let me die my own way. He's my heir. But
no! it's: "I wouldn't if I were you," or: "You'd better
not, old man. . . . Not now! . . . Wait a bit!" All
the time. . . .'

He sipped again.

'The *fine* illustrates what I mean,' he said once more.
'This finishes it. Ordinarily I should say: "Cyril I must
have some more '57 brandy next week." . . . Or, as it's
difficult to get I might say to myself that I must get it
myself. . . . As being more sporting, you understand.
I use Cyril for routine and do difficult things myself. And
it's difficult nowadays to find difficult things to have to
do.'

He put his hand on Henry Martin's forearm.

'What's become of religion?' he asked. 'I suppose that
when one contemplated death in the old days one wondered where one was going. Now one doesn't. . . . Why?
. . . One is irritated that one won't be alive. One thinks
of injustices one would like to put right. . . . You know.
. . . There are housemaids you think your butler isn't

130

nice to. Or women whose husbands were killed by grind-stones in your works. . . . There's a Mrs. Taylor now . . . I had a letter from her at Nice last week. . . . Her husband worked for the dad and me, man and boy for over fifteen years. And was killed . . . like that. . . . She says she's fifty-two and doesn't get about as well as she used to. . . .'

His hand, as if persuasively, grew heavier on Henry Martin's forearm. . . . 'In the old days,' he said, 'one would be afraid of going before one's Maker. . . . If one hadn't jolly well seen that injustice was remedied to widows and orphans . . . and housemaids. . . . Now. . . . I don't know. One forgets to think about one's Maker. . . . Why? . . . Why does one, as it were, postulate that there's nothing after death? And just feel amazed that one will be powerless? . . . It's very disagreeable to feel that one will be powerless.'

He reflected for a second or two.

'One can make a will,' he said, 'or add a codicil to one. As you saw me doing. But wills and codicils are tricky things. Suddenly they go off on a wrong side-road. One would want to put them back on the track. One would want to do it from where one is floating in . . . what is it? . . . infinity. . . . But one won't be able to. In the old days one thought, I understand, be-fore one popped off that if one were one of the elect one would have the ear of God. . . . So, if one had left money for a scholarship at Magdalen, say, and the wrong sort of fellows were getting it you could speak to God and He had the thing put straight. . . . Am I right? Or isn't that pukka . . . eh . . . theology. . . .'

Henry Martin was only half listening. Not half! He was distracted, resentful and engrossed. This was a shadowy affair. He felt as if he were continually being

131

grabbed by the shoulder. By a small boy. This distracted Englishman with a pain in his head was of the mental calibre of a small boy. He grabbed one's shoulder and gabbled irrelevant nonsense whilst one was engrossed. Gazing into clear sea water at *infusoria*. He didn't know what *infusoria* were. . . . He said:

'In the Roman Catholic days the saints were supposed to have the ear of God. So if you were one of the elect. . . .'

He didn't know what *infusoria* were. But during the last month at Carqueiranne he had several times spent half an hour or so looking down into rock-pools. There were rocks below and to the left of the hotel. There was practically no tide in the Mediterranean but waves came up now and then. They left pools when they receded. In the stereoscopic depths little beasts ran about and opened and waved tentacles. He considered himself to be, now, gazing into a still pool at the bottom of which was Mrs. Percival. Amongst the wavering weeds of course, Alice was somewhere wavering about her. . . . As the male spider desultorily wavers around the female. . . . Until he makes his final dash. . . . He had never before thought of Alice as detrimental. . . . Nefarious. . . . He did now! That was probably her secret.

Well: he had six hours. . . . Five and a half! He had wanted to spend them thinking in solitude about the rock pool. And this lunatic was perpetually grabbing at his shoulder. He did so now.

'I don't suppose,' Hugh Monckton was burbling, 'that one could pray to a saint to give one back Gloria Sorenson? The saint would probably think it immoral.'

Henry Martin said testily:

'You don't pray to a saint. You ask him to pray for you. That's what *ora pro nobis* means.'

Hugh Monckton said:

'Ah, you know everything!' and remained looking broodingly at his extended feet.

'What a hope!' he exclaimed.

That was probably Alice's secret. . . . Like the 'nice girls' of New York she preferred a woman to him! He had danced and not given pleasure. . . . Nefarious! That was what it was. Alice was like a beast of prey wandering in the jungle around Mrs. Percival. . . . Who was obviously the soul of innocence! . . . But was she? What did 'soul of innocence' mean? An innocent soul, no doubt. . . . As you say 'Man of sorrows.' Meaning sorrowful man.

Hugh Monckton was pouring brandy into his glass. And still talking. He appeared to be talking about his happy childhood. Or perhaps it had been an unhappy childhood. He seemed to have had an interfering father. . . . Who had wanted to bring him up like a prince of the blood-royal. . . Solitary! . . . He had had no friends. Had never had any friends. . . . But always great possessions! . . . He had never had anyone to talk to. . . . Till Madame Bumplesomething . . . Gloria Sorenson! . . . Now she was gone! . . . Rough luck . . . But now he had Henry Martin to talk to. . . . He felt instinctively that Henry Martin was someone he could talk to. . . .

Damn the fellow. . . .

Someone he, Hugh Monckton, could trust in. . . .

You couldn't trust in anyone. . . . There was Mrs. Percival!

It came suddenly over Henry Martin. . . . When father had left Paris . . . in 1919 . . . June 1919 . . . he had taken Alice with him. He had developed gastric ulcers. Naturally! He had lived like a rhinoceros in Paris. No doubt it had been worth it. . . . But he had

133

had to be accompanied and looked after by his attached daughter-in-law. Henry Martin had not been allowed to go home. He had been sent to the army on the Rhine. . . . There had been something queer about that. Someone had certainly blocked his being sent home. There had been nothing for him to do on the Rhine. . . . A few accounts for him to keep. Otherwise nothing. . . .

The dark girl who had lived with Leopold Kuhn had come to the Rhine. Kuhn had had enough of her. She appeared to resent it. She and Henry Martin had passed a day or two together. In Coblenz. She had put it into his head that Kuhn had cast his eyes on Alice and for a day or two Henry Martin had been furiously angry. He imagined that Kuhn had sailed with his father and Alice. Of course his father would not be able to chaperone Alice.

But a few days afterward Henry Martin had had a picture postcard from Kuhn. From Paris. Kuhn was still in Paris trying to get the claims of his firm against the French Government settled. . . . Henry Martin had parted with the dark girl who had gone to Heidelberg to find a fellow called Luther Cary of Baltimore. . . . They had not found much in each other. . . .

Henry Martin had been kept over a year on the Rhine: he had come to the conclusion later that it had been, after all, Kuhn or his politically powerful firm that had had him kept there. He had seen the sewing machines and typewriters in the hold and cabins of that White Star liner. But that had all seemed vague and quiet. He had arrived at the conclusion when Kuhn had introduced him to his all-powerful uncle who, in the Algonquin dining-room, had given him that disastrous financial advice. . . . Yes, he had come to the conclusion then that Kuhn had taken him to lunch either as a reward for having kept his mouth shut or as a return for the inconvenience he had suffered for being kept away on the Rhine whilst easy fortunes were being made in America. . . . That was no doubt the way grafters worked. They probably didn't, when they handed you out your share, explain what it represented. He had often wondered how people could face the fact of talking about graft when they got together to plan. The one or two really big grafters he had met socially had been very serious minded, silver haired persons with markedly white hands and clean linen. . . . So they probably never talked about it.

That was quite unimportant. What had burst upon him like a bomb just now – since he had been in that room! – had been his relationship with Alice after his return from the Rhine to Springfield. It had been then 1921. . . .

There had been no relationship between them.

And Mrs. Percival had left Springfield!

She had been on a just-after-the-honeymoon visit with Percival – to his father and mother. At that time Henry Martin had not seen her. She had been in the town for a couple of days and Alice had certainly seen her. He himself had been settling in. And going round the Pisto-Brittle works and into Pisto-Brittle affairs. With father. Mrs. Percival, he had vaguely understood, was already beginning to get on badly with her husband. He was reported to have every bad quality. . . . But if Alice and Mrs. Percival . . . had even then begun . . . oh, a love affair. . . .

Hugh Monckton, who had been going on tiresomely about something or other, pressed his hand insistently on Henry Martin's forearm.

'You'll of course not talk about it,' he said earnestly. He was staring intently into Henry Martin's eyes. His face was appealing. 'But of course you are not the sort

135

to talk about it. . . . I felt that the moment I set eyes on you. . . . Even in Orderly Room in the old days I saw that the most confidential returns went your way. . . . I daresay it's partly our having so nearly the same names. . . .'

Henry Martin said:

'I don't exactly know what you're talking about. I daresay I'm to be trusted.'

'About our A's,' Hugh Monckton said. 'I've been telling you what I wouldn't tell anyone else in the world. Or I was just going to tell you. . . .'

Henry Martin exclaimed:

'I wish you wouldn't. . . . I can't be of any use to you or anyone. I don't even know what your A's are.'

Hugh Monckton said:

'No, you wouldn't of course understand. You use such different words. . . . They're our ordinary shares. There's a saying that there's one man at least that ought to have a statue in England. . . . That's the Ordinary Shareholder. The mug who first subscribes to a company. . . . And his statue ought to be set up in the Workhouse Yard. . . . But our A's. . . . Next Monday week. . . . Après demain en huit as the French say. . . . Or it should be really demain en huit since we've talked into to-morrow, Sunday, the sixteenth. . . . Then they're going to declare. . . .'

His disjointed phrases were working Henry Martin into a rare state of nervous distress. He had never liked Englishmen. He could never see how any American could ever like any Englishman. The English sometimes like Americans. But the other way round, never! They did not seem human, those fellows. They made you uncomfortable. They did not see things as you see them and you never knew what they would say next. They were worse than negroes because they were whiter and colder.

But this insistent fellow. . . .

Hugh Monckton's hand was heavier and heavier on his forearm:

'A final dividend of a hundred per cent,' he said. He added: 'Making a hundred and twenty per cent for the year. . . .'

He remained silent a long time looking intently at Henry Martin.

Henry Martin remembered – There was no end to the coincidence in this affair! But no doubt coincidences always crowded into your last hours! – the solitary and final row he had had with Jack Percival. It had been, precisely, about the taciturnity of the English.

That would have been unbelievable; but they were shaping for a row in any event. It had been on an occasion – at a table outside a disagreeable café near the Panthéon in Paris. There had been some idea of effecting a reconciliation between Mrs. Percival and that fellow. His disagreeable accent was still in Henry Martin's ears. He spoke – he looked! – like a bull frog with a brick throat. He had brought an enormous bouquet with white paper frilling – like the petticoats Sister Carrie had used to wear in Springfield. When they had been children, and father with his gold-headed cane had taken them for walks on Sundays. . . . A quarter of a century ago. . . .

Hugh Monckton said:

'Damn it all. . . . Aren't you *any* kind of a business man? . . . That's inside information.'

Henry Martin said:

'Not much. . . . Not much of a business man, I mean. . . . Information about what? . . .'

The bringing of the bouquet . . . for Alice! . . .
had been a rough sign of grace. On the part of Jack
Percival. He affected the rough diamond. He had
once passed three months as a cowboy. Somewhere.
When his lungs had been touched. So he had offered the
bouquet to Alice with simulated awkwardness. . . . As
if to show a bashful, he-man's sense of his gratitude for
her hospitality to a wife he ought to have looked after
himself.

A rough diamond. . . . Henry Martin felt a revulsion.
. . . At the thought of a rough diamond in bed with the
soft flesh of Mrs. Percival! Then. . . .

But perhaps Mrs. Percival . . . and Alice . . . were
wronging that fellow too! A tenebrous affair!

He wondered where he had got the word 'tenebrous.'
Probably from a translation of the Russian author Turgenev. He had been reading Turgenev at that time.

But it had been tenebrous all right. The terrace of
the café had been too narrow and ill-lit. They had sat
close together, in gloom. Their faces had appeared rather
pallid when they had been three minutes there. Jack
Percival had already been in a hell of a temper. . . .
Jerking his arms about alongside his frog's head. . . .
Obviously, Mrs. Percival's revulsion from him had been
sufficiently justified. He couldn't see that Alice's had
been . . . from him, Henry Martin.

Yet obviously she had felt revulsion. From the very
minute when he got back to Springfield. Coming from the
Rhine!

From that date they had never lived . . . *Maritalement*
the French called it. . . . Except after drinking parties
when there had been lots of straight alcohol. . . . Twenty-
one to Thirty-one. . . . Say to 1929. When they had
already agreed to divorce. . . . Nine or ten years. . . .

Only after drinking. . . . Perhaps, then, Alice had had justification. . . .

There had been in those tenebrousnesses outside the café two who hadn't given pleasure. . . .

And two who presumably had. . . .

He perhaps had been the only blind one in an electric charged atmosphere. Percival may have seen through it. That was perhaps why he had treated him, Henry Martin, like a moron.

There had been no talk of reconciliation between Jack Percival and Mrs. Percival. She had behaved like a perfect English lady. It had excited his admiration!

Think of that! It had excited his admiration! . . . He had thought that that was what it was to have been born into diplomatic circles in Europe. She had sat, tall and drooping, playing with her glove buttons. Of the four of them she had been the only one to secure space enough in which to droop. The others had been all three jammed together. And, as it were, all listening to her. Though she only spoke once. But that had been enough.

Percival had been blustering about a film from one of his stories that Hollywood had released a couple of months before. He had got, from the Gaumont agency probably, a list of bookings for it. He had said to Mrs. Percival:

'We could see it at Innsbrück on the fourth. Or in Castellamare on the twenty-first. . . .'

They had all hung on Mrs. Percival's lips. She had sat looking down at her hands a long time. . . . It had appeared afterwards that Percival had proposed to take his wife on a renewed honeymoon tour – a third one! – through the Tyrol to some Italian sea-shore village where they were to spend some months. . . .

'Hang it all. . . . I knew American business methods were pretty unsound. . . . But I thought you all just doted on a flutter. . . . You could make a million by Monday week. . . .'

'Ah! I once had financial advice from a millionaire in the inner ring. It cost me my eye-teeth and then some.'

He was astonished at his rudeness. The searchlights went on whirling their arms behind the dark windows. He was dizzy. Hugh Monckton had recoiled to the end of the sofa. He was dim.

The two women had told him nothing about Jack Percival's proposal for a third honeymoon. They had told him readily enough when he had afterwards questioned them about it.

The third honeymoon. Henry Martin didn't know very definite details of the Percivals' married life. He didn't for instance know where they had spent the first honeymoon. It had not lasted long apparently. After it there had come the time when the fellow had left her to support herself by dancing in hotels! Apparently they had come together again. Then they spent a second honeymoon. In Springfield. In 1921. With his parents. Percival père had been born in Denver. In 1875 or so, during a gold rush. His parents had trekked there in blizzards in a prairie schooner. Something like that. It was from that fact that Jack Percival drew his claim to behave like a rough diamond . . . . To roar and wave his hands over beer-schooners outside Paris cafés. He claimed that he could not be expected to support a quiet life in Springfield. He was of pioneer ancestry. He had spent six months on a ranch. During the war. . . .

After a long pause, Mrs. Percival had looked at Alice and said slowly:

'We shall be in Chester on the fourth, shan't we? . . . And Edinburgh on the twenty-first.'

Jack Percival had hurled the bouquet with its frills amongst the cigarette butts beneath the table and had ground it under his right heel. This had seemed to be a gratuitous exhibition of coarse vindictiveness. . . . At the time it had seemed that. Colorado gold-rush manners. Mrs. Percival had seemed perfectly justified in giving such a fellow a peremptory *coup de grâce*. The fellow had had the presumption to ask that tall, delicate creature to share once more his savage caves with him. He had been properly rapped over the knuckles. Quietly and with dextrousness. . . . He had retorted by crushing flowers into the concrete of the café terrace. . . . Alice's flowers!

At the time Henry Martin would hardly have been able to express all the reprehension of this grossness that he felt. His gorge had risen. This was a fellow who warred with women . . . as if he had struck them.

He had not had any chance to express his reprehension. He had not yet spoken and within two minutes the fellow had been at his throat. Calling him a moron!

Percival had said with bitter contempt to his wife and Alice:

'Ah, you *would* want to get away among hysterical people like the English. When you have the chance to get among sheer, hard personalities.'

Henry Martin, feeling like a Perseus defending two Andromedas, had plunged into asking Percival if he meant that Italians were more restrained than the English. The reverse was generally considered to be the case.

Percival had retorted that no one but a moron believed in accepted ideas. The English were hysterical. And completely without manners! They were verbally constipated in mixed company because they were hysterically shy. But get an Englishman alone in a railway carriage on a long journey and inside of ten minutes he would be rehearsing to you his most intimate, private grievances. And his entire autobiography and parentage and all about his father's Oedipus complex. It was only Americans, Italians and the yellow races that were reticent in face of the disgusting problems that life offered you.

Henry Martin had countered by asking Percival what he could know about it. He had never been in England. He had been being an amateur cowboy whilst Henry Martin had been at Magdalen and in the British Army. He flattered himself that he had had opportunities of seeing sides of the English character that were closed to most people. And he considered the English to be unimaginably reticent. They never spoke of their private affairs. That was what made them so misunderstood by the rest of the world. No one knew anything about them.

Percival had let out a maddened laugh – a sound such as might be presumed to be made by an Atheist in Hell.

'Opportunities,' he had yelled. He had waved his hands over his head. 'Yes, you have opportunities enough, you fellows. I know a drummer who had peddled stove-pipe elbows all over China from the Great Wall to Tibet and sold them to the Dalai Lama. During the Boxer Rebellion. And there he was back in Cincinnati. Having seen as much as you see here. . . .' He drew in his breath so sharply it was like a sob: 'Opportunities,' he had repeated. 'You have them. And you don't see what's as near to you as your moron's face to your moron's nose!' He had stood up, hammering the ham of his hand on the tin table top. 'You,' he said, 'couldn't talk about the indecencies of your personal relationships in a railway carriage. You haven't got the brains to see them.' He had rushed away, waving his arms, all across the rue Soufflot. . . .

The three of them – he, Alice and Mrs. Percival – had walked home rather silently. As if they had been sobered by a shock!

It had occurred to Henry Martin that that fellow must have been jealous . . . of Henry Martin and his wife! And out of that had grown his attraction to Mrs. Percival. He had not much noticed her before.

Hugh Monckton had exclaimed mournfully and as if with reproach:

'It's not too damn decent of you, old bean. . . . You'd think you regarded me as a confidence-trick man. . . . It's too damn well known who I am. . . . And, God, I don't want anyone's money.'

Henry Martin said:

'I don't know what all this is about. . . . These circumstances are rather extraordinary. . . . And, let me tell you, I'm not myself.'

Hugh Monckton said:

'We *were* in the same regiment. . . .'

Henry Martin exclaimed:

'For the Lord's sake. . . .' He added: 'I've already told you I'm *not* myself. All this is extremely odd.' He said finally, 'I guess it's where I get off.'

Nevertheless he did not move. He found that he wanted to do something for this fellow. His distress had swum up even through Henry Martin's humiliation.' . . .

This Englishman was obviously trying to do what in Springfield, Ohio, used to be called telling you his middle name. To that extent Jack Percival was vindicated. He was also vindicated – for his apparently unseemly emotion. What his emotion was about had not come through to Henry Martin then. . . . Now he saw that he had been a dull fool. . . . A moron!

Now, what this fellow was in a state about did not come

through to him. It might in ten years' time. . . . But there would be no ten years. . . . He would be an eternalized moron! He said:

'I'm sorry. I'm not in a position to do anything for anyone.'

'Hugh Monckton had sprung to his feet.

'What the devil do you think you could do for *me*!' he said contemptuously. 'I asked you, it's true, a favour. . . . But damn it! . . .'

He strode beside the secretaire and out of a waste paper basket pulled by a long strap a polished leather-case of an irregular leg of mutton form.

Henry Martin said to himself:

'By God! that's a gun! If he shot me it might be a solution!'

It swung, jerking at the end of the strap.

'One would have imagined,' Hugh Monckton said, 'that you'd have seen that exceptional circumstances demand exceptional offers. . . . Let me tell you the favour I asked you. . . .'

'I don't understand . . .' Henry Martin was beginning. He certainly wanted to do the fellow a favour. But how could he? You can't do favours from the bottom of the Mediterranean. You become a nullity.

Under glass! Still he seemed to show sympathy. . . . But with what?

Hugh Monckton was shouting to drown his voice:

'It wasn't for myself. It was for the memory of Gloria. These dancing people leave no memories when they are dead. . . . Imagine you'll see clearer when you read my letter. . . . She has sung and danced. . . . And given a great deal of pleasure. But these things are so fugitive. . . . So, as you'll see, those other permanent things are to go to the Museums as the Gloria Sorenson Collection.'

. . . He waved his free hand toward his packing-cases and grips. They were like a mournful mound in the dim room. His voice had fallen after the first sentence. He was swaying a little on his long legs.

'I offered . . . the . . . the other stuff to you. . . . For a flutter. . . . It was meant to go . . . fugitively as you might say. . . . In giving Gloria pleasure. . . . So I wanted it to go in giving pleasure. . . . To someone, as you might say, in the regiment. . . . It struck me as odd that someone who'd been in the regiment should turn up to-night. . . . The first I've seen in donkey's years. . . . Gloria, you know, was like a great butterfly. . . . You've seen her of course. . . . The symbol of the soul, you know. . . . It should be immortal! . . . But you want to go to bed. . . . Death and his brother Sleep. . . . I daresay I go to a better place. . . . Don't mind me. I'm drunk. . . .'

He swung his wrist, coiling the strap of the revolver around it. He strode toward the door. Henry Martin was unwilling to move.

'I don't mind sitting up with you,' he heard himself say. He had had no idea of saying it.

Hugh Monckton faced him smiling:

'No, old bean, you don't,' he said. 'This is where you get off as you put it. . . . Makes you feel queer to be sitting with a confidence trickster. . . . You'll understand better to-morrow. . . .'

He slapped the hand with the gun in it against his thigh. He laughed as if he were neighing.

'It's a good joke,' he said. 'I suppose you thought the products of the Old Lady of Threadneedle Street were cuttings from the Yellow Press. Ten to one you never saw a flimsy of that size before.'

He went on laughing, swaying backwards on his legs

145

like an actress playing intoxicated parts on the opera
stage. He beckoned with his gun:

'Come on,' he laughed. 'Let's carry the good news
from Aix to Ghent. That'll knock 'em on the old Carqueiranne highway!'

Even on the dim staircase he stopped to laugh and
nudge Henry Martin:

'Good old confidence game!' he said. 'You hand me
your wallet to walk around a block with. Just to show
your trust. . . . And I hand you my twenty thou. of
wrong ones. . . . One can see there ain't no flies on
you. . . . I learnt that in New York when father was
there about the Dekobra affair. . . . Oh, you deep
ones. . . .'

On the silent quay he tapped Henry Martin on the
shoulder.

'In ten minutes,' he said, 'I'll be a snortin', rarin',
ravin' blade. . . . But in nine you'll be on your hotel
doorstep. . . . Then let the wind blow high. . . . Don't
worry, it's only twenty-seven kilometres. . . . Didn't
you know the Monckton sixty did five a minute?. . .
That's why we're declaring a hundred per cent on our
A Shares on Thursday week!'

Henry Martin reeled a little on the bare boards of his skeletonly clean bedroom. He stood listening. And extremely displeased with himself. He had taken two steps towards the door. In the conviction that he ought to go down again and look after that agonized lunatic. His ears still ached with the roar of the unthrottled Monckton car. Even when you were inside, it made the noise of a hundred aeroplane engines tearing sheets of satin. His knees still ached with wedging himself in, his eyes were strained with peering into the blazing darkness. . . . The fellow had driven like . . . like a lunatic in agony. . . .

Apparently he had not yet gone. He had said that he wanted to tune the car of torture up for what he had called Dick Turpin's last ride to York. His language had grown completely incomprehensible. . . . The thing to do was to ask him in to have a drink. . . . You couldn't ask a man to your room at one in the morning and not ask him to have a drink . . . . But the only drink he had was a very small flask. He had reserved that for the very last. To-morrow morning. . . . No: *this* morning. In case he needed heartening up.

But that fellow was probably going to commit suicide. You can't let a man commit suicide. That is perhaps the only thing you actually cannot do. It is a sin to commit suicide. If you connive at it it is doubly a sin!

He was already outside his door, clumping along the long wooden corridor . . . . It might perhaps help him with the Recording Angel if he sacrificed his last drink to keep a man from committing suicide. A Russian story came into his head. He had heard it years ago. He didn't know where. . . . A skinny old peasant woman was before the Recording Angel. Just behind her back was the bottomless pit. It was filled to the brim and in it swam and struggled the desperately damned. The Angel asked her if she could remember one good deed in her long, grasping life. She could remember none. The Angel cried: 'Think! Think! Not one!' And he was pushing her towards the pit. At the brink she screamed out: 'One! Yes, one!' . . . She had once given a rotten onion to a starving woman. The Angel pushed her into the pit. He held down to her by its stalk a rotten onion. She grasped it and was being drawn out of the pit. But other desperate souls grasped at her skirt and were being drawn out. She kicked with her legs and screamed: 'No; this is my onion. Let go! This is my onion!' It broke and she descended for ever into the bottomless pit.

He was descending the pitch-dark stairs. At the bottom he stumbled and fell on his knees. He was making noise enough to awaken the whole house. And the dead!

There was very little light in the dining hall and he couldn't find the switches. A nickel coffee machine behind the bar at one end of the darkness glimmered in the starlight from a little window that gradually showed itself high up. He was thus oriented and found the door fastenings to fumble with. He was in a desperate hurry. He was convinced that Hugh Monckton intended to do away with himself. The thing to do was to sit up with him through the night. He remembered to have heard of two men who had taken it in relays to sit up with some fellow for a fortnight. After La Belle Otero had thrown him over for Edward VII. . . . It was a parallel case.

Of course Gloria Sorenson was not La Belle Otero. But neither was Mr. Bumblepuppy something-or-other, King Edward VII. . . . Nevertheless a great poet is sometimes regarded as bulking as largely as a king. . . . If he, Henry Martin, had persevered with his writing he might have become as important as a king. . . . But kings were no longer very important. He was barking his knuckles on the invisible fixings of the back of the door. It was immensely heavy and cumbersomely fashioned. It swung back at last, noiselessly on its greased hinges. A square of the dust of starlight existed. That starlight was like dust. Then the door struck against the wall and its fixings went on tintillating. . . .

A rumble of a car, speeding, came to him from up behind; beneath the hills. It ran with the engrossed sound of something that went on an errand, the noise streaming out behind. It died away, rose . . . died away. At last you could not hear it at all though you strained your ears. . . . It was probably nearly at Hyères by now. It was at least going in that direction. If it had been going towards St. Jean du Var there would have been some hope. . . .

It seemed to Henry Martin that, as long – and only as long – as he heard that sound Hugh Monckton would be alive. . . . He was probably making for cliffs over which he could dash into the sea. Henry Martin could not remember any cliffs along that coast – not as far as the Italian frontier. The road went high on leaving Beaulieu for Monaco – and near the sea. But you could hardly crash a light car through the stone wall of the Corniche. . . . However fast you went at it you would glance off. There was not breadth enough of road to let you charge at right angles. . . . The picture of the road was brought before him – like nostalgia. The sea intensely blue, with gentle fleeces of unimaginably white foam. The road of the Corniche dove-colour, the balustrade pinkish. . . . He was never going to see that road again.

And perhaps Hugh Monckton was not going to kill himself in that way. He might object to smashing up that car as Henry Martin recoiled from the idea of humiliating his boat. He would choose some other way. . . . Yet Hugh Monckton had talked . . . raved! . . . about setting the Monckton sixty at a bullfinch. He had been boasting about what the car could do. At the moment, shaken to pieces, Henry Martin had not known what a bullfinch was. Now he remembered to have seen a rider in a top hat – in a sporting print. The horse was plunging through a thin plantation of something like sumach in an earth wall. He seemed to remember that the print had been captioned: 'Tare an' 'ounds at the Bullfinch.' . . . A fox-hunting procedure. . . . Perhaps that mad fellow intended to try out his adored car in some such way. It was as if that had been the last thing left to him to take a pride in. . . .

As they had passed a little side-road going toward the sea Hugh Monckton had laughed out that there was a goodish bullfinch down there. The road, Hugh Monkton knew, ran down to a tiny cove between high granite cliffs. . . . What they called a *calangue* about there. But he could not remember what that particular calangue was called. It was between the sea and Le Pradet. Or perhaps the place was not called Le Pradet. At any rate it was not so far as St. Jean du Var.

The cove contained only a cubical blind brick building in some way connected with the electric power supply of the districts, but there was a little strip of sand of extraordinary whiteness. The people of the town bathed and swarmed there on a Sunday. Pullulated was the word. But during the week it was quite lonely. A place where sirens might have disported themselves!

The red rocks forming the calangue rose precipitously from the strip of sand but a path at not too steep an angle mounted like a bandolier across their face. On the top there was a coppice of umbrella and stone pines, the ground soft with the pine needles and the light between their mournful trunks dim as it is in a cathedral. Henry Martin remembered to have gone there three times. Once, about a month ago he had gone there to think out a letter to his father. His father had replied to it opprobriously a week ago. Once he had put into the cove in the boat and had tried fishing for *rascasses*. . . . That had been on his first visit. He had had so little success with the *rascasses* that he had climbed the hill to look at the view. That was how he had discovered the thicket.

On the third occasion he had come through the thicket after calling ingloriously on M. Lamoricière. M. Lamoricière was the real estate agent who, it now appeared, had been negotiating the sale of *Le Secret* to Hugh Monckton. That was another coincidence. . . . Below the thicket and beyond the road that led to the main route from Le Pradet – if it was Le Pradet – was a stretch of grassland on top of the cliff. It was unusual to have pasture in those parts but the local property-owner interested himself in sheep. He had two hundred and fifty in a long byre in a wood a little inland.

On top of the pasture stood the villa of M. Lamoricière. M. Lamoricière was a thin, jet-black bearded sympathetic person who wore black glasses to protect his weak sight from the sunlight that poured itself over that upland. His manner was extraordinarily gentle and he made faded-like gestures with his thin white hands. He had, like every one in those regions, been at one time a colonial administrator somewhere in French East Asia.

But even through his gentle kindliness there had penetrated a tinge of disappointment at Henry Martin's call. He had expected another Mr. Smith – it was quite easy now to see whom. The other Monsieur Smeez was expected to make great purchases. Henry Martin had come merely to look for a job. . . . He had not taken the blows of destiny entirely lying down. He could score that to himself.

It had occurred to him that he might not be un-useful in the real estate business. He had a perfectly good knowledge of commercial French. Indeed his father had at one time contemplated opening a Pisto-Brittle agency in Paris and Henry Martin to oblige him had opened negotiations with several firms in the larger cities of France. He had even had an office and a clerk of his own for some months. The experiment had faded out, but Henry Martin imagined that it had given him insight into French commercial frames of mind. He also knew Americans.

He had called at M. Lamoricière's office to find that that amiable gentleman was confined at home with a severe attack of neuritis in the forehead. He had, however, made a date to receive Henry Martin at his own house the same afternoon. The interview had taken place in a dim room whose light filtered through the slats of jalousies on to innumerable Napoleonic relics. . . . Eagles in gilt, brass-headed swords; a standard or two and some uniforms in glass-faced cupboards. . . . M. Lamoricière seemed like a fabulous monster. His first remark had been to the effect that the road to his villa would never be supportable until some member of the Bonaparte family was Dictator of France. He was a Corsican and a Bonapartist. . . .

Henry Martin had at first been taken for a gentleman whom he supposed to be called Ash-Hammersmith. He had been received very cordially. The real estate agent's tense features had slackened into smiles. Henry Martin realized by now that he was supposed to be bringing what, for France, must appear to be the tidy sum of two and a half million francs. For the part-purchase of *Le Secret*. M. Lamoricière was imagining himself to be meeting Hugh Monckton . . . H. M. A. Smith. If you pronounced those initials in the French fashion. . . . 'Asch . . . Em . . . Ah . . . Smeez' you made a name something like Ash-Hammersmith. . . .

The interview really proved the death blow for Henry Martin. M. Lamoricière lost hardly any of his cordiality when he learned that Henry Martin did not desire to buy a two and a half million franc yacht. Nevertheless an almost tragic sadness fell upon his high features. . . . Sadness for the sake of beloved France.

It was delightful and sympathetic, he said, that Henry Martin should desire to pass the rest of his days in their beautiful land. And certainly depopulated France had need in her desperate state of new citizens as loyal as they were energetic. Such a young man as Henry Martin was just what France needed to supplement her disappearing birth rate. Nothing could be more advantageous.

But alas! . . . with the ruin of the approaching Crisis . . . which M. Lamoricière could assure Henry Martin was merely at its beginnings! . . . with the Bourse falling, the Government venal, incompetent and rhetorical, how could France support more mouths? No doubt Henry Martin with his special capacity, his admirable knowledge

153

of French and his social gifts might increase the business of the country. But that was a speculation. And who would take the risk? It was no time for taking risks. The State itself made it impossible to take such a risk. Henry Martin would have to provide himself with a *carte-de-travail* . . . a permission to work in France. And that permission would be refused him.

M. Lamoricière had seated himself behind his high, knee-well writing desk. Its black leather indented top was covered with bronze eagles. Six points of light gleamed in his black spectacles. Even, he said, if Henry Martin proposed to put capital into his business he could not advise such a course. He would carefully consider the offer from his own point of view but he would not advise Henry Martin to take any such step.

He asked Henry Martin to consider several points. The business at present just supported him, M. Lamoricière, his wife, his partner M. Flobel and *his* wife and the single girl secretary whom they employed. If Henry Martin put capital into the business it might be possible to extend it. On the other hand it might not be possible. The English on that coast where they had formerly swarmed were selling their properties very rapidly. That made business active. But it grew in proportion less remunerative. Prices fell and purchasers were less easy to find. Henry Martin of course knew more about American affairs than he. But, for his part, M. Lamoricière did not believe that any rush of American buyers was to be anticipated for several years to come. He had had unfortunately reason to follow the American markets. He had invested a moiety of his savings during his colonial career, in American undertakings. That had been a disastrous affair. The French Bourse had been more propitious. But that too, God knew, had been bad enough. So that after years of industrious, honest and, he trusted, efficient labours beneath the suns of the tropics he found himself forced to work at an office desk. He had hoped to have leant back and rested on his oars. He was tempted to say that he had almost a right to lean on his oars. . . . But there he was, with deteriorated health, almost, as you might say, at the beginning of his career again. It was tragic. It was almost more than tragic. . . .

His thin features on which the polished skin lay in tight folds were for a moment convulsed with pain. He had been talking in a long monologue – monotonously and with resignation. Now he drew his breath in between his teeth so that he hissed. He rose rather precipitately for a man usually deliberate in his movements. He conducted Henry Martin with little pats on the shoulder to the door. In the blaze of light on the veranda he covered his brows with his left hand. He pointed with his right away over the pasture lot. Where it rose again, waving towards the sky, was the thicket of pines on a mound.

'Go and observe the view from there,' he said. 'If I had to advise you I should say: "My young friend. Buy that hillock with its grove of pine trees. Erect in their shade the most modest shelter that you consider compatible with your needs. Then realize whatever your fortune may be. In gold! Put it in a stocking. Bury it. And take out from it once a year just sufficient for your needs. In that way you might live to see better times. . . . But you might not, of course".'

Henry Martin had gone round the pasture. In the grey-blue light beneath the tree trunks he had first felt death in his heart. He had just lately written to his father. He had said that, with a little capital something might be done with real estate in that part of the world. He had said that he was at the end of his tether and had asked his father to make him the loan of some thousand dollars. He had no great hope of his father's acceding. But, till that moment, he had thought that he could with a little trouble find a job.

But with the words *carte de travail* of M. Lamoricière he had felt a sudden falling of the heart. It was as if the world situation had come home to him. For the first time he really felt himself a part of the world situation. He sat amongst the purplish . . . greying . . . reddish, large-scaled trunks of the pines. He was on a knoll with the Mediterranean below him. But actually the kingdoms of the earth stretched before him. And particularly the republics. . . .

That had been a fortnight ago.

He had for the first time known that he was up against it. Till then he had perhaps believed that one might become one of the destitute millions of the world. But he had not taken himself to be such a one. He had really no hope that his father would make him a loan. His father would say: why couldn't he return and drum for Pisto-Brittle again? There was some reason in that . . . for his father. He had failed at everything else. The grey mountain of a man, sitting behind the table in the Pisto-Brittle office and raising and dropping alternately his spatulate, white fingers on each side of Henry Martin's letter that would lie before him, would ask himself that question over and over again. Then he would write, heavily, a contemptuous cable.

Up in the pine-thicket Henry Martin had known that that was what would happen. And it was what had happened. His father had cabled:

'Try another star. No possum up this tree.'

He was prepared for it with his determination of suicide.

The solitary session in the pine-clump had prepared him for the fact that he would find no job in that country-side. Faint investigations had absolutely confirmed that conviction.

He had imagined that, at the worst he could work in the field for a peasant or drive a delivery van for one of the department stores. He was not above earning his living in that way. He had washed dishes and waited on tables at Dartmouth. He would be only beginning all over again – like Mr. Lamoricière.

The great stars at last existed for him. Over the motionless sea! They wheeled, motionless. The last sound of the motor that he could hope to hear died away. He went to the edge of the terrace. The sea did not lap on the pebbles. Nothing existed but black masses . . . black masses of the pine trees: of the distant islands. Even the red light at the end of the little pier was hidden from him by the limpid blackness of a pillar that supported the story above the veranda. As it was mid-August the very frogs were silent. And the nightingales. By August begettings and parturitions of all birds, batrachians and insects are over for the year so none gave voice. All such sounds are love-calls. . . .

He imagined that it was like that when you are dead. You were motionless in black space. There would of course be great stars. Wherever it was perfectly black the light of the stars pierced the blackness. From the bottom of a deep, dry well in Indiana he had once seen the constellation of Cassiopeia though the sun was torrid above between the well-head and the sky.

If it were no worse than that it would probably be

quite as well to be dead. Perhaps when you were dead you worried. He had figured that Hell might really consist of endless mental worries. . . . You would be in blackness with great stars, worrying eternally. Or perhaps you would only worry in proportion to your wickedness in the flesh. You would earn oblivion by worrying.

You worried probably about what went on happening to your dear ones on earth. He hadn't, however, any dear ones on earth. There were Mrs. Percival and the dark girl in the café. He had given her his mother's ring. . . . He didn't care what happened to Mrs. Percival if she did not belong to him. His feelings for her were physical. Apparently her physical feelings went in another direction. He didn't know.

It worried him that he did not know. Perhaps afterwards, he would not be permitted to know. . . . By the Recording Angel! What, if Alice and Mrs. Percival were Lesbians, was Lesbianism? Possibly a desire for a higher union. . . . Perhaps his next-world torture would be worrying because he did not know what Lesbianism was. That would be grotesque. . . . But why should you not be grotesque?

Who else were his dear ones? . . . There was positively no one. He certainly wished no ill to his father but he could not imagine anything happening to him that should make him, Henry Martin, worry about him from the interstellar spaces where he drifted. . . .

He was worried at the time about Hugh Monckton. The fellow, standing beside his car had looked extraordinarily lonely. . . . Actually he was no lonelier than Henry Martin. But Henry Martin had the idea that that fellow had wanted to communicate something. And apparently Henry Martin had failed him.

He had taken it very hard that Henry Martin had not

jumped at what he called his tip about the A's. Almost his last words had been:

'Of course, old bean, I was exaggerating when I said you could make a couple of million. But you could make a tidy bit. . . . And, damn it, don't you understand what I was offering you? . . .'

He had immediately afterwards said that his old bus needed tuning if she was to take the bullfinch in style and with a mournful good-bye had dived under the machine on his back.

Exactly what the fellow's offer had been had not got through to him. The whole interview came back – at any rate the later parts of it – as if it had passed in dumb show. He had been overwhelmed by the thought of the intrigue that must have been carried on against him: that fellow had been mostly incomprehensible. Jack Percival had been right to the extent of at least one Englishman. Hugh Monckton had certainly communicated a good deal of his private affairs. . . . The trouble was, the English talked a language no one could understand. What with the childish slang, the pronunciation, and what they left out! You had to know their life story before you could understand them. . . .

That fellow had been like an agonized dog. Gazing into your eyes and trying to communicate with every fibre of his being. . . . Apparently because they had both been in the same regiment. . . .

A cross between a large-eyed dog and a schoolboy. For it was a schoolboy's idea that, if you had been in the same collection of lousy fellows in mud-colour you formed tender associations that lasted a lifetime or could be taken up again after twenty years. As if you had been in the same school! Though even that was school-boyish enough. . . .

159

All the same, the fellow had got through to him a sense of mental agony and loneliness. . . . And physical pain. . . . He had had an acute pain in his head. . . . Like M. Lamoricière. That real estate agent had hardly been able to see where he was going because of brow ague. . . . Perhaps Hugh Monckton hadn't really known what he was saying.

On the whole Henry Martin no longer wished that he could exchange identity with that fellow. He himself was calm, in no pain and drifting through space. The mental bitterness at least of death was past. He stood there amongst the immense stars that he felt to encircle the earth. And he felt the earth drifting in the blackness. . . .

There must be a low mist because the stars did not shine down the sea. A mist only a foot or so above the water. As you see it above alligator tanks in zoological gardens. That meant that the water was very warm. It meant that it would be about flesh-heat when he stepped into it in an hour or so. That was satisfactory. A gift of Providence. He remembered to have heard that if you wished to drown kittens you should do it whilst they were still blind in tepid water. They would then know no shock.

So Providence was being humane . . . to a blind kitten. It had warmed up the bath. . . .

It was odd how little part Providence played in his psychology. He seemed to have lost his faith by a process of painless extinction. He could not remember how long it was since he had prayed, but he was certain that now he never did. Even at that moment when, if there were supernatural governors, he had absolutely no impulse to prayer.

'Requiem aeternam dona eis, Domine, et lux perpetua luceat per eis. In memoriam aeternam erit justus: ab aestimatione non timebit.'

'Give them eternal rest, oh Lord, and let light perpetual be upon them. The just man shall remain for ever in the memory: he shall not fear the reckoning. . . .'

He liked to quote the words – in the Latin – because of their sound and the memories they half recalled. But he had no wish to utter them for himself. Nor had he any that they should be uttered for him in a day or two.

It was not that he disbelieved in the existence of a Deity. He felt indeed extremely aware of a First Cause. But he believed that the Deity was as indifferent to his existence as he himself was indifferent to that awful Presence. He could not believe that God cared enough about him even to punish him. Possibly some of the less important female saints might care about him rather indifferently but with pleasant manners of a stereotyped kind. As the Sisters do when you go into hospitals. . . . It astonished him to find that he felt towards the supernatural economy much as he felt towards the efficient police of a good republic. They had their function, but they were nothing to him and he nothing to them.

He could not believe that an august First Cause would take cognizance of his existence. It had more important tasks. . . . What had he done to make notice of him worth the while of the Deity? He had been drunk once or twice. That was defacing God's image. But he had never been drunk in Europe. That was the real test. At home you had to drink from time to time. Or appear Pharisaic. Pharisaism was a worse sin than an occasional jag. Beside it was a political demonstration. He had never taken pleasure in drink.

He had committed adultery – or fornication, for he did not know the difference. Three or four times. But so very dimly! He hardly remembered the women or girls. They had been dull. Infinitely dull. And they too had been social demonstrations. You had necked to show independence. Almost more in order to aid the girls to assert their freedom. And to shame Pharisaism. . . . Adultery then became little more than the exercise of a corporeal function. God had given you corporeal functions to exercise. He had never taken pleasure in adultery.

As far as he could remember he had broken none of the other commandments. He had coveted no man's goods. He had wanted to be someone else: but that was rather in the desire for salvation. He had done no murder. He had not even fired a rifle in the late war. On the contrary he had superintended a saw mill and a canning outfit . . . in the effort to end war. He couldn't say that he had not honoured his father and mother. He had at least loved his mother and admired his father – even when father had most tried to coerce him he had admired his spirit. Even now he took a sort of covert pleasure in his father's cable. It made the joke all the better that it was his death-blow. He imagined his father chuckling. That exhibition of stubbornness was something he could admire. . . .

He imagined besides that if Providence really took the trouble to punish any man it would be Napoleon. Or the politicians and big business men who had ruined the United States and so the world might well burn in endless fire. No one had escaped the desolation they had caused. It had sought out him, Henry Martin, on solitary shores four thousand miles away. Remorselessly. But Providence had to swing a million stars each populated by a million million beings. It probably would view the ruin of three or four hundred million human beings and their anxieties and distractions as a giant the size of Mount Everest would view a child of four sticking a branch into an ant heap, the size of a pudding-basin and agitating the inhabitants.

It was more likely that Providence let remorseless effect work out the punishment of individuals. Then he might well worry about his future. He had danced capably and given only mediocre pleasure. That was Sin. It was Sin, too, to have to say that, when he floated between the outer stars, there would be no dear ones here on earth for him to worry over. That was bad. Bad!

There was Sister Carrie. She had things to worry her. But he did not know what the things were. She had become more and more the European great lady, apart, cold, incomprehensible. She worried perhaps because her husband was not received with sufficient honour at the Court of the Grand Duchy of Luxemburg. Or maybe because he had not received promotion in the Garada Nobile at the Vatican, or because the Pope had not sent her a golden rose or a medal, or because her husband had not received the hunt-button of the Duchesse d'Uzes. Or because he was unfaithful. Or they had no children. They had plenty of money.

But Carrie had chosen to become European. An American could hardly sympathize with her troubles. On the last occasion he had seen her she had been out of her mind with indignation. Some Cardinal attending some function in her neighbourhood had chosen to lunch at a neighbouring château. Not at hers. She had come to Paris to avoid the slur's appearing too public. That was how Henry Martin had seen her. Her husband, the Comte de Pralinghem, had made very good use of the capital with which Sister Carrie's marriage settlement had provided him. Her château though it dated from 1169 was as modern as most New York hotels. She had there every imaginable kind of electric fixing, elevators and bathrooms. You might as well have been in Minneapolis, at a Beer Lord's before Prohibition. And she had innumerable servants. Her husband was a very keen business man – for a feudal landowner. He owned admirable quarries, sawmills, a ham factory. His estate in those distant woodlands fairly buzzed. In spite of world depression.

So Henry Martin could not see himself worrying about his sister. It might be that, having been granted supernatural insight into psychology – which would mean infinite capacity for worrying – he might appreciate what her tragedy was. And worry. At present her funeral was too much her own affair. . . . It might of course be cancer. . . . That was not so easy. Mental distress was more comprehensible.

It was difficult to sympathize with physical pain. Hugh Monckton had been suffering. So had Lamoricière. His black-bearded, pale face had been drawn with it once or twice. No doubt some of Hugh Monckton's more incomprehensible ejaculations and failures to finish sentences had been caused by pains in his forehead. You could not have a whack like that from a cavalry sabre and not feel after-effects. But it was only now that he realized it. It began to seem to him atrocious that he had been so indifferent.

All the same he was almost more worried about the dark girl. . . . That too came over him like a wave. Almost a pain in itself. She had been in prison. How was it possible to put a girl like that in prison? It was a sin. As if you kept a brilliant flowering plant in a cellar.

The flowers and leaves would grow pallid. Etiolation it was called. . . .

He wished he had had a long conversation with that girl – one of those conversations that last for days and weeks. He might have restored her faith in life. And have developed his own personality. She had a high, flaunting colour on her cheeks. And defiantly marked eyebrows. Artificial but precise, like black and white drawing. If he could have lived at her side it might have made a man of him. He seemed to hear her hard, clear thoughts. Stimulating him. Like a bitter apéritif!

It was considered to be a sin not to use your talents. . . . How did he stand under that heading? He presumably had talents. He had done nothing with them. . . . If he had been able to live with Wanda he might have made some mark with his art. Or if he had had physical contact with Mrs. Percival. He *had* lived beside her and the sexual irritation had made him do the only work he had ever accomplished. . . . His unfortunate book!

After all, he had written a book and it had been published. But it had been so snowed under by the illustrations and the way the disgusting publisher had put it out that it never occurred to his mind. Not even when he was summing up his life. That proved that it had been the product of sexual irritation caused by the proximity of Mrs. Percival. Whilst that proximity had continued, the book had seemed alive. The moment he left her it had simply faded. Like something on the stage when the spotlight goes off it. . . . He had never thought of that.

His feeling for Mrs. Percival had been purely physical: as far as he knew his feelings for the dark girl had been quite intellectual or sympathetic. That was queer, for the one moved as it were in the grey light of cloisters and the other was like a black panther in sunlight. . . .

He knew he had begun to think of his book and the physical seductions of Mrs. Percival at the same moment. That moment had been whilst Jack Percival had been calling him a moron outside the café. In quite fiery resentment he had said to himself as if he were answering that fellow: 'Ah, you think yourself damn fine because you've written some lousy books in slang. You wait! I'll yet do something that will prove to your wife that I'm as good as you!' And immediately he had been aware for the first time, of how desirable it would be to mingle his limbs with those of the silent woman on the other side of the tin table top.

His book had been addressed to her. It had consisted of a long argument with her on the subject of gossip. It had been a book about gossip.

They lived amongst crowds of Americans in Paris. And all these people gossiped unceasingly. They seemed to have no other vocations. . . . And Mrs. Percival shuddered at all that. . . . It was almost the only thing about her mentality that came back to him. She was normally exceedingly silent. He knew that she liked green and dark blues for her clothing and the music of Debussy and the pictures of Toulouse Lautrec. Advanced but sober works of Art! Otherwise, except that she was deliberate, he knew nothing about her. . . . But indeed she had rendered their household rather silent. She so disliked gossip that she left practically nothing for him and Alice to talk about at meals. It was no doubt because she thought she had been a great deal gossiped about and had suffered. . . . Or perhaps she shuddered at the idea that when her relationship with Alice became manifest there would be a good deal of spiteful comment.

166

There had really been very little talk about her either in Springfield or in Paris.

So he had written his book. It had been astonishing how easily it had come to him. It had arranged itself: a part on gossip in the Classics from Theophrastus to Lucian; a part on gossip in the Middle Ages from Robert of Gloucester to Montaigne; a bewigged part ending with Madame de Sévigné, Horace Walpole and various biographers of George Washington: a final modern part which took in the Yellow Press and the *potins* of Montparnasse. When he thought how easily it had gone he was astonished that he had not continued as a 'writer'. Even the Introduction and the Exordium had come easily. In them he had really countered the objections of Mrs. Percival to gossip. He had done it quite consciously, holding one or two arguments with her. He had put down her objections fairly and had contented himself with pointing out that without gossip there would be no knowing anything about the lives people lived. A good deal of gossip was malicious, but most listeners discounted automatically what they had heard. So you got something like the truth.

He had written his closing pages with some feeling. He was already thinking about a novel and realized that he would find it very difficult simply because he did not know enough of how people lived. Then almost simultaneously Mrs. Percival had turned him down; he had left Alice in preparation for the divorce. And the storm about his book had burst upon him.

The storm had been mostly the work of the agile and lewd publisher. Henry Martin had had no idea of writing salaciously. The publisher and the illustrator together had made him appear a sort of Casanova. The publisher had found the title BE THOU CHASTE, the motto on

167

the title page being: 'Be thou chaste as snow and cold as ice, thou shalt not escape calumny,' misquoting Othello. The illustrator had decorated the pages with vignettes of revolting lewdness. Mostly they represented nude revels in Montmartre and Montparnasse studios. In addition, the publisher had provided cheap reproductions of the eighteenth century prints of bedroom scenes that you buy for a sou or two at the open-air bookstalls along the Seine quays in Paris. So Henry Martin had found himself a purveyor of pornography.

It might or might not make it better in the general storm the volume aroused, that Henry Martin never received a penny for the book. The publisher had promised him a couple of hundred dollars on publication. This had never even been paid. A month or so after publication, Henry Martin had written to the fellow asking him for the money. He had received no answer. He had not even had a copy of the book. He wrote again more pressingly. Then he had threatened to put a lawyer to work. By that time he had seen a copy of the book in a shop window in the rue de Rivoli. It was surrounded with a band bearing in scarlet letters the inscription: 'What goes on in Paris studios.' The full invidiousness of the publisher had burst upon him. . . . The illustrations! The title! He had all but been sick under the arcades of the rue de Rivoli in the Paris sunshine.

He had communicated his emotions in the letter to the publisher that demanded payment of the sum due on publication. The publisher's jocular answer had expressed grief at the idea of an author's taking so commercial a view of his art as to demand payment. He also professed amazement at the idea that Henry Martin should desire to make money out of the book. On his own confession it was a pornographic work. The book was by now in the

168

windows of a great many Paris booksellers. Every time that Henry Martin caught sight of it it was as if he had been kicked in the stomach. His café acquaintances had begun to feign not to see him when he came into those establishments.

A man called Grimaud had attacked him very violently one night. He was a New Yorker of French extraction, a painter with a studio in Montmartre. He accused Henry Martin of having revealed the intimate secrets of his life. . . . And in addition the secrets of the lives of twenty . . . thirty . . . sixty Paris American expatriates. The illustrator of the book had apparently made recognizable portraits of actual American artists and their wives. In depictions of nude debaucheries and recognizably in their own studios. . . . The fellow with copper hair and a mouth as large as a coal scuttle had been held by two waiters whilst he gesticulated in front of Henry Martin's table.

Paris-America had however seemed to calm itself. Henry Martin had got himself invited to the weekly lunch of the Anglo-American Journalists' Association – by a man called Pritel whom he had known as a friend of Mr. Kuhn, a correspondent of a Detroit paper. Pritel, who was an amiable fellow, had introduced him to a number of the correspondents and reporters. Henry Martin had explained with care and moderation that the letterpress of his book was in no way either salacious or personal. He did not even know the illustrator.

One or two men there had confirmed what he said. They had looked at the book and had found it rather dull.

They had been pretty decent about it. Notes depicting Henry Martin's distress had appeared in one or two English-Parisian papers, one or two London ones and in some Paris letters of papers at home. Three times strangers in cafés had come up to him and commiserated with him as to the misunderstanding. He had been asked to an extremely dull party at a woman's club across the water. It had been distressing to him because the only people he had known there had been Alice, Mrs. Percival and a man called Josephson from Cincinnati who appeared to be squiring them. They had acknowledged each other's existence in the coldest possible way. He had been tempted to leave. But he had gone on for an hour listening to a lady with blue-white hair and a bronze-powdered face. She carried lorgnettes and came from Terre Haute. She was writing a book on period furniture. . . . Mostly as to its effects on morals. It was self-evident, she said, that the curves with which you surrounded yourself and the angle at which you sat or reposed must have an influence on your character. If you sat in a wheel-back Windsor kitchen-chair you would incline to a New England conscience. If you reclined, like Madame Récamier, on a day bed you would lean towards lascivi-ousness – like all the French. Henry Martin had inclined to believe that there might be something in it.

He had by that time of course separated from Alice and from Mrs. Percival. And he was leading a sufficiently lonely life in a small room in the rue Jacob. He went out for most of his meals. Sometimes he found an acquaint-ance to talk to him. As often as not he did not. He imagined that some people still avoided him – but he might have been mistaken. A determined maiden lady called Cameron from Dorchester, Mass., upbraided him with having treated Alice badly. She was now attending lectures on law at the Sorbonne but, as a young girl, she had known his mother. Henry Martin had been able to persuade her that it was Alice rather than he who wanted the divorce. After that he sat, most evenings, at the table of Miss Cameron in a café! She had a rather noticeable moustache and occasionally she drank far too many *petits verres*. Then she became voluble and hoarse-voiced about the wrongs of women. Her usual attendants were a New England Presbyterian minister who, at sixty, had abandoned the ministry and was attending life-classes, an English Colonel who was doing the same, and two very bespectacled young girls who were working at the Bibliothèque Nationale. They sat huddled together for hours in a corner of a rather noisy café. . . .

Paris apparently had forgiven him for BE THOU CHASTE. Springfield had not. By that time Henry Martin was nearing the end of his tether, financially. He had little more than a thousand dollars left. The rest of his money had either gone into housekeeping or into the hands of Alice. For years she had insisted on his making her a large allowance for housekeeping and dress. She had not spent nearly as much and had regularly banked the remainder. She had no doubt timed the divorce to come fairly exactly when his pockets should be nearly empty. He felt no resentment. During the divorce proceedings he had had to go through the formality of an attempt at reconciliation. He had been shut up alone with Alice in a bare anteroom of the Court. Alice had reminded him that he still owed a gas bill that had come in after his departure. The bill had seemed exorbitant but she had brought it with her and there had been no disputing it. She said that she was looking for more economical gas fittings in the kitchen. He had said that, if you could get the electricity people to install a certain type of fixing and a certain meter, electricity was nearly as cheap as gas and much cleaner.

At any rate he had heard so. From a pastry cook from whom he brought his *croissants*. . . .

To the judge who had asked him why he would not return to his wife he had answered succinctly:

'J'aime une autre femme. . . .'

The judge had burst out:

'Ah mais ça . . . mais ça . . . C'est un peu trop fort. . . .' When one has a charming, amiable and gifted lady for one's spouse one does not say one loves another!

Henry Martin had maintained an obstinate silence. The thing had gone through without further words. . . .

But he had begun to be pinched for money very soon afterwards. He had intended, during the months of separation, to write another book. A novel. But the annoyance connected with BE THOU CHASTE had too much distracted his thoughts. And the fact that he was approaching pennilessness paralyzed him. He presumed that showed he was not an author. Real authors are said to write away more furiously the poorer they are. But he, with all the strength gone out of him, had sat watching Anacondas until they passed their dividend. Then he knew that he was finished.

He had made one effort. He had written to his father asking him to put his lawyers on the publisher. Sangster, a sanguine Paris author, had computed that the publisher must owe Henry Martin five thousand dollars. Louis Trench, also an author living in Paris, but a pessimist, put the probable sum at seven hundred. The actual amount was somewhere, no doubt, between the two. On the lowest sum he would have been able to live for a year. Five thousand would have kept him going for two or three. Because of course with more money in hand he would have lived more largely. Probably with a French mistress.

172

His father's answer had been curious. Henry Martin had written that he was reduced nearly to pennilessness.

That, father had answered, was only to be expected. It was unfortunate too that he could not at this juncture be invited to take up again his position of drummer for Pisto-Brittle. Henry Martin could hardly expect to come back to Springfield for a year or two. Unless his hide was tougher than father believed.

BE THOU CHASTE had done that. According to father the book had been reported as a best seller in twenty-seven principal cities of the United States. Springfield, Ohio, considered that that meant that it was being held up to ridicule in twenty-seven of the forty-eight States of the Union. Its most intimate, scandalous and painful affairs were being laid bare to the inhabitants of that vast expanse of territory. The most prominent citizens of Springfield were the most enraged. Public action had been threatened against Henry Martin if he dared to show himself in that city.

It had indeed, the old man said, been taken against himself. Henry Martin seemed to hear him chuckling as he wrote that the Ku Klux Klan had waited upon him. They had told him that if he did not dismiss all his Roman Catholic foremen they would prohibit the sale of Pisto-Brittle in all the villages within a hundred miles of Springfield. The old man had insisted on employing always former inhabitants of Luxemburg as foremen over the boilers in his works. He considered that job as peculiarly suited to the Luxemburgish, phlegmatic temperament. He had several times received from the Klan missives informing him that they objected to this policy of his. Each time he had replied by dismissing a worker whom he suspected of belonging to the Klan and

173

replacing him by an Irish Roman Catholic. So, for a long time, the Klan had left him alone.

Now, he guessed, Henry Martin's outrage on the city had emboldened them to more open threats. They probably imagined themselves assured of prominent supporters. Prominent women who thought that their avarices, evil speaking or adulteries had been revealed in BE THOU CHASTE had half-publicly incited the Klan to direct action.

'I don't suppose,' father had written, 'that Springfield, Ohio, is any less chaste than any other American city. But they seem here to have taken the exhortation of your title as being addressed directly to them . . . and probably as being needed by them. Mrs. Prendergast in particular says that your story of the meanness of her ordering when the Schultz's were coming to stop over for a week-end can only have been told you by Sylvia Groen. So she has let out a lot of unsavoury hot air about the behaviour of Sylvia and the Younger Married Set.'

He added a little later:

'Suppose the K.K.K. to be degenerate descendants of earlier He-Men. Told them: "Very well gentlemen. Am aged over the Psalmist's limit and perfectly prepared to shut down Pisto-Brittle works should city desire it. Might or might not re-open in New York State. Or Luxemburg. Or England. But imagine such very considerable addition to already terrible hunger-lines of unemployed in city might render the corporation disliked. Stated should take that step if evidence should be forthcoming that sale of one packet of P. B. had been hindered by their activities".'

He said that he had concluded by telling those fellows that his will gave instructions for closing down the works, no member of his family desiring to continue in the industry. His aged body was at their disposal but he still took leave to imagine that his clandestine removal would not be applauded.

He concluded that part of the letter:

'Do not have to tell you that sale of P. B. has not been interfered with. Nevertheless I' . . . the 'I' occasionally crept in . . . 'should not advise your return here in search of a job. You remember how intensely you felt your unpopularity when you were suspected of murdering so-called Huns. And recollect that as you have chosen to jettison your wife she will not be here to make your peace with local Hun-ocracy.'

That was true enough. When Henry Martin and one or two others had returned from the occupation of the Rhine they had found themselves completely cold-shouldered. The local German population had boldly called them murderers and what few people there had been of English or allied descent in the town had already had cold feet about the War. Those ex-heroes had had to avoid even being seen talking to each other for a long time. He remembered that he and a young red-headed dough-boy had wanted to tell each other how queer that all was. . . . Not to exchange reminiscences of sawmills in the Cevennes and fighting in the Argonne but merely to discuss their present situation! . . . They were obliged to make a date in a wood ten miles from the city. The red-headed boy's name had been Adams or Quincy or Lowell. Or possibly all three united. In spite of that he had been forced to leave the city.

Henry Martin had had the mortifying experience of being protected by his wife's mother. That blaring, Teutonic housewife had proclaimed everywhere that Henry Martin had taken care to be an *embusqué* as the French called it. He had joined the A.E.F. as a gesture.

. . . As the majority of the German-born of Springfield had done when they were not over age. Most of the sergeants, top-sergeants and a good proportion of the officers of the local units had in early life served in the German army. But they had all done their damnedest – and then some! – not to be sent into the fighting line. Some of them had even deserted, their absences being covered by sympathizers in the ranks. Henry Martin, the vigorous lady had proclaimed, was then precisely on a level with those of true German origin. . . .

So doors had begun to open amongst the houses of the All-High in the city. At first only Alice had been asked. But gradually Henry Martin had begun to receive invitations. And then the non-German population, seeing that he was received by the principal German citizens, had begun to invite him too.

Henry Martin had borne the ostracism very badly. He would have liked to think that he disliked even more the manner in which the closed doors had been opened to him. That had not been so. He would have liked to think that he was of the heroic mould. But he had accepted admission to Society with relief even at the cost of being proclaimed practically a traitor to his country. He needed, in fact, human contact if life was to be tolerable to him. He had no great friends in Springfield; but then he had never had great friends anywhere.

Now he recognized that his home was closed to him. It was ridiculous that Springfield should believe that his book was written against its inhabitants. He had never once given that city a thought during all the time that he had been writing the thing. The formidable Mrs. Prendergast had gone shopping with Sylvia Groen one day when she was expecting the Schultz's and lobsters had been dear. So a two thousand five hundred year old scarcity of that crustacean in the market of Athens under Pericles had risen up and contributed to Henry Martin's end.

Real writers that he had met in Paris told him that they also had been plagued by members of the general public. Almost anyone would manage to recognize him or herself in almost any character in any book that was at all life-like. It was an absurdity one had to put up with. A novelist called Pink had told him that he had actually been sued by a lady called Christine Pfeil from near Terre Haute, Indiana. Pink had called a dissolute Swedish chambermaid in one of his books 'Christine Pfahl.' And apparently Mrs. Pfeil had the habit of visiting male guests in their bedrooms after the rest of the house retired. It had cost Pink a pretty penny.

So he might accept Springfield's dislike of himself as a tribute to the life-like nature of his book. It was contributing none the less to his end. His contacts with his father had been always one long struggle between differingly desperate types of obstinacy. It was no doubt nothing but pride that made father insist upon his returning to Pisto-Brittle – and by now nothing but pride made him refuse. He was no writer by vocation: that seemed certain. And he could not even make a living by his brains. Father had put his lawyer on the publisher of BE THOU CHASTE. . . . According to his books the publisher owed Henry Martin sixteen hundred dollars. But that, the lawyer said, meant nothing. He could doctor his books how he liked and, since he owed a great deal to his printers and binders, those people would give him any kind of vouchers he wanted. It made no difference for the fellow flatly refused to pay Henry Martin a nickel. He said that he had had two tremendous successes the year before and those two best sellers had practically ruined him. He had to pay printers, binders, and publicity and other overhead charges on the nail; the booksellers would take anything from nine months to two years before they paid for the copies he sold them. So there was no chance of Henry Martin's touching any money for a long time, if ever.

Father said that Henry Martin could of course bankrupt the fellow. But if he did so he would make himself very unpopular and could not expect to get more than two cents on the dollar. And that in two years' time, considering the congestion in New York Courts. . . . And that action would be approved by nobody. The whole New York book trade was, like everything else, in a completely rotten condition. Everybody – publishers, bankers, binders – was bolstering everybody else up. In the hope of one day realizing something. The bankrupting of any one of them might bring the whole caboodle to the ground. In that case none of Henry Martin's fellow-authors would get anything. By Henry Martin's action. The old man imagined that Henry Martin had already had a sufficient bellyful of unpopularity.

PART THREE

CHAPTER I

HE could not be certain whether the motor was running
quite smoothly. Usually its sound was an agreeable mur-
mur. But perhaps, just as colours will not have full
brightness if you are financially worried so the sound of
engines will not be altogether soothing if you have been
up all night.

Dawn had come very suddenly. It is the misfortune of
certain landscapes of great beauty that human arts have
banalized their most wonderful or unusual effects. On
the stage when an actor lights a candle the whole large
stage will be flooded as if with sunlight. It was so with
this dawn of the fifteenth of August, nineteen hundred
and thirty-one.

You cannot spoil dark night and immense, wheeling
stars by any parody. In such a place when the air is just
flesh-heat you are conscious only of being at one with
immensity. You are no separate being and even to you
your weightiest preoccupations are without importance.
You say: 'If I had acted then in another way my situation
would now be less unfortunate. . . .' But your regrets
have little poignancy.

But that dawn flickered suddenly into existence. The
islands were illuminated. A white sail showed on the
horizon. Sea birds called. The sea itself, as if awakening,
threw a single, long-resounding wave along the miles of
shingle. The stage was suddenly set. You could no
longer commune with infinity. These were the great
boards on which to enact tragedy.

A grotesque – an almost abhorrent – message from Destiny opened the ball. An immense, skeleton-grey bird was flying slumberously along the edge of the sea. At little more than the height of a man. With dawn its labours were no doubt ended and it was going to rest on some solitary crag. With the slow beating of its vast spread of wings it had all by itself the air of a portent.

It was sleepily almost upon him . . . six feet away. It screamed with rage and fear. Its immense wings beat the air in untidy panic: it towered. Straight up. Towering and screaming it let fall a small fish. The fish struck smartly on Henry Martin's left shoulder. . . . An omen!

If a raven in those regions dropped excrement on the left shoulder of a Roman it was the best omen of all. He did not know what that bird was. . . . A stork, possibly. A pelican? A flamingo? . . . A fish dropped by a stork might be of better omen than excrement from a raven. The fish was silver . . . a fortune must be coming to him. . . . It was a grim and atrocious pleasantry on the part of Destiny. It struck him as something indecent. Destiny had driven him to death. His end was tragedy, not mere death. A hundred slowly converging things were forcing him over the edge of the boat. Not mere despair because you had lost a woman. Or a million dollars.

He had been doomed in his mother's womb. It had been decreed that the seed of a wild boar of the Ardennes meeting the lymphatic stock of over-old New England should beget one who danced without giving pleasure. That was reasonable. . . . As it were within the rights of Destiny. Destiny had the prerogative of dooming you within the womb.

But to conduct you within a foot or two of death and

then, grinningly to throw a fish at you. That was execrable. In execrable taste. . . .

He ran suddenly into the gloomy cavern of the inn-door. He clumped up the dark, carpetless stairs. . . . On the staircase at least he had recovered the night. Shadows.

It had struck him when the dawn had fallen suddenly on him that he had taken his call too soon.

He ought to have descended two hours later into a brilliantly illuminated stage. He would have received the plaudits of the islands, the innumerable smiling wavelets, the pine trees, the pebbles. Of the sirens too, perhaps! He would then have been the hero of tragedy, stepping gallantly to his doom. Then he would have danced. And all that applause would have shown that he had given pleasure.

As it was, the curtain – the dawn – had gone up too soon. He had been without make-up – cothurnus, parsley fillet, pine cone sceptre. And Destiny, in the audience had chucked fish at him! . . .

He had actually been prepared enough and might then have taken his call. . . .

In his bare room his papers were all burnt, his grips packed. His drawers all stood open as witness of the fact that, the night before, he had taken the proper precautions to leave nothing.

There hung nevertheless on the wall a little card calendar. It had been given to him last year in return for his *étrennes* to the postman . . . his five-franc tip. It had a pink and grey picture representing children feeding pigeons beside the Medici fountain. In the Luxemburg Gardens. . . .

The incredible thing! . . . It was incredible! . . .

He had mistaken the date!

It was to-day, Sunday, August 16th. . . . He had taken it to be the 15th . . . the feast of the Assumption. . . . It stood there on the Calendar.

15 S. ASSOMP
16 D. St. Roch

The Assumption in good fat capitals. St. Roch in tiny type.

It was disillusionment. He had imagined himself going up to heaven in a festival of glory. The Assumption was regarded as the most important feast of the French year. Gipsies from all over the world came to celebrate it to the Stes. Maries, a few miles away. . . . Gipsies, cardinals, *vaqueros*. . . . The tenders of the wild bulls of the Carmargue. They swam their wild bulls across the Rhone and back and were blessed by the Cardinals. . . . The bulls for the bull fights. . . . For the *Salta della Muerta*. . . . The dance of death. . . . They placed, those bull fighters, their feet on the horns of the charging bulls and sprang right over them. . . . *Salta* . . . the spring . . . *Saltaverunt*. . . . They sprang amidst wild applause. If they didn't die they were lucky. If they did they got more applause. . . .

He had taken pleasure at the thought that, whilst he drifted over the waving fronds at the bottom of the Mediterranean, those excitements would be taking place over the blazing pebbles of the Carmargue. Almost within sight.

But S. Roch . . . who was Saint Roch! . . . He was represented as fainting, with a dog licking his hand, a great loaf and a bamboo cross. There was a statue of him in the church of his name in the rue St. Honoré at Paris. As far as Henry Martin could remember he was a local saint. . . . Local to Marseilles and these

184

parts. He must have been born in Montpellier. . . . Yes, there had been a pestilence and M. Roch had gone about curing the sufferers and probably feeding them from the great loaf. He had been himself succumbing to the plague. But the dog had rescued him.

How could a dog rescue you from the plague? . . .

Was that the sort of story you wanted to have attending on your extinction? . . . It was another grin of Destiny.

On the other hand . . . perhaps if a local saint had been appointed for the day of his death his soul might expect to receive more immediate attention. . . . *Anima . . . vagula . . . blandula.* . . . Little, pale, wandering, new wet soul. It might be glad of a dog and a big loaf. . . . A more homelike reception than to have all the Archangels and the morning stars singing in glory.

He pulled down the sheets and laid himself full-dressed on his bed. He didn't know why he wanted to stage his end in that way. But he certainly desired to leave the impression that he had spent his last night in bed.

Why should he desire to leave impressions? It was nevertheless a strong urge and no doubt there is something vital in all strong urges. Something going to the root of life. An intimation perhaps of immortality.

If hell consisted of floating between the tides of the winds and worrying, one might as well worry about what happened to one's reputation as about anything else. It might be agreeable to hear them say: 'He was hard boiled. He slept in his bed before the rash act – as if nothing had happened.' . . . Or rather it might be extremely disagreeable if they said he had been in such a stew that he *hadn't* slept.

185

That was no doubt it. He had examined the bill-fold twice already and he felt that he was about to do it again. That was because he extremely disliked the idea of having his body searched by whoever found him. That wallet contained – A: his passport and identity card. B: a letter to Alice. C: a cable to his father. D: a hundred franc note. E: a letter to whoever found him. He begged them to send the cable to father – a night letter costing thirty-five francs; to mail the letter to Alice; to believe that there was nothing else in any of his other pockets and to retain the remaining sixty-five francs for any incidental expenses they might be put to. He said, too, that his heir and next male representative was his father and that he had nothing against anybody. The Crisis alone was responsible for his taking his own life.

He could think of nothing else to add to that collection of exhibits. He had done everything he could invent to keep his body from being handled. He had even tried to invent some way of leaving his wallet attached to his hand so that they might not even need to visit his pockets. If he had been going to shoot himself that would have been simple. If you died by a shot in the brain your hand closed irrevocably on whatever it held. He imagined himself lying on the ground – on the pine needles under an umbrella pine. Then the first thing that met the eye would be the oiled silk wrapping of the wallet. . . . Or no, it would be the wallet itself. If he had not been going to die in the water there would have been no need for the wrapper.

Some people had all the luck – the people who shot themselves. They could lie with their proof of identity in their hand. . . .

He lay with a nearly vacant mind till a ray of sunlight touched the extended fingers of a branch of the stone pine that grew at the house-end. He had long since hocked his watch. And it was odd how little he needed it. He had, of course, gone native: he had pretty well acquired the ability to tell the time by the sun. A year ago he would have laughed at you if you had told him he would one day live watchless. The watch was the badge of American manhood. . . . Free, male and twenty-one: complete with timepiece. . . . Incomplete without. How could you make dates? You could not be American and not make them.

Four days ago he had verified by the *salle à manger* clock that the sun just touched the branch at five-fifty-two. Giving the sun two minutes a day of delay, this morning it would touch it at six.

When the dark needles grew suddenly golden he started. He could not remember what he had been thinking of. He must have dozed off. That gave him pleasure. He had actually slept. Then he would not be obtaining applause by false pretences. He was indeed hard-boiled. Before the rash act he had really slept in his bed!

He took his call from the end of the little pier at six-fifteen. It had taken him a quarter of an hour, accompanied by old Marius Vial, to walk there from the bed in which he had slept. He had a sense that the mountains and islands 'Ho-ho'd,' the innumerable wavelets clapped, the umbrella and stone pines waved commendations.

Somewhere the sirens smiled. Heartlessly! He remembered a picture he had once seen, of a smiling siren plunging down, beneath the sea. A classical-featured youth was tight bound in her arms. As if there had been a hundred ropes twining round his limbs. Iridescent bubbles shot up through the air. Her smile was gleeful but aloof. As if she were thinking of something else. . . . If you were carrying down to your grotto a stalwart youth whose blood you were going to suck it would be more polite to think of him. . . .

So there he stood amongst all that applause!

On the terrace of the inn the silver fish that the bird had dropped had still lain on the gravel. . . . Destiny could hardly have been pelting him off the stage with it. He had acted as became a hero of tragedy. He had slept with refreshment and come there for all to see. Spectators, mad with enthusiasm, throw to a great torero in the arena fans, cigarettes, hats, jewels . . . whatever they have to hand. So Destiny had thrown the silver fish. Silver you observe!

The sheaf of thousand pound notes that Hugh Monckton had thrown to him the night before had for some reason or another seemed to represent great quantities of silver. Perhaps because they were silvery white. So Destiny might have been trying, with silver, to persuade him not to commit . . . the rash act. Destiny might very well think him the hell of a fine fellow.

Well, wasn't he? There he stood on high amongst the applause of a world. Nothing Destiny might have done had been able to deter him. He had marched there to his end, Nordic hero. Taking his call.

He was not wrong in calling it that. An author took his call when the curtain came down at the end of his play. And the curtain had come down on the end of his tragedy. Of that he was both hero and author.

He bowed to the right; to his left; before him. As if he had been an Oriental saluting the sun. His mind was full of sardonic gaiety. He remembered to have read somewhere that trapeze performers felt hatred for a public that applauded their living in mortal danger. So he hated that heartless, smiling landscape. When he had finished bowing he ran down the steps to his boat.

His left foot was poised above it, his right was still on the granite of the quay when he thought: 'This is my last contact with dry land.'

He imagined that his soul had shrunk within him to the dimensions of a shrivelled walnut. A walnut in a cavern. That was his soul. It was already dissociated from his body.

Marius Vial appeared to be speaking. Henry Martin did not hear what he said. The boat floated free. He went forward and pulled back the starting lever. Marius Vial had already set the engine running. Henry Martin turned the wheel on its joy-stick. He considered that a minute ago he had been mad. You do not bow to mountains, islands and waves. It is not done.

He had secretly wondered for a long time how fear would take him.

It had made his throat horribly dry. At this moment, too, he noticed that the engine was not running smoothly.

It annoyed his head. It was as if a mourner had behaved indecorously at his funeral. He had been used to take pleasure in the deep tones of his motor.

It was perhaps no more than the hangover after a sleepless night. . . . But it had not been sleepless.

He had had five very small drinks of that amazing *fine* the night before. Minute drinks because it had been so precious. It would be treason to that sanctified liquor to think that it had given him a hangover.

Then this was fear!

The boat had rounded the rocky bluff and opened out the great bay. The 'port exterior 'as they called it. He thought that in English they called it 'roads.' 'The English fleet lay in Toulon Roads.' The level sea spread before him, between the headland and the mainland.

189

The headland was a peninsula parallel with the mainland. Those words brought back to him moods of his young boyhood. 'Mainland.' 'Headland.' 'Roads.' 'Bluff.'

Well, his bluff had been called all right.

'Oh, little did my mother think the day she cradled me
Of the lands that I should travel in and the death that
    I should dee!'

His mother had been proud of the fact that he had never been rocked in a cradle. His first crib had stood in the sun-parlour. It gave on to the garden that was behind the drug-store. It had the model of a caravel, time of Columbus, that mother had brought from Fall River after Grandfather Smith's death. But before his -- Henry Martin's birth. He supposed Grandfather Smith had had some movable property in Fall River at his death. Mother must have gone over there to collect it.

She had had the proud idea that rocking babies injured their brains. He could still hear the inflection of her voice as she told other mothers that Henry Martin had *never* been rocked. . . . That was the baby-raising craze those years. . . .

Perhaps that was why he and the boys born about then were now the Lost Generation. They probably needed rocking to form their characters. Well, Providence was about to make up for it. He was going to be. . . . What was the old song?

'Rocked in the cradle of the deep!'

His throat was deplorably dry, the missing beat of the engine exasperated his brain. He might go ashore in the little cove called St. Mejean where there was an *estaminet:* he might stop the engine and try sailing. There was a bright little breeze from behind.

If he went ashore it would look as if he were faltering in his purpose: if he took to sailing he would appear to be playing for delay. Besides he had not a penny in the world beside the hundred franc note in his bill-fold. . . . Hugh Monckton had not in the end returned the three hundred and ninety-four francs . . . was it three hundred and ninety-four? He could not remember. The momentary recollection of last night gave him pleasure. It reminded him of the dark girl. He wondered if she was wearing his ring or had hocked it. He would never know.

There were five bright sails in the bay before him. Pleasure craft. It was Sunday. There would be hundreds of them before the day was done. There was a very full-membered sailing boat club at a little place called Mourillon that had a seventeenth-century castle and a tiny harbour behind a mole. The little space of water was as thick with them as if they had been sardines in a tin. Before noon they would be all out and the bay would be as gay as Miami in a record season.

He was glad of it. It pleased him to think of going out of the world in a sort of watery Coney Island. Besides he might be seen to go overboard. . . . Then they would be fairly certain to look out for his body. It was his body he was anxious about.

Dreadful fear beset him at the thought of his last minute. He imagined that you struggled, suffocated. At last you breathed. What happened then? When the water entered your lungs? Apparently you died then. You became for the rest of the world no longer 'he' but 'it.' But what exactly happened to you? A desperate running together of thoughts. Panic? Regret? Your lungs no longer supplied your heart with air and the want of aeration of your blood stupefied your brain.

191

. . . So you died poisoned. . . . He had wanted to avoid dying poisoned. Poison distorted your face and caused pain like flame. Similarly he disliked the idea of cutting his throat. It would make you repulsive. So would death by shooting. Besides he had hocked his gun long ago.

He would not have been averse to putting his head inside a gas oven and turning on the gas. But he disliked the idea of dying in a room. He wanted to see a bright sky with his dying eyes. . . . And he had heard that the drowned had serene faces. He had never actually seen a dead man. Mother's coffin had been screwed down before he reached Springfield from Dartmouth. He had imagined that that had been an act of spite on the part of father. But, of course, it had not been. He heard afterwards that mother had had a look of terrible agony and father wanted to spare his children.

He had misjudged father. Father had told the cook to cook Luxemburg-fashion and had taken his gold-headed cane out of the drawer immediately after he had come back from the funeral. That had looked like callousness. It hadn't been. Long after, father had told Sister Carrie that he had done it as a tribute to mother. He had been so certain of her saintliness that he knew she had gone straight to Heaven. If he had had any doubt or considered that she had earned a period in Purgatory he would have waited till he thought that period had ended. But, in Heaven, she would see all things in the right light. She would see that Luxemburg-fashion cooking was the best for him, and that gold-knobbed canes became men of his generation. She would be glad when from the battlements in the sky she saw him eating his first *plat de côte* and Kramyk.

A queer old fellow, father – In some ways his mind worked singularly like his son's.

Of course Henry Martin had thought that death by drowning would be the most painless.

He stopped the engine and throwing up one of the deck boards took out two heavy pigs of iron ballast. He dropped one into either pocket. That was to show that though he might be delaying his death he was still determined on it. After all there was no hurry. If he had set six o'clock for the hour of his rising he had set none for his death. And he had all eternity before him. And a lovely day. He had always luxuriated in that sort of brightness. He imagined that Heaven would be all sunlight and little bright objects.

As soon as the boat had lost way the scarlet, triangular sail bellied out nicely. Henry Martin had never ascertained what such sails were called in English. 'Lateen' he imagined. But he had a vague idea that lateen sails were made of rush. Probably that was wrong. He was pretty sure that the rig when there were several masts was called 'felucca.' A brave word, felucca. It made you think of Salee rovers, corsairs. He was familiar with the look of the rig from a set of nacred tea-trays that his mother had had. They showed Mediterranean scenes with the curved felucca yards bending romantically this way and that.

It was a nice rig. So extraordinarily easy to handle that he had often wondered why it was not used all the world over. This particular boat had the disadvantage that, when the sail was furled, if you had forgotten, or if you had not had time, to secure the yard it would swing round and round on the mast and might catch you a tidy crack if you were in the way – say in the rounded seat behind the joy-stick. Then it swung round again and caught you on the other side. Precisely like a vindictive boxer delivering a left and right.

That had happened to him three days ago, the nose of the yard catching him such a crack on each shoulder that he had two immense bruises on his upper arms.

He retreated to the stern where there was a tiller that he used instead of the motorwheel when the engine was not running. The stern seat was the more comfortable. You could stretch your legs to the full with one arm over the bar. It was one of his favourite positions. From there he could handle the sheet of the main-sail without getting up.

He lay for a long time with a completely vacant mind. The very high bow of the boat towered up to a sharp point and hid the greater part of the roads before him. It was complete luxury. This was how he had imagined it.

After a time the wind fell completely. The sail flapped now and then against the mast. Why not be delayed when you could suffer it in complete luxury? The sails of the approaching flotilla of pleasure seekers grew brighter and brighter. He could see them beyond the side of the port bow if he leaned his head over to one side. It pleased him to see them. They were like a gay fleet coming to lead him to a feast of garlands.

The sunlight grew whiter and more white. The day hung breathless. The sea was like a looking-glass: infinitely blue and getting bluer and ever more blue against the bright green of the promontory. He was by now well into the roads.

But, by Jove, the water was not blue between him and the mainland. It was a reddish chocolate. And opaque! There must have been an immense rainstorm somewhere in the mountains during the night. Old Marius Vial's *trombio*. Henry Martin had seen the water looking like that once already after an immense storm, taking up exactly half the inlet so that, from above, it had seemed to be two streaks . . . of red-brown and blue. The storm had gone pounding along the foothills of the Alps and then out to sea beyond Hyères. Cyclonic! These storms with a circular itinerary were not unusual in that neighbourhood during early August. The amount of water that fell during one of them was incredible. You could tell that because though the actual number of days on which rain fell in that neighbourhood was the lowest in all Western Europe the rainfall itself was the highest in all France. It was of course practically the tropics.

A feeling of unease was coming over him. He felt as if someone was watching him from behind his back. That was absurd. But the feeling grew until it was as if the something was an immense feline creature. That was more absurd. You should not yield to these feelings. There was no knowing how your character might not deteriorate if you did! . . .

With his face looking backwards, his right hand, mechanically, but with frantic speed, released the sheet of the sail from its cleat. He had seen three boats against a grey curtain – slate grey triangles of supernatural leaden-whiteness! They had stood out against the leaden curtain. One: two: three! They had gone over, flat. One: two: three! It was incredible that they could have capsized. But the air was moaning for them.

The immense grey-black curtain towered up to the peak of the heavens. It advanced with unbelievable rapidity. Before it the white villas half hidden in the tropical trees, the fort of the top on Cap Brun, the white semaphore over the highest part of St. Mandrier – all these things sparkled and were distinct in the sunlight. When it reached them they disappeared. There was nothing but the leaden grey pall with the fringe of sea beaten into an agony of whiteness.

It threatened unimaginable horrors. It advanced with the speed of a racehorse. God knew what went on within it. Lightning tore it and glowed from within. The screams of the drowning were thin but incessant. Those three sails had gone over, flat, with the precision of flaps on the edge of a machine. . . . It was Hell that was advancing – the hell of primitive imagination.

If he could get the boat round! He had sprung to the engine. There was no time to let down the yard. The sail, let free, might not exercise much leverage. Not enough to turn that large boat over. The noise was now so great that he could not hear if the engine responded. . . . It had sounded out of order! . . .

It had sounded out of order. But, if he could not get her head round they were lost. Her stern was so low that those white seas would poop her, without a chance of escape. He jammed and jammed at the starting lever. He cursed but could not hear his oaths. The sounds advancing were like the screams of demoniac birds. . . . Like the scream of that bird. He did not dare to look behind him. He had been contemplating a sin – Hell was advancing on him.

She could never run before it. She had a trick of speed: she was a good filly. They must not be lost: they must not be lost. Time moved so slowly that when, in the now steaming heat he moved his hand from the wheel to wipe his wet forehead with the back it seemed to take whole minutes to get it up to his head. . . . One day is as a thousand years in hell. Then perhaps the engine was not refusing. It was time that had broken down.

There was a faint vibration on the wheel in his hands. . . . He felt his body sway back in his seat. If he could get her round. She must know she could never stand those seas on her broadside. She had way on. She was starting

196

engrossedly over the still placid sea in the sunlight that was already livid.

He said:

'Now for it, old girl.'

He pressed on the wheel a little but steadily. A big boat like that could not be turned very sharply. It was at any rate not one of her virtues. Besides, if that sea caught her heeling for the turn it would swamp her in a minute.

To his breathlessness her high bow moved slowly to the right. Along the flank of the mountain that is over Les Sablettes. Behind the inner harbour. A heavy, squarish mass of cloud was attached to the peak, going away to the right like a shock of hair. The bow moved round, obscuring in its deliberate motion, grey-white ravines and little trees each of which had its separate shadow. He was then in the shadow and chill of what was advancing. But out there the sunlight still fell. Objects were amazingly distinct: seven miles away. But the shadows were ink-black.

On the beach at Les Sablettes there would already be a thick, gay, unsuspecting crowd of Sunday holiday seekers. As they said there: You would not be able to smell the sea for the babies. . . . And unsuspecting!

She had come half round. The bows were obscuring the flowered gardens and the palms and pines of the mainland. He had made the inland turn. He would have preferred to make for the open, left-handed. But there might be some shelter near the land. He was about a mile out. People in white clothes were running in crowds along the smugglers' path. Along the face of the rock.

Suddenly he looked at the approaching *trombio*. She was now broadside on to it and turning slowly. As if unconcernedly. Like a woman occupied with her cooking during a bombardment. He still lay back. Luxuriously! Leaning slackly on the tiller. He considered for a moment and then sprang for the wheel. The tiller might be jerked out of his hand in the approaching torrent.

That Thing of God appeared to go perfectly straight across the inlet. Like a great wall with a whitewashed foot. It towered completely up into invisibility. But, as she moved slowly round, he saw that the face of the wall was in vaporous motion. It was as if cloudy beings rushed violently to right or left or upwards. Or as if. . . .

He said:

'By God!'

It was now that he was taking his call before the mocking beings of the Universe. It was now . . . now . . . now that he was going behind the curtain.

As soon as she was round he had unthrottled the engine. The sea was now agitated. She had come alive. Under the new force she seemed to spring toward her doom. He discovered that he was panting.

Darkness descended on him. It came like a whip. With a roaring rush. The air was full of missiles. It was as if a hundred pails of wheat had been hurled at him. Just before the darkness he had looked at the compass. Whilst he could still see the land. By steering due east with a little south to allow for drift if the wind beat inshore he ought just to shave the headland behind which lay Carqueiranne. But he was blinded. Heavy veils of water were in his eyelashes as he shivered. They seemed glutinous, one succeeding another as he brushed them away with the back of his hand. The rain drove straight through his shirt. It was icy and impelled him to rage. He would best this damned imbecility of the elements.

And save the boat. It was as if she trusted him to save her. He exclaimed:

'By God, she is the only friend I have.'

Damn all women ! A woman by now would have been shrieking or fainting. Not Alice perhaps. But she had gone Lesbian.

The noise was as if a thousand lunatics were rubbing sheets of corundum paper one on the other. The rain was solid on his skin. It was as if he were at the bottom of the sea.

He remembered the little flask in his pocket: the one he had not offered to Hugh Monckton the night before. *That* was fiery, cheap stuff. Having drunk half of it he seemed to be on fire within and frozen outside. What pastry-cooks call a *chaud-froid*. It seemed to fill him with savage gaiety.

She was labouring slowly into the teeth of the wind. She took the short seas as if she were a hunter at a horse-show taking in and out fences. It was impossible to see what progress she made if she made any. He steered to the left, towards the land. Very gradually. She shipped a little water. He imagined himself to be about level with Cap Brun.

He knew all the beaches along there. But he was not enough of a sailor to know how she would take landing on the shingle in this sea. He was, however, certain that she would be all right if she struck a patch of sand. Or, if he got under the lea of Carqueiranne mole he might risk landing on the hard stones.

Suddenly land loomed up before him. Reddish perpendicular rocks with the spindrift shooting before it. She was going at it, nose on. And travelling rather fast.

That would not do. Even in smooth water she would stave her bows in if she charged red granite rocks. He wanted her to come off without a scratch, and he felt full of confidence that he could do it. He headed her seawards. It was no doubt the brandy that had given him confidence. But that did not matter. He caught, near his left hand in large white letters the word RESERVE. He must be within ten yards of the land but the water was deep there. He knew the place but not its name. He was more than half way back to Carqueiranne and he knew approximately the pace at which they were travelling.

Out of the shelter of the land the storm blew again more furiously. She began once more her gait of the jumping hunter. It made his teeth chatter. He reckoned it would cut her travelling down to about half. They would have to stand it for a full hour more.

The wind howled: the rain beat upon him: the engine ran well now. He could feel its pulsations on the wheel. The monotony grew insupportable. Once there was a moment of calm in the air. He put her at it, cramming in the gasoline. He imagined himself to have made three hundred yards at racing speed. Then she washed into it again. As if she had gone at. . . . What was it called? A bullfinch. The sort of hedge Hugh Monckton had said he was going to put his car at.

There must be a pocket of calm travelling in the middle of the storm. He thought they called it the cyclonic centre. That must mean they were in the middle of the disastrous affair. They would have to go through as much again as they had already gone through. He doubted if he could do it. He was insufferably weary and cold. His hands on the wheel ached with cramp. His eyes were painful with gazing into the wind. He would have given anything to lie down on dry land. On pine-needles. . . . What a hope! as Hugh Monckton had said.

The fumes of the brandy were surging up within him. . . . You had to remember that his stomach must be quite empty. He had eaten nothing since dinner-time last night. He remembered to have read that, taken on an empty stomach brandy reached its maximum effect in a quarter of an hour. After that it acted as a soporific. Weakening you.

It was perhaps half an hour since he had taken that gulp. Then he must be feeling the weakening effect. That was damnable.

Suddenly he put her about. It was perhaps the recklessness of brandy. He must have underestimated her seaworthiness. The la Seyne boatbuilders probably knew their job and those waters. She was like a cork. Even when she was broadside on to the direction of the wind she shipped next to no water. Before the wind she fairly raced the wave crests.

He felt wild elation. Like a drunken motorist racing through traffic. Or like Hugh Monckton charging his bullfinch. Well, he was probably the better man of the two. It was unlikely that he had done what he said. Whereas he, Henry Martin, was actually charging an unknown obstacle at breathless speed. . . .

He would have to borrow some money of Hugh Monckton. So as to be able to sleep for two days on end. He would have to have two days' sleep before he would have the nerve to commit suicide again.

Well, why not borrow of Hugh Monckton? They had been in the same regiment! Besides, Hugh Monckton had offered to lend him twenty thousand pounds to have a gamble with. Surely he would let him have five hundred francs for a sleep. . . . One five-thousandth of the sum!

He exclaimed suddenly:

'Good God!'

They had leapt into perfectly still water. They were doing very likely thirty! With a furious kick at the pedal and pushing the lever completely over he reversed the engine. He did not dare to go about in the effort to reduce speed. They must have struck the mouth of the little cove beneath the stone pines. He was thrown against the wheel as the reversing engine began to take effect. All the breath left his body. The cove was perhaps two hundred yards across and a quarter of a mile deep. The sides were lined with red granite but at the bottom was the stretch of silver sand. The very thing to land on if they were not going at express speed.

But there was no knowing how far they were down the cove. The cove it must be because there was no other. But the rain falling direct into the windless space hid everything. He might well be going to crash her on to that sand with a force that might stave her bottom. What a thing to do to your only friend!

But perhaps Hugh Monckton was also a friend. He seemed to hear his voice say: 'Old Bean!' . . . Male and female created He them. . . . The boat was a female. . . .

There appeared dim and wet through the glassy rods of the rain a red brick blockhouse, a hillside and a white path that divided it at a slant. It was indeed the cove.

These things came toward him rapidly. But the reversed screw had taken hold. Every half second the speed decreased. He stood up to see exactly at what moment to stop the engine. Some men were running out of the red blockhouse. If the engines ran after she was stopped they might strain their bearings. He thought so.

She checked glutinously as she were on the bottom ooze. He half fell forward. She proceeded: then checked more determinedly. He felt a violent, an incredible blow on his cheek. Incredible pain.

The yard that had been completely divested of its canvas had swung round on the mast at the checking of the keel. The end of the yard was bound in iron.

The blow knocked him sideways. Immediately a fearful sear of pain existed in his right temple. That flail had swung completely round on the mast. He screamed. He fell desperately forward on to the hood that covered the engines. . . .

The only thing that existed was pain. Men stopped him on the sand and told him he was bleeding.

'Vous saignez!' . . . 'Mais vous saignez!' . . . 'Saignez.'

He struck at them and ran. He thought that if he ran fast enough he could escape from the pain. And they were barring his way. . . . What sort of life was this?

They shuffled back stupidly. He ran for the foot of the path. He must obtain insensibility. He desired to bite at the tufts of rosemary that on the pathside brushed his cheek. He was past them before he could bite.

He came to the top and sat down on a ledge. The rain had stopped. The sunshine fell on the island of Porquerolles – the high blue island over the ruffled sea. He could do no more.

He held his hand to his right temple. It came down glutinous and scarlet. He held his other hand to his other cheek. He desired to vomit. To have escaped war, tempest and self-given death and to come to this! The impulse to vomit made him remember his brandy flask. It was still half full.

The men on the sand below had given up looking at him and had gone back to the blockhouse. With the impulse of the brandy within him he stood up. The day was growing brighter and brighter. He must be going on!

CHAPTER II

HUGH MONCKTON was lying on his face. On pine-needles.
Henry Martin said:

' "Men fall on their faces when shot through the medulla: on their backs when. . . ." ' 'Medulla' was no doubt not the word in the quotation.

Some people had all the luck! Hugh Monckton was lying on his face in the place where Henry Martin had meant to lie. When he had thought, in the boat, of lying on the ground on pine-needles, that was where he had meant to lie. Undoubtedly!

The umbrella pines towered up. A light breeze shook their tops. As they moved pools of sunlight moved over the still, wet needles.

His passport was in some sort of celluloid casing. Stamped with a large plaque of gold. The Smith arms perhaps. Or the British Royal ones. It was in his left hand. His gun had the barrel and the carrier curiously damascened. It was in his right hand.

The Mediterranean shone through the trunks. From that height he could see that around the semaphore on the promontory across the water there was a brown open space. In the early spring no doubt it had been a green lawn.

It was troublesome to attend to immediate details. The alcohol he had lately swallowed probably confused him. He had never seen a dead body. Mother's coffin had been screwed up when he got back from Dartmouth. He did not know what you had to do for the comfort of the dead. He had an idea that you put pennies on their eyes. He had read that somewhere. In this case you could hardly do that.

What was he to do then? It was troublesome to think. He ought presumably to call assistance. That would mean that his friend's rest would be the earlier broken. Rough and careless men would eventually disturb him. Let him lie as long as he could.

It was evident that he had desired his body to be as little as possible rifled. He had had the same idea as Henry Martin, his passport being in his hand.

That fellow had succeeded in killing himself when he, Henry Martin, had ignominiously failed.

Henry Martin had been considering that matter when he had come into the grove. He had said to himself with bitterness:

'Here's the sort of fellow I am. I set out to drown myself – then run away from a storm that would have drowned me. What sort of a spectacle shall I present?'

He had said to himself that that was all one with his grotesquely futile life.

Then he said fiercely:

'Damn it all: I didn't run away from the storm. I fought it as few men not six feet in their stockings could have fought it. And precious few who were!'

There was no one but himself to whom he would present any spectacle. No one else knew that he had set out to commit suicide. It was merely with himself that he had to argue for it was only before himself that he could be ashamed. He was not going to be! His fighting the storm had been a courageous action. He was saving the boat. You had to save boats. There were two of them. He and the boat.

It was all very well to say that he had set out to commit

suicide. But his pact with Providence had been to do it in a warm still sea. With the sun on the island.

He took the passport from the leaden fingers. He had touched a dead friend! How quickly Hugh Monckton had become his friend. In the boat he had said that she and Hugh Monckton were his only friends. It had then seemed a little fantastic. Now it seemed the exact truth. At any rate as regarded Hugh Monckton.

They had had exactly the same idea. The celluloid casing! Those were certainly not the British Royal Arms stamped upon it. The crest was recognizably a pelican of the wilderness. There were two quarterings of things like hammers. Punning heraldry. The motto was *Sine Fabro Ars Nulla*. . . . There is no art without a Smith. . . . There was an old saying: 'By hammer and hand all Art doth stand.' . . . Father had said that in Luxemburg his crest had been a mailed hand holding a hammer. . . . Henry Martin felt towards the arms stamped there a sort of intimacy. As if they ought to have been his own arms. Perhaps he and Hugh Monckton had been related! That might account for their sudden friendship.

The celluloid casing, then, contained a blue British Passport inscribed in a little slot: H.M.A. Smith, a thousand franc note and a letter addressed: 'A celui qui trouvera mon corps!' . . . 'To whoever finds my body.'

The letter said:

'Je préférerais. . . .' 'I should prefer.' . . . That no one should search his body! His pockets were completely empty. He died by his own act. He had no ill feeling towards any human being. If French law insisted on an autopsy it must be so. But he would prefer to be buried in his clothes as it were. He died because the after effects of the late war had become too intolerable to him. He was completely useless to man or beast and suffered terribly.  He begged whoever found his body to communicate with his relatives – *communiquer les nouvelles à ses parents* . . . and war comrade – *comarade de guerre* . . . Henry Martin Aluin Smith of Springfield, Ohio, at present staying . . . *qui demeure actuellement Hotel du Port, Carqueiranne, Var.*

*Monsieur Henry Martin Aluin Smith trouverait sur la cheminee de la chambre seize, Hotel des Negociants.* . . . Henry Martin would find on the mantelshelf of Hugh Monckton's room a letter containing a codicil to his will.  It begged him as knowing all the circumstances better than another to take care of the disposition of such of his property as should find itself in that city. . . . It came with a sort of tranquillity to Henry Martin to turn the page and to see a rough design. . . .

✠

CI GIT
UN ETRANGER
OBIT
XVI.VIII.MCMXXXI
MISERERE MEI DOMINE
QUIA MULTUM AMAVI

He desired to be buried in the graveyard of Le Revest des Eaux, looking over the Mediterranean and to be covered by a single slab of granite bearing the inscription: 'Here lies a stranger who died on the sixteenth of August, nineteen hundred and thirty-one.  Have mercy on me O Lord in that I have loved much.'  Hugh Monckton made that request in that letter that might be made public because he did not wish the inhabitants of that countryside to think his heirs niggardly in giving him such simple sepulture.

For a moment Henry Martin felt that that was himself writing! And then that it was himself lying face downwards there. A sharp spat of noise came from the paper. It was a gout of blood that had fallen on the signature. It seemed to cement whatever was the odd relationship since it related Henry Martin's blood with the other's name. The signature was extraordinarily like his own.

The pain which had ceased at the discovery of that body now began again. The sight of the blood had recalled him to himself. He must go somewhere and get something done to himself. His chest was covered with blood that had streamed from his cheek and his temple. He imagined Hugh Monckton was shot through the right temple but not through the left jawbone.

Now was the time to commit suicide. But he admitted that he had not the nerve. He must have a couple of nights' sleep. He could not face it as he was.

He was wretchedly worried by the spot of blood on Hugh Monckton's signature. How would the people who found him account for that? He had the strongest possible revulsion from the idea that it should be he who denounced Hugh Monckton to the police. It would be denouncing ! Those ravens would fall upon him; they would drag him about and shout in his silent presence. They would perhaps accuse him of cowardice. . . . But there was one incontrovertible excuse for suicide. To be abandoned by a woman. That was the one absolute finality: your whole being was halved. The very reason for your existence ceased.

No: he would not be the one to do the denouncing!

Then the blood on the letter? How would they account for that? Blood on a letter inside a celluloid casing! And he, Henry Martin, bleeding and having passed that

208

way. . . . Hugh Monckton must have a clean letter. . . .

He thought of substituting his own letter from his own passport. . . . It was just such another letter. . . . The throbbing in his head became intolerable. He heard voices. He ran to the edge of the clump of trees and looked down on the path. He had his own celluloid wrapped passport in his right hand because he had just taken it out. Hugh Monckton's was in his left.

Four fat men in black were beginning the ascent of the path. They pointed to Henry Martin's blood on the track and interrogated each other. Henry Martin panted. He felt himself a hunted animal. He ran. He staggered a minute ago. Now he ran.

Hugh Monckton's fingers were cold. He pressed them. That was the last time they would be pressed on this earth.

He ran across the pine-needles, and, in the blazing light of the sun, down the slope that gave on to the meadow beneath the real estate agent's villa. Hugh Monckton's car was standing in the field. Henry Martin's passport was in Hugh Monckton's fingers! He had a clean letter.

The slope was slippery, the sun blinding. His miserable feet slipped: slipped again. They would not sustain him. They slipped away beneath him. For a moment it was ease to fall. He rolled over and over, he did not know how far. The jabs of pain at each turn made eleven!

He rolled over the hard roadway with the impulsion and into the meadow. He was escaping from the fat men in black! He climbed to his knees: then to his feet. He was screaming with rage and waving his arms with madness of fury. He ought to have been spared this. It was indecent. To make a sport of him when he had just lost his only friend. Destiny was indecent. . . . He was running towards the car. You do not take liberties with people who owned cars. He was running on a serpentine track. The car was as good as his. Hugh Monckton would lend it to him. Hugh Monckton had left all his property at his disposal. He was as good as Hugh Monckton himself.

He staggered two yards to the right: he was erect again but the earth was trying to strike him. He fell in mounting the step of the car. He gripped the metal but his hand had no holding power. He was on the ground. . . .

A gentle voice was saying:

'My wife with her opera glasses which explored the harbour. . . .' . . .'Ma femme avec ses lorgnettes qui explorait le port. . . .' But it must be the plural: 'exploraient.' It was extraordinarily luxurious to lie on the ground in the sunlight. . . . Or it might have been the wife not the glasses which explored the port.

This black-bearded undertaker was trying to make him get up. He had a large, shining car.

After a time they were in the car. The undertaker, in black alpaca, was driving it with one arm round Henry Martin's shoulders. They were going very slowly.

Henry Martin said:

'You will spoil your alpaca!'

The funereal fellow said:

'That will make nothing.' . . . Meaning that it did not matter. He went on: 'Make yourself comfortable my dear Monsieur Smeez. Lean heavily upon me.'

He had a gentle voice. It was M. Something or other, the real-estate man. Henry Martin hoped that his migraine was not troubling him. He said:

'You recognize me? You are very kind . . . très gentil. We are going to Carqueiranne?'

M. Something said:

'No: Carqueiranne is near. But they have little accommodation there. I thought it better to go to your own hotel in the town.' He added: 'I should not, my faith, have recognized you. . . . But I saw your name on the silver plate in your car. And I am naturally familiar with your figure. . . . You, of course, mistook your road in the storm. You must have charged right through the hedge at the turn of the road. . . . Famous cars that your House builds! Your specimen appears very little injured.'

The pain of someone cleaning his face with gentle dabs was very sharp. The pungent odour of an anaesthetic burned his nostrils. A man in white was hanging over him. A voice said:

'This is Monsieur Monckton Smeez. . . .'

Another:

'Vous ne le dîtes pas! . . . You don't say! I wish I had his money. But not at the moment his face.'

Henry Martin said:

'Non . . . non. . . .'

He was no doubt repenting of his rash act!

If he wasn't at the bottom of the Mediterranean he was at the side of a road under some plane trees and he had changed his identity. The firm husky voice said:

'It is necessary, Monsieur, that I get the gravel out of the wound. Otherwise you will have a very great scar.'

The voice of the man in alpaca said:

'Monsieur has already a very great and most honourable scar. From a Boche sabre.' He was one of the first hundred thousand of his compatriots to land in this country in 1914.'

Henry Martin writhed. This was one of the consequences of his act that he had not expected. He tried to say:

'You must not say that.' But they were binding his jaw over his head with a lint bandage. . . . After all he had wished to be Hugh Monckton. Now he was.

A mournful face with brown eyes immensely magnified by the lenses of spectacles was gazing at him from very near. . . . A square brown beard. A black skull cap. All in white. He said – in English:

'Be assured, sair, I weel hairt you as leetle as is not necessaire. . . . C'est vous qui avez sauvé la France. . . .'

Henry Martin remembered the canning factory in the Cevennes. And the Syphilis Inspector! They might between them have saved France. . . . With preventive instruction and canned salmon from the Rhône! But he tried to remember himself standing up to a mounted figure in a blue uniform with silver buttons. Galloping upon him with a waving sabre. It was a less satisfactory way of saving France. But more likely to be applauded by a wayside druggist.

The man then said he would give Henry Martin a composing draft. He was still in the automobile. There was a little crowd round it. Monsieur Lamoricière, the real-estate agent . . . that was his name . . . was explaining with grave unction. . . . This was Mongtong Smeez. The famous proprietor of the Mongtong car and a hero of the first water – during the Great War. During the storm he had mistaken his road and the car had charged a wall and hedge. At right angles. Monsieur Mongtong Smeez had been thrown out of his vehicle. But the car and the hero had each been very little damaged. . . . Monsieur Smeez appeared to have no broken bones. . . . A tribute to the build of both car and hero! Madame Lamoricière surveying with her opera glass the *port extérieur* for relics of the great storm had turned it negligently on the field. She had exclaimed to Monsieur:

'Tiens, mon ami. . . . There is a car in the meadow. . . . And, yes . . . the form of one recumbent half hidden by it. Go quickly. Be sure there has been a terrible accident!'

He had hurried down in his car and had found the hero, recumbent indeed, beside it. . . . Insensible!

The soft clear voice going on in its precise monotone was punctuated by gentle, applauding interruptions from the crowd. The thick shadow of the plane-boughs was black on the road. Monsieur Lamoricière went on to make a few remarks on the negligence of the local authorities who had set up no indication post at a most dangerous angle. Thus they had risked depriving the world of one of its great industrialists and France of one of her saviours. At a time of crisis when the world needed more than anything great leaders of industry. And France all the heroes that could be found!

To Henry Martin with the sweet taste of an opiate in his mouth this seemed agreeable and even touching nonsense. The chemist had introduced the syrup between his teeth by means of a syringe. He could hardly move his jaw. He wondered why they did not start. After a time they did, going very gently along a very smooth road. M. Lamoricière's arm was again about his shoulders. It was agreeable.

It was dim in Hugh Monckton's room. It had the air at once of a cathedral and a home. A closed in portion of a cathedral. He seemed to have passed at some time a large part of his life there. It was familiar. . . . The treasury of some cathedral. Because of the fantastically unique objects in the packing cases and because the spirit of Hugh Monckton was looking over them.

A great many people seemed to have followed him into the room. But he had had the first glimpse of it in its solitude and dimness.

It was odd that it was dim. The heavy curtains of course did that. But who had closed them? He could not remember Hugh Monckton doing it. And the night before he had watched the searchlights from the couch. And sure enough the hotel people were saying that they had not known Monsieur had not slept in his bed. No one had entered the room. They congratulated Monsieur on his escape. Volubly! They volubly lamented the storm. Thirty-two poor holiday makers had been drowned in the exterior port. In the roads. . . . Well, he knew something about that. But they were not to be aware that he did. . . .

Above the curtains a little light filtered. Through the rings. A single gilt streak ran diagonally across the dusty roses frescoed on the ceiling and vertically down the puce-coloured, faded wall beside the mirror. Like gilt. In the dim mirror he saw white things reflected. Bandages on a man's face. You saw only the eyes, the nose, the moustache. And a very little of the chin. It was like the head of a crusader in a helmet of lint. He could not remember if any of the crusaders had set sail from that port. They might have. The Pilgrimage of Children might have passed close by there! . . .

The question pressed upon him suddenly: Was he going to continue this. . . . What was it? A farce? A crime possibly? It seemed to be his only chance of rest. That he needed desperately. . . . A couple of days stretched on a bed. He did not suppose Hugh Monckton would object to his sleeping in his vacant bed. . . . Well, he was sure he would not. The alternative would be a French hospital. No: damn it! Hugh Monckton would not stand for that. Then. . . .

The people round him were full of solicitude and repeated over and over again the same exclamations as to the magnificence of his car. A magnificent car! It had jumped a hedge! It had jumped a hedge. A magnificent car! *Une auto magnifique . . . cela sautait comme un cheval.* . . .

It was their laudation of him as Hugh Monckton that most worried him. . . . But if they did not applaud him they would be pitying him. Or censoring. He was at least keeping alive that part of Hugh Monckton that was his name and excited applause. Without that there would be for him, so shortly, nothing but oblivion. . . . Vice-regent here on Earth. . . . That was what he was . . . Hugh Monckton's earthly representative. Receiving in his name their homage for having saved La France! Literally in his name.

The *patronne*, an aged dumpling in black, discovered on the mantelpiece a letter addressed to Monsieur. She began to cackle over it like a hen over an egg. 'Une lettre à l'adresse de Monsieur. . . .' A letter addressed to Monsieur. . . . A fat letter addressed to Monsieur Henri Mungtong Smeez. . . . A letter that crackled. . . . With *billets de banque.* . . . What a thing it was to be rich! . . . In times of crisis. . . . People left for you letters that were fat and crackled. . . .

'Fat and crackling,' the waiter repeated; the fat chambermaid, the thin one: and the little *chasseur*; and the husband of the *patronne* and the friend of the husband of the *patronne* who had been having a glass of syrup and water. . . . They all, in different tones, repeated the word. . . .

Monsieur Lamoricière and a silver-haired, tired man

215

were driving them out of the room. Monsieur Lamoricière said:

'This is my friend, Monsieur Smeez. . . . Monsieur le docteur' . . . Something!

He was holding the large letter. They were inviting him to recline himself on the bed. . . . The doctor had acknowledged the introduction with the air of a judge condemning you to death. The French doctor's bedside manner! He was a tired doctor. And easily annoyed!

Henry Martin glanced at the superscription of the letter. It was addressed:

'Henry Martin Aluin Smith, Esq.' 'To be called for.'

Yet the *patronne* had read 'Martin' as 'Mongtong.' . . . Nothing would ever make French concierges or *patronnes* recognize the superscription of letters. Either they gave you all the letters for all the inhabitants of your apartment building or they refused to believe that by any possibility 'Smith' could read 'Smeez.' Madame *La Patronne* was of the generous type. It was perhaps just as well!

These then were Hugh Monckton's testamentary directions. . . .

The doctor snatched the letter from his hand.

'It is me you have to attend to. Not your correspondence.' He said irritably to Monsieur Lamoricière:

'Make more light. How can you expect me to see a patient in these tenebrousnesses?'

The curtains, admitting a golden blaze, ran back, jingling on their rings. The light fell strongly from the left. The room faced due south. It could not be more than ten o'clock. The gilt dial of the clock with gilt mermaids on the mantelpiece said however a quarter to four. That was frivolous.

Was it possible to imagine that all that had happened

had taken at most four hours? . . . The setting out for suicide: the endlessly lasting storm; the actual suicide. And his complete change of identity. If he tried to prove to these gentlemen that he was Henry Martin and not Hugh Monckton they would certify him as a madman!

A supreme test must however be coming.

The doctor began his investigations – searching for internal injuries. Henry Martin did not see how he could have internal injuries. He had been clouted on each side of the head and had rolled down a little bank. Then he remembered that he had been thrown out of an automobile. After jumping a hedge in it!

The supreme test was however coming!

The doctor tried him for leg injuries apparently. He pushed up Henry Martin's feet till his knees hit his aching jaw. Then he tried the arms. His bending them was supportable. But when he tapped the outside of the upper arm Henry Martin groaned.

The doctor became as excited as a terrier by a stackside when you are ratting. He cut Henry Martin's shirt open right down the arm.

'It is better for you not to move,' he said, 'and you can apparently afford a shirt.'

He grew angry at the sight of the bruises on the upper arm.

'This fellow must be injured somewhere,' he said. 'It is unreasonable. Even his contusions have the air of clearing up. . . .'

*That* was not unreasonable because they were three days old.

Monsieur Lamoricière began with his sober, oratorical manner:

'If you consider that Monsieur Smeez was one of the. . . .'

That was the supreme test. If that grave voice had once more got out the statement that Henry Martin was one of the Old Contemptibles Henry Martin knew that he would have sprung from the bed and shouted that he was nothing of the sort.

The doctor cut the other short.

'That has no bearing on a man who has been thrown from an automobile.'

'You *were* thrown from an automobile,' he said angrily to Henry Martin and held his ear close to the patient's mouth.

Henry Martin found that he could not speak. His voice made sounds like the rasping of sticks.

The doctor said triumphantly:

'He says he doesn't know what happened. That's at least evidence of shock. . . . You can't be thrown out of an automobile in a hurricane and have nothing happen to you. That would be unreasonable.'

He was removing the face bandages with extraordinary rapidity and gentleness.

'Now for those face scratches,' he said. 'The pharmacien says they are serious. Pharmaciens always exaggerate. They seek to magnify the importance of the cases that their luck lets them be first at. . . .'

Henry Martin's jaw hurt him execrably when it was no longer supported. His temple hurt him relatively little. The doctor, peering and fingering, was for the moment silent. M. Lamoricière was looking intently at Henry Martin. Then down at a small, thin, dark-blue book. . . .

Henry Martin's heart stopped beating. By that he knew that he was passionately intent on assuming that other identity – that he had been intent on it the moment when he had placed his own passport in Hugh Monckton's fingers.

The moment before he could not have told you that. Now he knew because the dark man with alabaster features was looking at the portrait of Hugh Monckton in Hugh Monckton's passport. And then at his – Henry Martin's face. And Henry Martin's face was lit up by the merciless reflections in the room of the full morning sun.

'You have a great deal of luck,' he said. 'It is lucky that I found this at your side for it is disagreeable to lose a passport.'

Henry Martin caught at the outside of his pocket where the trouser was. . . . It would have been intolerable if that man had come upon Hugh Monckton's farewell letter. The passport he had had in his hand. But he remembered stuffing the letter and the note that were in the celluloid case into his trouser pocket. . . .

'Now I am not hurting you. . . . You cannot say I am hurting you,' the doctor said. 'You think I will and you shrink. But I am not hurting you. . . .'

The crackle of the celluloid made itself felt under Henry Martin's fingers.

'And,' M. Lamoricière said: 'if one were humorous one might say that you have almost as great luck in your portraits as in your life. The passport photographs of most of us resemble as a rule dejected pickpockets or atrocious brigands. Yours at least, monsieur, resembles an honest man and not a disagreeable one. The resemblance is also striking.'

At that Henry Martin must have fainted.

He heard the doctor say sardonically:

'It will not resemble him for long. If I am not mistaken this gentleman will have to join your confraternity of the bearded. Some good bromides now and a beard in the hereafter. . . . I will send a woman to cup him. After that for two days he had better sleep. His nerves are. . . .'

But after that he remembered only that they seemed to be moving him and the voice of Lamoricière:

'J'ai entendu dire qu'il a une petite amie. Mademoiselle. . . .' 'I have heard that he has a little female friend. Mademoiselle. . . .' And a name Henry Martin did not catch.

And after that the voice of the doctor booming unnaturally. He must have been fixing something quite close to Henry Martin's ear. He thought the words were:

'Ah! Elle se console!' And: 'Tonkin-Saigon. He might have done worse.'

After that it was, rather blissfully one o'clock in the dim room. One at night. A tiny light above a hung watch showed him that. Hugh Monckton would have that sort of contraption on his bedside table.

His jaw ached a good deal. . . . But he had decided to adopt the personality of Hugh Monckton. That was proved to him by his fainting. He had fainted with relief at the thought that the real-estate agent had identified him by Hugh Monckton's passport photograph. Then he had acted of set purpose – of set purpose in his subconscious mind – when he had fixed his own passport in those cold fingers. . . .

It opened up a whole vista of problems in criminology. His conscious mind had had no idea of his motive – the mind with which he framed words, caught trains, and decided what to eat in a restaurant. But the motive must have been there. Otherwise he would not have so revolted at the thought that the subconscious plan might not succeed.

A problem in criminology! . . . But he denied energetically that he was a criminal. So far he had asked no man for anything. And no woman either. They had handled him as if he had been a brown paper parcel. Without his yes or no.

His subconscious mind must have been mad for a bed. For sleep! For silence! It had realized what would be the quickest way to get its desires. He had been conscious only of running from the fat men in black on the path below. He had substituted the passport, as far as his conscious mind had been concerned, as one performs other odd actions when one is in a hurry or panic. . . . As people escaping from fires select eccentric objects to save. Or as he had crammed those documents into a trouser pocket. Instead of the natural breast pocket of his coat.

That chance action had preserved his reason. He was assured of that. If his fingers had not found the feel of those things when his hand had gone to his side. . . . There was no knowing what would have happened to him. He would have been convinced that Lamoricière, having read the letter, was awaiting the dramatic moment at which to denounce him. . . . Then he would have gone mad. At the thought that he was not to sleep in Hugh Monckton's bed. . . . At the thought that he would not, for a day or two, have the chance to rummage amongst Hugh Monckton's gadgets. That fellow had had the inventive mind. The bag, stapled to the floor and painted like a harlequin was proof of that. And now this watch, hung to the tiny electric globe. . . . And there were probably hundreds more in the half visible pile of Hugh Monckton's travelling effects. . . .

So that his conscious mind had now to take charge of a situation created for him by its partner. Its partner was no doubt the part of your brain that took charge when you were drunk and did odd things that, next morning, you could not remember to have done. But he repudiated angrily the idea that he had been drunk. He remembered his actions perfectly well. And he was aware of his motives.

He had now to take charge.

What was to become of Henry Martin? Of the Henry Martin who had been left lying on his face under the pines on that knoll? He had to think of who would be hurt at the news of his death. He imagined no one. No one seriously. Sister Carrie not much beyond the inconvenience of having to go into Continental mourning for a year. That might be disagreeable.

Alice would care nothing at all. Brother Hal might give him an hour or two of thought. He might be hurt that Henry Martin had not applied to him for assistance. Father. . . .

Henry Martin had long ago made up his mind that father would take the news with grim humour. He would lean back in his chair with his two hands on the edge of the table before him. He would say:

'My! The boy sure hitched his wagon to some star after all.' And he would be proud of his son's spunk. He was an old man. To him separation came gently enough. Besides they had been separated. They could hardly have been more apart. . . . Then. . . .

Someone was sobbing. And then moaning. Five sobs and a moan. . . . Six sobs and a moan. It was impossible to locate the direction from which the noise came. It seemed to pervade the night. He wished it would stop. It was like what he would like Mrs. Percival to do on hearing of his death. There was no soul in the world whom it would affect. Hardly anyone would say so much as: 'Poor fellow.' That rather let him out. He did not have to worry much over the grief that his death would cause.

For the matter of that, in a day or two he could cable to his father and the rest to say that the news of his suicide was . . . say, premature. He was by no means out of the wood.

The fat letter was still in his hand. In fainting he must have gripped it as Hugh Monckton had gripped his passport. It was another trait that united them. And French people would never take a letter from anyone's hand. They regarded letters with the superstition that savage tribes attach to objects under a tabu. A concierge who gave to a husband a letter addressed to his wife might be sent to prison.

In lifting the letter to within the range of his sight he was aware that his chest and upper arms smarted considerably. On his arm near the shoulder where the doctor had slit his shirt were half a dozen brown rings. Within them the skin was as dark brown-purple as if he had been a negro. His chest would be in the same condition.

They had been cupping him. That is another amiable mania of the French. They will cup you on every occasion for which the English will prescribe a nice, hot cup of tea. Queer people, Europeans!

From the heavy relief and dark colour of the rings Henry Martin knew that they had called in a professional . . . probably a domineering old woman in black who had pulled him about as if he had been a mattress she was turning on a bed. . . . It was queer to think that what he had dreaded happening to his dead body should have happened to him alive. . . . It was perhaps now happening to Hugh Monckton.

That thought was so disagreeable to him that he switched on the light above the bed and tore open the envelope of the fat letter. To escape from the thought of Hugh Monckton's body which had become his own!

CHAPTER III

THE first thing to come out of the envelope were eight
pinkish mauve notes. They were pinned together to a
slip of paper that bore a scrawl: 'For Mademoiselle
Virginie, next door. Beg her to accept as souvenir – at
one thousand francs per day – of our being neighbours.
Tell her can take from the dead what would be inaccept-
able from living.'

The sentiment seemed sympathetic to Henry Martin.
He himself had thought of nothing as sympathetic with
which to mark his departure. He had left twenty francs
on the mantelpiece at Carqueiranne for Mademoiselle
Simone the tuberculous chambermaid. Twenty francs
to him had been more than eight thousand to Hugh
Monckton. But he had not devoted an ingenious and
kindly thought to that lady. It was good to be able to
devote ingenious and kindly thoughts to others at the
moment of your own supreme trial. . . . Still, he could
say for himself that he had thought of leaving his room
very tidy. To save trouble for Mademoiselle Simone.

It was queer. Everything attaching to Hugh Monckton
resembled all his own attributes . . . but on a grander
scale. Eight thousand francs to twenty. The battle of
the Marne and a sabre cut to a canning factory in the
Cevennes and some water colours!

Well, now that he was Hugh Monckton for a day or
two perhaps he would do things on an equally grand
scale. . . .

The sobbing had begun again. He wished it would

225

not. What was the good of being Hugh Monckton if you could not have silence in the night? . . . It went on; became stifled: burst out again.

It interfered very much with his comprehension of Hugh Monckton's codicil. That he read first because it was the shorter document. The letter attached to it appeared immensely long. Seven pages of solid handwriting.

The codicil was fairly succinct. It gave and bequeathed to Henry Martin Aluin Smith all his property personal or otherwise that, at the moment of his decease found itself in room sixteen of the Hôtel des Négociants. In trust for the following institutions. . . .

The institutions were the British Museum, the National Gallery and South Kensington Museums. The distribution of such property was to be at the sole discretion of Henry Martin, but the testator desired that everything that South Kensington would accept should go to them and should be exhibited in one collection as the Gloria Sorenson bequest. . . .

That seemed rather complicated. Henry Martin's head was swimming a great deal. The sobbing had ceased for the moment. The suspense of waiting for it to commence was almost as distracting.

Henry Martin was fairly acquainted with the purposes of the British Museum and the National Gallery. But South Kensington seemed to him to be more amorphous. As far as he could remember it exhibited everything imaginable from rudimentary locomotives to pictures by Titian and stuffed owls. . . . There would no doubt be some way round. . . .

The joke of it was that he was actually a pauper and would be dealing in millions. . . . The manuscript from Mount Athos alone must be worth a King's ransom.

And he dimly remembered that Hugh Monckton had spoken of some crown jewels. . . . Something of the sort.

And then. . . . By Jove, he wasn't a pauper. Hugh Monckton appointed him his sole executor and residuary legatee. With absolute power to dispose as he chose or to retain possession absolutely of such works of art, *incunabulae* . . . What did that mean? . . . as those institutions should refuse to accept. . . . And also with regard to the sum of francs fifty thousand (50,000 francs) in French notes of one thousand francs. . . . Nos. . . . So and so to So and so. . . . There was no following the figures and letters. . . . The notes were in the flap of the grip. . . .

Besides, the sobbing had begun again. . . .

He was then assured. . . . Fifty thousand francs was two thousand dollars. . . . He could live . . . luxuriously. . . . As if leaning back on the cushions of an automobile. . . . He put the codicil down on the bed beside him.

He could accept the fifty thousand francs. Any man of honour could. He was to undertake an office of considerable trust. One that for him at least would be laborious. . . . Then. . . .

It was a reprieve. . . . But the queer thing was. . . .

Destiny, sure, was one up on Henry Martin. . . . To the tune of sobs. . . . That was perhaps what you called a *memento mori*. . . . . The Egyptians used to have a mummy case at their feasts. To remind them that one day they would die! The Romans called that a *memento mori*. . . . So the sobbing might have been invented by Destiny to remind him that he would come to the end of the two thousand dollars.

It was perhaps not real sobbing . . . a noise in his bandaged ears.

One two three four five sobs. And a long, high moan.
. . . One two three four five six seven eight nine. . . .
Why in hell didn't she moan? It was a woman sobbing.
*Memento mori.* . . . *Memento homo quia.* . . . What?
*Mortalises.* . . . Thou art mortal and money flows through
your fingers like quicksilver.

There was perhaps even an Egyptian Book of the
Dead amongst those packing cases. There might be anything. He could not remember. He had not attended.
Hugh Monckton seemed to have gotten together all the
rare things of the world. To attend on his voyage to
the Isles of the Blest. With Wanda Sorenson on the
yacht called *Le Secret* . . . he imagined them reclining
on cushions in the soft brightness of the tropics. . . .
Beneath the Winged Victory. And Wanda Sorenson
playing with unset jewels in her lap. Picking up a handful
and letting them trickle through her fingers. . . .

However, she would probably not want to do that.
She would be reading a second folio Shakespeare. Besides,
the gods would not let you know Paradise.

What a lot of people meddled with you. Destiny,
the gods, St. Roch. . . .

He had an extraordinary sense of Hugh Monckton.
He was standing astride his leather case. Smiling: a
high-featured melancholy smile. Like an actor playing
Hamlet astride Ophelia's grave. He was holding a skull.
No, it was a leather case containing a hundred grand.
He was just about to say:

'Here, old bean. . . .'

Instead of:

'I did love thee once, Ophelia.'

But it was Ophelia who had got him. Hugh Monckton
ought to be floating down a brook holding poppies or
whatever it was. . . . But he was otherwise engaged!

The room had been lighter last night. Or the light had been redder and had fallen on Hugh Monckton from above so that his face had been more illuminated. . . . But it was a tangle. Hugh Monckton could not play Ophelia. It was Wanda. . . . No, Gloria who was Ophelia. She was Danish. Or something Scandinavian? So had Wanda been. . . .

What was Wanda now? It was twelve . . . no, thirteen years since he had seen her. He had not seen her the last time he might have because that woman had had the grippe. . . . He had not thought of her for a long time. . . .

Gallia Considine. . . . A pretty name. A born New Yorker. . . . Welsh-Irish-French. He had known her before he had known Alice. Sitting about in the Ritz bar when Paris had been full of American troops and their women. He knew very little about her. Tall and dark and silent. . . . He had apparently always been attracted to silent women. Or to very talkative ones!

When Alice had as it were gotten into his bed he had regretted Gallia Considine. He had had a sudden urge toward her the first moment he had seen her. She had been leaning back in a lounge chair talking to a waiter who had been standing behind her shoulder with a tray of cocktails.

She had wanted to know how to get to Fontainebleau. Henry Martin had taken her there and they had spent an enjoyable quiet day. Both liking the same things. Pictures of royalty and period furniture. She had seemed to like him. But they hadn't seen much of each other alone. They met at the bar most afternoons. And then Alice. . . .

They had met afterwards when Alice had gone to

229

Springfield to see about her inheritance from her mother. And they had each revealed that they regretted the other. . . . They had seemed to have very similar minds. . . . Queer! Queer!

Queer, these sudden attractions. . . . He had had one or two in his life. . . . And two last night, by Jove. . . . He was getting to say 'By Jove.' Like Hugh Monckton.

Then, by Jove again, he had two thousand dollars. He would be damned if he let anything come between him and the dark girl as long as they lasted. . . .

The silver fish had been a valid omen. A fish, according to psychiatrists, had a sexual significance. . . . Well, the dark girl was obviously not unsexed. . . . No: no one should come between him and her. On his side of the bed at least. He was through with this damn Hamlet mood!

The silver fish. . . . He had taken it to mean the leather case with the twenty white banknotes that Hugh Monckton had been chucking about just now. . . . No, that had been last night. But he could not get out of his head that Hugh Monckton was in the room. It seemed to smell of his peculiar language.

But the silver fish. . . . There was nothing about the twenty thousand pounds in the codicil. He was aware that he had skimmed it through to see that. No doubt technically that might come to him as residuary legatee. But you could not take money like that. Not such a large sum. Even if Hugh Monckton had had as strong an urge towards him as he towards Hugh Monckton. . . . Still, the twenty thousand pounds.

He picked up the long letter from the bedspread beside him. It might give some information. . . .

The sobbing was beginning again.

'You may think this damn extraordinary.' . . . 'Uncommon spunky three-quarter back. . . Remarked you in O.R. . . .' O.R. meant Orderly Room. He was running through the large, sprawling writing. It in no way resembled his own though their signatures were singularly alike. But men who dash at the body of their writing are often careful about their signatures.

He gathered Hugh Monckton began by explaining why he had placed such singular trust in him. . . . Apparently he had been more observed in the British regiment than he had known. . . . And particularly as being trustworthy with returns. That had given Hugh Monckton the idea of entrusting the dispersal of his relics to Henry Martin. He had been thinking of looking for a man. He had even had the idea of giving the job to M. Lamoricière. But it would have taken two or three days to have explained the matter fully to him. And Hugh Monckton was in a hurry. He said that Henry Martin could not know what his sufferings were. His mere physical sufferings.

So Henry Martin had appeared to him as a godsend – a man he knew to be trustworthy. Exceedingly cultivated! With an immense knowledge of the world. And wealthy. . . . Then it was not the mad thing it looked. The only doubtful feature was whether he would take the job. He might find it a bore. If he did he trusted that he would place the whole thing in the hands of M. Lamoricière. And pay him handsomely out of the twenty thousand pounds. Hugh Monckton only hoped that the French Government would not get too much out of it in the way of Death Duties. . . .

It was difficult for Henry Martin to keep all these details in mind. The sobbing had continued; he had pulled one of his bandages back from over his ear. The sound came from the next room. The one from which the girl had last night emerged.

The phraseology of Hugh Monckton's letter was not as insular as his language last night. It was, nevertheless, extraordinarily redolent of his personality. It seemed to fill the whole, dim room. And Henry Martin was continually looking up from the letter. As if to see whether Hugh Monckton was not standing over his grip with the full light on his face. . . . And suffering.

And wanting what with regard to that girl? . . .

She was supposed to have slept with him. He gathered that from what the doctor and Lamoricière had let drop. But he didn't suppose that she had. As much from her passionate gesture when last night she had thrown the money back into the room as because Hugh Monckton had been passionately in love with Gloria Sorenson. If the girl had slept with him she would no doubt have accepted the money as her due. The passion in her gesture probably came from the fact that she considered herself disdained. And after all Hugh Monckton must have had so many little *poules* at his disposal that he could have done very well without her.

Then if the lady were sobbing with financial embarrassment he supposed that Hugh Monckton would have wanted him to knock at least on her door and tell her that the money was still at her disposal. She could now very well accept it. . . . You can take from the dead what you cannot from the living. . . .

But he wanted to discover if there was any mention of the twenty thousand pounds in the letter. The night before Hugh Monckton had talked of letting him have that money to speculate with. At the time the idea had seemed absurd. Or as if there were some trap in it. There had been something about the A shares of the Monckton Company. They were to declare a dividend of a hundred per cent.

It was queer. It was the dear things that were affected by the crisis. You noticed in Paris that the expensive shops in the rue de Rivoli had their windows full of placards announcing tremendous reductions in the price of expensive luxuries. But people clung to some luxuries. So whilst necessaries and costly things fell in price and still more in consumption, things like the Monckton Car and Pisto-Brittle even increased their sales.

He came, in one paragraph, on something about a widow, a Mrs. Taylor, about whom Hugh Monckton said he was going to talk in a moment or two. He wanted her provided for. . . . Henry Martin remembered vaguely that he had actually talked about some widow of a workman in the Monckton Car Factory. . . .

Henry Martin's heart gave a leap. . . . There was 'twenty thousand pounds' looking up at him from the sheet of paper. . . . But the passage only said that if Henry Martin would not accept the distribution of the trust the expenses of forwarding and M. Lamoricière's costs were to be paid out of that sum. . . .

The idea of lending Henry Martin the money to speculate with had then only been an afterthought. . . . That perhaps let him out.

It was nevertheless an enigma. . . . He was in possession of a bit of secret information. By it he ought easily to make a small fortune. But unless he took the loan of that money he would not be able to make anything out of it. And there was not a great deal of time to be lost. He thought he had till Thursday. It was now Sunday.

That Hugh Monckton wanted him to take it he knew.

One of his most vivid discomfitures was the thought of that fellow standing beside his car and saying:

'You hadn't ought to have done it, Old Bean.'

He had said that he was going to tune up his car and, from somewhere under the footboard he had dragged out some spanners and a pair of enormous gloves. And then he had stood, wavering a little, silhouetted against the glare of his headlights. They illuminated half the little port with the boats sleeping and the front of the Douane, the great white house, sleeping too. He looked extraordinarily gauntletted. And solitary.

That had been the last time Henry Martin had seen him. Outside the inn at Carqueiranne, before he had gone up to his room. Last night. . . . Was it last night or the night before last? It was now a quarter to two by Hugh Monckton's watch. Was 'last night' the time up to last midnight – two hours ago? Or was it the night before the day before? . . . It didn't matter. It must have been exactly twenty-four hours since he had taken leave for good of that poor fellow. His newest friend. . . . One of his oldest, too. There could not be many men he had known for sixteen years and who had kept him himself in mind for as long. . . . As being trustworthy enough to handle million's worth of knick-knacks!

Gauntletted! So as not to soil his hands!

It was queer to think that a man who was just going to commit suicide by disfiguring, in the most awful fashion, his features should care about whether his hands were dirty. But people who were about to commit suicide did the oddest things. And that poor, dear fellow. . . . He must have been nearly demented. . . . Intense physical pain – and passionate longing that was no good!

He felt himself luxuriate in the strength of his own life. He was almost without pain as long as he kept still. The bed was extraordinarily comfortable. It was probably Hugh Monckton's own property. That is, his, Henry Martin's. . . .

He said:

'Damn it, what a swine I am!'

But, in the end, a living dog *is* worth a dead lion. . . . And he, Henry Martin was wearing the lion's hide. . . .

What had happened to the other fellow? Was he still lying face downwards with the light of the great stars filtering through the pine tops. At least he would not be cold. The night was still and warm. . . . The great stars of last night and of for ever! Please God, Hugh Monckton was sailing amongst their tides. And not worrying too much. At any rate, he, Henry Martin, would see that his Gloria had her name handed down by that bequest. Of her at least it could be said:

*Saltavit et placuit.*

And maybe Hugh Monckton's lavishness would secure for her a measure of immortality. So they need not say: *Mortua est.* . . . Alms for oblivion they called it.

The phrase came to him:

'Nothing is here for tears. . . .'

Perhaps there wasn't.

The sobbing had begun again. He was going to do his best to alleviate that girl's sorrow. He seemed to have adopted Hugh Monckton's individuality with some thoroughness. Then he must do what Hugh Monckton would have done. Hugh Monckton must have made her acquaintance in that selfsame way. He had heard her sobbing through the night. . . . For the governor of French Cochin something or other. A Hell of an attractive fellow that governor must have been to exact such steadfast lachrymosity! But now he could go to her and tell her that she could quite appropriately accept that sum of money because it was the bequest of a dead man.

He had one leg out of the bed. The movement, oddly, hurt his jaw more than a little. He nevertheless persisted, moving the other under the sheets. He became motionless.

He could not tell the girl the money was from a dead man. He, the dead man would be alive before her. Here was a dilemma.

His impulse to do something for that girl was, all the same, very strong. He got as far as the middle of the room, level with Hugh Monckton's harlequinade grip.

Damn it, he must give up thinking of it as Hugh Monckton's grip. It was his own grip! These things were all his! Except the antiquities!

'*My* grip! *My* watch! *My* bed!' Hugh Monckton would have said: 'Mäi kit-bag!'

Damn it, too, if the girl on the other side of the door had slept with Hugh Monckton she might well be a danger. She would presumably know him better than even Monsieur Lamoricière or the hotel people. He circumnavigated the baggage. His legs were unsteady and his head and the muscles of his neck ached. He held his bandaged face close to the glass. He was strikingly like that poor fellow! He tried frowning. The bandages over his brows remained unmoved and his expression was not changed. He thought if he displaced his 'h's' he might seem more English. He said:

'Some people as hall the luck, ol' bean!'

But practically no voice came. The crack on the jaw might account for that. And the bandages. They had the bluish tinge attributed to the dress of ghosts. . . . Decidedly it would be better not to come personally in contact with that girl. He could send her the money by Lamoricière who could no doubt be persuasive enough. And he would allege himself to be too ill to see her.

Of course Hugh Monckton did not misplace his 'h's.'
And the 'ah' sound in his 'i's' had been hardly noticeable.

Destiny must have watched over that affair with singular minuteness. Henry Martin imagined that he had no particular accent. One cannot tell. But no one had ever mimicked him as they would have if his speech had been at all outrageous. On the other hand in French he had no doubt a strong American accent just as Hugh Monckton had a strong English one. The difference was very marked. Apparently to the French the English accent was what they called '*zézayant*' . . . a little childish and appealing. The American on the other hand they considered harsh and overbearing. The boat had been then a good friend to him. He had at first imagined that those two strokes of her yard had been a sign of enmity. Now he saw that the one in the temple supplied him with a necessary scar. That on the jaw gave him an excuse for speaking for quite a time with a voice that was no voice at all. When his natural voice returned his French friends would accept the change as being a product of the accident. As for his English friends Henry Martin would have to avoid them. Destiny had begun its job very thoroughly: it was unlikely that that august Force would now spoil the ship for want of a ha'porth of tar! But it would be better to avoid the girl next door. Her ululations had an ominous sound: like a dog baying the moon.

> A dog that howls at his master's gate
> Foretells the ruin of the state

Something like that! But he was tired for the moment of Destiny. He desired to try a little freewill. As if he proposed to take the bit between his teeth.

There came from the next room a crash: a thud: half

a dozen more crashes and the tinkling of broken glass sliding down. Then moans. Gradually becoming stifled. Lasting a long time. Then silence. . . .

You can of course produce a devil of a row in the middle of the night. With comparatively few effects. . . . But when you have knocked things over and smashed, say a wash-basin and a tooth glass you generally start picking them up. Then they clink. . . .

He found that he was hammering on the communicating door. . . . She couldn't have cut her throat because of the Governor of Cochin-Saigon. She ought to have gotten over that by now. . . .

He was pressing the button of the bell by the door. . . . The door giving on to the passage. He was in the passage, ringing at the same time the bell and shouting. The bell resounded from dark distances: his shouting was inaudible. . . . There was a horrible smell. . . . He was not too steady on his legs. But they would serve.

The smell in the girl's room was atrocious. He dragged her by the hand along the floor into his own room. Hugh Monckton's. It *had* been a basin that had smashed. No doubt as she staggered. She was lying among parti-coloured fragments. A basin and a ewer! She must have grabbed them as she fell. . . . Parti-coloured herself too. In a Cochin-Chinese bathrobe. . . . Batik they called the colouring. She was flattened into his floor in a way only the dead have. And not all of them. Hugh Monckton had not looked flattened. Rather in what you call high relief.

She wasn't breathing. She was like a little mound of stuffs.

He drew deep breaths. He thanked God for his large lungs and the cool air that came into them, yet the night was hot. He had held his nose with his left hand, dragging her with his right. He could not have lifted her. She had poisoned herself by turning on a gas jet. . . . She must have held her head over it. And then fallen against the wash things.

He had closed the door between the two rooms. That ought to have settled it. Of course it hadn't. The slightest spark and half the house would be blown to pieces. His head ached and all his limbs. It hadn't been without damage that he had rolled down that slope. He wetted a towel in his ewer and covered his nose and mouth. It was a weary business.

He was back in his room, the gas-tap was turned off. He had not drawn a single breath. But his head swam. He sat down on the horsehair sofa. He wondered if, having changed identity with Hugh Monckton, he had inherited his physical disadvantages. Supposing it was to be all pain and neither wine nor women! That would be . . . oh, poetic vengeance.

He had been sitting with his elbows on his knees and his hands over his eyes and bandages. He might have been sitting there a long time. He might have been asleep. As he had been that morning when the sun had touched the fingers of the stone-pine branch.

The girl's arm which had been over her breast was stretched out. She lay in the form of a cross.

An impulsion of intense weariness went over him. He would have to set about reviving her. Of course she was not dead. It was wrong to imagine that every one in that countryside had the knack of successful suicide. But apparently those who did it for the sake of love were more persistent than those who were beggared.

You revive, don't you, those who are suffering from gas poisoning by the same thing you do for the nearly drowned? To expel the gas from the lungs! He didn't believe he could do it. . . .

The bell rang in distant darknesses. In the corridor he hammered on several doors. From behind one came a somnolent man's answer, but no result. . . .

He was on his knees at the girl's head. He worked her arms up and down. The small wrists were quite warm. The batik gown, with the up and down motion divided itself gradually. Her form became plain. And rather agreeable. The Indo-Something Governor must have been a connoisseur in night-gowns. . . . No thinner fabric could have been imagined. . . .

He worked unceasingly. It seemed unceasing! All the sinews of the back of his neck ached, going down into his shoulders. . . .

Seen from above her unconscious features were very regular. Of course you cannot tell what a woman is like till you've seen her eyes. . . . Her figure was extremely symmetrical. The small feet stood up; bare. Their nails were reddened. Her hair exhaled an agreeable, oriental odour. . . . She was no doubt a completely uninteresting *poule* but the Governor would have seen that she had a good figure. . . . Governors can be trusted to see to that. And agreeable, preferably regular, features!

It was no doubt because of his lech for the dark girl that he found no physical attraction towards this one. Or because of his physical exhaustion. Or because he was annoyed with her for causing him the extra fatigue. Or because she was upside down to his eyes.

But there were white limbs just sheathed and shining. . . . One ought to feel attraction. Or at least curiosity. Physical attraction was mostly curiosity of an exploring kind. . . . There must then be something wrong with him. Perhaps it was poetic vengeance – no, Justice! – once more. Perhaps like Hugh Monckton he was never again to know what is called love of woman. . . . What a hope! As Hugh Monckton said. He himself wasn't mad about women. But that would be a dumb outlook. . . . Yet he had been hit over the head just as Hugh Monckton had been. He didn't know how the yard of a boat compared with a German sabre.

'. . . Not as deep as a well or as wide as a church door. But 'twill serve.'

Why did he have to think of gloomy quotations?

A single large drop of moisture was on the girl's forehead. It must be his own sweat. He was panting by now. That was perhaps a direction. Try water. When he rose he reeled right over to one of the packing cases. The harlequin grip was at his feet. . . . It was perhaps a sign that brandy was indicated.

He opened it. Just like that! . . . Without having to pause to think he had pressed a stud. The jaws of that monstrosity went apart with a faint sumph like a sigh. It had acknowledged its master's hand. . . .

He was drinking a minute sip of the *fine de la République*. . . . Hugh Monckton had recommended him to finish it with his girl. . . .

Damnation. Was it possible that he was never to drink again? And that he was to be impotent? . . . Or afraid to risk it for the fear of death? Because of the crack on his skull.

He knelt on one knee beside the girl. He placed the mouth of the square case bottle to her lips. . . . Any other alcohol would have done as well. He elevated grudgingly the end of the bottle. She certainly swallowed.

He lifted up her head with his arm underneath her

dark hair. He pressed his lips on hers. . . . A man must want to explore.

Her arms of course were round his neck. They would be. Her eyes remained closed but she said distinctly:

'C'est toi!' and, 'Ah que je suis contente!'

She must be taking him for the Indo-Something Governor.

He said:

'Do you think you could stand?' The floor must be very hard.

She was of course going to sleep in his bed. There was no end to this nuisance. But perhaps, then, he might feel at least some physical attraction.

She said:

Je croyais que tu t'étais suicidé . . . à cause de l'autre.'

She thought he had suicided. Because of the other. . . . Then she must be taking him for Hugh Monckton. Her eyes remained closed: her head hung back over his arm. They must have made a romantic picture. He kneeling. Her voice seemed to come from remote distances of her inner consciousness. It said:

'Pourquoi as tu fermé ta porte à clé? . . . Alors je me suis décidée à me tuer. . . . Je te croyais mort derrière le cloi. . . .'

You would have said that she was suffering from the effects of a narcotic. She could not finish the word which was no doubt 'cloison'. . . . She thought Hugh Monckton had locked the door against her. Then she had decided to kill herself. . . .

It began at least well. She had taken him for that fellow. . . . There was no knowing what their relationship had been. But so far he, Henry Martin, had made a satisfactory substitute. After all, why shouldn't he?

The clothing had fallen right off her shoulder. Her

skin was brown. Over the armpit it was quite dark. In creases. It was at least a change from the skin of Alice which was *mat* white. And wearisomely unattractive. Some blood showed at least under this skin. . . . Why did he have to think of Alice?

If he had opened the window in her room he could have taken her back. She was trying to help him to help her to rise. But listlessly. . . . But he had not opened the window. . . .

Her eyes opened for a moment. She was on her feet holding her hand to her hair as if to be sure that it was tidy. Her eyes were blue-grey. They closed ineffably. She said:

'Pardon que je t'ai tutoyé. . . . Je vous aime tant.'

She was asking for forgiveness for having said 'thou' to him. As you do to children or your lover. Then she had said: 'I love *you* so much.' It proved she had a tidy mind to think of that at that moment. . . . Then Hugh Monckton had only been kind to her. As he would have been to any stray.

He was getting his breath to make the formidable journey to the bed. He supposed it did not matter to these girls where they slept. She exclaimed:

'Vous . . . si fort . . . si courageux . . . si généreux. . . .'

He was going to have some job to live up to that fellow. Well, he would tackle it. He would be strong: courageous: generous! Why not? He owed it to Hugh Monckton.

She sat crumpled together on the side of the bed and took off her batik covering. There was nothing to her. She was smaller than Alice. She had an oval face and the slightest moustache. Like any other girl of that country where they descend from the Phoenicians or God knew what race. She said drowsily:

243

'Vous savez je vous ai jeté l'argent dans le visage parce que vous m'aviez ignorée . . . mais main . . .' and collapsed sideways on the pillow. . . .

*That* difficulty had solved itself. Those eight thousand francs were disposed of. She had thrown them at Hugh Monckton the other evening because till then he had ignored her . . . Her charms presumably. But now apparently she could take it.

CHAPTER IV

THE dark girl was sitting in a round-backed arm-chair just on the other side of the night table. She was reading the *New York Herald*. On his shoulder Henry Martin felt the breath of the ex-lady of the governor of Cochin-Something. It was exceedingly still in the room. The eight thousand francs lay on the night table. The dark girl was wearing his ring on her wedding finger.

She had broad shoulders, high breasts. A green jewel showed on the lace insertion of her black dress. It went up and down as she breathed. The clock ticked.

Her dark eyebrows and her high colour expressed a capability of anger. Of passion. When she touched the hair just above her ear with her ring hand he felt extraordinary pleasure.

She looked at him and said:

'Is there no end to human madness? Surely the gods intend the destruction of humanity. . . .' She added. 'But why should they destroy us who are sane?' She tapped the newspaper as if some paragraph in it had aroused her animosity. She looked extraordinarily sane. He almost regretted that she had spoken.

He said: 'You read English?'

She exclaimed:

'You need not whisper. The opiate I gave *la petite* should keep her doped for an hour or two yet.'

He had indeed whispered: he did not know whether it was because his jaw had been fractured or because the injury had affected the muscles of his throat. She lowered her newspaper and crossed her legs.

'La petite tried to suicide?' she asked. 'She said that she would. So I gave her that heavy opiate. Under the pretext that it would drown any pain.'

That was evidently what had happened. He might have gathered from the girl's voluptuous drooping, that she had been doped, not poisoned by gas which was probably disagreeable. She had looked like an enraptured flower.

'It is amusing,' the dark girl said, 'all these failures to suicide. . . . And indeed suicides! For that other *pauvre* has succeeded. And a man at la Cressonade has killed himself and his mistress and three children.'

She added, in English:

'It was good dope that. My boy friend gave it to me. In case I should be sleepless in the cells.' And then in French: 'But I supported all that with equanimity.'

Henry Martin whispered:

'Another has suicided?'

'Encore un Smeez,' she answered. 'Another Smith. A New Yorker. I saw you with him, night before last. I too am a New Yorker. I shall attend his obsequies. He was down and out.'

She counted on her fingers:

'Two Smiths. Mademoiselle Becquerel. The man at la Cressonade. He was called Amontillado or something like that. From Genoa. And four he killed.'

Henry Martin said:

'Becquerel?'

She answered:

'The participatrix of Monsieur's couch is Mademoiselle Jeanne Becquerel.'

Henry Martin managed to get out: 'Virginie!' rather louder. In alarm! Hugh Monckton's note had said: 'Virginie.' The eight thousand francs were to be given to Miss Virginie. If he had given them to a Miss Jeanne he would have to make it up himself.

The girl said indifferently:

'Jeanne – Virginie. Virginie – Jeanne. It is all one. That nasty fellow called her Virginie so I call her Jeanne ever since though I called her Virginie before. . . .' She added in English. 'He was the sort of quarter-tipper that would call her Virginie. I bet he never tipped a cloak-room girl more than a quarter in a speakeasy.'

Henry Martin whispered:

'He at least was not a New Yorker!' He imagined she was talking of the ex-Governor.

'No, sir! Il est un sale Moco . . . et un sale monsieur. . . .' A Moco was a local inhabitant. 'But if Jeanne's mother had not sufficient sense to see that she had a reasonable settlement when she became his *maîtresse en titre* I don't see why he should make up the deficiency. . . .'

He asked:

'She was very hard up?'

'She was in the cart,' the girl answered. 'Dans la misère même. And she had not the spirit to go out and do the requisite. She could no doubt have got a speculative lawyer to make that sorry fellow cough up. It was I who handed her all her food through the door. Except her *petit déjeuner* which is provided by the hotel. And that comes to an end to-morrow.'

She added.

'There were days when she would not open to me, myself. . . . The truth was, I imagine that she loved that monsieur! She would not hock the jewels he had given her.' She added again. . . . 'We are like that, we others. . . . A ring, a necklace, becomes sacred. More fools we.'

A waiter in his shirt sleeves with a yellow-striped waistcoat and a face like that of a stupid racoon came in with two round trays on his left arm.

The girl said:

'You can put Mademoiselle's coffee on the divan. She will not wake yet. I will heat it over the gas when she does.'

The waiter put the tray on the night table, having first taken up the notes. He laid them on the *croissants*. He said they had made Monsieur some gruel in case his jaws would not work. If he did not eat the *croissants* they would be allowed for in the account.

He took up his station behind the curving mahogany foot of the bed and looked without interest at the face of the girl on Henry Martin's shoulder. He had a short lock of darkish hair that fell over in front of his eyes. He said nonchalantly that an emissary of the *commissaire de police* was waiting to know when it would be convenient for monsieur to receive him.

The personality of the dark girl had so overwhelmed Henry Martin that he had not begun to put two and two together. He had not got over the improbability of the dark girl's being a New Yorker. His brain was probably not working very fast because of the opiate he had had the night before. . . . But he feared the French police.

The waiter said:

'It is because you were the last man, probably, to see that poor mad man alive. He sprang out of a boat in the storm and tried to murder Marius Guiol and Marius of the Reserve. He threatened them with a revolver. Then he shot himself under their eyes. There was a third man too.'

The dark girl said:

'They say he demanded their money. But no one believes it. They are a couple of fat Mariuses.'

She said in English:

'You best see the Commissaire at once. Then they will close the *enquête* very quickly. There are seventeen *enquêtes* to-day. On seventeen poor drowned ones of the cyclone. . . . If you put it off. . . . Well, the police like to make *ennuis* for millionaires. It pleases the democracy. And they will have more leisure later on. See him at once.'

The waiter said:

'It appears that monsieur was the last man to see him alive. He was the monsieur that monsieur brought in with him the night before last. I have recognized the body. There is no mistaking it, though the face is much injured.'

Henry Martin felt as if at every minute he was being handed banknotes. This was a product of crowd madness. . . . He imagined that the two Mariuses even believed their story. They might even have *seen* a revolver when he had sprung out of the boat. One of them would have invented that fire-arm. The other would have contagiously believed it. Then he would have communicated the contagion to the first and the two of them would have infected the third. . . . They would say they had run up the path after him. He had seen them creep. They were the fat Mariuses of the Marseilles district. Incredible boasters and liars. To the extent that they were capable of believing themselves. With truthful asseverations. . . . So much the better. . . .

What worried him was the dark girl. She became more desirable with every flash of her teeth. They flashed when she smiled and her lips, drawing up, showed them when she spoke viciously. She had only smiled once. She was more given to denunciations. . . . He wanted to live with a woman who denounced people. It would be like a tonic. A woman like a tonic was what he needed. . . .

He had two thousand dollars. Certain. Would that keep them for. . . . Six months? Two? One? It would depend on what her scale of extravagance was. . . . One month might not be enough to exhaust his . . . his curiosity as to her. Perhaps not two. Perhaps not six. . . . Even eighteen months might not be sufficient. Usually a skill at denunciations grew tiring after eighteen months or less. . . .

But how was he to provide for eighteen months. . . . There were the twenty thousand pound notes. He had been thinking about whether he could make use of them. He imagined he had thought that matter out but he could not remember what he had decided.

Half a policeman was in the room. He wore a great cloak in spite of the stifling weather. He had a pink and white face like those of the waxen dummies in the cheaper tailors on Main Street. He said nothing. He held a slip of paper.

The dark girl said:

'Monsieur will see Coco at once.'

She said to Henry Martin:

'They call that guy Coco. . . . No not this guy. . . . The Commissaire.'

The policeman removed his cap and with stiff swaying came to lean over the foot of the bed alongside the waiter. He stared down with expressionless and glassy eyes at the face of the girl on Henry Martin's shoulder. It irritated Henry Martin that he could not see her face. He would have disturbed her if he moved.

The policeman cleared his throat. He must have been very husky indeed before. It occurred to Henry Martin that the ex-mistress of the ex-Governor – particularly if he was a local man! – must be more of an object of curiosity to these people than himself. . . . Than Hugh Monckton that was to say. He felt a pang of jealousy. If you have exchanged identities with one of the great rich in the world you ought to excite curiosity!

The policeman said to the waiter:

'Apparently she is not for the Red Light quarter this journey.'

The dark girl said:

'Sale flic,' and put out the end of her tongue at the policeman.

Henry Martin thought that if you said 'Sale flic,' to a French policeman he immediately clubbed you. This policeman merely laughed, leaning back and catching his thumbs in his belt.

The girl beside Henry Martin suddenly sat up. She wiped the sleep from both eyes and, in the same gesture, leaning across his chest, she took the sheaf of notes from the bedside tray and waved them towards the dark girl.

'These are mine,' she said, 'Eudoxie, do you see? I have earned these!' She lay down again and went to sleep.

It appeared that the dark girl's name was Eudoxie . . . Eudoxia! It seemed to be a name for rather majestic women. . . .

The policeman was leaning back on his heels and, with his face towards the ceiling was roaring with laughter.

'I will tell you,' he exclaimed, 'where for fifteen. . . .'

The dark girl might have moments when she was majestic. At the moment she was not being so. She had caught a pair of scissors from the table beside her and held them as if they had been a dagger.

'Dare to say it!' she exclaimed, 'and you shall see your eyes lying on this table top.' She threw the scissors down. 'Besides,' she said, 'I shall report you to Coco. You are a disgrace to my family.'

She could certainly appear disdainful.

The policeman and the waiter were again regarding the girl beside Henry Martin with a serious attention that might never have been interrupted.

'After all,' the waiter said, 'one does not see every day one who in a single night can earn francs by the thousand!'

The policeman said:

'In a single night!' with an awestruck expression. 'I thought it was in eight.'

'I tell you, in one,' the waiter said. 'Should I not know? I, Marius Paline!'

M. Lamoricière was tranquilly in the room. He seemed to be more in black than ever. He had brought the aged *patronne* with him. Or perhaps the *patronne* had introduced him.

He removed his black glasses, looked at Mademoiselle Jeanne Becquerel as if with satisfaction and said:

'I hope you had a good night. . . . I took the liberty of locking the communication door as there were so many valuable objects lying about.'

'That was thoughtful,' Henry Martin said. As soon as they saw his lips move everyone in the room became as still as a mouse. 'But it was quite unnecessary.'

He intended that to give pleasure to the dark girl.

The *patronne* whose small black person was hidden from Henry Martin by the waiter and the policeman brought out shrilly:

'Indeed it is quite unnecessary to lock doors in this hotel. I accept none but impeccable clients. You, at least, Marius, will say that there has never been a robbery in this hotel.'

She was addressing the policeman, not the waiter, for the policeman turned to face her.

'Not,' he said jovially, 'not since the German poet was robbed by the two women.'

The *patronne* protested more and more shrilly. That gentleman had been a German. And a poet. And he had introduced the two women into the hotel. You cannot refuse a poet. And if he brings women with him. . . .

M. Lamoricière was introducing a very sleek, very tall dark gentleman who had a scarlet button in his nosegay buttonhole and who introduced himself sideways, thrusting his left shoulder forward as if he had the habit of penetrating crowds.

M. Lamoricière said:

'My good friend, M. Eugène Gaudin of the police.'

The dark girl raised her eyebrows and said:

'Bon jour, Coco.' Mademoiselle Jeanne Becquerel sat up in bed beside Henry Martin. She occupied herself with arranging her hair.

M. Lamoricière waved a formal white hand:

'My distinguished friend Monsieur Ash Emmà Smeez!'

The sleek gentleman spoke with such rapidity that Henry Martin had difficulty in following him. M. Lamoricière was also saying that Henry Martin was one of the heroes who saved our dear France. Henry Martin nevertheless gathered that the tall, sleek man desired to see Henry Martin's papers and to know what he knew of the deceased. His heart beat heavily. But he was unconscious of fear. M. Lamoricière picked up the passport that remained on the table where he had dropped it the night before. The police official snatched the passport, read out 'Asch Em Ah Smeez. Correct,' coldly and with immense speed. 'Tiens! The initials are the same as those of the deceased!' He glanced at the inside of the passport: at Henry Martin imperiously. He said: 'Likeness sufficient,' and threw the passport back on the table. 'Passport No. 374,875. Last renewed in London, June 30th, 1930. . . . You last saw the deceased?'

He fixed Henry Martin with his imperious dark eyes. He had been dictating to a little dark fellow who had a note book and was half hidden by the other.

Henry Martin whispered as well as he could for the beating of his heart.

'Last night. . . . No the night before last.'

It was ridiculous of his heart to beat perceptibly. There was no danger. His heart made noises in his dry throat.

He was made to say the deceased had been in the same regiment with himself. Was distinguished for trustworthiness. And valour. Had many decorations. More than himself. Certainly more than himself. . . .

The statements were coming out of him like contrary happenings in a delirium. . . . But they were all true.

The Commissaire said:

'Yet he was American. . . . Well there were some good Americans.'

The dark girl said:

'Be careful what you say, Coco. Je suis New Yorkaise!'

The Commissaire said:

'Well we know it!' With his eyes firmly on Henry Martin. 'Did he beg money of you?' Did he seem outrageous? Were you aware that he was ruined? Did he appear poor? . . .'

Henry Martin said:

'On the contrary.' Far from demanding money he had paid Hugh Monckton's bill. . . .

The dark girl said:

'That is true. I saw it. Monsieur, here, went across the *dancing* to ask him.'

The Commissaire said:

'Trust you to see things, Yu-Yu! . . . Did the deceased appear disturbed? . . .'

Henry Martin said: 'He appeared perfectly calm. He was perfectly well dressed. I understood that he was a very rich man. . . .'

It was confusing. He could not collect whether he was speaking well of Hugh Monckton or of himself. . . . It would be inappropriate to speak well of himself. But that poor fellow. He said urgently:

'Could you not give him a military funeral? He deserved it. He was immensely brave. And suffered terribly. For France.'

The dark girl said:

'He was a splendid fellow. I would rather have had him penniless for a lover than any man here. He appeared calmer than any man here. He came across and spoke to me. About the Antibes youth who danced and gave pleasure. He gave me this ring! To be sure that gave pleasure. And in an hour he was dead.'

'You are always romancing, Yu-Yu,' the Commissaire said.

Henry Martin said:

'Yes, yes . . . he gave her the ring. . . . I saw it.'

She gave him a quick, pleased glance. He forgot what he had to say.

The Commissaire said:

'That closes the *enquête*. . . . That is characteristically American. He gives his ring to a chance woman, lends his last sou to a friend. And suicides. It is convincing. The two fat Mariuses were lying. It is a banal affair. A ruined man suicides. A product of the crisis – *Voilà tout!*'

The little black man snapped his notebook to. The Commissaire-adjoint was edging away.

'A military funeral. . . . Military music, at least.'

Henry Martin's voice was apparently audible to all the room. The Commissaire shrugged his shoulders.

'For that,' he said, 'you should apply to the municipality. And it is not militarist here!' He added: 'Besides funeral processions are not popular with the police. There are too many of them. Every dead grocer has a procession a mile long. Walking. It causes great anxiety to the traffic policemen. They also have to be considered. Their tasks are already sufficiently onerous.'

Henry Martin found himself to be desperately anxious that Hugh Monckton's body should not be treated as if it were his own. He would have been thrown into any kind of ditch. But this was a splendid, fortunate youth. He must not be treated as if he were a down and outer. . . .

'Something must be done about it. Can you not feel that?'

He had a sense of extreme loneliness. Everyone of these faces was blank. As if they could not see why a pauper who had shot himself should need an expensive funeral. At home – whatever could be said against them! – they would understand that a hero had earned a funeral march. Only the dark girl looked at him sympathetically. She had said she was a New Yorker.

He exclaimed:

'I will provide all the expenses. I will conduct the obsequies myself. . . .'

256

The thought of Hugh Monckton – his image, his dark and outraged soul seemed to brood above that appalled and stupid multitude. More people were coming in.

An energetic voice said:

'You will do nothing of the sort while you are my patient.'

It added:

'What is this? . . . The *lever* of the King and Queen? . . . Just because monsieur is a King of finance. . . . Is this the eighteenth century?'

At each of his barking questions an individual left the room. The French may be hail fellow well met with a policeman. Or they sink into the ground before him. According to his mood or the occasion. But before the doctor they all tremble. Always! And he addressed them as if they were mean church robbers of deficient intellect. They were alone with Lamoricière and the two girls. The doctor towered over him as a chef above the joint on which he is about to operate. Beside him sat Mademoiselle Jeanne. She was still doing her hair. She had procured a comb and a hand-mirror. Presumably the dark girl had passed them to her.

The doctor said to the dark girl that he wanted towels. Two towels. And clean!

It was the first time she had stood up. So it was the first time he had seen her on her feet. She was tall. And erect!

The doctor had several nickel instruments. He said:

'It would be better if Madame got up. The hour is presumably sufficiently advanced!' The girl laid her comb and mirror on Henry Martin's chest. The décolletage of her nightgown was almost excessive. It was perhaps as well that it was long. She threw back the bedclothes and stepped over Henry Martin's legs, sliding to the ground. He did not understand why he should feel a proprietary interest in her. The dark girl drew the nightgown down as she slid to the ground.

'La petite is used to the tropics,' she said to M. Lamoricière.

'We are all used to the tropics,' M. Lamoricière said. He was like a perpetual undertaker at a feast but his manner was approving.

The doctor shook his large, white finger at Mademoiselle Becquerel. She was draping her butterfly-robe about her. She made a little grimace at him. She tenderly embraced the dark girl. They whispered. Beside the dark girl the other was mouse-coloured.

Henry Martin supposed that these amenities attended on the lives of European millionaires. But he had anxieties at the back of his skull. Perhaps because he was not to the manner born.

The dark girl said, after a whisper of the other.

'He saved your life then. That was chic. He is a chic personage.'

The other whispered.

'And courageous! And generous! And handsome!' the dark girl repeated aloud for her.

M. Lamoricière said:

'Surely monsieur is all these?'

The doctor said:

'If these ladies would assume the functions of modern nurses instead of that of the chorus of the ancient Greek Theatre! I should have thought M. Lamoricière would have had more sense!'

The dark girl answered:

'It is true we are like a Greek Chorus. Strophe and anti-Strophe. But it should not be disagreeable to you, Monsieur le docteur Grouault!'

The doctor said:

'I did not say it was disagreeable to me. But duty combines ill with pleasure. Put a towel on the pillow to receive the face of Monsieur. Madame will relieve him of the jacket of his pyjamas. He will lay himself on his face. I must examine his back.'

Hugh Monckton's pyjamas were of a vivid dark green silk. On either breast was a Japanese embroidered stork. The silk was very heavy. The dark girl approved of them. But his skin? It was eroded and bruised and no doubt covered with dark cup-marks. . . .

He said to the other:

'Mademoiselle is not very acquainted . . . intimate!'

The doctor said:

'It will do her no harm to see an admirable torso.'

M. Lamoricière said:

'It is true. Monsieur has the figure of a Greek athlete.'

He was stripped to the waist and made to lie with his face in the towel that was on the pillow. He wondered why the doctor wanted the towel on the pillow. But it was restful. On his back the doctor hammered. He pressed to it his ear and his heavy head. He addressed himself obviously to Mademoiselle Becquerel.

'Madame,' he said, 'Monsieur has admirable lungs. His liver is completely sound. . . . What I don't understand. . . .'

He clasped something round Henry Martin's upper arm. There was a noise as of pumping a bicycle and the pressure increased.

It was agreeable lying there and having your physical fitness recounted item by item to the dark girl. The doctor spoke to the other but the dark girl heard. Both girls tittered now and then. Lamoricière said:

'What did I tell you? A Greek athlete. Of the type

that saved the world at Marathon. And two thousand years later, our dear France.' He lowered his voice to say: 'Mes félicitations!' He was no doubt addressing the girl who slept in Henry Martin's bed. . . . He imagined that sympathetic Lamoricière, like half that city, had been concerned over the fate of the ex-mistress of the ex-governor. They all undoubtedly knew that she was shut up in the room, grief-stricken, refusing to emerge, having her meals handed through the crack of the door by the dark girl. No doubt they informed themselves from day to day as to her progress. Some would be of the opinion that she would commit suicide; others that she would die of grief. The less kindly would call it all comedy. . . . Now, because she had passed the night beside Henry Martin, the kindly Lamoricière offered her his felicitations. He imagined her again, *casée*. And with the perfect male animal. . . . Well, she had eight thousand francs. A girl alone can live a long time on eight thousand francs. For long enough to recover herself. And to form new connections. . . .

He wondered vaguely as to the class of such a girl. She was delicate-limbed, dainty in person. She spoke French beautifully. Her voice was precise. He had discovered no trace of coarseness about her. Yet she sat with complete unconcern in a strange man's bed. Under the eyes of quite a crowd and exposed her limbs with as much unconcern as if she had been alone in her own room. That was the product, obviously, of some brand of purity. Or at any rate of innocent fearlessness. And all the others accepted her. Apparently at her own price. He had been towards her in a proprietary position of sorts. He accepted as much responsibility for her as he would have done if, say, he had invited her to dinner at a good restaurant. He had felt very little embarrassment and no anger at all. Yet if Alice exposed herself in the slightest he had always felt deep – as it were fundamental! – anger. And she had had a sort of passion for adopting lascivious attitudes and exposing her legs in company. Whenever she was at all lit. And your real nature came out when you were lit! . . .

The girl at any rate came of a better race, with a better tradition and training. Alice no doubt took after her German forbears. She had a natural coarseness and desire to display that the appropriate male would have suppressed with a club. But she had been born into a society where clubs were no longer used. That must be it.

Yes, this girl was a step upwards. . . .

It annoyed him that again he should be comparing her to Alice. It was hardly fair to her. She also was no doubt careful of money. She had grabbed those eight notes. As Alice would have done if they had been lying about. But she had put them down again. She was a sufficient judge of men to know that they were safely hers. Alice would have thrust them into her bosom. . . . Displaying her bosom to do it!

Indeed this girl had apparently only held them for a moment to display them to the dark girl. In sign of a victory. . . . Over Hugh Monckton's resistance to her charms. No doubt they had discussed the matter for a long time. Perhaps after she had thrown the notes back at Hugh Monckton. She would have told the dark girl about it and Eudoxie would have told her she was a fool not to keep the money. Then she must have boasted that she would earn it. Or die! . . . That was good enough.

She had neither earned it nor died – if the earning it meant that she was to arouse sentiments of desire in Hugh Monckton! Or in himself who was in possession of the other's identity. But she had at least come into

261

all the apparent right to be regarded as the . . . oh, they call it *maîtresse en titre* – of the man who was in possession of Hugh Monckton's identity. She had attempted a gallant gesture and, to all appearances, had succeeded. She had every right to triumph. Good for her!

As compared with Alice's acquisition of himself it was a dashing affair. Very similar but more ingratiating. Alice had got him by lumpishly exhibiting herself to the eyes of father – who, compared to these others, was only an obstinate Luxemburg-Ohio peasant. But this girl had done the same thing with prayer and fasting and at the cannon's mouth. . . . Over a gas ring which, being of shorter range, is more deadly!

He was smiling. He had not expected to smile into his pillow. He had expected all this to be an affair of anxieties. It hadn't been. Destiny had indeed done the thing in style. Or he had selected the occasion well!

If you wanted to attempt suicide with subsequent change of identity where else could you select better to do it than that landscape of stone pines and illusions? It was there inevitable that fat men should see a revolver in your hand. It was a country to keep pace with which you had to boast of your unflinching courage. Those fat Mariuses had to have faced revolver muzzles without paling. So they had to invent the revolver. Old Marius Vial's special line of boating was *trombios*, water-spouts, and incredible catches of fish due to his wisdom. He would never have invented a revolver. Yet, in those parts you were safe to find someone who would.

And indeed in those parts you were safe to find classically featured dark girls beautiful enough to make you cross a room and present them with rings. . . . That was the entrance into siren-land, that region. You were safe to find a siren there. As well as a *poule* with a cold.

262

The dark girl's bit of evidence had come in very handy. Her assertion that he – Henry Martin – had that night been perfectly calm had undoubtedly saved him – Hugh Monckton! – at least a good deal of cross examination by the commissaire. It had settled it that the *enquête* would be closed then and there.

The exact spot: the exact climate! Without that white sunlight wouldn't Lamoricière have been able to do without black spectacles and so to have recognized that there were certain differences between the down-and-out American who had asked him for a job and the corpse of the Englishman in the mortuary? And the hotel waiter. . . . In that land of dreams and islands he must have dreamed the identity of that corpse with the monsieur who had visited Hugh Monckton the night before last. For he had pulled the cordon in his sleep when he had admitted them. And he had been fast asleep with his face to the back of the sofa in the hall when they had passed him on their way upstairs! Yet he had sworn that he recognized the corpse as Hugh Monckton's friend! Illusions! Dreams! The desire to be of assistance or to be in at the death to the wonder of the crowd!

He might well smile. There he was, face down on a bed instead of face upwards drifting over the Mediterranean ooze with its *oursins* and sea-flowers and foliage. . . . And wasn't it a refutation of the Catholic's denial of perfectibility? Or even of progress?

There he was, rather ludicrously, in something of the same situation as had been his a year or so ago. . . . In apparent possession of a woman who in no way interested him whilst another woman – who might, he had thought, have been the making of him was not his! But he had progressed.

If his available money were merely fifty thousand

francs – with whatever additions the residuary legatee-ship of Hugh Monckton's possessions might bring in – it was more than he had possessed very lately. And if Mademoiselle Jeanne Becquerel did not interest him very much she was at least an *article de vertu* – a Dresden shepherdess! – as compared with Alice Heinz.

And the dark girl was certainly an improvement on Mrs. Percival. On the Considine girl. Even on Wanda. She at least was alive. They were shadows. And he himself, now that he was awakened – was as you might say enlightened – he did not mean to let himself get into any false position again. It was all very well for Lamoricière and the rest to imagine that he was in the possession of Mademoiselle Jeanne Becquerel. He wasn't and did not intend to be.

With age a man did make a certain progress. In his worldly circumstances and wisdom. He must gain in powers of selection and determination to get what he wanted. He himself was no longer a chicken. And he had now a second start.

Eudoxie was the centre of that group of three. Mademoiselle Becquerel was seated on the arm of her chair and had her right arm over the back behind Eudoxie's head. Her left hand fondled the other's right. Mr. Lamoricière stood behind the two at a little distance. They were talking of the late storm with its seventeen drowned in the *port extérieur*.

The doctor had turned him over and was continuing his meticulous and impatient investigation. It was as if his indignation increased with each progress he made over an organ. He said, as if contemptuously:

'Well, and now the bandages. . . . Your blood pressure is disgustingly normal considering the life you lead.'

The others were talking in low, audible voices. Henry Martin wondered if he ought not to protect Hugh Monckton from the imputation of having led an outrageous life. . . .

But the dark girl held the floor. M. Lamoricière had been in church. The other girl had of course been shut up in that room. M. Lamoricière had only been soaked to the skin. Between the corner of the rue Émile Zola and the cathedral door. The sheet – of rain – had fallen on to him at the corner of the rue Émile Zola. Without a premonitory drop. In the next room there it had grown as dark as night. Jeanne Becquerel had been going through her papers. She could not distinguish them. Then she had observed that the surface of the *rade* was like a gigantic nutmeg grater, the flat steel-grey water thrashed into agony by the rain.

But Eudoxie had seen the storm. She had been out in it. To her they had to listen.

She had been walking on the Chemin des Contrebandiers – the path that leads half way up the cliff when there is a cliff or on the shore when there is none, all the way along the indentations of that land. From the Spanish border to Italy! Whenever she was on that path she wondered what it would be like to travel it all over. Some called it the Chemin des Douaniers. It was a matter of taste. Those who were in favour of law and order called it the customs officers' path. The others named it after smugglers. For herself, she was among the others. No doubt both the *douaniers* and the *contrebandiers* used it when they needed it.

Well, she had been going along that path. As she did every Sunday. To go to Mass with Aunt Véronique. At Ste. Agathe. They knew her custom. The other two said: 'Yes! Yes! . . . But yes!'

She had, naturally, witnessed Henry Martin's struggle with the waves. In common with several hundred others. The half of the city's population that did not go out on the waters, went, on a Sunday morning, along the Chemin des Douaniers. Henry Martin had seen the crowds, dressed in white, running for shelter. As he had gone round.

She had been round a corner. Under Les Jarres. So she had not for the moment seen the storm in the sky. But she had seen the leadenness of the atmosphere. And three white triangles going suddenly flat down. And a large launch with a red sail, going about. With the red sail streaming out.

That had been when Henry Martin had let the sheet go. . . .

The doctor said irritably:

'Why are you panting? . . . What are your sensations?'

The dark girl went on:

'It may possibly have been the embarkation of the poor deceased. But that would be too romantic. Considering how, as I have told you, the night before I would willingly have become his mistress. . . . And I do not become the mistress, as they say in the United States, of the first guy to hit the sidewalk . . . le premier venu.'

The other two said simultaneously:

'But assuredly not, Eudoxie!' And Mademoiselle Becquerel:

'It takes for you the beginning of a true passion.'

The dark girl said:

'Voilà!' As if she were accepting a deserved tribute.

She had got to the top of the crag under Les Jarres. Then she had understood.

'It was not, my children, my first trombe. Nor my tenth!' She had been out with her cousin, the police sergeant that had lately been in the room. In the great storm of 1924. So she knew. . . . 'I called to that man in the launch with the red sail: "Come in here. You can land in the lee of the rock here. Before it strikes you." . . . And, if it had been he, there would have been the romantic situation for you! Me with his ring on my finger and his picture in my heart. Calling: "Vous serez à l'abri, ici," "Vous serez à l'abri, ici" . . . You will be in shelter here! You will be in shelter here! "As if on my breast." ' She added: 'But it was probably not to be. The boat of Marius Vial at Carqueiranne has, it is true, a red sail. . . . But they all have red sails. . . . A hundred. . . .' She had taken off her *fichu*. And waved . . . like Isolde!

M. Lamoricière said:

'Like one of the sirens. . . . No one can say we have no sirens in our cerulean waters whilst we have our Eudoxie.'

She exclaimed:

'Like Circe, then. Not just any old siren. . . . La première venue des syrènes.'

M. Lamoricière laid his hand over his heart and bowed.

'You at least, Madame,' he said, 'never turned man into a beast.'

She reflected a moment and said:

'No, I believe I never did. . . . Still it was probably not he.'

Henry Martin found that he was writhing on his pillow. White lint was flashing before his eyes. The doctor was undoing his bandages. He was trying to push the lint away. And he was exclaiming: 'C'était . . . C'était. . . .' 'It was . . . It was. . . .' He was trying to tell the dark girl that it had been Henry Martin in the boat.

He didn't care. It was perhaps dangerous. They might ask him how he knew. They had heard everything that had been told him about the suicide. . . . And he did not care. He had harmed no one. He wanted to establish that relationship with her. To show her that Destiny had intervened!

This was all getting into a tangle. . . . If the dark girl really felt a tenderness for the dead man. . . . Then. . . .

The doctor said harshly:

'I do not believe you are a Mons hero. . . . You writhe like a baby at the undoing of a bandage. . . . You said just now: "It was . . . It was. . . ." What was it? A little stab of pain. . . . I swear I have caused you no pain. . . . All you pampered people. . . .'

He must be a fierce democrat.

Henry Martin's features felt naked. And stiff. All the bandages were off and he had to shade his eyes from the light.

The doctor called to the others:

'Come here and look at a hero.'

The doctor had put on gold-rimmed pince-nez to examine the wounds. His yellow-foam coloured hair was rumpled as he passed his fingers through it with invitation. His little, white naval beard bristled.

'This is an incomprehensible and vexing case,' he said. 'I, as you know, was on Admiral Séné's flagship and escaped only by the intervention of God! . . . So I have seen the seriously wounded . . . I have also . . .'

The dark girl's brows had come down into a straight line. All their eyes gazed at him. It was perhaps the crucial test.

The doctor continued:

'I have also, God knows, attended on drunkards and

idle wastrels. . . . This gentleman was till four yesterday morning . . . it was yesterday morning, was it not? . . . till four yesterday morning drunk. At Hyères. Writing letters furiously. In spite of the remonstrances of the waiter. . . .'

Mademoiselle Becquerel said:

'It was because of that then that your room was empty.'

She was across his chest, her arms around his head. She kissed the wound on his temple. She said:

'Why did you absent yourself? . . . I thought . . .'

M. Lamoricière laid his hand over his heart.

'It is thus, fittingly,' he said, 'that beauty heals the scars of valour!' He added: 'The one scar has singularly displaced the other.'

The doctor snorted:

'Valour!' with unexpected violence. 'You call it valour, Lamoricière. I took you for a serious man.'

'This gentleman,' he addressed them, 'mad drunk. . . . Writing. . . . Writing. . . . Is it the hour? . . . And the unfortunate waiters. . . . They I suppose are clay? Furniture? Spittoons? . . . Those poor fellows in this time of crisis. . . . Whose earnings are derisive! . . .' He addressed Henry Martin: 'Let me tell you, monsieur, on one of those men I had enjoined rest. . . . Now he is a case of nervous breakdown. . . . Are you aware those poor fellows must be at their duty at six? And you keep them till four. Attendant on your frenetic writings. . . .'

That was why, in the darkness, he had heard the long, intermittent roar of the car, making towards Hyères.

Mademoiselle Becquerel was looking at him with reproachful eyes:

'Mongtong!' she said, 'why could you not have written

in your room? I would have sat and held the inkstand to you. . . .'

That miserable fellow! . . . He saw him being hovered over by the miserable waiter, in a lugubrious, ill-lit café. . . . In atrocious pain. Brushing the waiter aside and saying:

'Laissez-moi seul, vieille fève.' 'Let me alone, old bean.'

The dark girl's eyes were still upon him, the brows still a straight line.

Mademoiselle Becquerel had stood up. The doctor wagged his pallid forefinger against her face.

'And you, Madame! . . . Have you no more sense! After that grave accident and his outrageous folly. . . . Let me tell you, if you desire to retain the affections of monsieur. . . . What do I say? If you desire to retain monsieur on this earth and in his full reason. . . .'

Mademoiselle Becquerel said:

'He is infinitely courageous! And beautiful as Apollo! And generous! She whimpered and took refuge in the arms of the dark girl who continued to look at him over her shoulder.

The doctor said:

'What is puzzling . . . the real puzzle is that the symptoms of this fellow indicate neither wounds, nor inebriations. Nor even lechery. . . . They are those of shock after a long period of financial misfortunes . . . *revers de fortune*. Heaven knows that with those symptoms in these days I am familiar enough.'

Eudoxie had retreated to her arm-chair with her arms still about the other girl. Her face as she looked at Henry Martin was curiously softened.

'*Chagrins! Préoccupations journalières*. . . . Grief!

270

Eternal preoccupations! Heaven knows the doctor in these days is familiar enough with the symptoms they cause. . . But this gentleman is famous throughout Europe for his resources. . . . Consider: before committing his madness . . . his rash act, he throws a *billet de cinquante livres sterling* – to the waiter. . . . And then charges a hedge, being too drunk to tell the twenty metre broad highway of *le Pradet* from a tiny *chemin vicinal*. . . .'

The dark girl said vindictively:

'What do you know of the anxieties of wealth, Monsieur le docteur Grouault? . . . May this unfortunate gentleman still not have known your *revers de fortune?* And *chagrins!* And *préoccupations journalières!* Are you such a communist that you have lost all sense of relativity? I thought you were more soft-hearted.'

The doctor said:

'That is true, Yu-Yu . . . I am perhaps carried away with indignation at the thought of the way in which those who call themselves great financiers – our Kings of to-day! – have with their incapabilities ruined the world. . . .'

Eudoxie said firmly:

'That is true. If you left it to me not one of those men should escape hanging. But that is not to say that monsieur, here, may not have known *revers de fortune!*'

The doctor said:

'I heard the other day of a King of Copper . . . Vainkell-hosare: some such Boche name. He was broken-hearted because his fortune of two hundred and fifty million francs – six thousand two hundred and fifty million dollars – was reduced by this crisis to fifty million . . . twelve hundred and fifty million francs. . . . But do you suppose that Vainkell-hosare gave any tears to his millions of victims? . . . Millions? . . . the sacrifice of his Vanity and incompetence.'

'That does not say,' she maintained, 'that monsieur here may not have had *préoccupations journalières.* How do you know he may not have had worries due to that very Boche? . . . These things all interlace.'

Henry Martin said:

'Yes, mademoiselle. . . . Yes, mademoiselle. . . .'

It was the first time he had spoken to her in a long time. But he imagined that he recognized in the doctor's singular phonetics the name of Mr. Kuhn's uncle. There was no other copper king with a German-sounding name and two hundred and fifty millions to lose. He had the momentary impression of the heavy jowl and contemptuous voice of that financier. He had threatened Henry Martin into ruin.

He suddenly thought that he would give not a little to be drinking near-beer in the hotel where he had lunched with the millionaire. It came over him like a wave at the thought of the stiff napery, the substantial silver that clattered fatly as it was thrown on the table, the wallowing in fat steaks, the roar of the conversation, the clatter of the waiters at the serving tables, the high ululations of the bell-boys. . . . He seemed to have heard nothing like it for years.

The millionaire he remembered had been infuriated at the service. He had slammed a heavy hand on the table and asked his nephew if he considered *that* to be civilization. The nephew had even obsequiously run to the waiter's service table and had fetched the great man the ketchup. The delay in bringing it had excited his heavy rage. . . . If then the waiter had brought that fluid more speedily Henry Martin might not have been so completely ruined. The financier would have been less violent in his commands and Henry Martin would have dared not to put all his eggs in one basket. As it was he had been too frightened to do anything else. These immense men of business excited an awe. Defying that man was more mysteriously frightening than it would have been to defy a Roman tyrant. . . . So all Henry Martin's capital had gone into those copper shares. . . . As all everyone's capital had gone into things into which they had been ballyhooed or tyrannized into putting them. . . .

The occasion had not been propitious. It had not even been agreeable. The great man had treated Henry Martin as if he had been a maggot on a lettuce leaf. . . . But at the moment he would have given not a little to be just rising from some such table over there. Rising and going out into the rattle and banging and overtension of the nerves and hell that flowed all round the noise in which he had been existing. . . . But that torrent of fluid noise was not for him. He had to remember that he was now an English millionaire. Those fellows' lots were cast probably in quieter places. . . .

The doctor was preparing some new bandages for his head.

M. Lamoricière was saying:

'And indeed we have to consider that even the Monckton car shares have not been immune. The natural instinct excited in one by contact with a distinguished figure has made me take notice that they have been dropping a point here and a point there. . . . So that – I saw it stated in passing in a financial paper – they now stand lower than they have done at any time since a month after the reconstruction of the company on its present lines. . . . '

Henry Martin was conscious of an extraordinary ringing

273

in his ears. If they now stood so low – an almost fantastic dividend was just about to be declared. . . . Why, that was fortune to anyone who possessed a certain capital. . . .

'It is all the more unusual . . .' M. Lamoricière was going on, 'in that shares of an apparently prosperous company usually rise towards the time of a declaration of dividends. . . .'

The dark girl said:

'Is it you that are going now to give us financial advice?'

'You mean to say,' M. Lamoricière said, 'that I have brought my own eggs to a miserable enough market. That is true. I little thought that after years of service in a treacherous climate . . .'

The doctor made an impatient 'Br-r-r!' of sound.

'We are all in the same boat, my friend,' he said. 'And monsieur here too seems to be of the same company. . . . Mankind has always been the prey of scoundrels. And survived. Now the scoundrels are not even sufficiently competent to feather their own nests. So mankind perishes. We used to live on the crumbs that fell from the rich men's tables. Now there are neither crumbs nor tables. There are not even rich men.'

Eudoxie said:

'When I listen to you men . . . to a crowd of men . . . it is as if. . . .'

'Why, yes,' the doctor interrupted, 'I admit that if the Ship of State were conducted by women as beautiful and as intelligent as you. . . . .'

'It would at least be a barque of Cytherea,' she interrupted in her turn. 'As it is it is a cargo of maimed. . . . And having brought the world to such a pass you chastise me for supplying the only sane solace.'

'It was not I that chastised you,' the doctor said. 'There are many things that should be suppressed before you and your snow. . . . For all I would do to stop it they may to-morrow put up a statue to you as the *Bona Dea* of Sirenland.'

He beckoned the Becquerel girl towards the secretaire on which Hugh Monckton had written his will. But he remained looking at the dark girl.

'All the same,' he said impressively, 'I should be guilty of ingratitude if I did not traverse your attack on our friend Lamoricière in his capacity of financial adviser. As it is hard on him at his age to have to set again his hand to the plough so it is hard on me at mine to have to give up my collecting of pictures. . . .'

Eudoxie said affectionately:

'You and your crusts!'

'My collecting of pictures and my leisure with dignity,' the doctor continued solemnly. 'To have to give up at once all my repose and the purpose of my life and to have to betake myself again to the scalpel and the bistouri! . . . But I owe it to the advice of our friend that I am not cast upon the streets and my beloved if incomplete collection dispersed.' Their friend possessed an instinct for the Bourse that could only be set down as a natural gift since he had passed so much time in their colonies. And in the most desperate positions he had shown the coolest of heads. When, a month ago, the incompetent criminals who managed French affairs had reduced the Bourse to a state of raging lunacy M. Lamoricière had managed the affairs of Doctor Grouault himself and his friends Escartefigue, Boyer, Decanis – and much humbler people too! – so consummately that, although they had all been seriously hit, not one of them but retained a good proportion at least of their holdings. . . .

He went on for a long time. . . .

Henry Martin was feeling extremely lonely. What sort of people was he amongst in this musty and mouldering room? He had no sort of clue. They appeared eccentric but extraordinarily real. And unrelated and unaccountable.

Here were girls – presumably of a certain class – yet they talked of Cytherea and Circe and Isolde. As familiarly as they would talk of their pet dogs. And with the evident expectation of being understood by their menfolk. It seemed incredible at this day and year. . . . And they were the cousins of police sergeants and mistresses of governors of provinces. And went to prison with good humour and without loss of self-respect. . . .

And the men talked as if they were addressing political meetings and handed each other testimonials. . . . Lamoricière had handed even Henry Martin a testimonial . . . in his character of Hugh Monckton. . . .

They seemed without rancour and tolerant of the hardships that life thrust them against. . . . It was nevertheless lonely. . . .

As far as he could see they would have to form his society. For as long as his funds lasted. They seemed to be on terms of easy intimacy with the dark girl. Presumably they would stroll in and out of the rooms – wherever they might be – that he and she would occupy. . . . It was perhaps a desperate venture. But it appeared to be what he was in for. A life without recognizable landmarks. Without, as it were, a Chrysler Building, a Brooklyn Bridge, a level crossing with petrol signs and a traffic jam. . . . Without even a Tour Eiffel!

How did you orient yourself?

It appeared to be obvious that he would have to live in a closed circle. . . . *Sicut hortus inclosus est soror est*

276

*conjux.* . . . He did not know what Hugh Monckton's social or vital contacts had been. Except for the Bumble-puppy Bumblesumpske's and Jeanne Becquerel he could not think of anyone who had known that poor fellow. He might have numbers of gay friends in the near neighbourhoods. And if he, Henry Martin, ran up against any of them he would be at a serious loss. He would not be able to recognize them. . . . He could of course feign loss of memory as the result of his accident. And there were no doubt other expedients. But he disliked the idea of active, false pretences. It was one thing to lie in a bed nearly voiceless, and have other people call you Asch Emma Smith. It would be quite another to sit, say, in a terrace of one of the Riviera palaces and, amidst crowds, boldly to declare:

'I am Hugh Monckton Allard Smith!'

Everything then forced him to a sort of disappearance. And a disappearance where he was. He had once seen some sort of crab sink straight into sand, apparently without effort or motion. He would have to perform some such operation. And there! . . . There at any rate he had an identity. Almost anywhere else in the world he might suddenly have to struggle to retain any at all. For, if he was not Hugh Monckton what was he? Henry Martin would be buried.

The doctor had by now installed himself at the *secretaire*. He assumed a pair of pince-nez, took a sheet of paper and placed the fingers of both hands, palm downwards, determinedly on the edge of the writing flap. So installed he regarded Mademoiselle Becquerel who stood humbly before him as an implacable confessor might regard a weeping penitent. That attitude is the delight of French doctors.

He said with a military voice:

'Madame; the case of Monsieur Smeez is serious but not desperate.'

Henry Martin felt a certain shock. After all he did not know how much injury might have been done him. He had certainly suffered from long strain and the accident had come right on top of it. It would be at least singular if, whilst inheriting the outward personality, he had incurred also the physical handicaps of Hugh Monckton.

The doctor went on harshly:

'It need not become desperate if you will observe exactly what I am about to enjoin on you. . . . But remember; it is the last drop that makes the barrel overflow. . . . You go on following certain detrimental habits day after day with little detriment. . . . Then . . . *Vlan!* . . . the superfluous drop! There is your barrel overflowing. . . . Perhaps irrevocably. . . .'

He regarded Mademoiselle Becquerel with re-awakened fierceness. She drooped before him like a flower in a waterless vase.

'Abstinence!' the doctor barked suddenly. 'You understand! If you value Monsieur's future happiness, abstinence must be the note of his and your existence for a long time to come. There must be no physical indulgences. *None!* Not a drop of alcohol! Not a drop! A most limited regime. Most limited.'

He readjusted his pince-nez to gaze fixedly, first at the girl, then at Henry Martin.

'There must be no toying with actresses in the draughts and small hours of the *coulisses*. There must be no stimulants either to the spirits or the corporal frame. Anxiety must be avoided. . . . If in fact you desire the return of Monsieur Smeez to a state in which the normal and usually

legitimate pleasures of humanity may be again his. . . .
The lawgiver seeks nominally to restore the moral health
of the individual by confining him between iron bars.
The physician says to his subject: "Here is a prison. It is
only by your voluntary entry here that your normal
health can be assured." . . .'

He fixed the girl even more intently:

It appeared to be the general impression, he said – and
that impression his own eyes had confirmed – that she
was sufficiently intimate with the patient to have considerable influence over him. Probably she considered
that their lives were, at any rate provisionally, a joint
affair. Then let her try to persuade Monsieur to seek some
rural retreat. This life of hotels was no thing for a patient
suffering with nervous disorders. A rural retreat. A
small establishment with none of the disorders attendant
on profuse wealth. They must live simply with a very
few true friends for all society. Monsieur must be content
to exist *en bon père de famille* – as lives a good father of a
family. . . . But even as a *bon père de famille* he must
acquiesce in shackling himself. . . . That is difficult
when one has just taken to oneself a young wife of charm
and grace in a district where the wine with its juices
grows in profusion. But the results of neglect of these
injunctions might be terrible.

There were already indications that the brain of monsieur had been too much tried. All his other organs were
impeccable. He had in truth the physique of an athlete
. . . a physique in which any woman happy enough to
engage his affections for however limited a time might
well revel. . . . But the master of all these organs . . .
of the heart, the lungs, the sense – that master tottered
on his throne. The brain!

This singular voicelessness for example. There was

nothing physical to account for it. It was a symptom of the failure of the brain to control the action of certain chords. Its nature was no doubt suggested by the sufficiently serious surface injury to the jaw.

Henry Martin had been observing the dark girl. She had begun, when Mademoiselle Becquerel had left the arm of her chair, by affectionately stroking the sleeve of M. Lamoricière. She was apparently trying to lessen the hurt feelings that her jeering at his financial abilities seemed to have left in him. Henry Martin had heard her say:

'Mais non . . . mais non! Everyone knows how your advice saved Freddi Champnouveau and Diane de Montsouris and the others Doctor Grouault was talking of. . . . Is it not freely said that because of you the *crise* has not come to certain quarters of the city? . . .'

M. Lamoricière had made some remark that Henry Martin had not been able to catch because of the doctor's peroration. In a pause she had said earnestly:

'It was said of someone else: He saved others. Himself he could not save!'

Apparently M. Lamoricière remained adamant in his hurtness for she continued to retain her hand on his sleeve and to look up into his face running through a whole gamut of little grimaces of affection, apology and deprecation. But at last the doctor's barking voice had had to master the attentions of the other two. She had remained silent. But again over her mobile features there had run a whole scale of expressions.

When the doctor had declaimed as to the seriousness of Henry Martin's condition she had looked at him with concern and pity. And then with a little *moue* as if to indicate that the doctor was a pessimist who must not be too seriously attended to. Her glance resting directly in his eyes was indescribably moving to Henry Martin. . . . Like a welling up of a beam of velvet-black light!

When the doctor with gesture and voice had harshly enjoined on Mademoiselle Becquerel the necessity for 'abstinence' she had made a comical little grimace at that lovelorn girl's back. . . . But when he had prescribed for Henry Martin the life of a *bon père de famille* under a regime in rural surroundings she had clapped together her pink-nailed hands, exhibited pleased hilarity with her mouth and eyes. . . . Henry Martin imagined for a moment that the idea of rural retirement appealed to her for herself. As if she had had enough of precarious life and desired nothing better than the society of a restrained father of a family in vineyards whose fruits were not used for the manufacture of intoxicating beverages.

But she pointed first to Henry Martin and then to the back of the Becquerel girl. She made a gesture of benediction . . . as if they were kneeling down before her and she imposing her hands on their heads. Then by joining her hands in supplication and looking up to Heaven she made him quite plainly understand that that was what her little friend had all her life prayed for.

The doctor had now arrived at the really luxurious part of his séance. He had for some time been writing fast in a minute hand. He held up the sheet of paper and from it read vindictively to Mademoiselle Becquerel. He tapped the paper sharply as he read.

'At six-thirty two water glasses full of tepid Vichy Chosal water. . . . At seven-thirty no coffee but infusion of lime-flowers. Some dry rusks without butter. Diet almost entirely vegetable. . . . Vegetable soup: the juices of fruits. Between each principal meal a coffee-spoonful of Passiflorine. . . . Extract of passion-flower

in an infusion of lime-flower and orange flower water.
. . . Before each meal a coffee-spoonful of . . .' something Henry Martin did not catch. In half a wine-glassful of red wine of not more than nine degrees of alcoholic content. Or preferably in a half a glass of pasteurized milk. . . .

The regime took a long time to read out. Finally the doctor said:

'If *that* regime does not cure him of the habit of keeping waiters up till four in the morning and then charging hedges like a Spanish bull there is nothing that will.'

He gathered his paraphernalia hastily and, in going, stood a minute before Henry Martin.

'You have probably a bad three days to go through. The third, fourth and fifth days after a shock such as you have had are probably the worst. You feel no doubt well enough now. But to-morrow will be bad.'

He added:

'Let me beg you to observe very carefully the regime that Madame will explain to you. The slightest departure from it in any of the major particulars will, I may tell you, cause inevitably the most distressing mental symptoms. They would be heralded by excruciating pains in the head. But it would then be too late to ward them off. . . .'

The dark girl and M. Lamoricière had apparently continued their discussion. Her voice became audible saying:

'My dear friend: If I were the King I would give you my fleets and my armies and my lands to lead and administer for me. If I were God I'd give you my waves and my clouds and my rivers and my hills and my olive fields and vineyards so that you might better administer a sad world. . . . If I had ten sous to invest I would give them to you. Or if I had two million, eight hundred thousand francs. . . . But since you are so ill-natured and grouchy I will not stay in the same room with you.' She added in English: 'Oh hell, take the chip off your shoulder.' And told her little friend that it was time she got some clothes on her.

PART FOUR

HENRY MARTIN lay looking at the grey Mediterranean. Across the satin water above the balustrade of the terrace were the wooded slopes and white villas of the peninsula of Saint Mandrier. Below his eyes was the exact spot at which he had gone about in the boat. To the left was the open sea, stretching out towards Africa. The woods were dark: the waters of the exterior port light grey: the sky cloudless and without colour. Suddenly the semaphore above the dark woods lit up. It became a candle of white flame. The first rays of the sun had just impinged on it. . . .

Well: that was that! They had moved into the villa the night before, the long and tiresome process finishing after dark. All the doors and windows being open, in the coolness, the slight warmth of Jeanne Becquerel, beside him, motionless in the bed, was not disagreeable.

But you cannot dismiss the Mediterranean with: 'That is that!' It remains with mercy, without heart. It smiles without malice as without kindness. But with more of malice! . . .

They were in the villa next to the farmhouse of Eudoxie's aunt. She was a bad old woman who had always been bad. . . . *Malin* as her admirers said. Now she was a farmeress. They said she was a miser about everything but food. She insisted on having twenty-two different kinds of fish for her *soupe de poissons*. . . . And she ate enormously. But the villa, which belonged to her, was in a state of dilapidation. She was broad. Broad-faced, broad-mouthed and appeared implacable. She was also loose and jovial. Apparently you never knew whether she would denounce you or shake her sides with mirth at the spectacle you presented. She was said to have been responsible for Eudoxie's having gone wrong . . . if Eudoxie could be said to have gone wrong. Eudoxie's father – the aunt's brother – was some sort of *fonctionnaire*. A functionary. Apparently he kept the accounts – or it might have been only the door! – in the French Consulate-General in New York. He was said to be terribly serious! . . . *terriblement sérieux.* . . . That was how Eudoxie came to be a born New Yorker. It appeared that there was a colony of terribly serious French people: a French quarter . . . somewhere between Hell's Kitchen and the bottom of Riverside Drive, according to Eudoxie. Henry Martin did not know New York well enough to be able to place it. He did not know even exactly where Hell's Kitchen had been though someone once driving driving him in an automobile had said to him amongst rather squalid streets on the West Side: 'This is what used to be Hell's Kitchen.' No doubt in the 'eighties it had been the resort of thugs with bangs and light women with bustles. Or with knives and guns and marked cards. On beer barrels in dancing saloons. . . . Something like that. It must have been Dennis – one of the chief Pisto-Brittle New York agents who had been driving him. He said he had been born in Hell's Kitchen. . . . And yes: one evening when he had been sitting on his mother's doorstep he had seen a lighted kerosene lamp descend through the air and crash in the roadway. . . . Thrown by some pimp at a kept woman on the third floor! But he had only understood that when, the other day, he had seen a similar episode in a play whose name Henry Martin could not remember. At the time the fellow –

288

it must have been Dennis! – had been only a child of eleven. Now he was the head of quite a big firm of chain drug stores. . . . If he wasn't ruined! Everyone there appeared to be ruined. Or it might be more correct to say that anyone might be. . . .

But you could not underestimate the Mediterranean. . . . It lay there grey and unwinking. . . A russet tinge was showing on the plateau at the foot of the semaphore on St. Mandrier. . . . He had forgotten that there was a plateau there. But, being now so high on the mainland and the dawn air so clear, he could see a flat space around the base of the white building that had become golden. A little tinge of blue was coming into the sky.

It had perhaps sirens – that grey, unwinking sea. You would imagine that high on the mainland you might be beyond its influence. . . . But no! its influence spread – to the land, the skies, the vegetation, the hearts of the people.

You could not call Eudoxie . . . the dark girl! . . . a siren! She asked nothing of you. She desired neither to suck your blood nor to rifle your purse. Nevertheless she was without remorse and without passion. Or so nearly. . . .

Her father had ten years longer to serve in New York for his pension from the French State. Keeping accounts. Or doors! Apparently he had not approved of New York. At any rate between Hell's Kitchen and Riverside Drive. He had thought it might be bad for his daughter's morals. Or perhaps not her morals . . . her *tenue* . . . manners, deportment, management of her voice. So when she had been twelve he had sent her back to have the benefit of a true French education. In care of her aunt who was avaricious except for food. And she had gone wrong.

Like her aunt who also had *mal tourné* in her youth. But she was now enormously rich, ferocious, jocular. And respected. She was permitted to provide the *pain bénit* in the village church. . . .

He could not make out whether, if it were still to do, he would do it over again!

The sunlight was creeping down the flanks of the peninsula. It was on the great, white villa half way down. The sea was becoming blue. And the sky. . . .

In Chicago when he had been drummer still for Pisto-Brittle, he had met a man called Smith. Casually. In the underground lunchroom at the Blackstone. Smith had warned him against copper. . . . A man with a red nose; but he seemed to know something about copper. He had said the Germans were coming into the market for the first time since the war. With immense quantities of the metal. The Cape Copper Mines also were about to treble or quadruple their output. Under American management. They had been bought by some big company. Kennecotts Henry Martin thought. There would be floods of copper on the market. And with shares at the immense price to which they had been forced . . . why with the slightest touch of Bad Trade – which was sure to come – the bottom would fall clear out of the market.

Henry Martin had taken red-nosed Smith to be one of those Americans who are always raising hell about America. There are such Americans. Nothing American is good to them. . . . The food: the interstate railway commissions: the House of Representatives. Even the merits of the plumbing, they say, are exaggerated. . . . That fellow had been the merest casual acquaintance. He had sat down next to Henry Martin in that grill room. And then had burst out into an attack on Copper. He had seemed a madman at the time. One of the bores you have to suffer when you travel. . . . But if he had taken Smith's advice. . . .

Well: what had he to grumble at? He had a villa on the shores of the Mediterranean. Tiberius had nothing better than that. And a great garden containing every kind of sub-tropical vegetation from spinach to pomegranates. And money to burn. And Hugh Monckton's bed to lie in. . . .

They had taken it from the hotel. You might trust a man like Hugh Monckton not to sleep in the beds of a one-horse hotel. He travelled with his own bed. . . . But Hugh Monckton was sleeping at the end of a deep valley. On a hillside under a place called le Revest. With his tombstone ordered. And might the Almighty have mercy on him because he had loved much.

He, Henry Martin, on the other hand had the luxurious bed, and a nearer view of the Mediterranean; and money. . . .

Hugh Monckton had probably lugged that bed about with him because he was an invalid. It was an incredible bed: it supported you as lightly as swansdown – you being the swansdown . . . And he, Henry Martin, was now lugging it around. . . .

Because he was an invalid.

He could not tell whether he was an invalid or not. He had two charming girls . . . one of them really lovely and meek like a dove and the other the most beautiful creature he had ever seen. He had their society day and night and they looked after him with a tender solicitude. . . . Eudoxie had stayed chatting with them last night till long after twelve . . . but the other lovely creature left him completely indifferent. . . .

He looked down at her sleeping face beside his upper

arm. Relief: absolute and warranted trustfulness – and no doubt happiness! . . . A mere fortnight of them! . . . had delicately rounded her cheeks and given them a tea-rose blush. Her eyes were lightly closed. . . . She was actually like a rose. And she clung to him like a clinging rose about a tree trunk.

She was fairer than he had thought. Or perhaps the constant presence of the dark girl made her seem to grow fairer.

On the other hand the mere contemplation of the dark girl in his more emotional moments made his heart beat and his brain swim. His heart would beat so fast as to be troublesome. Occasionally he would have tears in his eyes. . . . But so, he would swear, had she. . . .

They were perhaps witnesses of pity. She knew he must have suffered for a protracted period, to get very little. . . .

But he had the makings of a harem: a luxurious bed in which to lie like a Sultan; no material worries. No moral ones even. . . . And to be rid of material worries was something in which no one who had not been through them could believe. . . .

Nevertheless if he had taken the advice of red-nosed Smith he probably would not have been there. Though if it had not been copper it might very well have been something else. No one had escaped. The dark girl had said she had had a letter from her father. He said that no one over here had any idea of how bad it was over there. Their connections – Eudoxie's and his – had had to close their flower-shop on Forty-second Street. No one bought flowers. Their sons had lost their jobs in the bank. Old Courit had been on the bread-line for a month. He had been seen there by accident by his niece. His bed-ridden wife had been without blankets for a long period. At the Consulate work had fallen to nothing. A spider had made

its web over one of the ink-wells in the chief-waiting room
. . . A week ago! They had let it remain to see how long
it would be unbroken. It was still intact. It was fortunately still August and warm. The bread-line stretched
from the Sister's hospital at West Eleventh right up Sixth
Avenue to West Fourteenth Street. God knew what would
happen when winter came. . . .

Reading the letter Eudoxie had looked up at him and
said:

'Think of that . . . from West Eleventh to Fourteenth. . . .'

Henry Martin had said that he did not know lower
Sixth Avenue very well. He had only been in New York
for visits. That was true. He tried to say only true things
to her.

She said:

'You don't say. . . . I have the feeling you are New
Yorkais. Like myself. . . . But one has the feeling that
everyone who does not speak French as a native language
is New Yorkais.'

She exclaimed:

'Listen to this. As you are not a citizen of New York
this may impress you. My father writes: "Your sister
Eugénie was last night coming home with her fiancé,
young Larbre, from a party in Columbia Heights. They
had in their taxi a young fellow . . . a millionaire
*quelconque*. When they got to Columbus Circle they were
delayed because the bread-line was all round the Circle.
'Isn't that a splendid sight,' said that young fellow;
'doesn't that make you proud of America?' They said!!!!!??
And he answered: 'They're all down and outs. Starving.
They have to wait four hours for a can of coffee and two
inches of bread. . . . Yet they are perfectly orderly.
No exclamations! No complaints! . . . What country

293

but America could show such discipline?' – And he added: 'But something will have to be done to stop them from going from bread-line to bread-line. Some of these fellows after they have been fed here will go on straight to another place. That must be put a stop to!' "

The dark girl's eyes rested contemplatively on Henry Martin.

'Do you know what I would do if you were such a millionaire?' she asked.

She answered seriously :

'I would come up to you and I would spit in your face!'

Her glance had, however, changed to one of soft compassion.

'But you are not a millionaire. . . .' And she added very slowly: 'Like that one!'

He had had a swift feeling of dread. . . . It seemed to him certain that she must know that he was not Hugh Monckton. . . . He had had the conviction before: that seemed to confirm it! . . .

St. Mandrier was by now all in sunlight. It would last only for a short time for that was the north slope. They were now in September. The first or second. Anacondas had passed their dividends. That did not matter to him. Moncktons hadn't.

He tried to gather his thoughts together. . . . He had been thinking of red-nosed Smith: and of his emotions when he looked consciously at the dark girl: and of Jeanne Becquerel here, a little. . . . And of course of his general situation! But all the others bracketed into that.

It wasn't red-nosed Smith so much. He had done with the memory of that lunatic. But perhaps he was not so much of a lunatic. When you heard of bread-lines from West Eleventh to West Fourteenth it made you think he ought to have been taken more seriously. . . . But when Americans have a down on America they speak so wildly they cannot expect to command much attention. . . .

But there had been another Smith. . . . If he had taken his advice he would not be here now. . . . That was Henry Martin Aluin Smith I. His surface-conscious self. . . .

His emotions when he had stood over that body were now clearer to him. They were perhaps clearer than they had been just after the event – the rash act!

There had been H.M.A.S. I with burly common sense. He had said that it would be an act of childishness to take passports from a dead man.

But in the eyes of H.M.A.S. II that British passport had looked extremely hypnotizing. Like a trinket. Dark blue: with the gilt plastering of royal arms. And the idea of celebrating his escape from death had been allur-ing. After having passed out of such a long period of shadow it was only fitting to make whoopee. . . .

And heaven knows how complex a man is! Henry Martin was aware that, but for another intercession, his conscious self would have won out. He was not, in his normal senses or even when a good deal agitated, the man to let himself be carried away by a childish reckless-ness. A gilt bauble was nothing to him. Either in itself or as a symbol of the sort of lawlessness that sometimes becomes a man! . . .

But under these two there had been a third Henry Martin. It was a stern being: the remains within him-self of the cave man: the latent possibility within him of the criminal. It was the part of him that was motivated by hunger, thirst, panic, the dictates of sex. And sleeplessness. It was as if that third presence at the conference had said: 'Aw hell: I want sleep and a Hamburg steak. And bandaging. And a woman. . . . Get to hell out of here. Give me two days of that and to hell with the consequences.'

He must have reckoned on a pretty certain two or three days of as much whoopee as his banged up frame could support. . . . No doubt not any of his subconsciousnesses had counted on more than two days of it. He – they! – had intended explaining the mistake and laughing the matter away. He ought to have known that that would not turn out so easy. . . . None of it had actually been easy. . . . To keep himself from making slips he had had to act to himself the part of Hugh Monckton. And it had proved easy. It had been like when you valorously set out on a course of lying. You come to believe yourself in the end.

And he had lied very little. Those people had displayed astonishingly little interest in his past. . . . None at all! He could not recollect that they had asked him a single question until once, in a sort of jealousy, he had described his father as an old, obstinate man. . . . The French are like that. For them there exist only France and the present. They are incapable of showing interest in your past in another land. . . . No, he had only lied once. When he had been pleading with Eudoxie. He had said:

'But you are wearing my ring!' It had slipped out.

She had turned it round on her finger and said:

'But it was given me by the other poor fellow!'

He had caught himself up with a readiness of which he might have been proud at any other time.

'None the less,' he heard himself say: 'It was I who

sent it you. You will see my initials on the inside of the setting.'

She had been sitting by his bed in the hotel.

She said:

'Yes: I know your initials are there.' She had looked at him with the first amusement she had shown at that interview. A queer, as it were sideways, amusement. At any rate her mouth had gone down only on one side. As when they say you smile on the wrong side of your face.

'Ah yes,' she said, 'Of course yes! You could not be seen talking to a . . . To one like me. . . . Yes, yes: of course. Much less giving me a ring. . . . So you sent it. . . . He would never have thought of that the poor fellow. . . . But you, you had your distinguished position. And of course. . . . Yes: Gloria Sorenson would not have liked it. She would have made the fur fly. . . .'

He had said:

'I loved you from the first moment I saw you!' He was by then a great deal worked up. But it had been true enough.

She sighed.

'It is a hard, cruel thing . . . life!' she said. 'If you had seen Jeanne the first time I saw her. In the playground of the Lycée. . . . She came running up with a button and a needle. . . . My tablier was too small for me. My aunt who was a scatterbrain had forgotten to attend to my school trousseau until the last moment. So there was no tablier. And an overall like that is prescribed by the rules of the Lycée. So that no girl should look finer than any other. So at the last moment my aunt found me an old tablier of my cousin Georgette. And there stood I, scowling like a fiend and a lot of girls jeering at me. Because I had burst one of the buttons of that garment. Girls will jeer for any reason at all if you are new and shy and speak French awkwardly. With a New Yorkais accent. . . . And Jeanne sewed on that button. And you would not believe it, seeing Jeanne now, but she bit one of the girls that went on jeering at me.'

She stopped to think for a moment.

'I would have you believe,' she said, 'that it was not long before every one of those girls would eat out of my hand whilst I called them names. . . . But Jeanne continued to worship me and carried my knapsack and spent her lunch money on buying me scent and did my devoirs for me, crying, whilst I was flirting with my cousin who is the police sergeant you saw. . . . So decidedly you are not the first one to fall for me on sight.'

Her features dropped.

'No,' she said. 'When I saw that red sail flash away before the gloom I knew that poor man was not for me. But it is true that that night I would gladly have slept with. . . .' She did not utter the last word.

The flying away of the scarlet sail seemed to have made a deep impression on her. She had referred to it several times. . . . As Henry Martin's boat had charged into the tempest the triangle of scarlet had flown away behind him. . . . Like an omen, she had said. . . . A mysterious stranger the night before had given her a ring. Now she saw a gout of flame or of blood whirl away behind him. How could you read that? And she standing on top of a rock, waving, like Isolde! . . .

Immediately afterwards she had had to run into the chicken house of les Jarres where she had crouched amongst the outraged hens.

It had been at that point in that particular interview that he had first known pain. . . .

He was getting confused. . . . At what point in what

particular interview? . . . His brain was turning. It was as if he had to hold himself down in bed.

He was lying looking at the sea above the balustrade of the terrace. The supporters of the balustrade were of stone. Pinkish. They were like a row of ewers of which you could not see the handles. Between them was the sea. The sea was like grey satin – with enormous scrolls of glutinously still water. The sun was gradually filling the world. . . . He almost prayed that the heat wave might be over. They had had now ten days of heat wave. Down in the town. But they had promised him that, up here it would be cooler. The sky was nevertheless without a fleck.

He was looking at the exact spot. . . . The spot where the scarlet triangle had whirled away behind the white launch. He ought perhaps not to have that spot under his eyes. It might bring on pain.

Pain. . . . He had never imagined such pain. He had never known pain before. Before he had always been healthy. A healthy animal. . . . Almost an Olympian athlete. . . . But that pain had been like flame going to the very sources of sensation. . . . In the brain. Not the pain of the wound in his temple. Behind that! . . . It drove him mad merely to think of it!

That accursed doctor!

It had come of course at the end of his first interview with her. After the long and tiring interview with that argumentative fellow Lamoricière. Tiring. . . . Two tiring interviews. At the end of the doctor's examination. And after the shock of the 'accident.' . . . Well: it had been an accident: the blows from the yard. Swinging round on the mast. . . . Right: Left! . . .

And then you can have any number of private thoughts

during interviews. Your other personalities are thinking for you. About suggested illnesses. All sorts of panics. . . . All his personalities had gone into his pleading with the dark girl. . . . But all through his interview with Lamoricière he had been thinking other thoughts. . . . About cabling to his father. . . . About, precisely, his health. . . . That had been by the doctor's suggestion, evidently.

That accursed doctor. . . .

They had said he was somebody tremendous! A great Paris mental specialist who had retired to live among painters and collect their pictures as they painted them. But the *crise* had hit him. He had had to begin to practice again. . . . Serves him right! . . .

Perhaps their declarations of that fellow's distinction had been all a product of the southern sun. They were all Mariuses down there. If they had nothing else to boast of they would boast about the miraculous gifts of the last stranger they had met in a café. . . . As Lamoricière had boasted to everyone on the road about his, Henry Martin's, valorous exploits on the Marne. . . . But of course they were Hugh Monckton's. . . . He had by now so identified himself with that poor dear fellow that the fellow in the blue uniform charging down on him on a roan charger was something that he might seem to see at almost any moment of the day. In a sort of substituted memory. . . . And he had called the hotel waiter: 'Old Bean,' half a dozen times whenever he brought in a meal. . . .

But of course they would exaggerate the distinctions of that doctor!

Nevertheless he had on his prescription headings a formidable list of distinctions. He was adviser to the Republic on half a dozen hygienic directions. And, after his name on the same headings was printed a whole row of things like bugs! Decorations. . . . From a great number of countries. . . . Sweden: Canada: Rumania. England even. . . . So he was an international big bug!

It was enough to frighten anyone into a nervous attack. . . .

Perhaps that pain was no more than a suggestion of the doctor himself!

These accursed fellows! In France they called them the New Inquisition. In earlier days it had been the priest allying himself with the woman on your hearth who held you down with bands of steel. Now it was the doctor. He curried favour with your woman. By forcing abstinence and economy on the *bon père de famille*. The woman on your hearth wanted that. It let her build up the *dots* of her daughters, the capital for starting up her sons in business. . . . So the doctor established himself as firmly in your house as the sucker fish fixes itself in the keels of ships.

New Inquisitors. . . . For, damn it all! The old Inquisitors were merely external. Their spies were outside the house; their executioners and torturers outside the body. But this new order was always within your doors and the woman of your hearth was their spy. The pains with which they threatened you were within you: they could create them by suggestion and the woman kept them always alive by reminders of the dread threats of their ally. They were inescapable. . . .

On the other hand that damned fellow may have been right. The pain may have come in the course of nature: consequent on the emotions aroused in him by that fatal and predestined scene with the dark girl.

And on the other hand it might well be that, in this case the woman of this particular hearth might object to the fiat of the doctor. She had already begun to say that it was hard on her little friend. . . . Of course it was hard. It was even indecent. Still she would have been in the same case if she had had a husband who had had an accident after a long period of. . . . He could not remember the French phrase . . . financial worries. . . . A bridegroom though! That perhaps made it indecent! . . . *Revers de fortune*: that was the French phrase. Well, she was suffering from the world crisis. She was not the first, nor would she be the last! . . .

And it was all fatal and predestined. . . . Eudoxie had so strong a feeling of the wrong millionaires had done by mismanaging the finances of the world that she would not take up even with so innocuous a millionaire as Hugh Monckton. She preferred to remain for her 'boy friend,' the dope merchant whose only attraction seemed to be that he was in gaol in England after having clumsily got her into gaol. He was English.

And he, Henry Martin, had had to change identities with a millionaire. 'A pound millionaire!' she had said. With an inflection as if by association with her boy friend she had learned to be contemptuous of the dollar.

A net, its bamboo frame shining in the sun, was moving along outside the balustrade, visible between the pink ewers. He felt sudden peace. He had always the dread that one day it would occur to her that the present situation was too equivocal. Then she would never come again. Apparently not even an idea that the situation was even unusual had so much as brushed her lucid mind. 'Equivocal' was probably a word that she did not know. As the dictionary of Napoleon had not the word of fear in it. Or perhaps that was Nelson . . . She was coming carrying a fisherman's landing-net. Of course she was going fishing with Jeanne Becquerel. To catch the twenty-two different sorts of fish that her aunt needed for her fish soup. She was said to make the most admirable fish soup in all the Var. The 'young couple' were invited to dine with her that evening.

The landing-net pitched over the balustrade. The terrace was very long. She preferred to run like a cat up the protuberances of the rocks that supported it. One black trouser came over the balustrade: then the other. She was wearing a great round straw hat. Bistre coloured. The sunlight touched the top of the balustrade along with her. Her hands were in sunlight. . . .

He said to himself:

'How is this? I am like the Indian who prayed: "O Shastriyama what is this creature that Thou hast given me. Seeing that I can neither live with her nor without her!'

Shastriyama had not given that creature to him. Yet, since sunrise he had been thinking incoherent thoughts. Because of his fear that she might not come. Now he could not get his breath because she had!

She picked up the fishing-net and walked in with it over her shoulder. In trousers she had broader hips than he had thought. She balanced as she walked with one hand on her hip. With the great hat the hoop of the landing-net made intersecting haloes behind her head. Above the immense bell-shaped trousers the top of her bathing-dress was light flame-coloured. It was not very low in front but a broad opening came right down to her belt behind. The belt was emerald green. He could not see the opening at her back. But he knew it was like that. He had no doubt seen it as she had climbed over the balustrade. He had thought he had shut his eyes. Obviously he hadn't.

She was leaning against the doorpost. Even then she

was defiantly rouged. At six in the morning! It was bad taste. She was got up to resemble southern beauty. A Carmen or, with the wide trousers, a Corsair's bride. With the provocative hips and the hand on one of them. Her lips were no doubt exaggerated in colour, but he could not see them. They were hidden by a purple aster! She was chewing the stem. It gave the effect of an enormous mouth. She was smiling.

Jeanne Becquerel groaned:

'Je me lève! Je me lève. . . . Mais je suis si bien!' . . . 'I'll get up! I'll get up. . . . But I am so happy here!'

The dark girl leaned her face over his face. The aster fell upon it, chastely sprinkling his cheek with dew.

'That is better than a kiss!' she said laughing at him ironically. He groaned. She bent again and kissed him on the lips. Her warm breath smelled sweet of coriander seed. Coriander seed is one of the chief ingredients, with saffron, of *soupe de poissons*. No doubt she had picked a grain or two out of the mortar in her aunt's great kitchen.

Jeanne Becquerel threw a possessive arm right across his chest.

'Mamour!' she protested sleepily. 'Mamour! No one shall have Asch Emma Smeez but me.'

The dark girl leaned back. Smiling at her as one of infinitely superior physical vigour may smile. Each time she had bent over Henry Martin she had done it without moving her hips from the doorpost. That was a piece of suppleness that Henry Martin much liked. Hugh Monckton had done it when he had bent down over his grip to take out the twenty thousand pound notes – which were by now more than doubled. . . . And that gesture had undoubtedly endeared him to Henry Martin. . . . That was not so unreasonable. A person who could do it must have lived cleanly, with moderation and sobriety. . . . And of course she was a beauty specialist. She said she could do away with his scar if he persisted in not wearing a beard. But they liked his beard, those two. It made him look more like a man who could beat them. French women apparently liked to think that their men could beat them up if they wanted to. With skill and attention, not breaking bones or disfiguring visible parts of the flesh. . . . Women of their class. . . . But of what class were they? Perhaps of a class like that of actresses who were never, on any account, 'received' in France. . . . He had forgotten about his beastly beard. Now it started tickling. He could not scratch under their eyes! Of course many Frenchmen wore beards. . . . And some English!

A nearly three weeks' beard! Past the absolutely revolting stage. . . .

He had not shaved since the fifteenth of August. It was now the fifth of September. He remembered that he had not shaved on the morning when those things had happened. That was scarcely polite to Destiny. It was perhaps why that august but humorous force condemned him to wear that unhygienic offence. It cut him off from his countrymen. He had gone native. Englishmen could wear beards. They had a king who was a beaver! . . . It was Eudoxie who was set against his shaving. She refused permission clamorously. She said that if he shaved at all he must go clean-shaven. He disliked the idea of sacrificing his moustache. He thought he had a weak upper lip. He must have. Anyway he was cut off from his countrymen. Expatriate! Eudoxie no doubt knew that! . . . It also made him less easily recognizable. That fellow Jimmy Stout had showed no sign of recognition at all.

'Get up and catch the rascasse. The rascasse! The rascasse!' Eudoxie laughed. Jeanne Becquerel hid her face almost under his armpit.

'You need never be without rascasse,' Eudoxie said. 'While you have my little friend. . . . She can always catch them. She is so lethargic. . . . As for me I can catch everything else but not rascasse.' *Soupe de poissons* needs rascasse before everything else.

'If you bait her hook,' Eudoxie said, 'and throw it in she will sit motionless for an hour. . . . That is why my little friend catches them. . . . All the other twenty-one kinds will only take moving bait. That is why I catch them up so fast. . . . I shall call you Monsieur Rascasse.'

Jeanne Becquerel sat straight up in bed.

'No one shall call my Asch Emma Smeez anything but Asch Emma Smeez!' she said. 'And they shall not even shorten it. He is Asch Emma Smeez.'

'You do not even know his name!' Eudoxie laughed.

Jeanne Becquerel made a face as if she were contemplating a bitter draught.

'You Mongtong . . .' she began hesitatingly.

'No it is not at all that,' Eudoxie said.

'Then it is Asch Emma Smeez,' the girl panted. 'My Asch Emma and my Smeez, too.' She curled one of her feet under her.

Eudoxie said:

'Rascasse . . . Rascasse . . . Rascasse I tell you. . . . If you do not come soon the rascasse will be too late for my aunt's soup. Then she will never give me another holiday. And I shall have to stop in Manhattan Beauty all my life. Never go out of the shop. Pass all my life giving fat Americans from Montparnasse physical lessons. . . . You without pity! . . . You know my implacable aunt.'

She stopped and then exclaimed very slowly:

'If you do not come soon the sun will be blazing into our cove. . . . Then it will spoil the nacreous skin that you think our Seigneur likes. . . .'

Jeanne Becquerel moved up suddenly on her foot. Her left leg was stretched straight before her, two inches above the soft bed. The nacreous skin was dead white under the shining, transparent covering.

'It will go rusty,' Eudoxie said. . . . 'And Monseigneur will take on another favourite!'

Jeanne Becquerel from her single foot sprang right over him. She was on tiptoe on the red tiles of the floor. . . . Like a Greek statue of a poised diver. . . . She poked her chin triumphantly at the dark girl. . . .

Eudoxie held her head back.

'It was I that taught you that!' she said with pride in her pupil.

There were yards of cream-coloured silk on a chair beside Jeanne Becquerel. She was out of her nightdress and the silk was whirling round her silver white person. As if she had been a scarf dancer. The heavy silk rustled about her thighs. She was draped, with a square end of silk hanging before her. She poked her chin again at Eudoxie.

'No, I could not do that,' the dark girl said: 'Little Malay girl. . . . We know you have been in the tropics. . .'

Jeanne Becquerel looked like a Greek boy in old alabaster and fig leaves. She bathed in a *sarong*.

They embraced rapturously. The dark girl's arms were like mahogany crossed over the other's skin. . . . Mahogany whose transparent surface contained luminous blood!

Jeanne Becquerel stood in the doorway, leaning back against the doorpost beside the dark girl. Since the light from the upper sky was intense she was not in silhouette and her skin was indeed nacreous as the dark girl said. Like mother of pearl. She stretched out one arm to hold the other doorpost so that it cut the doorspace in half, like a straight bar, obscuring St. Mandrier. Her head was turned to gaze into the south. The shadows beneath her arms, armpits, breasts and knees reflected the blue of the sky; there was a little pink on the base of the neck, the ribs and the lower limbs. But most of the flesh was rice-white. . . . A Hellenic figure done in nacre! The dark girl was like a drop of luminous blood! . . . She would no doubt one day fly away. . . . Like a scarlet sail before disaster.

They had perhaps arranged that contrast so as to be alluring to men. They had perhaps arranged to shade or expose their flesh so as to be the one in red bronze, the other, rice. . . . Why shouldn't they? The allurement of men is the business of these seas and skies. . . . They had to leap and give pleasure. Then to die. Or maybe sufficiently to economize to unite their wealth to that of a rich, tamed farmer and to capitalize a Manhattan Beauty Shop where you could employ your niece as adviser in reducing calisthenics. That was what Eudoxie's aunt had done. It was no doubt relatively death. But in her youth she was said to have danced and given pleasure.

The dark girl pointed her thumb backwards towards the face of her mate.

'What wouldn't you give to know what she is thinking? . . . She will stay like that till there is an earthquake.'

She slipped under the rigid arm. Out on the terrace she juggled with oranges. With one hand she kept six in the air at once. As one fell out of range she caught it with her net and took another from the table beside her. So there were always six in the air at once. Those high up caught the sunlight and were illuminated and golden. Behind her pyjama trousers, from below the terrace the orange trees pushed up their formal and emotional foliage. He could not be certain that Greek women wore pyjama trousers. Perhaps the Cretans did. At Cnossos. Or he seemed to remember an outline on a red platter. In the Louvre.

At any rate the boy of Antibes who danced and gave pleasure had probably juggled six oranges in that way. Perhaps on that very terrace. It was an unchanging landscape. . . .

When the last of the oranges had gone beyond reach of her hand and had been caught in her net she disappeared from the field of his vision in that doorway. He saw her for a moment through the other. In full sunlight there. But a momentary cloud went over the sun.

He was left alone with Jeanne Becquerel. Her face was averted.

No he had no curiosity as to what she was thinking. He had practically never felt curiosity as to what Alice had thought when she went into one of her trances. Actually she must have thought of miles of pictures in the Louvre. . . . Very likely Jeanne Becquerel thought about the salaams of Cochin-Saigonese or whatever they were. . . . Apparently, out there of an evening, she had mixed cocktails of unusual fruit juices for the Governor's male friends. In a Batik wrapper of unbelievable intricacy of colour and a Japanese sash wound round and round her. Like the *sarong* now. Only the Japanese sash would be in great bows behind whereas the *sarong* was knotted or draped or something, in front. She would stand in a dim, shining room and as each man took his drink he would kiss her hand. Or the Saigonese would raise it to their foreheads. . . .

Maybe she was thinking of that. . . . Perhaps there had been incense – joss sticks – and gongs and paper lanterns and things. . . . But Eudoxie had said that she dreamed of a future in a farmhouse in that countryside. Beside a *bon père de famille*. . . .

He wished he did not have to think of Alice every time he thought of this girl. This girl was in no way like her. . . . She had long, well moulded, slow moving limbs. Alice had been by comparison squat. And about this girl there was no avarice at all. She had not yet asked him for a penny. Not even for the cable she had sent to father for him. . . . The eight thousand francs had trailed about the hotel room for days. At last Eudoxie had taken them to open an account for her. In some bank that was said to be sound.

Apparently, like so many French people, the ex-Governor had been close. In every direction but one. He had given the girl no money and she had taken none though she might apparently have had the resources of a province to play with. In the way of bribes and exactions. On the other hand the governor had fairly buried her under silks, large conglomerations of jewellery-like cat's-eyes and moonstones and objects in brass. Perhaps she liked that. At one moment she would be in a garment, black in base, with emerald green, orange, scarlet and purple scrolls. When you next looked round she would be in a scarlet jacket with black, blue and gold-wine embroidery. With her hair as if glued back under jewelled combs. . . .

In that, if in no other way, she was an improvement on Alice who would wear the same stuff gown without change for a couple of months. She had had one Indian printed muslin that had driven him fairly batty because she would wear nothing else. Yet she had bought frocks fairly often. . . . Perhaps for the charming of Mrs. Percival!

When they moved up to the villa Jeanne Becquerel's kimonos and bales of silk and large jewel cases had hardly left them room in the car to sit in and it had jingled like an old iron cart with her hammered brass pots and ash trays and vases. And he must already have seen her in fifty different, clinging dresses. It was rather agreeable. It was agreeable too to see her flesh under the clean sky. . . . As if you were beginning to collect statues. . . .

The dark girl came back with a tray. A ewer full of ice cubes and another of red-orange liquid.

'A l'Americaine,' she said. . . . 'Though of course you are not a New Yorker. Still here's the juice of ten oranges. . . .'

She slipped the net over Jeanne Becquerel's head and went along the terrace dragging the shrieking girl after her.

In a minute she was back in the doorway. Her face was grave enough.

'That old letter,' she said in English. 'The one I gave you last night. . . .'

He said:

'No, it was a very good old letter. . . .'

She exclaimed:

'I was afraid it told you where you got off. . . .'

He answered slowly:

'No: it solved the last of my moral doubts. . . .'

She said:

'You'll admit it looked like blue ruin. . . .' And then: 'But a moral . . . oh, la, la. . . . Isn't my little friend moral enough for you? Is your urge for New England schoolmarms? . . .'

She added:

'It is true. You are a good boy. . . . And he did not wish the news of his death. . . .? That is of course why. . . .' She was rather breathless.

Jeanne Becquerel was dragging her by the bare arm.

'This is not *convenable*,' she said. . . . 'You shall not send me to catch rascasse and creep to my man. . . .'

They went from that doorway and then appeared at the other, further down the room. They had their arms about each other and stretched their free hands towards him in a Roman salute.

He lay for a long time looking at the amethystine blue sea. The slopes of the peninsula opposite were dusky. The sunlight had gone round to the other side. The cleared space round the base of the semaphore showed as a green lawn. He sipped his orange juice from a thin, frosted glass in which ice tinkled. . . . They had looked like sisters of the Roman decadence moving in long steps. . . . Or of course like mannequins on the terrace of a Riviera resort.

That was all one.

'The point is,' he said, 'that that really is Alice!'

The taste of the orange juice had reminded him of the dining-room in Albany station. You eat rather well there. He used to think so.

One morning towards five, coming from Buffalo when he had been drumming for Pisto-Brittle, he had got out of the train and drank three glasses of orange juice on end. Afterwards he had had a real American breakfast. . . . Perhaps he would never eat a real American breakfast again! It looked like that. . . .

He lay for a long time, regarding the white triangles of sails over against St. Mandrier. Even the cataclysm of three weeks ago had not cured them of their passion for catching minute sea-creatures. Perhaps because that was something for nothing. If they went to New York the first thing they would ask as the boat approached the Twenty-third Street Quay was whether there you could catch small fish for a *friture*. . . .

Alice at least had never paid him the compliment of even simulating jealousy when Mrs. Percival had deigned to give him a moment or two of private interview. This girl called him '*mamour*' with a pretence of possessiveness! . . . One progressed! The species remained the same, the genus underwent modification.

THE night before she had handed him a letter just as they got into the car to leave the hotel. It was addressed to 'Henry Martin Aluin Smith'. The waiter indignantly protested that he had not been able to read the name. And the *patronne* had lost her spectacles three weeks ago on the day the letter had arrived. Henry Martin had expected so little trouble from letters that he felt no shock at receiving this. But when he saw that the postmark was 'Hyères' of the sixteenth of August he had a shock. It was as if the dead had risen. He had held it in his hand on the wheel when he had been driving to the villa. All the while she had been looking at him with anxiety and sympathy. And all the while they had been sitting in the little saloon, by the light of a single candle she had looked at him. . . . Perhaps with panic. He was aware now that it had been at least with sympathy and anxiety. He was warranted in believing that was because she had just said that she had been afraid it was where he got off. . . . Then she was with him!

It was difficult to know what she thought. She knew he was not Hugh Monckton. Of that he had been aware from the very first. At the very first whilst the doctor had displayed his damaged face.

He had felt a moment's alarm. That secret might be worth money. She too might want something for nothing. But he had long known that she didn't want money at all. She wanted only that Jeanne Becquerel should be provided with a *dot*. So that she might be married to a wealthy farmer when he, Henry Martin, was ready to dispense with her society. . . .

She would gain nothing by hurting him. She would only hurt Jeanne Becquerel.

All the same their conversations had had a certain piquancy. . . . As if she knew that she could make him jump at any moment. For fear she should laugh at him because she had so easily penetrated his disguise. . . . And within a very short time he was sure that she cared for him a great deal. So that those *tanquineries* – the teasings – were mere by-play of intimacy. They showed they had a secret known to no one else in the world.

And her zealous retrieving of the letter showed that she watched out for his good.

No letter had come for Hugh Monckton. . . . No communications at all. He had perhaps a private box at the post office. Or perhaps on first setting out with Gloria for the Islands of the Blest he had cut himself adrift from his kind. That was most likely true because no one had called to see him. He had left no address. Probably he was in that obscure hotel in order really to cover his tracks. And wasn't it likely that in confiding to Henry Martin so considerable a trust he was showing that he had lost touch with his social kind? That neighbourhood even now swarmed with English. Rich English. Hugh Monckton must, if he had wanted to in the ordinary course, have been able to find half a dozen men he knew better than Henry Martin.

That he should have so confided was not as extraordinary as it appeared. It is not at all unusual to meet men whom one would trust on sight with one's most vital affairs. It would be too much to say that it happened every day and one doesn't very often trust strangers with one's intimate secrets. But it is not at all unusual. . . . In a very short space of time he himself had met Hugh Monckton, Eudoxie and Lamoricière. . . .

And Hugh Monckton had been as ready to trust Lamoricière as Henry Martin had been – and almost as much on sight. That man was made to be trusted. . . . You even trusted him in spite of yourself. As it were unconsciously. He, Henry Martin, had made up his mind not to indulge in that speculation. Then, next moment, he had heard himself putting all that money into the hands of that black-bearded fellow. Unconditionally. For the purpose of conducting a speculation.

That dreadful day that had ended in pain! . . . The seventeenth of August.

Jeanne Becquerel had gone into her room just after the doctor had finished re-bandaging his face. M. Lamoricière had apparently not made up his quarrel with the dark girl. He stood with Napoleonic folded arms over by the window. His sunk head made his black beard stick forward like a brush from his chest. His forehead was rather – not very – bald.

He had advanced immediately upon Henry Martin. He was between Eudoxie in her chair and Henry Martin's face. He began at once an apology. The introduction was very long and stately. It disclaimed on the part of M. Lamoricière any claim to interfere into the affairs of Henry Martin. . . . It took Henry Martin some time to realize that he was begging forgiveness for having locked the door between Henry Martin and Jeanne Becquerel the night before.

He said he had been in a quandary. He did not of course know what he knew now. The hour had been late. There had been large – very large! – sums of money lying about. And valuables worth even more than

316

the sums of money. . . . He knew of course that the English were more careless in these things than his own countrymen. Still it had seemed a little exaggerated. . . . There was an unlocked drawer in the secretary. . . . Hugh Monckton went everywhere with a Napoleonic officer's travelling bureau. It was an ingenious piece of walnut-wood furniture. . . . Ingenious in the heavy way of the eighteen-tens.

As M. Lamoricière did not finish his sentence as to the contents of the unlocked drawer Henry Martin took it that they had been of great value. He made a sign that he wanted to speak. He said he could not remember what had been left in the drawer. Shock had driven it out of his mind.

M. Lamoricière had made a note of the contents. He had a large notebook and sat stiffly. There had been two books of notes of French currency: one for fifty thousand, the other for sixty thousand francs. He had taken the liberty of introducing into it: . . . He began to read a list of jewellery: a gold watch: a valuable pair of cuff-links: a lapis-lazuli signet ring. A number of. . . .

Henry Martin had waved his hand. He might be taken to know what his personal effects consisted of. In his creaking whisper he asked that M. Lamoricière should put his ear next his own mouth.

The doctor had suggested that his voice-failure was self-induced. But it grew more and more difficult to speak. He said he wanted to see Mademoiselle Yu-Yu's face. M. Lamoricière placed a hairy ear next Henry Martin's dry lips.

These things had been difficult of arrangement. His head had been again swimming. But he had kept on. He had a desperate desire to know what the dark girl

thought of him. M. Lamoricière signalled to the dark
girl to move into another bergère that stood near the foot
of the bed. His composure was unbreakable. He seemed
to think it the most natural thing in the world that Henry
Martin should desire to see the dark girl's face. . . . But
he seemed to think that everything was the most natural
thing in the world.

Henry Martin directed his words towards the dark
girl. M. Lamoricière kept his ear close to Henry Martin's
lips. Whilst Henry Martin spoke M. Lamoricière directed
his eyes pensively towards the carpet. Before he himself
spoke he erected himself, rigid and black, in his cane
chair.

Henry Martin addressed them both. He said: they
had heard the doctor's directions as to his immediate
future. He intended to follow them.

The dark girl leaned suddenly towards him, her lips
parted.

He whispered on:

He desired to find a villa. . . . But modest. . . . Fit
for a very small establishment with an income at the most
of fifty thousand francs a year. . . .

That should settle it. It should show the dark girl
what she had to accept. She could take it or leave it.
On the spot. . . . Her lips were more widely parted;
she sat further forward; her glance seemed to penetrate
his eyes.

M. Lamoricière sat up, rigid against the back of his
chair.

'That seems very proper,' he said. 'That seems appropriate.' He made notes in his large black book. He said:
'You would like it high up. For the sake of a view of the
Mediterranean. And to avoid heat which would be
pernicious to you in your condition.'

He asked if, for the sake of his eyes, he might close the curtains. The sunlight had been streaming in. He came back in a soothing dimness. He said he hoped that did not prevent Monsieur's seeing the face of Mademoiselle.

He produced his notebook again. . . .

He said:

'I presume you desire that the lease should be in the name of Mademoiselle Becquerel . . . of Madame. . . . That would be the usual course.'

A convulsion moved Henry Martin's throat. The dark girl was nodding. She wanted the lease to be in the other's name!

M. Lamoricière went on: he had few such villas on his books. The estates he dealt in were usually much larger. But with good-will. And with the aid of Mademoiselle Yu-Yu. . . .

The dark girl said:

'Oh, I'm a good scout!'

'You will perhaps desire,' M. Lamoricière said, 'to pay one or two years' rent in advance. . . . To secure it. That is not unusual. . . Or to take it à volonté. . . . With the option of purchase. In case the arrangement proves permanent. . . .'

Henry Martin said:

'Whatever is usual. . . . Generous. . . .'

He lay back on his pillow. . . . He felt faint. . . . It was perhaps misleading the dark girl. . . . As to his resources. . . . He had fifty thousand francs. No other certainty. . . He heard her say that that was swell. He was a swell guy. Her voice for the moment was a deep contralto with emotion. . . . He understood that she was indeed a New Yorker. At that time he had not known her history. It was the first time he had noticed

her English. If she spoke English in a moment of emotion
– spontaneously – she must be a New Yorker. That
soothed the part of him that was homesick. As if he would
be less expatriate! . . . A swell guy too. . . . That was
what he was! . . .

The others began talking villas. . . . One at Dar-
dennes. . . . Too inland. No view of the Mediterranean.
The Villa Pavia . . . Mon Répos at La Vallette. . . .
Not the one at Bon Rencontre of course.

She said:

'My aunt has the Villa Niké at disposal. . . .'

*Niké* meant Victory! He wanted the Villa Niké! He
kept his eyes closed. To rest his voice. . . . He must have
more money. She was a New Yorker. At that time he
thought she must have contracted a New York demi-
mondaine's habits of expenditure. . . . She would make
do with less. He had had a Scotch porridge mug as a
child. It was yellow. But with brown, as if burnt in
lettering it said, 'Contented wi' little but canny wi'
mair!' . . . He must get her a good time. Damn it,
she deserved it. Father and mother had brought the
mug home from a honeymoon voyage. They had been
in Luxemburg and the Rhineland and had returned
over Scotland. . . . She deserved . . . she deserved
*Le Secret*. . . .

It was odd. How often hadn't he seen *Le Secret* off St.
Mandrier. With her high spars and tall black hull? . . .
Her screw was so powerful that when you saw her from
a height beating into the *port extérieur* against a strong
mistral – with only the mizen set – you saw behind her a
great trail of blue-green whitish water. A hundred and
fifty yards long. But it had never occurred to him that
one day he might come to think of that marvel as a
wedding present for a New Yorker!

M. Lamoricière said:

'It is too ramshackle. It is almost a ruin. . . .'

Henry Martin found that the thought of the twenty silver-white notes was burning into his being. From behind his right shoulder! He must have left the painted grip open last night.

Eudoxie said:

'We will make the old she-devil diminish the rent by half. With the other half we can arrange it tastefully. Besides, that will much lessen the taxes. . . .'

Henry Martin found he was trembling. He clenched his teeth. They had been knocking together and had hurt his jaw. It was perhaps in that way that thieves felt at the thought of easy hauls of great booty. He had once been on a jury in Springfield. A burglar who was being tried for burgling Mrs. Von Augsburg's had explained. He had successfully made off with half the diamonds of Mrs. Carl Busch next door and had been having a good time at Miami. But in coming away from Mrs. Carl Busch's he had noticed that Mrs. Von Augsburg's would be extraordinarily easy to break into. The thought had so distracted him that he had lost all taste for Miami and eventually he had come back. So the cops had got him.

M. Lamoricière said:

'If you have sufficient influence with Madame your Aunt the Villa Niké would be admirable.'

'I can always blackmail my aunt when I really want to,' Eudoxie answered coolly: 'I have only to threaten to leave Manhattan Beauty Shop. Or if the case is really serious I can say I intend to open an opposition business. I am all the Manhattan there is in the establishment. And eighty per cent of the beauty. And I have enough capital. And the wholesalers will trust me. . . .

Besides the title of the firm is registered in my name. . . .'

M. Lamoricière had wondered that the old lady had fallen into that trap. For himself he would have thought that the 'New York Beauty Shop' would have been a better title.

Eudoxie said:

'No, *sir!*' in English. All French people knew that Manhattan was a cocktail and all Americans that there must be a real live New Yorker behind that gilt name. . . . Little old Manhattan was good enough for her.

. . . And so the cops had got that burglar. Henry Martin kept his eyes closed. It was perhaps that he was contemplating. But it wasn't! . . . It was a puzzling affair. He had hurt Hugh Monckton's feelings by refusing to take those silver white things. Then, now that he was a ghost it was his duty to appease that ghost. . . . By doing what he had asked. . . . But Henry Martin being dead. . . . No, Hugh Monckton! Being dead his property became no longer his. He had no right to dispose of it. Not even his ghost had. . . .

Eudoxie was saying remarkable things. . . . Her aunt hadn't fallen into a trap. They had arranged that Eudoxie should register the name of the firm under her own name. So as to avoid death duties. Her aunt would probably die before she did. Then the name of the firm being Eudoxie's all its essential value would be hers. There would be no death duties. The extraordinary mania of the French for evading death duties. . . . They took precautions against those payments even before they had earned any money. They would rather earn no money than make the payments.

They were talking in low tones. They thought he was going to sleep. . . .

It occurred to him that, if he was committing any offence against the law it was that of evading these death duties. . . . He ought to pay on the fifty thousand francs. And to see that it was paid on the rest. . . . But then he was acting in the spirit of the country. Every Frenchman would applaud that. . . . He could chance it.

Eudoxie was apparently talking about her traffic in snow. She was going to abandon that. It would be dastardly.

Apparently in a back parlour of the beauty shop she slipped tiny papers of snow into face powder packets. . . . She had clients who trusted her. She would not let them down. Was there so much happiness in the world? She was carrying on a crusade against the imbecile wickedness of Authority that hated happiness! The police had put her in prison for six weeks. Because her boy friend was a foreigner. And to placate the English police who had discovered the international supplies. . . . It was understood they would not touch her now. As long as she was discreet and the traffic did not assume unreasonable proportions. She was in partnership with her aunt. Her aunt's political pull was fairly considerable. The police preferred to let her alone. Besides Eudoxie would rather spend the rest of her life in prison than let down her favourite clients. The whole countryside, too, was with her. They all doped. Every other man in the Arsenal and half the personnel of the Navy. Every day she had been in prison she had received half a dozen bunches of flowers.

If what she said was true Eudoxie was a very bad, dark girl. An enemy of Society with the applause of the Nation. If you evade death duties you are also an enemy of Society – with the applause of the Nation. Fifty million Frenchmen can't be wrong. All the same there seemed to be something – what the French called *louche* about the situation. His head could not exactly distinguish nice differences. As regards the French tax-collectors he could say, couldn't he, that the fifty thousand was pay for work done. And, if he handed over the Bank of England notes to the principal executor that fellow could settle about death duties. . . . The chief executor was, he supposed, the man called Cyril Monckton. That was the simple course. . . . But . . . there was an obstacle. He could not think what the obstacle was. . . .

M. Lamoricière was gravely applauding Eudoxie. . . . Could you entrust twenty thousand pounds in banknotes to a man who applauded a trafficker in cocaine? With nothing but what they call a note of hand as security. . . .

Of course the obstacle was that, if he returned the silver-white banknotes to Cyril Monckton that fellow would have to be told that Hugh Monckton was dead. . . . But it was Henry Martin Aluin Smith who had blown his brains out. That was on the passport. What do you know about *that*? . . . Of course he could return the notes through a bank which would say that the payment was made by the order of Mr. Asch Emma Smith! Certainly he was never going to sign Hugh Monckton Allard. . . . Changing your identity was more difficult than had at first appeared! Eh, old Bean!

Yes, return the notes by way of a bank. Speculation was too risky. The 'Monckton A's' would have to be bought before next Monday. The shares apparently were dropping in fear of a bad dividend. But the dividend to be declared on Monday was to be one hundred per cent. . . . It would be an unparalleled opportunity! No one had ever had such a chance. If you bought the stock with dividend you netted one hundred per cent at once. With naturally the *pro rata* diminution for the price above par of the stock. By spreading out the money carefully, on cover, you could make. . . . You could make more than double. Not more than double. With stamp duties if there were any in England. And Lamoricière's fees. . . .

But before next Monday. . . . How did you **operate** from that place? God only knew. It was obvious that he could not go to London. Not even to Paris. . . .

He opened his tired eyes. The dark girl was holding the door open. For Lamoricière to go. Henry Martin said: 'Hi!' Desperately. His voice had completely broken. The dark girl did not hear him. She seemed to be ages coming towards him. It was God's mercy that she had not followed that fellow.

He whispered desperately in her ear:

'Get that guy back . . . *Prompto Subito*! For God's sake get him back. . . . Tell him Big Business. . . . Big. . . .'

Why in God's name had he sent for him? The girl had gone. She had said they had thought he had been asleep. . . .

How could he trust that fellow? What did he know about him? He looked like a Chief of Department in a French Ministry. No chief of department in a French Ministry could be trusted out with twenty thousand pounds in cash. Two and a half million francs! It was unthinkable. . . .

The fellow was a long time coming back.

And there was something *louche* about the whole thing. It was too much like getting something for nothing. That was said to be the American sin. Americans were jeered at all the world over for that. . . . He would be damned

if he would add to the National discredit. The straight
and proper thing was to return the money to the Cyril
Monckton man. . . . Obviously! And work out the
morals later!

He could tell Lamoricière that he had brought him
back to give him a tip about Monckton A's. Out of
gratitude. That ought to please Lamoricière. He might
put ten out of his legitimate fifty thousand francs. Or
twenty thousand. . . . Twenty-five! That was the
proper thing. The right thing! That would give him
another six months with Eudoxie. She seemed to be
willing to accept a fifty thousand a year scale of living
. . . In eighteen months he could turn round too. . . .
Write a book about French morality. Sympathetically,
of course! . . . It was wonderful how calm it made you
to have found the right way. . . .

M. Lamoricière was indeed like the French Chief of
a Ministerial Department. He ought to say:

'En quoi puis-je vous être utile?' . . . 'How can I be
of service to you?' That was exactly what he did say.
Whilst he was still holding the doorknob.

He must have got some way down the stairs. Eudoxie
was still slightly out of breath. She went first to the communication door and then to the window after she had
peeped in. She remained looking out on the *rade*
intently, through a little division she had made in the
curtains.

M. Lamoricière bent his ear to Henry Martin's
lips.

There could be no doubt that to give up all idea of
using those banknotes was the right thing. Everything
pointed to that. Every circumstance clamoured that. It
was only in that way that he could find the peace of mind
that was now necessary to him. He said:

'Next Monday Monckton A's will declare a dividend of a hundred per cent.'

He had not intended to say just that. But with so little voice it was difficult to beat about the bush. If he wanted to do a service to Lamoricière that was the quickest way. He said:

'Of course, in confidence!' He managed to add. 'I have no objection to your personally . . . using . . . the information.'

His heart was beating *too* fast. He got out:

'Discreetly!'

M. Lamoricière was sitting like a ramrod. Looking at him! He made with his head a motion to indicate that Lamoricière should put his ear down again. He whispered – with extraordinary speed:

'The big grip is open? . . . Yes. . . . You did not close it last night. . . . I wish to benefit. . . .' His head swam. . . . 'A young friend. . . .' Well he wasn't old!

M. Lamoricière whispered:

'Yes. . . . Yes. . . .' Excitement was perhaps gaining him too.

'You will find in the grip. . . . In the left hand . . . side flap.' Between each group of words his heart beat violently. . . . 'A small . . . square . . . pigskin portefeuille. To hold English banknotes. . . .' He could tell the man to mail them to the executor! They were not safe there anyhow. . . .

He had read constantly in French novels that in moments of excitement men's brows drip with sweat. His brows were dry. Prickly!

Lamoricière was a long time gone. Behind his head.

The notes were gone! . . . They must be gone. . . . His heart stopped beating this time! His brow was

dripping. . . . There would be only the little wads of
French notes. It was too little. . . . He had lost
Eudoxie. . . . It was no doubt the waiter. . . . Or
the old woman who had cupped him. . . . He had lost
Eudoxie!

M. Lamoricière was standing beside him, looking pas-
sionlessly down at the pigskin note-case.

He whispered:

'They must be put in a place of safety.' That was all
that was in his mind. They must be put in a place of
safety. . . . They were the future of himself and Eudoxie.
He whispered: 'Open it. . . . Count the notes. . . there
should be twenty. . . .'

The case was too high above his sight for him to see
the notes. He heard them rustle. Lamoricière was
fingering them deliberately. He said at last:

'Yes: there are twenty. . . . I have a safe at the
Crédit Lyonnais. . . .'

Henry Martin said:

'You understand. . . . For the benefit of my little . . .
no, my young . . . friend. . . . Any profit you may
make in Monckton A's. . . .'

M. Lamoricière bent his head forward and erected it
again. A sign that he understood. He said:

'A little speculation . . . a safe one! . . . For a . . .
a dependant. . . . That seems very proper. . . .'

Henry Martin said:

'Not in my name. . . . I do not wish to sign papers.
. . . The capital to be returned. . . . Intact . . . your
commission. . . .'

M. Lamoricière said:

'I do not take commissions when operating for a friend.
That is not my métier. I am a real-estate agent.'

Then there was nothing more to be said.

M. Lamoricière began an oration: He appreciated Monsieur's trust in him. It was a pleasure to be connected with interests so vast. He would avail himself of Monsieur's information. It would be of the greatest service. And Monsieur could be sure of his discretion. Were their interests not the same? It was obvious that any divulgence of information to third or fourth parties would defeat their joint aims. . . .

It all seemed very satisfactory.

The dark girl had turned him down. He might have expected it. But not for the reason she gave. It was just his luck. He presumed he had not given pleasure. . . . Not at all. . . . If it had been the night before last! If it had been before the sail blew away! If it had not been to that room he had contrived to be brought. . . . If he had been brought to her all bruised and bleeding. . . .

He expressed blind passion for her. She whispered:

'I had thought it. . . . Jeanne Becquerel was asleep just now.' Her face was extraordinarily fixed. As still as a Japanese painting. He said that at the first time he had heard her voice. . . . She said:

'They say that. . . . But I believe you. . . . For as long as it lasts. . . . But I believe you for as long as it usually lasts. . . . If you had chosen to be anyone else. . . . Or any other room. . . .'

He did not understand her. She said:

'If you had not been a millionaire. . . . If you had not chosen that. . . .'

He swore he was a beggar. . . . With enough for a year's happiness. . . .

She said:

'Yes, I know. . . . But one does not get a year's happiness. It is not what one is here for. . . . Not people like you. Or me. . . .'

His voice had come back. He was half out of bed trying to catch her hands! He exclaimed loudly:

'That is nonsense. . . . I have just come out of Hell. . . .'

She gave him her hand to soothe him and stood looking down at him. She was cool and good-humoured. She said:

'Moses saw into the promised land. . . . We are like Moses. . . .'

He exclaimed, again loudly:

'I shall be rich. . . . I promise. . . . In a day or two I will buy the yacht *Le Secret* . . .'

She said, as if she were afraid:

'You must not do that. . . . You must not be mad. . . . I do not like rich people. . . . There are too many poor to think about. . . . I should be unable to think. Out of fear for you and because of the bread-lines too. . . .'

He said:

'I swear I am not a thief!' so loudly that she looked back over her shoulder, drawing at her hands. . . . At Jeanne Becquerel's door. She said:

'I have, of course, known some thieves. One was afraid for them. . . . But we are made for renunciation.'

Her looking backwards had stung him. He said contemptuously:

'You talk like a Protestant. One would say you had read that fellow's book. . . . "Strait is the path and narrow the gate. . ."'

'Does it astonish you?' she said. 'I am a Lutheran. . . . We are in great strength here. It is our country.'

That stunned him. He said:

'But . . .' Then he found no words.

She was a light woman. Up for sale to the highest bidder. Or he had thought so. Yet she talked of renunciation. It did not hang together. . . . He tried to check all she had said. . . . If this had been the night before last, she had said. . . . If it had been before the sail blew away. . . . If it had not been to that room that he had contrived to come. . . . Perhaps it hung together. . . . There might be reason in her madness. But she was mad.

He said:

'You are mad. . . . You love me. . . .'

She said:

'I think so. . . . As these things go. . . . If it is a consolation, I feel for you as I never felt for another. . . . But that is perhaps more torturing to you.'

He said no, she must tell him. He tried to draw her down towards him. . . . She looked again towards the door behind her, the strong sinew of her throat rigid beneath the skin. She nearly laughed.

'Of course we can speak English,' she said. 'I had forgotten. Lie down. You may kiss me before Jeanne Becquerel. . . . Lie down. . . .'

She said:

'Listen, honey. . . . These things happen. . . . I guess I felt as strong a lech for you the night before last. . . . And it has gotten stronger. That's O.K. . . .'

She was speaking calmly and dispassionately. Her American hurt him.

'These things do happen,' she said. 'I guess you may call it love. I guess that's what love is. Having no experience. . . .'

He said:

'Speak French. . . .'

She answered:

'No, no. . . . If Jeanne Becquerel heard. . . .'

He cursed that girl. She said:

'You cannot save a life . . . if it is a suicide . . . and then torture worse than the Third Degree. Even a cop wouldn't. And you're too swell a guy. . . .'

He said:

'The hell I am. . . .'

She said:

'I'd have slept with you. . . . Jesus, I would. . . . Till what happened last night.'

He exclaimed: Christ, she didn't think that he. . . .

She said:

'A gentleman doesn't kiss and tell. . . . An honest to God gent doesn't *not* kiss and tell. It's even less genteel. . . .'

He said he swore that. . . . She leant down and took his head in her arms. She whispered:

'Listen, honey,' again. It was torturing. She spoke French like Prosper Merimée, English like a Caféteria waitress. . . . Was that what New York did for loveliness?

'I guess,' she went on, 'with us French girls in sex it's all the same as with liquor. We get wine as kids so keeping on the water wagon's no effort. . . . It's an effort to keep off you, honey. . . . You're too swell a water wagon for it not to be. . . .' She was stroking his sound cheek. . . . She said: 'You can see for yourself, lovebird. . . .' She had left New York when she was twelve. . . . She said: 'Mamour, mamour. C'est la tragédie inscrutable de la vie humaine . . . Qu'il faut. . . .'

She held her head back so as to look at him down the lane of her black lashes. They were heavy with. . . .

He had forgotten the name of the stuff. He had known it well once. . . . His head was not on her breast. . . . He had once helped Mrs. Percival put it on. . . . For a costume ball. She was going alone with Al. . . .

The world stopped. . . . It was as if it went to the centre of the world. . . . That doctor had said. . . . Pain. . . .

She said:

'It would be too damn hard for the kid. . . . She's a swell kid. . . . Oh, hell, she's been through hell too. . . .'

Her voice was like thunder. He was sobbing on her breast. You could not believe such pain was. . . .

She called out:

'Jeanne Becquerel. . . . Jeanne Becquerel. . . . Viens vite. . . . Ton homme est. . . .' 'Come quickly. . . . Your man is. . . .'

There was nothing but the knife going through the temples from side to side.

That had been exactly three weeks before the day on which he had watched the dawn from his bed. No . . . exactly twenty days. It was three weeks to the sixteenth. He did not remember those twenty days too well. The fifteenth and sixteenth were clear enough in his memory. It was like what they say of old men, they remember the events of their youth better than the day before yesterday. . . . He was certainly not an old man. . . . Free, male. . . . But was he either? . . . At any rate he was rising thirty-six. What you called the prime of life: though until you had been through it yourself he did not see how you could tell!

And no doubt those two days had aged him. . . . What could you expect?

It is the desperate thing about human life that sorrow

never comes and goes alone. You suffer; then you have to suffer more because you have suffered. . . . They call it 'sorrow leaving its traces!' It had certainly left its traces on him. . . .

Though you wouldn't say so, to see him lie in a gorgeous bed, with a scented beard, in green pyjamas of heavy silk and a Japanese crocheted white stork on each breast pocket. Looking out over the Mediterranean – with houris kissing their hands to him every time they left him for ten minutes. . . . Those girls made him scent his beard!

But Destiny is probably virtuous and reads the gospels. . . . It hands you bouquets with its right hand; but its left, not knowing that you are a favoured individual, socks you one that damn near leaves you down for the count. And certainly inappreciative of the plaudits! It had done that for Hugh Monckton – 'Some people as *hall* the luck.' . . . Now it was presumably doing it for him, Henry Martin . . . It wasn't true to say: 'Never the time, the place and the loved one all together. . . .' They were all there. . . . But. . . . What a hope?

He drew Hugh Monckton's letter from under his pillow. It was the final gift of the right hand of Destiny. . . . The propitious one. God knew where the left was going to sock him next. . . . Long Melford, they used to call it. The Straight Left! . . . But he had his charter. . . . To himself. The stuff to ease the New England Conscience! . . . He had awakened extraordinarily cheerful that morning. As if overnight he had been proclaimed Emperor of China. . . . Well it had been something like that. . . . He was secure in bed and board. And he hadn't had something for nothing. Hugh Monckton had begun his immense, sprawled letter by saying right away that Henry Martin had killed him and you have to accept

334

favours from the people you have killed. Just as you have to split yourself to serve those whose life you save. . . .

Nothing less than that!

The letter began:

'Look here you Yankee! You put the kibosh on this Johnnie. You've got, in honour bound, to do what you can to appease his wrathful ghost. . . .'

Twenty days. . . . For three of them that doctor had kept him under with a strong opiate. Then for twelve more he had bromided him into a moron. He knew that because when Lamoricière had come in with an authorization to bearer from the head office of the Crèdit Lyonnais to draw for six million odd francs he had felt as if it had been Hugh Monckton's valet coming in to say that his bath was ready and his eggs had been on four minutes and ten seconds. . . . He had spent two days trying to reckon what six million odd francs made in dollars, pounds sterling and other fancy currencies. On the next day the doctor had taken him off bromides and he had spent it weeping on the breasts alternately of Jeanne Becquerel and the dark girl. That was the thirteenth day. On the fourteenth day they had taught him to play *belotte* on an invalid table attached to his bed. On the fifteenth he had taught them rummy at a table near the window. The waters of the *rade* had been like viscous glass: dove-coloured. He had seen *Le Secret* come in and be moored under the window. On the fourteenth, against the doctor's orders, but accompanied by that Inquisitor, M. Lamoricière and the two girls he had been driven to the local branch of the Crèdit Lyonnais. His beard was like a hedgehog's spines but his temples were still in bandages. At the head of his cortège he had been received like the chief mourner at a swell funeral. He had hardly been able to keep his mind on the conversation of the

335

bank-manager but he hoped he had succeeded in paying two and a half million francs to the account of Hugh Monckton Allard Smith at the Bank of England. . . . By direction of H.M.A.S.

That had been such a load off his mind that he had seemed well enough to let Jeanne Becquerel and Eudoxie by turns drive him to see the Villa Niké. In his Monckton! . . . He had not been strong enough to climb up the hill to the villa. It was pink: standing a hundred yards up off a side road. Eudoxie had driven timidly; but Jeanne Becquerel had taken the car like the very devil over atrocious roads behind a mountain. He had seen on the roadside under le Revest the grave. . . . It was a bare square, all alone in a dry field they had lately added to the cemetery. Eudoxie had cried. Their white wreaths had gone brown under the torrid sun. But from where he lay he could see the Mediterranean, miles down the valley. If he was any more interested in the Mediterranean. . . .

When they had got back to the hotel Jeanne Becquerel had taken cables to his father, and sister Carrie and Alice. To each he said, 'Newspaper reports erroneous. Feel no anxiety.' He had signed 'H.M.A.S. . . .' Jeanne Becquerel had asked to be allowed to send the wires. The post office was just round the corner. She wanted to try the streets. She had not been in them for six weeks!

Whilst she was gone he pleaded once more with the dark girl. She told him to remember his head and begged him to vouchsafe a few endearments to Jeanne Becquerel. She made him understand that if he pressed her again he should never see her alone. She said certainly she loved him.

When Jeanne Becquerel came in again he offered her

336

an account of her own for fifty thousand francs; a platinum wrist watch; a Monckton eight or a Packard. She refused them all. She said that on the night he was well she would take a diamond ring.

Eudoxie said she would take the fifty thousand francs and bank it for Jeanne Becquerel. On a former occasion Jeanne Becquerel's mother had been too dumb to ask for proper settlements. But she, Eudoxie, was a New Yorker with no flies on her. Men would now find Jeanne Becquerel a different proposition. Jeanne Becquerel said there would be no other man. Eudoxie said that that was all the more reason to take the fifty thousand. . . .

It was queer, when they went into the great café on the Rade under the hotel Americans ignored Henry Martin. He might not have existed. . . . He was a bearded Frenchman with two French girls. The place was full of Americans, nights, because of the heat-wave. When they stepped on Jeanne Becquerel's toes or knocked his hat off the table they never apologized. . . . A fellow he had known rather well because he had been one of the literary squad at Dartmouth – called Harold Cripps – told him he had once dressed up as a plumber. He had been aiming at Journalism. He said it had been like being dead. Because no women looked at him. When dressed as a sophomore or a dry goods drummer he could catch glances – ranging from glad eyes to dulled casualness. But, as a mechanic, he was one with the refuse boxes at street corners.

Henry Martin had thought at the time that had been because, anyhow, Harold Cripps, was rather an unpresentable little rat. Now he knew! It was not so much that women avoided his glances. All did not. There are American women who will take up with niggers or any native. But with the men it was universal. He was a Dago.

He had gone native. The Declaration of Independence no longer applied to him. All men are *not* born free and equal. . . . In the brilliant illumination outside the buzzing shades of the café the polyglot, polychromatic crowd of the port drifted by against the moonlight. It was full moon on the twenty-eighth. . . . Innumerable niggers in khaki with scarlet fezzes, Algerian carpet-sellers, little Indo-Chinese women: Hawaiians, unimaginable Germans; little sailors. . . . He was one with them. He wondered any French were allowed in that café. . . .

There was a Montparnassian called Jimmy Stout. Henry Martin had known him once and then had ceased to know him. Alice had been behaving rather freely one night at the Dôme. Mr. Stout had misunderstood her intentions. As she had not been very canned on that occasion Alice had complained to Henry Martin. . . . At any rate Mr. Stout had every opportunity of knowing Henry Martin by sight!

On the night of the third of September Jimmy Stout, a squat, heavy jowled ignominy in a very tight béret, had been sitting two or three tables away from Henry Martin and Jeanne Becquerel. Eudoxie had been up at her aunt's to arrange about the moving into the Villa Niké. They had obtained a lease of the place for an almost infinitesimal rent. The old lady had considered that she would get it back in the repairs they would effectuate and the perfumes Jeanne Becquerel would buy.

Henry Martin had been in the inside of the café. When he came back Jeanne Becquerel complained that the fat man had insulted her outrageously. Henry Martin had sat down and stared straight at Jimmy. Fixedly. For nearly a minute. The fat man had fidgeted, rubbing his right hand over his cheek and trying to return the stare. There had been no sign of recognition about his furtive glances. When Henry Martin had half risen rather precipitately the fat man had bolted into a knot of his countrymen who were occupying half a dozen tables at the other end of the long terrace. . . .

On the other hand several American women – usually stout – bowed and smiled ostentatiously at Eudoxie. One, very stout indeed, came up to their table and addressing Eudoxie as if she had been the Queen of England, said that she had reduced three hectos. She said Madame Eudoxie's method was marvellous. She wore as many diamonds as the wife of a French wholesale greengrocer. Her be-paunched husband in white ducks sucked at an immense cigar behind her. The ash was two inches long. He managed at last to get in that he had met Mr. Hugh Monckton Allard Smith, v.c., in New York with his father Sir Charles. . . . His wife bustled him away, shockedly, into the middle of the American group. Faces from there turned towards them frequently. . . .

Jeanne Becquerel distinguished herself that evening. Eudoxie always blazed. She had returned from her aunt's wearing a black satin, skin-tight vest above her immense pyjama trousers. Her lips and cheeks were scarlet: her lashes so heavy that you would have said she could not raise them. She had brought in a tiny white paper a minute portion of snow for Henry Martin to try. It had had no effect on him.

But Jeanne Becquerel had been in white. No doubt white *crêpe de chine*. But on Eudoxie's mentioning a dress of some Eastern Queen she had jumped up and run into the hotel.

While she had been gone Eudoxie had revealed that Henry Martin had been in luck to meet her at that

339

*dancing*. He had been trying to find out whether she had been there again. She said that, on Saturday evenings when the farmer, her aunt's husband, came into town she looked in at most of the respectable places of entertainment after half-past eleven. If she saw her uncle she got one of the waiters to telephone up to the farm and held her uncle in conversation until one of her cousins came and took him home. . . . Henry Martin remembered that he had first seen her in conversation with an earthy man and a dull girl. Her uncle might go to the Red Light quarter or even to Marseilles once a month to *faire la bombe*. But, for the rest, he was as avaricious as his wife and next day was grateful to his niece for having caused him to save money. Besides the old peasant was not insensible to the prestige it gave him to be seen sitting in a semi-public place with any one so striking and well-known as his niece Eudoxie. . . .

Jeanne Becquerel came hobbling, with short steps, between the impressed tables full. She was in Cardinal's scarlet with azure blue dragons in embroidery that climbed amorously all round her figure. She had narrowed her eyes with Kohl, and her hair, mucilaged straight back, was transfixed with foot-long pins that had carved, jade tops. . . . The Americans she ignored but she scattered smiles on the French tables and got a sufficiency back. Henry Martin realized that she was not above reaping the fruits of an innocent triumph. She was showing the inhabitants of the city that she had more than kept her end up. . . . She put her arms about his neck for an instant. To show that the English Milor was hers.

He had gone native indeed. And he was beginning to penetrate the habits of his fellow savages. . . . He ought, of course, to have known that a girl who was one of the

340

principal commercial ornaments of that place and whose salary and share of the profits of an expensive establishment amounted probably to more than those of the admiral commanding the station would not sit for hire in a *dancing*. But he hadn't known it.

What he could never have penetrated on his own was why she should sit there at all. It was democracy. He had once asked a Southern girl with a deep and earnest contralto voice why when she got among other Southerners she – and they all! – elevated their voices into shrieks that were hardly believable. As if they had been calling to distances, along cliffs, against the wind. The girl had said: 'Well, they're not all First Families of Virginia here. But most of us have been to Kids' school together. So we mustn't high hat the others.'

It had been like that with Eudoxie. She made opportunities to go into the *dancings*. On weeks when her uncle went to Marseilles she would get the *commis* of big perfumery firms to take her there to dance and would nod at the girls who sat there for hire or make up their faces from her own vanity accoutrements, in the cloakroom. It was she said: 'le coq qu'elle devait à Esculape' . . . the cock she owed to Aesculapius. . . .

So that he had next to all that he wanted, for he took all the rest of her to be a compound of virtues and spices!

As they drifted past the American quarter a voice said: 'That's the Madame of the Beauty shop.' It seemed to be produced by a throat of parched brick. 'The other's the chief mannequin of Call-lo's.' Voices said: 'No, Chanel's. . . . No, Poiret's. . . I seen her there. . . .'

A voice like Stentor's roared:

'He's hiring the Queen of Sheba for a third. . . . We can't all be Rockefellers. . . .' Another: 'But we can keep from being beavers. . . .'

They strolled past those people as if they had been third class passengers.

And, next day the last of the difficulties solved itself. With the letter that Eudoxie gave him and that he held under his fingers on the driving wheel. . . .

A year or so ago he had been at a reception. A French royalist deputy had been there, a high-nosed, red-faced Norman. He had spoken English better than Henry Martin. The moment he had heard that Henry Martin was American he had begun to pick at him. Gradually he had worked himself up to an oration. Shouting. He had said that America had ruined the world. Because she wanted something for nothing. Others gave genius, labour, civilization, lives in millions. America had given nothing and hoarded up everything. He had gone on for a long time, citing innumerable instances. . . .

How that might be Henry Martin did not know. He was unacquainted with the ground. If other nations were such fools as to let one nation get something for nothing he didn't see why it shouldn't.

But for his own person there had suddenly spoken within him – the New England Conscience! It would be too much to say that that problem of life had become with him a morbid obsession. But it had worried him. He might, for instance, have taken proceedings against his publisher; but the thought that the sales of BE THOU CHASTE had been really due to the illustrator had stopped him. No doubt if he had actually begun proceedings the fellow would have paid him at least something. Then he would not have been driven to commit suicide at the same moment as the other fellow. His whole life would have been changed. He would have been still at Carqueiranne, holding the knitting work for the old ladies and pottering about the shores in the boat with the scarlet sail! He had mildly pleased that little group, just as now he had another little group that liked him. He picked up little groups so easily.

It was without doubt due to his hybrid origin – He was a product of a wild boar of the Ardennes and a First Family of Fall River. The New England Conscience could be acquisitive enough. Boston, according to Southerners, had grown rich out of the Slave Trade and as soon as the Slave Trade had become obnoxious to world policy it had howled for the walloping of the South to whom it had sold the slaves – slave-manu-factured products competing with those of its own cotton mills.

No: he had no illusions as to want of acquisitiveness going along with a delicate moral sense. The trouble was that the New England Conscience was critical. New Eng-land would reconcile with its conscience the sale of slaves as long as the sale of slaves was practicable. But, while it could do that, it considered, say, buccaneering as most reprehensible. It would have no truck with that Central American practice. It was Nordic and don't you forget it. It excelled at drawing lines! Before all things else.

The devil was if you inherited half your blood from Buccaneers and half from Fall River First Families. Father and mother had been able to run their ship all right because when occasions called for buccaneering father could attend to it and when you had to remember that you were a First Family of Springfield mother took you in hand and made you put away your gold-headed cane. But when you had the two strains inside yourself. . . . You could not buccaneer efficiently because your left hand considered it indelicate to go beyond selling slaves. It was as if *Le Secret* went yawing all over the bay. Instead of sailing near the wind!

343

He would be damned if he was irresolute. He would face anything. The times were out of joint but the cursed spite was that he was not the fellow that was called to set them right.

It was perhaps that that was the matter with America. . . . With the world. There was too much hybridization. Affairs were no longer in the hands of people who ran true to type. Eighty per cent of the population of New England was of confused Dago origin. Yet the critical power of the region remained in the hands of the Hill. . . . And was paralysing!

Over the body of Hugh Monckton, Henry Martin III had eventually triumphed over H.M.A.S. I and II. I, was no doubt the normal Henry Martin of Fall River Psychology: II, which had wanted to take the passport for a lark, was father's product: the child of the wild boar of the Ardennes. (The aristocrat of poor mother's family had naturally to be a refined bandit who refused to take something for nothing. Taking from the rich what he gave to the poor and so getting to heaven in true New England fashion!) . . . But Henry Martin III who had eventually won the day had been the acquisitive instinct that was at the bottom of both Luxemburg and Massachusetts – of the cave man that was at the bottom of all types.

So there Henry Martin had walked – a milor, a Rockefeller – before a parterre of ragtag and bobtail, with, on each arm, a whore of surprising costume and grace. . . . And expected to acquire an even more dissolute and alluring third!

But underneath that magnificent, international figure there had still been the lean, troubled Henry Martin of Fall River Conscience. He had money and was afraid to use it. He had actually said to Jeanne Becquerel that they must keep within a margin of fifty thousand francs a year. Not out of a spirit of economy, but because he shrank from the fiercer pleasures that might be earned from the millions – in francs – that he had gotten, for nothing! He could not see how he had earned even the use of the twenty thousand pounds with which he had speculated. . . .

Those two girls had accepted his orders with delight. They seemed to make him almost French. That was what they wanted to complete their idyll. . . . He could see, however, that Eudoxie was puzzled. It appeared to her not to fit in with the spirit of a gentleman who gave away gold rings on sight and presented his last three hundred and ninety-four francs to a mere acquaintance! . . . She had taken him for a bold and ingenious thief. That had troubled her because she had thought she might have to worry over his arrest. . . . But thieves squandered. One who, having millions at his disposal, proposed to live with a lovely mistress on a sum fitted only for a comfortable but careful middle class family – that puzzled her. It ravished Jeanne Becquerel, who asked for nothing better than comfort based on economy.

But Eudoxie had arrived very near the truth. By the morning on which they went fishing! It was obvious to her that he was not a thief. That he had been given a moderate sum that he might conceal from the world the fact that Hugh Monckton had committed suicide. . . . For the sake of the shareholders of the Monckton concerns! . . . And she had felt immense relief when he had told her that that ominous letter had made things all right once and for all.

It was whilst re-reading Hugh Monckton's letter that he had the full sense of her perspicacity! With an immense amount of beating about the bush, army slang and endearing epithets Hugh Monckton asked that Henry

Martin should do his best to conceal his suicide. That request was the occasion of the letter. Whilst speeding between St. Jean du Var and Hyères the idea had come into his aching head. If the startling news of his death by his own hand were broadcasted across the world there was no knowing what effect it might not have on the Monckton concerns. . . . His shareholders were mostly old-fashioned, quiet investors who would be so troubled by sudden fluctuations that he almost thought he had not the right to kill himself. But, relying on Henry Martin, he was going to take the chance. If he didn't kill himself by putting his Monckton at the bullfinch he would do it with his revolver.

But he begged Henry Martin to do his best to suppress the news. Temporarily at least. For good if possible. It would do his father's memory no good; it would militate against all that he stood for. It might even hurt Gloria. And, Henry Martin knew that he would give away everything that he possessed rather than that for one second Gloria's white brow should be wrinkled by pain.

What Hugh Monckton wanted was to drop out. Unnoticed. If all trace of him could be lost so much the better. He had already done what he could to cover his tracks. That was why he had been staying in that unspeakable hotel. He had told his boring cousin Cyril Monckton that he was going away for years – with a woman unnamed. . . . At the end of years, the English courts would give leave to 'presume his decease.' . . . It was doing Cyril Monckton no great injustice. He was rich enough already and in due course would come into his, Hugh's, shekels.

There was money in lashings to effectuate this. Henry Martin could buy up the reporters; he could bribe officials wholesale. As residuary legatee all the money lying about was at his disposal. . . . There was no end to the considerations that Hugh Monckton produced. . . . It was tragic to hear his lamentable voice pleading!

Henry Martin read the sixteen scrawled pages of the letter by the light of a single candle in the dim saloon of the Villa Niké. As happens in France the electric light had not yet been put on. And it was as if, from standing astride of the grips in the hotel room, Hugh Monckton had come to stand in the shadows of that place. Henry Martin could see his very hand, with the strap of the gun about the wrist, move in that passionate pleading.

And there was the final plea. . . . It was Henry Martin who had killed him. Until they had been walking across the painted Place du Théâtre in the deathly sirocco there had seemed still one possibility of escape for that tormented mortal. But the contempt in Henry Martin's voice when he had uttered the words: 'The Foreign Legion!' – that had made Hugh Monckton see that there was only one means of escape! How indeed was he with his destroyed physique to stand the business-like gruelling of that life under a torrid African sun? . . . What a hope indeed!

'Then,' Hugh Monckton adjured, 'do me this favour, old bean. It is all one whether I die to-night or after two months of hell in Oran. I shall go certainly to a far better place than that stink-hole. I have no remorse. But do this in expiation. Old bean, I have never been so grieved. Surely my awful shade shall be unappeased in Phlegethon. . . . Good old Achilles, you know. . . . Then to appease me – For indeed old bean, you're the first man I felt I could talk to – unburden myself – in donkeys' ages – donkeys' and donkeys' ages. . . . Except Gloria and she took insufficient pleasure in my unburden-ments. . . .'

He begged Henry Martin to hire *Le Secret* – or any equivalent abode of bliss on the earth, the waters of the earth or the waters under the earth. And to take any little piece. . . . And the remains of the *Fine de la République*. And any oddments and spondulicks as he believed they called it beneath the folds of the star-spangled one. . . . And so to prolong for Hugh Monckton, here on earth, the jolly old beanfeast that, by all odds his own mortal career should have witnessed. . . .